THE RIVERWOMAN'S DRAGON

Also by Candace Robb

The Owen Archer mysteries

THE APOTHECARY ROSE
THE LADY CHAPEL
THE NUN'S TALE
THE KING'S BISHOP
THE RIDDLE OF ST LEONARD'S
A GIFT OF SANCTUARY
A SPY FOR THE REDEEMER
THE CROSS-LEGGED KNIGHT
THE GUILT OF INNOCENTS
A VIGIL OF SPIES
A CONSPIRACY OF WOLVES *
A CHOIR OF CROWS *

The Margaret Kerr series

A TRUST BETRAYED
THE FIRE IN THE FLINT
A CRUEL COURTSHIP

The Kate Clifford series

THE SERVICE OF THE DEAD
A TWISTED VENGEANCE
A MURDERED PEACE

* *available from Severn House*

THE RIVERWOMAN'S DRAGON

Candace Robb

SEVERN
HOUSE

First world edition published in Great Britain and the USA in 2021
by Severn House, an imprint of Canongate Books Ltd,
14 High Street, Edinburgh EH1 1TE.

Trade paperback edition first published in Great Britain and the USA in 2022
by Severn House, an imprint of Canongate Books Ltd.

severnhouse.com

British Library Cataloguing-in-Publication Data
A CIP catalogue record for this title is available from the British Library.

ISBN-13: 978-1-78029-136-9 (cased)
ISBN-13: 978-1-78029-825-2 (trade paper)
ISBN-13: 978-1-4483-0563-6 (e-book)

All Severn House titles are printed on acid-free paper.

Typeset by Palimpsest Book Production Ltd.,
Falkirk, Stirlingshire, Scotland.
Printed and bound in Great Britain by
TJ Books, Padstow, Cornwall.

In memory of my dear friend Joyce Gibb,
soul friend, wordweaver, inspiration,
a Magda tale

Owen Archer's York

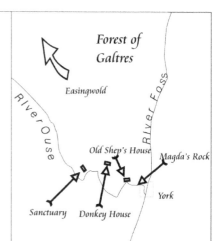

Forest of Galtres

Easingwold

River Ouse

River Foss

Old Shep's House

Magda's Rock

York

Sanctuary

Donkey House

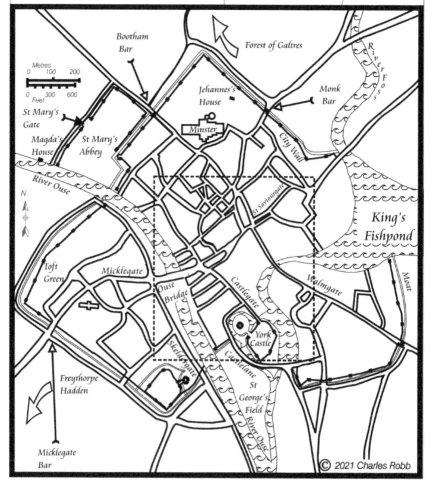

Bootham Bar

Forest of Galtres

River Foss

Metres
0   100   200

Feet
0   300   600

Jehannes's House

Monk Bar

St Mary's Gate

Minster

Magda's House

St Mary's Abbey

City Wall

River Ouse

St Saviourgate

N

King's Fishpond

Toft Green

Micklegate

Ouse Bridge

Castlegate

Walmgate

Moat

Skeldergate

York Castle

Coppergate

Freythorpe Hadden

St George's Field

River Ouse

Micklegate Bar

© 2021 Charles Robb

1. St Helen's Churchyard
2. St Helen's Church
3. York Tavern
4. Wilton Apothecary
5. Lucie's and Owen's House
6. Hempe House
7. Poole House
8. St Crux Church
9. Cooper House
10. All Saints Church
11. Wolcott House
12. Ferriby House
13. Toller House
14. Graa Warehouse
15. Brown House
16. Old Bede's House
17. Franciscan Friary
18. Graa House
19. St Denys Church
20. Fuller House
21. King's Staithe

St Saviourgate

Coney Street

River Foss

Foss Bridge

Walmgate

Ouse Bridge

Castlegate

York Castle

If you ignore the dragon, it will eat you.
If you try to confront the dragon, it will overpower you.
If you ride the dragon, you will take advantage of its might
    and power.

                         — Chinese Proverb

PRO LO GUE

A s the days lengthened and the pale green leaves of early spring, delicate as an infant's fingers and toes, swelled to complete the forest canopy, a cruel visitor wound its way north along the roads and the waterways, sowing fear and sorrow. All knew of its coming, for it had called on a few unsuspecting households near York in the golden light of August past. The two youngest Wolcotts, an infant and a toddler, had succumbed. The manqualm taking the most precious members of a family disrupted the balance of affections. But Magda Digby had sensed trouble brewing among them long before, the Death merely coaxing out the poison. Other families were touched as well – children, parents, elders. All knew that it was merely a taste of what was to come as summer returned. The pattern was known: warm weather ripened it until it burst forth, spreading its seed. All were wary, looking for scapegoats on whom to hang the blame.

Memory of the first visitation stirred a deep, ancient fear in the folk that lay dormant in good times, a fear of the Riverwoman's healing skill. For she was ever the outsider, the wise woman living just beyond the city wall, on a rock in the Ouse guarded by a dragon. She blamed no one for the shunning, having known the risk when she chose her path. Born of a long line of healing women on the moors who served their community with ancient roots in the wild hills, she had been raised to follow in their footsteps. And then, in the midst of a year of disasters, a shabby friar intruded on their peace, his beady eyes slithering and twitching as he preached of a vengeful god who would continue to punish them with sicknesses that thinned their flocks and disastrous summer rains that ruined their crops until they cast out the healers and wise women, worshippers of Satan, daughters of Lucifer.

Neither Magda nor any of her kin knew of such a being as this Satan or Lucifer, much less worshipped him, yet one by one, household by household, the folk turned on the healers, threatening to burn them all unless the women set aside their evil practices. It was a choice between what the friar called the dragon, Satan, and the lamb, the Christian god. Magda was confused – the god he described sounded far more the dragon than the lamb, and he seemed indifferent to the welfare of his 'children' – but her questions were received as attacks and she was cursed for them. All the while the slovenly, corpulent snake slithered through the community, forcing himself on the young women. Magda was ready for him, burning the arm that reached for her with a red-hot knife. For that she was ordered to submit to whatever punishment he commanded for her penance.

Magda chose banishment, walking off into the forests to the north, where she lived a long while in a community who practiced the old ways in peace. The only dragon they knew of was wise and fierce, a powerful protection. In time she returned south for the sake of a child longing for her brother. But she kept to her path of healing, ever wary of Churchmen, especially in times of loss when their worship of a god of vengeance separated folk from their own wisdom about the earth and their own bodies. She would bide her time, ready to depart if truly threatened. Over the years she learned that eventually the clerics grew so fearful they bolted their doors against the community, and then the folk remembered how she'd helped them in the past, once more seeking her aid.

For now, as she exited Bootham Bar in a soft rain, she bid the city farewell. The poor were her priority, particularly those living without the walls of the city and in the forest of Galtres. The city inhabitants were well served by physicians, barbers, and midwives, but the poor had only her.

The line to enter the city straggled out past the walls of St Mary's Abbey. Bedraggled, already weary, many having risen long before dawn to make the trek, the folk stood in small clusters, eyeing the others with unease. They searched for signs of illness, fearing this might be the day the manqualm walked among them. The fear would be stronger in the throng at Micklegate Bar, on the King's road from the south, where the Death already wakened.

ONE

A Dragon, a Raven, a Newcomer

York, mid May 1375

Water was her element, despite the fiery reputation. In the liminal light of late evening she played in the River Ouse, leaving a trail of silver droplets as she arched and dove, reemerging from the peat-brown water, shaking her head, arching and diving once more, circling the rock that had been her home this long while. The ease, the grace, the joy of movement reminded Magda Digby of a time when her own body sliced through chilly waters alongside the most beautiful man she had ever known. She followed the happy memory as a scent on the wind and a taste of salt in the brown water signaled the turning of the tide in the loamy water of the Ouse. Until the gentle splash of an oar called her back to her seat in the doorway of her home on the rocky island in the Ouse. Slipping back onto the roof, the dragon gave one more shake, droplets raining down on Magda, and resumed her watch.

A coracle emerged from the fog thrown up by the dragon play. Magda wondered whether it would be Sten. For why else the recent tidal wave of memories? But he had doubtless died of old age years ago. Their son? She walked to the edge of the rock, calling to the passenger to toss her the line. As she secured it on the stake driven into the rock she noted that the river lad's companion was too short to be Sten. Their son? Grandson? There must be a reason Sten haunted her dreams. But as he turned to toss the line she saw that her visitor had nothing to do with her distant past.

It was Sam Toller, Guthlac Wolcott's factor, or agent for trade, his face creased with worry as he disembarked. She might guess that at last old Guthlac had let go the incompetent leech attending him and sent for her but that Sam pulsed with fear for himself, his family . . . and her. Perhaps the leech had stirred up more trouble? Or was she sensing Sam's fear of the pestilence? Both, most likely.

'I will wait for you here, Master Toller,' the lad called.

Sam lifted a hand to acknowledge him and followed Magda to the house. He crossed himself as he passed beneath the stern visage of the dragon, then hastened across the threshold.

'Hast thou news of thy daughter's baby?' Magda asked. Several weeks earlier she had guided the young wife through a long, difficult delivery, her firstborn, pitifully small with a mewling cry that bespoke a weak heart. Magda had stayed with mother and infant in their home in the north of the forest of Galtres for several nights until her husband returned from taking goods to market.

'No. No news from Mary,' said Sam. 'But here.' He thrust a small money pouch toward her. 'She would want you to have this.'

Though Magda sensed his relief in the gesture, his shallow breathing indicated an accompanying unease. Mary might approve, but that was not her father's purpose in coming, nor was this his or his daughter's money. 'Many thanks for this generous offering,' she said. 'Come, sit down, warm thyself.' She drew him to a bench near the fire, poured him a bowl of ale, and handed it to him as she settled so that she might see his face in the firelight.

He tasted it, then took a longer drink. 'Bless you. I needed this.' He stared at the fire, his gaze taking on a faraway quality.

'With the sickness threatening the city, thy mistress will be reminded of her little ones,' said Magda. She spoke of Beatrice, the young wife of his employer, Guthlac Wolcott, for whom Sam harbored a strong affection. The Wolcotts' young son and infant daughter had died of the pestilence at the end of the past summer.

Sam nodded. 'And Guthlac's health is failing. Yet he was hale and hardy in winter. How is it that no one speaks of what is so plain, that he began to fail the moment the leech Bernard appeared? God forgive me, but I blame Guthlac's son for this.' Gavin, the old merchant's son and heir, born of an earlier marriage, a few years older than his father's young wife and rumored to have no affection for her. 'You would not know the old man now.'

'Alisoun told Magda of his decline.' Her apprentice had been shocked by the elderly Wolcott's condition when she saw him on the street leaning heavily on the arms of his wife and a manservant. So much change in the fortnight since Magda had been in the city was indeed cause for concern. Alisoun was at present assisting in Lucie Wilton's shop while the apothecary accompanied her husband Owen Archer to London on royal business. For convenience she was lodging in the couple's home.

'She must have seen him on one of his last outings,' said Sam. 'He no longer leaves his bed.' He crossed himself.

'Is it concern for thine employer that furrows thy brow?'

'Yes, but— In truth, at present it is my concern for you. I came to warn you that the leech Bernard means you harm. He has poisoned the hearts of Guthlac and his son Gavin against you. I pray you, do not come into the city.'

'Magda has no thought to do so. With the sickness surrounding the city she will be busy with the poor and the folk of Galtres. But rest easy, the leech Bernard will not have the leisure to think of Magda.'

'They say Bernard demands such a high fee that few in the city can afford his services.'

'The desperate will do so.' She heard a timid knock on the door. 'That will be the lad waiting with the coracle.'

'My wife is grateful for all that you did for our daughter.' A gentle lie, for his wife Gemma resented charity of money or spirit spent outside her home. But Sam was a kind man accustomed to compensating for his wife's sharpness.

Magda escorted him to the door and watched as the lad rowed him back, skillfully maneuvering against the current of the outgoing tide. He was of an age with the others who assisted her, seven or eight winters, strengthened by the rowing and other work, on the cusp of being sent away from home to seek his way in the world. Her brave lads. She paid them well.

It was a busy evening on the bank. Magda noticed a man standing upstream from the spot where Sam would disembark, watching her. She had sensed this person often of late, sometimes accompanied by another, but not tonight. Another pair of watchers stood closer to the landing but farther from the bank. Hostile, menacing, but watching the coracle, not her. It seemed Sam Toller had cause to be ill at ease. She watched until he disembarked and walked away without incident.

Once alone Magda tucked the pouch of coins in a hidden place so that it might be safe until she decided who needed it most, then resumed the chopping of roots to add later to what was left of the coney stew. She was about to serve herself when Alisoun appeared, pausing in the doorway, eyes closed, inhaling, her exhale a long sigh of release.

'Thou art troubled,' said Magda. 'What news from the city?'

'A woman in All Saints parish has died of the sickness the morning after returning from her sister's home to the south. Her husband burned all that was in their bedchamber. But God watches over them. Neither he nor the children have taken ill.'

All Saints parish lay in the center of York. 'They have not been attacked for fear they carry the sickness?'

'No. It is not like that this time – or not yet.' Alisoun bent over the pot to sniff. 'Mmm.'

'Thou art welcome to sup with Magda.' Kate, Owen and Lucie's housekeeper, would feed her well, but her apprentice was fond of coney stew.

'Gladly.' Alisoun set her basket on the worktable, lifting out a loaf of bread. 'Kate sent this. And I bought this for you.' She set a jug on the worktable. 'Tom Merchet's ale.' The owner of the York Tavern next to the apothecary brewed the finest ale in the north.

'Many thanks. A bowl of the ale, then stew?'

They settled by the fire, speaking of their days, small matters, news of shared acquaintances. Alisoun's blushes told Magda that she was enjoying her close work with Lucie's son and apprentice, Jasper. The two had declared their love for each other several years earlier, but they were often at odds, she easily believing herself betrayed, he withdrawing into himself when uncertain of his path. It was good they were at peace for now. Yet something troubled the young woman. After some hesitation, she came to the point.

'There is yet another new healer in the city,' said Alisoun. 'A woman. And the leech Bernard has turned several of our customers against us.'

'Sam Toller spoke of him, warning Magda to stay away.'

'I saw Sam glancing over his shoulder as he was rowed to the bank, peering into the twilight as if sensing trouble.'

'But he departed safely?'

'Yes, of course. Who would wish him harm?'

'Magda noticed a pair watching him. She could not see who they were.'

Alisoun nodded absently.

'What dost thou know about this new healer?' asked Magda.

Alisoun drank a little of her ale, cleared her throat, and looked at a corner of the room rather than Magda. 'A gray-haired woman, tall, walking with a cane. I have seen her on the street, not in the apothecary. She does not seem friendly. Folk say she is from Lincoln, or Peterborough, or from up on the moors. Ned Cooper says she is attending his mother since his father forbade her to come to you.' The young man worked for Owen Archer, captain of the city bailiffs.

'Magda is glad to hear that she has sought a healer.' Some women transitioned out of their childbearing years with a gradual easing of the monthly cycle, a slow cessation, hardly noticed until it was gone. But such was not the lot of Ned's mother, Celia. For the past year she had endured weeks of bleeding, an unfortunate, not uncommon way a woman's body adjusted to the changing season of life. 'Is she in much distress?'

'The long bleeding comes more frequently, weakening her.'

'This new healer is helping?'

'Ned thinks not. He says her potions sicken Dame Celia, flushing away what little food she has managed to eat. And while she sits at his mother's bedside the healer draws images in charcoal on paper that fill his mother with unease and give her bad dreams.'

'What frightens her about them?' Magda asked. She began to understand Alisoun's unease.

'He brought a few to show me, to see whether I agreed. There is something about them. They seem to change. Grow. I did not find them frightening, but strange.' Alisoun handed Magda a page crowded with images, creatures and plants intertwining, spreading, twisting, seeming to grow out of the drawing and into the room.

It was as she had suspected. 'Magda has seen such images before.' She handed back the paper. 'Why art thou reluctant to say her name?'

'But I—'

'Was it Jasper who told thee?'

Alisoun blushed. 'I heard a rumor that she is your daughter

Asa. Then I asked Jasper and he said he had heard she made no secret of it. But as you have not spoken of her—'

'When did she arrive?'

'I think about the time you left the city.'

Magda thought back to a gray-haired woman supporting herself on a cane. She had seen her from behind and felt a tug. But so faint.

'She has not come to you?' Alisoun asked.

'No. Art thou worried she will supplant thee?'

'She is family.'

'She would prefer it were not so.'

'Then why come to York?'

'Magda does not know. But thou needst not fear. Thou art more daughter to Magda than Asa has ever been. This is thy home as long as thou wishes it.' She rose to fetch the stew, giving her apprentice a moment to regain her composure.

While they ate, Magda led the conversation toward the proper seasoning of a coney stew and the items Alisoun should put aside in the shop for her next assignment.

Afterward, while sharing a touch of brandywine, Alisoun returned to Celia Cooper, concerned that Ned's father, learning that Asa was Magda's daughter, had threatened to replace her with the leech Bernard. 'Ned has seen Guthlac Wolcott's decline and warned his father against him, but the man is stubborn,' said Alisoun.

Edwin Cooper was the worst of hypocrites, spouting pious nonsense and loudly condemning others for their sins while bedding the maidservants and casting them out when they became pregnant. Magda knew of this from young women who had worked in his household and come seeking her help.

'Ned might suggest that his mother ask to go to St Clement's Priory,' said Magda. 'The infirmarian has experience with women of Celia's age. She would be safe and well cared for.'

'Why would Edwin Cooper agree to that?'

'Is the young woman with the red hair still serving in the household? If so, he will feel free to be with her.'

'I see. But is that not a cruel use of her?'

'This one is wise to his ways and uses him to her purpose,' said Magda.

Alisoun considered for a moment. 'I will tell Ned.'

Only as Alisoun rose to depart did she speak again of Asa. 'She claims to be a healer. Did you train her?'

'No. Asa believed she should be able to heal without the long study. She believed that as it was in her blood her mother must be punishing her by instructing her to study and observe, that she was hiding the craft from her. She was ever impatient with a world that did not bend to her idea of how it should be.'

'Much like me when I first came to you.'

Magda laughed. 'There were echoes, yes. But that was long ago and thou hast come far.'

When she was alone Magda returned to the fact that she had not sensed Asa's presence in the city, nor had she recognized her on the street. She wondered how that connected to her rush of memories of Sten. Their children were the twins Yrsa and Odo. Asa had a different father. Was the other, more frequent watcher somehow connected to Sten? She was now quite certain it was Asa who sometimes joined him. But how would they have met? Sten and the twins had been long gone from Magda's life when she met Asa's father Digby. Stepping outside, she settled beneath the dragon and let the quiet of the night calm her. Only then did she go to bed.

Just before dawn the cry of an owl wakened her, its claws scratching along the roof. After a long pause, it took flight. No more sleep for her. As Magda prepared her basket of healing remedies for the day's visits she considered who might have died in the night. But by day's end she had heard nothing to explain the portent.

Several days passed without news of the death of which the owl had warned. Magda let it be. Nothing to do until the prophecy came clear. She continued to be curious about her watchers. The one most often about was male, she sensed cautious interest. And she was now quite certain his occasional companion was Asa, wary and angry. Whether the man was also kin she could not tell, but after sensing him she often thought of Sten. That, too, she let be. Her days were busy, and that would be so through the summer. When Lucie Wilton returned to her apothecary, likely within a fortnight, Alisoun would move on to Lucie's family manor in the

countryside south of York to care for the couple's children, who
would remain there until the manqualm quieted in York. It would
ease the minds of the couple to have a competent healer in the
household should the Death find the manor. Magda was happy for
Alisoun to go, but her absence meant she would continue to care
for folk outside the city by herself. Just yesterday a family north
of Easingwold had been struck, an infant sickening in the morning,
dead by nightfall. The news spread quickly. Magda had learned
of it as she began her rounds.

In late afternoon, with her physicks dispensed, roots and herbs
gathered, Magda turned toward home. But she did not hurry. The
warmth of the day enfolded her in a pleasurable caress, inviting
her to stray off the path here and there in search of tender shoots
she might have missed. A cluster of coltsfoot in the ruins of an
old shed rewarded her. Humming to herself and absorbed in
harvesting the bright plants, she did not feel the weather shift until
the wind whipped her skirts about her legs as she turned back
toward the forest track. A briny wind. Glancing up, she saw the
canopy of trees being whipped by the gusts, though there was blue
sky beyond. Clear now, but not for long.

Caw! A beady eye studied her from an overhanging branch.
Caw! Caw! Raven. When Asa was a child, Raven had watched
out for her. *Caw!* With a ruffling of feathers, the bird rose to the
sky just visible through the woodland canopy. Magda quickened
her pace, all temptation to step off the path in search of plants
gone with the wind and the raven.

By the time Magda emerged from beneath the cover of trees
into the fields before the abbey walls, clouds chased the blue
westward, chilling the air. *Caw! Caw!* Raven tacked into the wind.
Tucking the basket beneath her cloak, Magda continued to the
riverbank opposite her home. One of the lads hailed her, offering
to row her to the rock.

'Magda will go by foot,' she said. The tide was coming in, but
it was not yet so high. 'Take thyself home. Shelter from the storm.'
She tucked her skirts up into her girdle and put her shoes in her
basket.

Caw!

She crossed over the shallow water using the smooth river stones pressed into the mud to afford a reasonably dry walkway. Once on the rocky outcrop she paused, watching Raven fight against the sharp east wind to at last alight on her dragon. Raven's battle with the storm reminded Magda of her daughter; so Asa had ever been, fighting against the elements, against anything.

Gazing out over the water, Raven fluffed her feathers, turning one eye, then the other on the Ouse, where the storm whipped the incoming tide into a boiling surge from the sea. *Caw! Caw!*

'Is Asa threatened by the storm?'

Raven did not respond.

Nor did Magda sense that her daughter waited within the house. Shaking out her skirts, she took shelter in her snug home.

All night wind and rain battered the house while the fire within snapped and chuckled, the varied woods in conversation. Now and then Magda dipped her finger in a cup of goat's milk and fed it to the kitten curled up in a basket on the edge of the table, the runt of a litter who had been handed to her by a young girl when she returned at midday. Magda had been given the goat's milk in payment just hours before. Nature's balance. Hungrier now, mewing for more, the kitten wobbled about in the basket, her gray, tan, and white asymmetrical markings reminding Magda of her own patchwork clothing.

'Thou'rt eager to thrive, little one,' Magda murmured. The kitten rubbed its head against her hand. The child would not return, her family would forbid it. No matter. A home would be found. 'Thou hast a good appetite.' From a shelf she plucked an old cloth glove that was missing several fingers. With a snip, it lost another. Filling it with some milk, she held it to the tiny mouth. The makeshift nipple was soon suckled dry. 'Enough for now.'

Magda settled to work, humming as she ground nuts and roots for a broth that sustained her when busy, kept in a small jug she carried with her as she traveled in her donkey cart to the farthest reaches of Galtres, her primary visitation routes. The cart and donkey were a treasured gift from Old Crow, the late John Thoresby, Archbishop of York. Her good friend in the end. He had not always been so.

A neighbor kept the cart and donkey for her, and when Alisoun was not available to groom Nip, her name for the ever-hungry being, the neighbor's daughter did so. For her, Magda prepared a tisane to ease the child's tremors, the result of a head injury when young. As the girl grew and explored the world the tremors were easing, but not yet gone, and she hid from the world in fear that folk would think her cursed or possessed by a devil. Foolish ideas from the same source as made some folk fearful of Magda's skills as a healer. The Church taught intolerance for the mysteries that did not serve it, and the people suffered. Turning her mind back to the child, Magda added angelica for sweetness.

A gust of wind found the chink between the door and the sill, sending the fire dancing. The kitten mewed. Magda found her trembling, and after feeding her another nipple full of the goat's milk she tucked her in her basket bed and softly sang as she stroked her asleep. Despite the storm, a peaceful moment, an evening of contentment. When she had prepared all that she needed for the next day's planned visitations, Magda lifted the kitten from her basket and held her on her lap while enjoying a cup of spiced wine in the fire's warmth. As they sat, the kitten purring, Magda's thoughts drifted to Wicket, the kitten with whom she'd slept as a small child, the being with whom she'd shared her dreams, her fears, her secrets. 'Perhaps thou hast come to share Magda's bed once more?' Setting aside her empty cup, Magda sprinkled sand over the fire so that it would die down, and slipped into bed with the kitten.

As she drifted off to sleep she sensed Raven on her shoulder, whispering of another who had slept with kittens long ago, and other small beings she would spend the day drawing. Flowers also Asa had drawn, covering the walls of the house with fantastical bouquets and vines out of which peeked the young beings she nursed to health. She created beauty, yet believed she had no gifts. A contrary child, always preferring what others had, certain all had more than she. From what she had seen of her present art, Magda guessed that Asa now drew what she sensed roiling the minds of the ill, but had not learned to draw from memory once she had left the patient's presence and then burn the nightmare to release that which poisoned the spirit. A mistake a teacher would have caught and corrected.

Sometime in the night Magda woke from a troubled sleep, thinking of the bank across from the swans' nest. She had dreamt a body floated there, swollen from time in the Ouse. In the morning she would walk the bank to see whether she dreamed true. The kitten mewed and touched her face with both front paws. Stroking her gently, Magda returned to sleep.

After feeding the kitten in the early morning, Magda walked upriver to the place in her dream. Father Swan glided by, a ghostly grace in the rising river mist, looking back toward something snagged by a fallen log that was in turn trapped by willow roots along the bank. She found the bloated corpse of Sam Toller, eyeless, one hand shredded, a wreck of the appendage with which he might in life have grasped on to the log and pulled himself from the waters. She guessed he had snagged on the log before the storm dislodged it and carried it here.

She bowed her head, thanking River for carrying him to a place where he might be found, grieved, put to rest. *May his spirit be at peace.* She remembered his daughter Mary speaking of him with deep affection. A kind, generous man, a caring father. She would take a calming draught to Mary when next she traveled north past Easingwold. And if his death proved no accident, may those responsible be brought to account.

Magda sensed her male watcher behind her. Not Asa. Today he was wary, as if unsure of her, even frightened, but also curious, almost eager. He stood beneath the trees a few strides from the bank, revealing himself with a movement as she stepped close to the water. Though she did not turn she felt him stretch out his arms as if to steady her, but stopped short of touching her. He might of course mean to push her in. He had been watching when Sam left her home, and the mix of curiosity and fear suggested this, that he might realize she could implicate him.

'Thou wouldst offer to assist this old woman in pulling the body from the river?' she asked as she turned to face him.

A step backward, brows pulled down in a frown, eyes wary. 'I thought you might need help.'

The young man was a stranger and yet familiar. She studied him as well as she could, with him still shadowed by the trees. He was not yet twenty years, she thought. Healthy. Ah. Now she saw it. It was the eyes. He was kin, of that she now had no doubt. That did not ensure he meant her no harm, but she was not worried. She smiled at him, hearing his name in her mind.

'You smile in the presence of death?' he asked.

'The dead take no offense.'

'You are not frightened?'

'Art thou? The dead cannot harm thee.'

He returned the smile. 'You are all they say you are.'

'They? Thou hast asked about the Riverwoman?' She waved off his attempt to answer. 'No matter. There is no need to assist now. The coroner must see him where he lies. Wilt thou watch him? See that he does not float away?'

'I— Yes, of course. For how long?'

'Not long.' With a nod, she left him.

Returning to the shanties of the poor, she chose the eldest of a clutch of lads who came out to see whether she had work for them this day. 'Go to Crispin Poole's home on Coney Street. What was the Swann home. Say that Dame Magda has need of the coroner of Galtres.'

The lad took off, several of the younger ones trailing after him. Those who remained asked what had happened, was there a body. 'In good time.' Calling the youngest to her, a lad called Twig who often helped her with animals, she asked whether he might care for a kitten while she was away for the day. 'A half penny and a potion for thy dam.' Beaming, he followed her across the still ebbing tide. She instructed him in the feeding of the little one, then left him cradling her as she fetched the basket she had filled for her day's visitations and departed. She would not neglect the sick for a dead man. Her part in the morning's grim discovery would soon be complete.

Back on the bank she thanked her watcher and advised him to go on about his day. 'Thou art welcome in the dragon's house any time. This evening after sunset would suit Magda. Come with an appetite. Asa is also welcome.'

'How did you—?'

'Magda has sensed thee watching, sometimes with Asa. After sunset, Einar.'

'You know my name? Asa came to you after all?'

He might be kin, her daughter Yrsa's grandson, judging by the eyes, but he was not gifted with the knowing of names. She would be curious to learn whether he carried any of the gifts passed down through her own or Sten's families.

'No. She has not yet come to see Magda. Go now.'

She kept her ears pricked until she could tell he was well away upriver, then settled on the remnants of a stone wall to await Crispin Poole, welcoming the memories stirred by the encounter. In the brown water of the Ouse she saw a child frightened by the fear in her father's eyes when he chided her for greeting a stranger by name. She had not understood, her mother having never told her this was a gift others did not share. She had not known she was different until that day when her father tucked her behind him as he told her mother of the incident. *Never tell anyone outside the village that you hear their names.* She saw her mother's fear. *They will curse you.* She had not known it to be a gift not all healers shared, had not known to ask. It seemed a useless knowing. A name told one little about a person, least of all what ailed them. But later she had understood – men considered a name a thing of power.

Low voices on the bank warned of two men approaching. Coroner and bailiff. She was pleased that Crispin Poole had collected the bailiff George Hempe on the way.

Rising to greet them, she gestured toward the body. 'Sam Toller.'

Both men crossed themselves and bowed their heads for a moment, then Poole bent for a closer look at the body in the willow roots, asking whether she was certain it was Sam.

'She's right. I recognize the tunic,' said Hempe. 'And the hair.' Long strands of brown billowed out from the ruined face. Sam had worn his thick brown hair long for a man of the city, a vanity.

'How did you find him?' Poole asked.

'Dost thou see the nest on the far bank? Each year this pair returns to birth their young. They have become friends. Magda walked out to see how they fared in the storm. The body was where thou seest it.' No need to speak of the dream.

Poole grunted as he straightened. 'Death by drowning. Looks as if he's been in the water a few days.'

'No one has seen him for two days,' said Hempe. 'His wife has been worried.'

'He came to see Magda three evenings ago,' she said, 'bringing a gift for seeing his daughter safely through a hard birthing. He did not stay long.'

'Perhaps in the river ever since then,' said Poole. 'Was the tide in when he left you?'

'Flood tide it was. But Magda watched him cross back to the bank in a coracle steered by one of the lads. It was not yet dark. Does Gemma Toller say he never returned home?'

'She says he told her in the morning that he would be late returning home,' said Hempe, 'and she did not see him again. Ah, here they are,' Hempe waved to a pair of young men approaching, carrying cloth and ropes.

Ned Cooper greeted Magda with warmth. 'My mother is safely at St Clement's. My father could not refuse her wish to give herself up to God for healing. Not after condemning you and Asa for worshipping false gods. My mother and I are grateful to you. But I—'

With the others hovering, Magda patted his arm. 'Good. That is good.' She stepped back.

The other young man nodded to her, mumbling something respectful, but clearly eager to see the body. Until he wasn't. Hand to mouth, he hurried away into the brush to lose his breakfast.

'I thought it time he was blooded,' said Hempe with an apologetic wince. 'Ned, take Peter to find some stout branches so you can carry the body back to town.'

Once they had pulled Sam from the river, Poole declared the cause of death uncertain – the damage to the back of his head was such as to be unlikely to have been caused by drowning. Floating debris in the rushing waters of a tidal swell might do such damage, but unlikely unless he were vertical in the water. Far more likely someone hit him, then threw him into the river. To Magda's eyes the latter was a certainty. Sam had been murdered.

'I wish Archer were here,' said Poole.

'Thy friend is on the road home,' said Magda.

'I am glad to hear it. Close enough to delay the burial?'

'No. Permit his widow to bury him. Thou canst record what Archer should see.'

'Peter can sketch the body for him,' said Hempe. 'Another reason to include him. I've had a bad feeling about Sam's sudden absence.'

With a nod, Magda took up her basket and set off down the path toward her next visit.

'Dame Magda.' Ned caught up with her, drawing her into the trees where they might not be watched. 'I must tell you about your daughter Asa.'

Remembering Raven's struggle, she said, 'She did not depart thy home in peace.'

'After she had been warned away my father found her at my mother's bedside. Gossiping about Bernard the leech and Guthlac Wolcott's decline. Wolcott is a good customer for father's barrels, and two warehousemen were below fetching some for him. I arrived as father chased Asa down the stairs calling her Satan's spawn, the Devil's own, accusing her of spreading rumors about a Godfearing leech and the Wolcotts. He knocked her cane out of her hands. She clutched the banister but started to fall and I rushed to help her. I caught her cane and threatened my father with it if he interfered. I've challenged him before. He knew I would not hesitate to carry out the threat. So he kept his distance. Raining curses down on both of us, of course. I helped her out of the yard but she shook me off once out on the street. Preferred to limp off on her own. Later I heard she had been attacked by two men, but onlookers had chased them off. They say she was hurt, falling badly on one leg as she walked away.'

Magda had listened with eyes closed. Now she nodded. 'Hast thou seen her?'

'No. Her landlady said she wished to be left in peace.'

'Hast thou told anyone else of this?'

'Hempe knows. I told him the whole story when I asked him if he knew where I might stay.'

'Thy father banished thee?'

'Again. My sisters will beg him to forgive me. But this time . . . Now that my mother is safe . . .' He gestured as if well away.

Magda knew that Celia Cooper was often the victim of her husband's temper. 'What of thy sisters? Will he now turn on them?'

'Their husbands would not tolerate it, and my elder brother's wife knows how to appease my father.'

'Thou hast found lodging?'

'Dame Lotta insisted I bide with them.'

Hempe's wife. Magda smiled, patted his shoulder. 'Good. Many thanks for the news.'

'Dame Magda, I am worried for you.'

'Sam Toller was as well. There is no need. Folk will not cross Magda's dragon.'

'But what of during the day when you are walking about?'

'Magda trusts that she will sense danger approaching. Her weapon is her knowledge of Galtres, every path and track, where it is dangerous to tread, the hidden places. See to thine own safety. Now go. Hempe will be looking for thee.'

She set off on her rounds. Asa might appear on her doorstep this night, and she wished to be ready for her. But her work came first.

At sunset, Magda's guests used the coracle to cross though the water was not yet high. Stepping outside as it touched the rock, Magda saw Raven circling overhead – she who flies against the wind. Against all. So Asa had come. Raven cawed three times and flew off.

Einar helped his gray-haired companion climb out onto the rock. She stumbled against him, then struggled to straighten on her own. She suffered, but she would not bend to it.

'Welcome. It has been a long while, Asa,' said Magda.

'A long while,' Asa said through her teeth.

'Thou art injured?'

'I am old.' Not a lie. Asa gestured to her companion. 'You have met my son Einar?'

Though his eyes were unlike Asa's, and his mouth prone to smiles, the dark hair and long nose were like hers. Still, Magda knew what she knew.

'Dame Magda.' Einar bowed.

'Go within while Magda speaks to the lad who brought thee across.' She would have need of Twig in the morning. 'How didst thou fare with the kitten, Twig?'

He grinned. 'She likes the milk. I sat out in the sun with her a while this afternoon. She slept on my lap.'

Magda gave him a penny for his day's work. 'Tomorrow?'

'Yes, Dame Magda!'

'Have one of the lads await the guests' departure in a few hours.'

'I will.'

Stepping within and shutting the door, she invited her guests to help themselves to the ale she had set out, and the pot of stew.

Einar served Asa, then himself while Magda saw to the kitten, who drank well.

'Your kitten?' Einar asked as Magda helped herself to food and drink.

'Mayhap.' She took a seat across from the young man, Asa between them.

'I have long wished to meet you, Dame Magda,' he said.

'Asa spoke of Magda to thee?'

'It was my father who told me of you.'

'Magda knows him?' She guessed that his father was Yrsa's son. Or perhaps Odo's, though he would know little about Magda. He had been very young when Sten left with him.

'No, he never met you, but he heard much of you.'

'From thy dam?' Magda asked, smiling at Asa, who would not meet her eyes.

Einar shrugged.

Magda sensed a deep, restless force held in check. Disciplined. Unlike Asa, though much like his grandmother, if she was right about Yrsa. Asa had ever been headstrong, impatient . . . Magda stopped the thoughts. Better to rein in judgement. Life might have taught Asa the wisdom of temperance.

'I took it upon myself to set the kettle over the fire,' said Asa. 'Would you prepare me a soothing tisane?'

'Thy leg is painful.' Magda knew better than to mention the attack. Asa must choose whether or not to speak of it.

'All my bones. The long walk, the coming storm . . .'

Magda set aside her bowl and fetched a powder, mixed it with hot water and wine, proffered the cup to Asa.

Her daughter placed a hand over Magda's and closed her eyes. Magda felt her reach out, and did as well, a mutual sensing that continued long enough to enable her to assess the extent of her daughter's injuries. A bruised arm, sore neck and shoulder, but the worst of it was the already injured leg, and her feet. She was most curious about the feet. This was an older, ongoing trouble.

With a murmured thanks, Asa freed Magda's hand and sipped. 'You are much as I remember.' A familiar bitterness in the low, arresting voice. Magda had never been to her daughter's liking. Knowing that her mother had uncanny gifts, she had hungered for signs of it in herself. From early youth Asa drew, later painted, landscapes to hold the eyes, then the heart and mind. Magda praised her gift, but the child felt it a paltry thing. She could not see how her drawings affected people – for good or ill. She scoffed at Magda's attempts to advise her to hold it close, making use of it only when nothing else would suffice. But the child said anyone could draw and blamed her mother for keeping her true gift from her.

'Magda is glad to see thee.'

A dark laugh. 'Are you?'

'If thou dost doubt it, why hast thou come?'

'A question for a question for a question.' Asa eyed her warily, yet her weariness softened the challenge.

'Magda has sensed thee near. Art thou lodging in the city?'

'I have been. But Einar has offered to share his lodgings.'

Magda looked to him.

'Old Shep's house. A villager upriver told me that his friend had died and left the house empty.'

'A good choice,' said Magda. It was near the river in a copse that hid it from curious eyes— Shep had his reasons. 'Art thou in need of anything? Cushions? Blankets?'

'Einar has been to market,' said Asa. 'But another blanket would be welcome.'

Her guests were wary, taking care with their words, sometimes glancing at each other, as if easing toward their purpose, fearful lest they say too much too soon. They spoke of the body in the river. Magda added little to Einar's description, admitting only to knowing Sam Toller. Some additional talk of the city, nothing of substance.

Uninterested in their dance, Magda rose. 'While Magda sees to the little one, decide who will explain thy purpose in coming to York.' She went to her worktable, taking her time preparing the nipple of milk, then resumed her seat, the kitten in her arms, and bent to the feeding.

'I was always the one to care for the animals,' Asa noted.

Magda said nothing, waiting for more, giving her attention to the life in her arms. Already she felt the bond, her own heart softening. Holda, she thought, the wise one.

'In Peterborough folk talked of pestilence, the certainty that this was the summer it would return, and I regretted waiting so long to come to you,' said Asa.

Einar mouthed the word Peterborough with a frown.

'And thou didst wait again once here,' Magda said, softly, without censure.

'The journey was difficult for me,' said Asa. 'I needed to rest before coming to you. And to understand how it went with you. I know that I come asking for your help when you have little time.'

'Help for thy leg?'

'It is an old injury made worse by a recent fall. For a long while I have eased the pain so that I might continue my work. But the comfort is now my curse.' She nodded to Einar, who knelt to her, removing her boots. Black toes.

'Thou hast eased thy pain with willow bark,' said Magda. Far too much. As a healer, she would have been aware of the danger.

'Yes.'

'Magda trusts there was none in the physick for Celia Cooper.'

Asa hissed. 'No. I know better. Who told you I attended Dame Celia?'

'Her son. The one who helped thee.'

'Then you know her husband attacked me.'

'And that thou wast beaten afterward by two men. The same two who had been in Cooper's yard and heard what Edwin said to thee?'

'I did not notice them.'

'A pity.' Magda lifted a hand to stop Asa when she would defend herself. 'Magda is not blaming thee. She would that thine enemies be apprehended.'

'Thee, thine, never using me and I – I wish you would speak as others do.'

Gently Magda drew the nipple from the sleeping kitten, smiling down on her, grateful for her presence. *Thou wilt be Magda's balance, Holda.* Meeting Asa's petulant gaze, she said, 'Rest. The blood must be allowed to drain from thy feet. A careful, gradual change in the physick to thicken the blood, but slowly. Thou wilt move little for a time. Better for thee to bide here rather than Old Shep's.'

Relief softened Asa's expression. So great had been her fear. Perhaps the journey from wherever she had been revealed to her the folly of her stubbornness. And the attack. This would not be easy. Magda knew her daughter, knew that soon she would regret revealing her weakness. Yet Magda was a healer.

'I did not wish to intrude,' said Asa. 'You have little room.'

'Easier if thou art here.'

'And Einar?'

'Magda prefers to keep a bed ready for one in need.'

'Of course,' said Einar. 'I am settled in Shep's cottage. It is close if I am needed.'

For what? Magda wondered. The young man interested her. It seemed he meant to bide there awhile, which meant he'd had his own purpose in seeking out Magda, something beyond escorting Asa.

'That young woman who comes,' said Asa, 'the brown-haired one, is she your helper? Would I be taking her bed?'

'Alisoun is Magda's apprentice. She will not be needing her bed here for a while.'

'But with the sickness coming—'

'Others need her more at present.'

'Perhaps I might attend you on your rounds, be of some use,' said Asa.

'Not until thou art out of danger.' Even then . . . Asa had ever been a lazy healer, preferring to satisfy her patients with spells and charms – the very things to stoke the fires of the pious against herself and Magda. Indeed it appeared she had already caused suspicion with her drawing. And considering her incautious use of willow bark . . . No. Magda would not be so foolish as to accept her daughter's offer. But that confrontation could wait.

'What of the dead man?' Einar asked. 'You seemed to know the men who came. Will they tell the people in the city it was you who raised the hue and cry? Will there be trouble?'

'Nothing Magda cannot bear.'

'If I can help in any way,' he said.

'Do not worry.' She returned her attention to Asa, who stretched her blackened toes toward the fire. 'Dost thou accept Magda's plan?'

'With gratitude.' She looked up at Magda. 'Do not look so surprised. I *am* grateful. I have given you little cause to love me. Though I did bring your grandson to meet you.'

Einar rose. 'I will fetch your things, *Dame Asa*.'

Asa reached for his hand, pressing it, but not in thanks, in warning.

Magda returned to her workbench, settling Holda in her basket so that she might gather what she needed for Asa's treatment. Her daughter might deny her suffering, but Magda would do what she could to ease it.

'Do you need help?' Asa asked.

'No. Rest now, daughter. Rest.' She would need her strength. Magda saw far more suffering for her daughter in the days ahead.

TW O

H om ecom ing

Late May

O wen was no stranger to leave-taking. During his decade of serving Archbishop Thoresby he was often away from home, and, before that, he had made his farewells to his family in Wales, some for a long while, some forever. But this departure was different, leaving his children at Lucie's family's manor, Freythorpe Hadden, after a brief reunion. Both mother and father riding away. They did it for love of those they left behind, yet never had it so wrenched his heart.

It was not that Owen did not trust the stewards of the manor, Tildy and Daimon. He knew they would care for his little ones as they did their own, and they were most excellent parents. Nor would the couple be overwhelmed by the task, for Lucie's dear friend Emma Ferriby would remain at Freythorpe Hadden with her sons until her husband arrived to take her to their own manor, bringing Alisoun Ffulford to look after Gwen, Hugh, and young Emma. Alisoun was not only beloved by all three children, but she was a skilled healer. All to the good. Yet with the pestilence awakening, Owen suffered continuous showers of needle pricks in his blind, ruined left eye. He prayed it was a natural foreboding in such times, and not a premonition, a knowing, riding away with

a heart so heavy he wondered that his mount did not stumble for
the weight of him.

Even so, his agony did not come close to that of his beloved
wife. Lucie rode with eyes unfocused, her journey happening
within. He knew the territory she traversed, her heart doubting
their decision to leave the children at Freythorpe Hadden where
the two eldest had safely sheltered from the last visitation of the
pestilence, rather than bringing them along on their return to York
and keeping them close, sheltered in their love. They had chosen
what had served them before, a decision they had made that time
because her firstborn, her son with her first husband Nicholas
Wilton, had died in York of pestilence. But what if this time were
different? Owen wished he might carry her worry for her, free her
to enjoy the return to her work, her garden, and Jasper, her stepson
and apprentice.

He owed her so much. Without her prescience he might have
stayed too long at Kennington Palace, ignoring the unpleasant truth
about why Prince Edward had summoned him. He had wanted to
believe the purported reason, that the prince valued his opinion
on the peace negotiations in Westminster. But almost from the
moment they arrived in early May there were signs that was not
quite true. Lucie had given a sympathetic ear to his complaints
about how the prince avoided discussing the negotiations, turning
the conversation to Owen's friendship with Magda Digby, her
respect for his insight, his curiosity about what she'd meant by
that, whether she believed he had the Sight. It was Lucie's account
of her conversation with the king's mistress Alice Perrers that had
shaken Owen out of his denial.

On the surface, Dame Alice presented herself as a chilly woman
of elegance, her gowns and jewels chosen to enhance her subtle
beauty, her voice modulated to caress when in the presence of the
king, express submission in the presence of the royal siblings and
their wives; yet when Lucie had chanced upon her in a garden at
Windsor Castle, away from eyes and ears, she found her warm
and engaging, eager to ask about the plantings in the apothecary
garden in York, what she might suggest for the king's failing
memory and increasing frailty, as well as her own exhaustion and
creeping despair. Her candor was a rarity at court.

Alice – she had asked to be called simply Alice – had apologized for all of her questions. 'Forgive me, but I hope you will soon return home and so I rush to ask now, when I may.'

Lucie admitted that she had been yearning for her garden, thinking of all that she would be doing in this season were she there, hoping that Jasper remembered all that she had taught him. But saying she hoped Lucie soon returned home suggested Alice was eager for their departure. Was she? 'You hope we soon return home . . . Have we offended someone?'

'Forgive me for being unclear. No, you have been the most delightful guests, patient with our demands and far more generous than we perhaps deserve. I wish it for you. I have seen how Prince Edward heaps praise on your husband, as he did me when his father began to fail. With Joan's cunning assistance Edward has discovered how to worm his way into your husband's affections. It happened to me. His praise feels like an intimate caress, touching on one's deepest sources of pride. For your husband, those skills he believes few notice, his observations about the powers in the North gleaned in a decade of serving the archbishop and, lately, the city of York. But the truth is that Edward is most keen to ask of your husband the sorts of questions I have asked you. He had heard of the Riverwoman's respect for the captain, that she believes his loss of half his sight opened his third eye, giving him the gift of a different sort of sight. He hopes that your husband can advise him in ways that no other man might. Yet I see how the captain squirms when asked about this, how he attempts to draw the prince back to matters of state. You must spirit Captain Archer away before he is hopelessly ensnared in providing a service that will endanger him in the dark times ahead, not only the weakening of the royal family but also the realm. We all know that the Death returns. Already there are rumors of it in the countryside. The Church sees the Death as punishment for our sins, a purging. Belief in those with special powers is heresy. When the prince dies – and we know from Dom Antony, who learned it from your Riverwoman, that he was poisoned too long to recover – your husband will be thrown to the wolves of the Church.'

Lucie had declared herself in Alice's debt, and asked how the prince had heard of Magda's talk of a third eye, for she was certain that neither Owen nor Magda would have mentioned that to the princess.

'By all accounts Bishopthorpe Palace and the grounds were so crowded during her visit that it was easy for a listener to disappear among the servants and gardeners. Her Grace learned much that was not meant for sharing. The royal family sees all the realm as their concern, and therefore nothing should be hidden from them. It is all to the good of the realm, if it be in their interest.'

Lucie used that insight in asking Princess Joan to convince the prince that it was time she and Owen returned to York. She couched the request in terms of the good of the realm, that the return of the pestilence meant that their places were in York, she seeing to the health of the citizens as an apothecary, Owen keeping order in the city. She was not immediately successful, but gradually Princess Joan agreed and spoke to the prince, who concurred with their arguments and arranged an armed escort for their return journey.

'I cannot have misfortune befall my eyes and ears in the North as he journeys through a countryside rife with fear.' Prince Edward spoke of reports that the road was teeming with people escaping outbreaks or rushing home to families, peppered with prophets of doom standing by the wayside preaching fear and repentance or bands of thieves preying on the desperate.

The prince had not been wrong, and they had been glad of the addition to Owen's two armed companions, Alfred and Stephen.

'I did not think I would miss the prince's men, but I do,' sighed Brother Michaelo, riding up to join Owen.

They had parted with the prince's retainers shortly before they reached Freythorpe Hadden, when one of the men fell ill with a fever. Lucie was quite certain it was not pestilence. No boils or blackened extremities. But she advised them to stay in the small priory in which they stopped that night. One of the brothers seemed skilled in healing. To be safe, Lucie, Owen, Michaelo, Alfred, and Stephen had spent a few nights in a farmhouse on the manor, watching for signs of fever. A difficult wait, with the children so close, but worth the peace of mind when they at last held the little ones in their arms.

'At least the king's men had wit, a quality sadly lacking in your own armed men,' Brother Michaelo declared.

Owen laughed, and, to his surprise and delight, so did Lucie.

'You miss all the trappings of the prince's court,' she said.

The monk sighed again, no doubt remembering the gorgeous

fabrics and tapestries, the precious stones, gold, silver, mother of pearl decorating the most mundane objects. And the fragrance of the fires, the scents of lavender and rose, the minstrels who softly played in the corners. Elegant, luxurious. Her Grace, remembering Michaelo's efficient management at Bishopthorpe, consulted him about her own household, seeking suggestions, including him in discussions with the officers of the wardrobe. For his pains, which he experienced as joys, she had sent one of the prince's tailors to him to fit him out in a new habit of silk and linen. It was packed in the bag slung on his saddle, handled as if precious cargo. The gift had softened the agony of departure. Princess Joan played his strings with skill, but with respect as well. Indeed, all five in the party returned with gifts. In gratitude for the physicks and instructions to the household in preparing more, as well as advice on dietary changes, the royal couple presented Lucie with a crispinette of gold thread studded with pearls and a brooch in the shape of a linden leaf studded with emeralds and garnets, princely offerings. She also came away with fabric for the children's clothes in appreciation for undertaking the long journey at such a time. Owen touched the hilt of the sword the prince had presented to him, marking him as a member of his household and that of his son when he passed away. Again he had been offered a knighthood, again he had declined. The prince had scowled for a moment, but then laughed that his wife had prepared him for Owen's obstinance. 'I respect you for it. And I trust you will always speak your mind, not what you believe will win you favor with me.'

'To live in the midst of such beauty even for a short while was a great gift,' said Michaelo, 'and I repent being greedy for more.'

'He would agree with you,' said Lucie, nodding toward a raggedy man with burning eyes standing on a log at the side of the road shouting, 'Repent, sinners!' as they passed.

'Blessed Mary, Mother of God, pray for all madmen who think themselves prophets,' Stephen grumbled behind them.

'I had hoped we had seen the last of them,' said Alfred.

'But of course they congregate on the road to York, a cathedral city,' said Brother Michaelo. 'They will flock to us, haranguing all the holy brethren and sisters in the city.' He wrinkled his nose. 'This one certainly smells as if he has been in the hell fire of which he cries. The king's men would have frightened him off.'

'God help us,' Lucie whispered.

Owen moved his horse close, reaching for her hand. 'What is it, my love?'

'I feel such dread of a sudden. What if Alisoun has fallen ill? Or Jasper?'

He knew that dread, but he reassured her. 'It is easy when weary to succumb to the fear such men hope to incite. If anyone in our household were ill, a message would have been sent to Freythorpe.'

'Yes, of course you are right, my love.' Lucie did not sound convinced.

The guard at the gate welcomed them with clear relief, saying that the mayor and bailiffs would be glad of his return. As they walked their horses on to Micklegate, Owen prayed the trouble had nothing to do with his family, only his post as captain of the city.

The apothecary garden was a riot of color, the beds ordered, neat. There were tears in Lucie's eyes as she turned round and round, smiling, thanking Jasper.

'Alisoun worked in it as well. And Kate,' he replied, shaking back the lock of fair hair ever in his eyes, standing straight and proud.

All three were well. And it seemed there was no sign as yet of the pestilence in the city except for a woman who returned from Doncaster already sick. God be thanked, though folk were flocking to the apothecary for the customary remedies against the sickness. Would the children have been better here? Owen shut the door on that thought as Jasper drew them into the kitchen, eager to hear about the court, the wonders they had seen. To Owen the fragrant kitchen was far more enticing than his memories of court. The boot bench against the wall, the hooks for cloaks and hats behind the door, the long table at which Kate stood, the kitten battling a small ball of string amidst the benches and stools by the fire – everything in the room conjured memories of family and friends tucked into its familiar warmth.

Suddenly shy, Kate stood back until Lucie rushed to embrace her. Then she burst into tears, sobbing how she had missed them all, asking after the children and her sister Tildy, wife of the steward at Freythorpe. She was more than a maidservant, she was part of the family, as was her sister.

'Brown as berries and learning a great deal from your nieces and nephews about the countryside,' said Lucie. 'And all of them are learning much from the Ferriby boys.' The pair were older, but had been kind to Gwen and Hugh and the others, including them in their work with the falconer brought from Emma's manor nearby, asking them to lead them round the property, introducing them to their favorite places. 'Has Alisoun been a help to you, Kate?'

'I was glad of her company. But I saw her only in early morning and in the evening. Sometimes in the garden. She spent most of her time in the shop.'

Lucie looked to Jasper. 'You have been so busy? Has Alisoun time to assist Dame Magda?'

'She did that as well. But she's been keen to be in the shop, learning how it works, ordering, how items are delivered, how stored. In the shop and the garden she worked with the plants she would not find in the woods.'

'I am glad she benefited,' said Lucie. 'I hope she will not regret having agreed to now go to Freythorpe.'

'I cannot speak for her,' said Jasper, 'but I think she's proud to have your trust.'

Owen lifted the pitcher of hot water Kate had prepared and nodded to Lucie. 'Time to shed the dust of the road.'

'Just to warn you,' said Jasper, 'George Hempe asked to be sent word the moment you returned. Crispin Poole has stopped in the shop several times as well. They are both concerned about the death of Sam Toller, the Wolcotts' factor, found floating in the river after a storm a week ago.'

'Why is Crispin involved?'

'Sam was found upstream, in Galtres. Magda sent for Crispin.'

Of course the pestilence was not the only threat to peace. But Owen had hoped for a moment's grace. 'They think it might be more than an accidental drowning?'

'They said little to me. But from their eagerness to know when you would return, it would seem so.'

Without a word, Lucie took Owen's free hand and led him into the hall and up the steps to the solar.

*   *   *

Dressed in fresh clothing, Owen stood on the landing listening to a soft rain on the roof, a fresh breeze drifting out from the empty nursery, slipping past him and dipping to find the long window in the hall below. A cart rattled by on the street, children screeched in pleasure, a bell rang, not a church bell tolling a death – not yet. The scent of damp earth rose from the window below. Kate hummed in the kitchen. A momentary solitude, something he had not experienced since leaving home. On the road he traveled in a company, and at Kennington Palace one never had a landing to oneself, for servants, retainers, clerks, dignitaries were ever rushing past, carrying on the business of the prince, of the realm. Yet it was there he had felt alone. Even Lucie had seemed out of reach when not wrapped in his arms, caught up in her own journey of discovery. Here he felt a part of the flow of life.

But he also felt the lack of his children's voices, the sticky hands reaching for his, the clatter of their wooden toys tumbling down the steps. In time, God willing.

Lucie joined him, offering a bowl of ale. 'Missing them?'

'For a moment I felt it more than I could bear.'

'I know.' She took a deep breath. 'But already we are called to our work. Alisoun said she has much to tell us before she leaves in the morning. Are you ready to resume your role as captain of the city?'

As if he had a choice.

As the afternoon unfolded Owen felt the weight of his duties in the city pressing down. From Alisoun he learned that folk were turning against Magda, blaming her not only for the return of the pestilence but for all manner of misfortunes, from dough that failed to rise to Sam Toller's death, some saying the healer made the river take him. He was not surprised to hear that Magda had not been within the walls for a fortnight. But when he learned that her daughter Asa was in York, he did wonder whether Magda's absence had more to do with that arrival. Alisoun continued the litany of woes with an account of Celia Cooper's illness, her husband's accusations about Asa, which seem to have led to an attack as she hurried home. She spoke of the trouble in the Wolcott home, Guthlac's decline under the care of the leech Bernard, how that might somehow be connected to Sam's suspected murder.

'I think Sam's wife was the one pointing the finger at Dame Magda,' said Alisoun. 'Or it might be the leech Bernard.'

'I am glad to hear that Celia is at St Clement's, that is good,' said Lucie, but she did not smile. 'In the coming darkness I fear for those deprived of Magda's healing presence. Have people come to you?'

'They have. I saw a few, but I have made it no secret that I am going away. For the rest I recommended other midwives.'

'Any change in how people behave toward you?' Owen asked.

'Some avoid my eyes when I pass. Custom in the apothecary is down, but only a little. With you here now, that all might right itself.'

Or it might not. He saw in Lucie's frown that she doubted they would be untouched.

'This Bernard. I feared he would cause trouble,' said Owen.

He had not met him, but Lucie had. He'd come to the shop in early April, introducing himself as a physician new to the city, buying a common purgative, leeches, a headache powder, crushed gems. He had said little, vague about where he had lived before but eager to name important names in the city, particularly the Graas – Thomas Graa was the current mayor – and Wolcotts. He had not returned, but he complained to the guild master about the impropriety of a female apothecary. The guild master informed them that he had assured the newcomer that Lucie was a member in good standing and suggested he curb his tongue if he wished to be accepted in the city. They had heard no more of him, but it was enough.

'Has Magda met him?' Owen asked Alisoun.

'No. All he knows of her is secondhand.'

'There are plenty who will feed him all he wishes,' said Lucie.

Owen steered them into the plans for Alisoun's departure for Freythorpe Hadden the following day. She said she would spend the night at the Ferriby home so that they might depart at first light. Peter was eager to see his wife and sons who had been away at Freythorpe Hadden for more than a month.

'Will you see Magda before you leave?' Owen asked.

'Yes. I have already packed all but the physicks that she is preparing. I thought to take my things to the Ferribys and go to Magda just before the closing of the gates this evening, I will be returning after they are barred, but I know the way along the bank at low tide.'

'No need for that. Carn is the Bootham gatekeeper at that hour. I will tell him to expect you.'

'Would you care to come with me?'

'It seems I have plenty to occupy me here. I will see her after you leave. You say Asa is staying with her?'

'Yes. Jasper says you once met her up on the moors.'

'I did. She wished to have nothing to do with her mother. What would bring her here?'

'I know little. She came with her son Einar. He is staying in Old Shep's cottage. Since they arrived Magda hurries me away. Will you— Is there a way you might set a watch?'

'Without Magda knowing?' Owen shook his head. 'But I will make a point of meeting them. What is it that bothers you?'

'A feeling. I do not doubt Einar is Magda's grandson – he has her eyes. But' – she shook her head – 'I cannot explain it.'

He found it all unsettling. 'I will wait for you at Bootham Bar on your return, walk you to the Ferriby house,' he said.

Alisoun made no protest.

Entering the York Tavern in late afternoon felt the final step in returning home, the innkeepers Tom and Bess Merchet awaiting Owen at the door. Tom stood back while Bess gave the traveler a welcoming hug.

'I've kept Jasper, Kate, and Alisoun supplied with bread and ale.'

'So I've heard,' said Owen. 'And I'm grateful. Lucie is eager to tell you about life in Kennington Palace.' She had laughed about it on the first days of the journey home, before the bleakness of their fellow travelers on the road had cast a cloud over all. *As I walked round Kennington Palace I imagined how I might describe it all to Bess – the fabrics, the patterns, colors, gold, silver, pewter, gemstones.*

'And the little ones?' Bess asked.

'In good health, and enjoying the countryside.'

'Praise God for that,' said Tom. He pressed a tankard of ale into Owen's hands and pointed toward Hempe and Poole sitting in the back corner. 'They arrived a while ago. Grim-faced, as they have been many an evening of late, casting a cloud over all.'

Owen took a drink. 'I tasted nothing so fine in the south, my friend.'

Tom nodded, then stepped closer, lowering his voice. 'Ale's not the only thing being brewed in the city at present. Someone's sickening folk with a dark, ugly mash of lies. I'm that glad you've returned. You're the one to find them and drain the poison before someone dies.'

'Any idea who?'

'Look to the friends of the leech Bernard.'

Thanking him, Owen threaded his way through the crowd, smiling at greetings, promising to pass them on to Lucie, all the while noting the ones not smiling about his return. Not that he expected to be welcomed by all, but he thought perhaps he might find some who could speak to the moment, help him understand what lay beneath the ugliness besides fear of plague.

His friends rose to welcome him, teasingly addressing him as 'Sir Owen.' Laughing, he lowered himself onto a stool, raising his tankard in celebration. Bess came to top up all three tankards, then left them. Before they distracted him with questions, Owen told them all that he'd learned from Alisoun about Sam's death, and Jasper's sense that there was more to the story.

'I have seen many a man with the back of his skull opened by a hard blow,' said Crispin. 'But I've never seen such an injury caused by drowning.' He raised his one hand to ward off argument. 'Debris in a rushing river might cause further injury, but to hit him just so, I don't believe it.'

'You think he was murdered, then tossed in the flood?' Owen asked.

Both men nodded.

'I doubted at first,' said Hempe. 'But now— There's the matter of his wife. She claims he went out to confront Magda Digby, to accuse her of poisoning Guthlac Wolcott, and she never saw him again. Implying Magda punished him. Trouble is, two witnesses swear they saw him return that night, heard raised voices in the house, and then him storming out, her rushing out the door and calling down curses on him as he disappeared. "You will be the ruin of us!" They both agree she said that. The curses I left them debating.' He gave a mirthless chuckle.

'You've asked her about their witness?' Owen asked.

'Not yet.' Hempe looked to Poole. 'We want to be sure before we go to her that they are speaking the truth, not making it up to defend Dame Magda.'

'I was the one to tell her of her husband's drowning,' said Poole. 'She showed no surprise, only anger. I thought at the time it might be that his being gone for a few days had prepared her. But she wasted no time in accusing Dame Magda. Nor has any new information moved her to change it. I cannot help but wonder whether she's protecting herself and her children with a lie. And there is the matter of the leech. My mother has lived all her life in York. I asked her whether she remembers any physician being the subject of so much gossip and she does not. "A physician's reputation is everything. They are careful." But not this man, a stranger in the city. I don't like it. He's too bold.'

'I agree,' said Hempe, 'as does Lotta.' Hempe's wife. 'As with Sam's widow, Gemma, the opinion about Bernard falls into those who defend him – Bernard's side, and those who distrust him – Magda's defenders. You see why we want to move with care.'

'And there is the arrival of Magda's daughter Asa. Folk do not trust her,' said Hempe. 'Odd thing is, some say she is the source of darker rumors about Magda than I have heard before, accusing her of sorcery.'

'Plague fear,' said Crispin. 'Even the sisters at St Clement's are anxious. Dame Marian tries to lift their hearts in song, but she struggles to engage them.'

'You have spoken to Dame Marian when you visit your mother at the priory?' Owen asked.

'She sought me out when she knew I was there to see Mother. Asked what she might do to support Dame Magda, who was good to her. I told her I would send word if I thought of aught, and if it seemed Dame Magda needed her help. She also said to tell you that she prays for you and your family every day.'

'I am grateful.' Owen sat back, drinking in all in. He was glad the nun had settled at St Clement's. He and Lucie had taken her in when she first came to York and he had grown fond of her despite a rocky beginning. 'Anything else?' he asked when he'd ordered his thoughts. 'Surely more has happened while I was away.'

'The usual thefts, brawls, a missing child – found the next day,

at her cousin's,' said Hempe. 'A few folk accosted at Micklegate
Bar for fear of bringing Death to the city, one a stranger, one a
tinker familiar to most of us. Troublemakers hear someone has
come north and accuse them of bringing sickness.'

'A family down on the river below Clementhorpe is being
shunned for rumors that the father returned from the south with
the sickness,' said Poole. 'The mood is tense.'

Hempe nodded. 'It's a tribute to you and Dame Lucie that you
caused no stir on your return.'

Owen had been thinking the same.

The business taken care of, they spoke of Crispin's new wife,
Muriel, and their daughter, Lucie. 'Beautiful as her first godmother,'
said Crispin.

Owen smiled, both at the compliment and Crispin's apparent
delight in his child. It mattered not a whit to the man that she was
the daughter of Muriel's first marriage, her father murdered shortly
before her birth. 'I will tell her godmother you said that. Though
I am certain Lucie will visit as soon as all is settled in the shop.'

'Alisoun leaves tomorrow?' asked Hempe.

'She does.'

'With Dame Magda avoiding the city, Alisoun will be missed,'
said Crispin. 'But I am glad your children will be well cared for
while away.'

'Please tell Muriel that she is more than welcome to take your
child to Freythorpe Hadden. It is a large home, and the Ferribys
will be traveling on to their manor.'

'I will tell her, and I know though she will be as grateful as I
am, she will refuse to leave the city.'

Owen understood. Pushing away his own doubt about the
wisdom of leaving his children in the country he had asked for
more detail about the rumors regarding Magda when a cry went
up at the door.

Tom Merchet had his hand on the shoulder of Timkin, an elderly
man, not a regular at the tavern, who was holding his head as he
cried out, 'Old Bede's house is burning!'

There was more, but Owen was already up and moving toward
him, thinking of Bede's widowed daughter Winifrith and her young
children, who lived with him. He bent to the man who was now
doubled over, gasping for air. 'Did the family escape?'

'Don't know,' the old man sobbed. 'I saw folk running to the river calling "Fire!" Rushed after them, saw what was burning. Someone said the men who lit it called it a plague house. A lie!'

Owen needed to hear no more. In a moment he was pounding down Coney Street, his companions falling back – Crispin needed a cane. At King's Staithe he joined Ned Cooper and several other young men who often worked for the bailiffs. He saw the flames now, licking at a much larger space than Old Bede's small cottage. Several small buildings in the lane behind the staithe were on fire, moving close to a large warehouse.

He whispered a prayer of thanks when he spied Old Bede, Winifrith, and the two children among a group huddled together as they watched the fire. Ned had paused by them, his fellows rushing on to grab the pots and buckets that neighbors were carrying out of their houses and rushing down to fill them with river water.

Some men were hacking at a burning wall near a warehouse. Beyond them folk were stretched along the staithe and down on to the mudflats to reach the water at low tide, passing along filled buckets in one direction, empty buckets in another.

Owen grabbed two of the axe-wielders and tossed them toward the shore. 'Water, you fools. Water is what you need.'

'We are paid to watch the warehouse.'

Picking up an axe, Owen growled, 'Water.'

The men stumbled off toward the staithe, sputtering curses.

A woman was wrapping Winifrith, Bede, and the children in blankets.

'You can sleep with us tonight,' she said. 'Devils, the ones who did this. We're all out on the street every day. We'd know if the great sickness was here. Someone did this for spite, they did.'

But who was the target? 'Did you see anything?' Owen asked.

Old Bede shook his head. Winifrith was busy with the children.

'No,' said the woman. 'I knew nothing until my son shouted "fire".'

'Is your house far enough from the flames?'

'I pray so, Captain. Go. Help with the fire. I will take them home.'

Four buildings burning, and the sparks were catching the thatch on a fifth. Owen directed a few buckets there, enough to wet it.

'Keep watch on that,' he ordered a young woman working the line, skirts hitched up, her eyes aglow with the fire. He moved through the crowd, helping where he could. So far it seemed everyone had escaped their homes, most of them working to put out the fire. Homeless, frightened, but safe. Owen helped the water-bearers until Crispin limped down to tell him that the fire appeared to be under control.

'Hempe says leave it to the men,' said Crispin. 'You need to rest up. You will be busy tomorrow chasing down the culprit.'

After passing a few more buckets, Owen sought out the woman sheltering Old Bede's family. 'Did your son see who started the fire?' he asked the woman.

A young man stepped forward. 'I heard someone shout "plague house," and "burn out the Death", but there was so much smoke.'

'Did you see or hear anything else that might help us find them?'

'No. I can ask my friends. Should I come to you if I hear anything?'

'Me. Or Bailiff Hempe. Good work, calling out your neighbors.'

Hempe waited beneath Ouse Bridge. 'Ned's taking charge for the night,' he said 'They will watch the fires, keep them low. That's one of the Graa family's warehouses at the staithe. His men complained that you ordered them about. I set them straight who you are. They whined that in the smoke they hadn't recognized you. As if I believed them. They'd note the patch no matter the smoke.' He spit off to the side. 'I set them to stand the watch with Ned and the others, told them if I heard they'd wandered off I would fine them.'

'Unwilling helpers can be more of a nuisance than a help,' said Owen.

'I don't much care if they guard only the mayor's warehouse. The others will be free to watch the rest.'

'Clever.'

'So off home with you.'

'First I'm off to Bootham Bar to see that Alisoun gets through,' said Owen, 'then home.'

THREE

A Deepening Mystery

Alisoun stood on the rock with Magda and Asa, watching the smoke. One of the lads who manned Magda's coracle had come to report the fire.

'A plague house, they say. Some say it's Old Bede's.'

'I saw him yesterday,' said Alisoun. 'He would have mentioned illness in his house.' But she remembered with what cruel speed the Death cut down her family, as if with each heartbeat she was more alone. She crossed herself.

Magda took her hand, pressing it for courage as she told the boy to set a watch with his friends through the night in case trouble traveled.

'Captain Archer returned,' said the lad. 'He will see to it.'

'He cannot be all places at once,' said Magda. 'Be his eyes on this part of the river tonight.'

She drew Alisoun back into the house, Asa following close behind. 'Bird-eye will see to it,' Magda assured Alisoun. 'He knows what to do.'

'All-knowing, all wise, most honorable Captain Archer,' Asa muttered as she limped past them. 'Sworn to the city and the crown. He will do as he's told.'

Alisoun bristled, but before she could compose a retort Magda nudged her back toward the worktable. She watched Asa limp over to her pallet near the fire, using her cane to ease herself down. Even if she had been so inclined, Alisoun knew better than to offer her assistance. Such gestures were met with sharp rebukes. *I am no cripple. Did I call for aid?*

Magda picked up the mortar and pestle she had abandoned when the boy knocked. 'Bird-eye does not require her approval,' she whispered.

Propped up on pillows, Asa resumed watching them, her dark eyes glinting with suspicion, so unlike Magda that Alisoun had to remind herself that this was her teacher's daughter. Strewn on and around Asa were drawings on bits of paper, women with branches rather than arms, their bodies twined in flowering vines, legs ending in long, tangled roots, stranger even than those Ned had shown her. No wonder folk whispered about her.

Alisoun had felt those eyes on her all the while she'd stood with Magda at the worktable gathering what she might need at Freythorpe Hadden, herbs, roots, barks not likely to be found on the manor lands, as well as sufficient supplies of what she might find to last until she could replenish them. As before the interruption, she struggled to ignore Asa and keep her mind on the work, the lists, Magda's instructions. Even now, her teacher must tap her hand to bring her attention back to the worktable.

'Sorry,' she whispered.

'It is wise to stay alert to a wild one,' Magda said softly.

Startled, Alisoun met Magda's gaze. The clear eyes held hers for a breath, then the instruction continued, and now she engaged, asking questions, seeking to understand not only what she must do, but why. Her heart raced as she took in the breadth of the responsibility she was undertaking, keeping Owen and Lucie's children safe from the pestilence and all other childhood ailments and injuries. She would have neither Magda nor Dame Lucie to advise her. Remembering her family, how quickly they had fallen . . . She used the fear to push her mind to the task at hand, thinking through every instruction, searching for anything that might be beyond her ken.

Finally Magda declared her ready, with the knowledge and the skill needed to protect her charges. 'When the Death took thy family thou wast but a child. Now thou art prepared. Thou wilt do thy best. There is no certainty.' She handed Alisoun the pack.

Slinging it over her shoulder, Alisoun yet hesitated, uncertain how to take her leave.

'Magda will come out with thee.'

Asa stirred, rising to join them. 'I wish you a safe journey,' she said, startling Alisoun by taking her hand. She whispered something unintelligible, blowing on their joined hands, whispering more until Alisoun yanked hers from the woman's strong grip.

Looking insulted, Asa said, 'You would refuse a charm against the pestilence, and a spell to assist you in keeping safe the children

in your charge?' The dark eyes in the strong-boned face
challenged.

'Behave thyself, Asa.'

'You might have asked permission,' said Alisoun.

'Come, Alisoun.' Magda drew her out the door.

Owen carried a jug of Tom Merchet's finest as he left the York
Tavern. He'd changed into dry, clean clothes at home, answering
Lucie's worried questions about the fire. He stopped first at his
friend Archdeacon Jehannes's home, hoping to warn Brother
Michaelo about the possibility of trouble on his nightly charitable
rounds among the poor who slept on the north side of the minster.
But Michaelo had already departed. Jehannes reassured Owen that
he had told him of the uneasy mood in the city.

The jug was to be shared with Carn, on duty at Bootham Bar,
a genial man known as the Scot for his brawn, his copper hair,
and his ability to drink long into the night without effect. Except
for the hair color, the rest had nothing to do with Scots blood in
Owen's experience, and Carn's family had lived near York and
guarded the gates for generations untold. Reaching the gate, Owen
called out, 'They tell me Carn the Scot appreciates a good ale.
I'm here to test that.'

A rattle as the door unlatched. 'Oh aye? Is that Captain Archer?'
Carn's bulk filled the doorway as he peered out, a tuft of red hair
standing up at the back of his head as if he'd been asleep. Yet
he'd heard Owen. 'What does a Welshman know of ale?'

Laughing, Owen entered, closing the door behind him as Carn
led the way up narrow stone steps to a chamber that looked out
on the far side of the gate. A small fire burned in a brazier, more
than the space needed. No wonder the man had nodded off.

'I'm awaiting Alisoun Ffulford.'

'Bailiff said she's to come through. You didn't trust me to
recognize the lass who's seen to Molly and the babe she carries?'

Owen set the jug on the table. 'As good an excuse as any. Drink
from the jug?'

'I can do better than that.' Carn plucked two cups from a bench.
'Will these do?' He sniffed the air. 'You were at the fire. Did
everyone escape without injury?'

While pouring the ale, Owen gave Carn a dramatic account of

the scene on the river. The guard noted that the location, so near Mayor Graa's warehouse, meant all the city would be called upon to come forward with any information.

'They'll soon sort it,' he said.

There was nothing like Tom Merchet's ale to loosen tongues. Owen learned much of interest in the course of emptying the jug – Carn drinking most of it, though when someone pounded on the door the man was quick on his feet, descending to the street and returning in short order without breaking a sweat. He cursed the leech who was turning people against Magda Digby, and those who would believe such stories from a newcomer who hoped to steal business for himself. 'Calls himself a physician, but I hear he does naught but apply leeches no matter the complaint. He's naught but a barber.' Of particular interest to Owen was a sighting of Thomas Graa returning from his Skelton property in the company of Gavin Wolcott on several occasions – a curious combination.

'Not far from there, a family lost their bairn to the pestilence some days past,' said Carn. 'I suppose the mayor believes he is protected by his wealth, but the rest of us folk are uneasy about the Death coming so near. I'll not go to Easingwold soon, of that you may be sure.'

Owen wondered about Magda. Would she be safe? And he meant to have a word with Mayor Graa on the morrow, about many things.

Out on the rock Magda nodded at the questions in Alisoun's eyes. 'Yes, Asa's preference for charms and spells caused the parting. She did not care for the work of learning the healing arts, far more interested in the trappings, being wrapped in a mysterious cloak of power, wishing folk to admire her, swearing vengeance on those who offended her, caring little about healing.'

'Is that why you discourage my curiosity about charms and spells?'

'Didst thou think Magda warned only thee from depending on such tricks?'

'Are they merely tricks? Is she not effective?'

'Seldom. She is a vagabond, moving on before word of her deception is on everyone's lips. Or her acts of vengeance.'

Alisoun steeled herself to tell Magda something she feared

might be construed as an accusation. She decided to be bold with the name of the one she actually suspected. 'Asa must be alone in the house often?'

'She is.' Despite the fading light Alisoun felt Magda's close regard. 'She stole something from thee.'

'Remember the mandrake root, the one I called a poppet?'

Magda frowned toward the house. 'She will see a use for that, money to be made. But thou hast mandrake in thy pack, and in several of the mixtures.'

'I do. I had not meant to use it, but I like to keep it by me, wherever I am biding.'

'A charm?'

Alisoun bowed her head. How to explain? At first she had meant to keep it, learn a spell or charm that would make use of her treasure. But in time she'd found it comforted her to know it was near. 'I feel better knowing it's beneath my mattress.'

'Thou didst not take it with thee while working in Dame Lucie's apothecary?'

'No. I feel safe there. Not that I do not here, but you are so often away, and the river . . .' she stopped. Everything she said made it worse.

'So thou hast not searched for it since Bird-eye and the apothecary went away?'

'No. Not until tonight.'

Magda touched Alisoun's shoulder. 'Such a comfort is difficult to lose. But thou art strong. Mayhap the need is gone. Magda is proud of thee, Alisoun. Thou hast applied thyself, learned from thy mistakes, dedicated thyself to mastering the knowledge. Do not doubt thyself.'

For a moment, Alisoun could not move, could not speak. Was this a jest? But no, she saw the light in Magda's eyes, heard the warmth in her voice. Words still would not come, so she wrapped her arms around Magda's slender form and held her close. After a few moments, Magda drew away.

'The tide comes in as the moon brightens. Go now.'

Now she heard the water slipping across the rocks, and sensed a watcher on the riverbank. Not like Asa's watching, but disturbing in its own way.

'Einar,' she whispered. 'Come to see his mother?'

'He is not her son,' said Magda, 'though she claims it. Wishes it.'

'He is not your kin?'

'He is the grandson of Magda's daughter Yrsa.'

'Asa's sister?'

'Half-sister. Yrsa died long before Asa's birth.'

But lived long enough to give birth to Einar's parent. Alisoun knew that Magda's history was complex, and had imagined several marriages, but not such an expanse of years between children. Of course it would be so.

'Why is he here with her?'

'Mayhap he came upon her and found her useful. Or she him. She was ever one to see to herself.'

'But why here? With you?'

'That is not yet clear to Magda.' She touched Alisoun's cheek. 'Thou art wise to distrust their purpose. Magda is not so foolish she believes her wayward daughter has come to respect her. Nor that a young man might be in awe of his elder.'

'Her drawings frighten me.'

A grunt. 'She would smile to hear that. Think no more of them.' A gentle push toward the stone pathway across the rising water. 'Go now. Walk in thine own wisdom, thine heart open and tender.'

Einar still stood on the bank. 'He hides behind a veil of courtesy,' said Alisoun.

'Yes. There is good in him, but greed as well.' Magda lifted her head, smelling the air. 'The fire is out. Now go. The water rises.'

Alisoun picked her way along the stone causeway. As she reached the bank, Einar held out a hand to steady her.

'Mistress Alisoun.'

'Einar.' She nodded, but ignored his outstretched hand, walking on past him, setting off for the city gate. She listened for his footsteps over the sounds of the camps of the poor as they settled for the night. There. He was following.

'I am sorry you are leaving,' he said as he caught up to her.

'Because we are such old friends?' She glanced at him as she continued, noticing a dagger at his waist and a bow slung over his shoulder, a quiver of arrows. His posture was proud, pleased with himself. 'A good day's hunting?'

A low chuckle. 'You learn Dame Magda's ways, speaking in questions.'

She did find it useful, serving a double purpose in avoiding inconvenient questions while disconcerting the questioner, unbalancing them. Choosing to ignore Einar, Alisoun called out to a group of boys walking a watch along the edge of the encampment, asking whether they had seen any strangers, other than the one annoying her. The boys had seen none. They offered to walk Einar back to Old Shep's cottage in Galtres. Laughing, she assured them she could defend herself.

'They know where I'm biding.' Einar's tone was not so proud as before.

'They consider themselves Dame Magda's retainers, ready to serve and defend her. You would be wise to have a care not to antagonize them.'

'I will remember that.'

The road was empty, the gate lit by a solitary lantern at the guard post door off to one side.

'Magda is nothing like Asa,' he said after a brief silence.

'Asa had not told you the reason they had not spoken in such a long while? Had you expected a warmer welcome?'

He laughed. 'More questions.'

She might say much about their differences, but she chose to say nothing, holding her observations close in an uneasy embrace, still seeking to understand. It pained her to recognize much of herself in Asa, the Alisoun that might have been had she not vowed to try Magda's way first before setting out in the direction that called to her, the way of charms and spells, far more alluring than committing to memory the lore of healing plants and observing, listening, assisting her teacher. Love and fertility charms, spells against the heir to an inheritance, spells against a competitor, charms to win an invitation to a guild, spells of protection against the pestilence – though such things seldom worked, the desperate still sought them, and paid well. But now, seeing Asa's bitterness, her inability to prevent her own physical suffering, Alisoun felt ungrateful and not a little foolish.

'Are you excited to go off to the country?' Einar asked.

'I grew up on the river, on a farm,' said Alisoun. 'It is the city that still excites me. But the hunting will be better. You want to

have a care in Galtres. It is a royal forest. Magda has permission
to hunt coney and such small game. A grateful sheriff arranged it
by royal consent years ago. If you are caught hunting, you will
be fined. Or worse.'

'Magda will vouch for me.'

'You asked? If not, I would advise you to do so.'

'But we're kin.'

Alisoun said no more. Let him discover the difference between
blind loyalty to family and a respect for the law of the
community.

Owen stood by the window as he listened to Carn describing the
foul rumors regarding Magda. 'What is the substance of the tales?'
he asked.

'You will not be surprised to hear the accusers seem unaware
of anything but their own fear that God will smite those who
seek the help of a pagan healer. He's not done that before. Why
now?' Carn took a long drink. 'Edwin Cooper cursed Dame
Magda's daughter for casting a spell that made his wife talk in
her sleep. Have you ever heard such a thing? His son Ned says
both his parents chatter like jays all the night. Always have. He
spoke also of drawings that cursed his wife's dreams. And there
was something about a charm tucked in his wife's bed, a pagan
thing.'

That interested Owen, knowing that although Magda held no
truck with such things, Asa favored them. 'So it is the daughter
who might cause God to smite him.'

'Ah, but Cooper says she does her mother's bidding. They do
say the archbishop has spoken out against Dame Magda.'

'Archbishop Neville is here?'

'No. They say he's written a letter.'

'Who is they?'

'Gavin Wolcott.'

'Graa's new friend?' Owen tucked that away. 'To whom did he
write the letter?'

'To the heads of the religious houses in York.'

Owen would ask his good friend Archdeacon Jehannes about
that. Turning toward the window he noticed a familiar figure
approaching the gate.

'I see Alisoun,' he said. 'She is not alone.' Carn joined him at
the embrasure. 'Do you recognize the man?'

'No. Cannot say that I do.'

Owen clapped Carn on the back and thanked him for the
company. 'If you would open the gate I might engage him before
he leaves her.'

'He cannot enter.'

'I know. I mean only to speak with him.'

Outside the gate Owen avoided the area lit by Carn's torch and
the one overhead, choosing to watch from the shadows. Alisoun
walked more quickly as she grew near, as if to shake off her escort.
The man, no taller than Alisoun, walked with the cockiness of
youth, a guess confirmed as he moved into the light. Dark hair,
light skin, nothing familiar about him. Owen stepped out into the
road. The young man drew a dagger and began to stride forward
as if to defend his companion.

'Captain,' Alisoun called out. 'How kind of you to meet me.'

The youth hesitated, glancing back over his shoulder, then halted,
sheathing the dagger.

'Forgive me, Captain. I thought someone meant to attack
Mistress Alisoun.'

'Folk in York know better than to threaten me,' Alisoun said.

Owen laughed. 'Indeed. You must be new to the city.'

'Einar.' He bobbed his head. 'I have heard much about you,
Captain.' He adjusted the bow slung over his shoulder.

'You've been hunting?' Magda had permission to hunt small
animals in Galtres, and Alisoun as a member of her household,
but the privilege extended to few others.

Einar had the good sense to look discomfited.

'Are you a good shot?'

'Fair enough. Though out of practice.'

'Come to St George's Field on Sunday,' said Owen. 'We practice
at the butts. For King Edward.'

'I would be welcome?'

'If I invite you, yes.'

Einar cocked his head, considering. 'I might.'

Owen nodded to him and turned to follow Alisoun through the
gate.

Carn stood behind him. 'Poor young fool. He's not won your heart, eh, Mistress Alisoun?' he laughed.

'I hardly think that was his intent,' she said. 'How goes your wife, Carn?'

'Bless you, young woman. Round as she is tall and humming about the house. Young Meg is excited to assist Dame Magda when the time comes. Glad we are we live without the gates.' He waved them on, wishing her a safe journey.

As Owen and Alisoun walked along Petergate she asked after Old Bede and his family. Already weary of recounting the evening, Owen was glad she did not ask for a full account. Indeed, she said little, seeming to have much on her mind, which he would expect the night before a journey. He welcomed the quiet, thinking about the small items he meant to pursue in interviews on the morrow. As they reached Christchurch, Alisoun told him of Magda's parting comments about Asa, and Einar's relationship to her.

'He has her eyes, did you notice?' she asked.

'No, but he was mostly in shadow.' He was curious about the youth.

'You will watch over her, Captain?'

'He worries you?'

'Both of them do.' She described Asa's drawings and how they affected her. 'The stuff of nightmares. Women becoming trees.'

'I recall nothing so disturbing in the house on the moors. But I do remember her animosity toward her mother. Small wonder Asa had forged her own path.'

'She is as unlike Magda as a daughter could be. She may have stolen something from me, a mandrake root shaped like a person. It was hidden, so she clearly searched the house.'

Remembering Carn's story of the charm, Owen wondered. 'Did you tell Magda?'

'I did. She was not surprised.'

Nor was Owen. Asa had impressed him as a woman who did as she pleased with no regard for others. To search her mother's house for items she might use seemed quite in character. He promised he would make time to visit Magda. His disappointment in the prince's purpose in summoning him was on his mind, and until he talked to her it would hang over him, clouding his thoughts. 'I will think how to keep an eye on Einar and Asa,' Owen said.

He sensed Alisoun's relief. 'The lads who take turns watching her coracle, do you think? I might ask them to do me a favor.'

'I should have thought of that. But coming from you, reporting to you, their hero – they will be proud to have your trust.'

He smiled, thinking how much the lads admired Alisoun, how in awe of her they were. *She shoots the bow like a man. No fear! No one has ever apprenticed to the Riverwoman.* 'Are you taking your bow?'

'It is already at the Ferriby house,' said Alisoun. 'When Master Peter saw it he asked if he had wasted his money hiring a few men to protect us on the journey. I reminded him that I would be stopping at Freythorpe Hadden, so he would need the men for the completion of his journey to his manor.' She laughed. 'My bow is for hunting, helping with the meat supply on the manor.'

'I count on you to have your bow ready to defend my children when out in the fields,' said Owen. 'Warning folk who might wander there that they are welcome to approach the gatehouse to ask for food or work, but should they choose to take without asking, they will pay.'

'You depend on me to protect them?'

'I do.'

She walked a few steps before responding. 'You may count on me, Captain.'

'We are grateful to you, Alisoun. I would not blame you for wishing you might stay with Magda in this strange time.'

'I promised. And I love your children.'

They moved down through the Shambles, quiet at this time of night. A stray dog scooted out of their way, a cat streaked across the wet cobbles after a rat. The stench of the butchers' street was subtler at night, the bloods washed down, the scraps fed to dogs or given to the poor, shops shut, housefires burning. The latter scent seemed stronger than usual. Or was it himself? Carn had guessed he'd been to the fire on the river. Had he smelled it on him despite his change of clothing? Perhaps, but as he turned into Hosier Lane, St Crux Church looming to his left, Owen noticed that the house next to the Ferriby's was shrouded in smoke.

'A fire at the Wolcott house?' asked Alisoun.

'I see no flames.' Smoke, yes. Owen blinked to keep his one

good eye clear as they passed. Peter Ferriby answered his door on the first knock, as if he had been watching out for them.

'Burning rubbish in the yard,' he muttered. 'Owen, it is good to see you.' Peter pressed his arm, an unusual gesture for the staid merchant. Though their wives were good friends and the families occasionally dined together on feast days, Peter had treated Owen with distant courtesy. 'Alisoun, let me relieve you of that heavy pack.' He set it in front of a collection of such packs piled round chests. 'I am glad I arranged for a large cart, and still I am uncertain it will all fit.' He rubbed his hands together. 'You heard about the fire at the staithe? A plague house, they say.'

'I was there,' said Owen. 'By all accounts there is no pestilence on that street, though there are several families who have lost their homes. How did you hear of the fire?'

'My servant saw it as he came across the bridge after making the arrangements for the cart.' Peter frowned. 'Not a plague house? Damn the gossips. But my neighbor had heard the same. Gavin said the victim was his laundress, Goodwife Brown. Poor woman. Folk will be wary of her. A pity. But with so much fear . . .' He spread his arms as if to say what can one do. 'I will be glad to escape the city.'

'Gavin Wolcott. I wondered whether they'd had a fire,' said Owen.

'As I said, fools were burning bedding in the garden this evening and failed to control the blaze. I ran out with a bucket of water to douse sparks on my gate.'

'Damage?'

'Nothing to speak of. They were more careful with the children's bedding in the autumn. A terrible loss for Guthlac and Beatrice.' Peter crossed himself.

'Why bedding?' Alisoun asked.

'When Dame Beatrice heard that the plague house was Goodwife Brown's she ordered the servants to burn the bedding delivered this morning. Lettice Brown is their laundress. Gavin – her stepson – was out there as well. A rare truce between the two of them – they are usually at war. He made a right mess of it, but soon had it under control. But enough of them. Sit, sit. Ale? Wine?'

Though Owen would rather head next door to ask about the rumor and then return to the scene to find out whether anyone had seen Lettice Brown – he did not recall any mention of her – he felt it would be discourteous to rush off without expressing his gratitude for Emma Ferriby's care of the children at Freythorpe Hadden and Peter's accommodating Alisoun on the morrow. Alisoun joined them, putting their host at ease with questions about his sons Ivo and John. He, in turn, spoke of his gratitude that Emma's favor for Lucie and Owen had sent her and the boys to the countryside before the mood in the city had grown so tense.

When the conversation wound down, Owen took his leave, repeating his thanks, wishing them both a safe journey.

As he crossed to the Wolcotts' door Owen considered what he knew of them. He had encountered Gavin's father, Guthlac, on occasion, a gruff elderly man who had been the gossip of the city four years earlier when he married a pretty young woman, a distant cousin. On all accounts, and much to everyone's surprise, the marriage was reportedly a happy one, producing two children in quick succession, Guthlac doting on them. And then tragedy struck when both children died of the pestilence in late summer. It was said that Gavin, a son by an earlier marriage, heir to the business, had distanced himself from the couple for the years of their happiness, but had hovered like a carrion bird since his father's loss, as if sensing that his time had come to take over the business.

At the Wolcott house Owen's knock was answered by a servant, who had him wait outside. Gavin appeared at once, clearly annoyed though courteous, explaining that his physician was there to see to his burn and it was not a good time to entertain a guest. Owen had noticed that his right sleeve had been cut away to expose a large area of blistering. He was otherwise well dressed, a slender young man with expressive eyes, narrowed now as he impatiently awaited an explanation for the interruption. 'What business might the captain of the city have with me?'

'I understand you heard earlier that the fire near King's Staithe had begun at Lettice Brown's. Who told you that? How did you hear that so quickly?'

Gavin took a step back, the slight sneer replaced by wariness. 'Dame Beatrice heard someone calling it out as they rushed past toward the river. Why do you ask? Was it not true?'

'I wondered how they knew that before they had been to the staithe.'

Gavin said nothing for a moment, his eyes moving as if he were calculating what was best to say. 'I see why you wished to know. It *is* unlikely. Was it true? I ask because Goodwife Brown has been our laundress for a long while so of course we are concerned.'

'As far as we can ascertain there are no plague houses in that area,' said Owen.

'God be thanked,' he said, but muttered a curse. Seeing Owen's quizzical look he said, 'Burned good bedding and suffered this burn for nothing. Silly woman. I should know better than to act on her word.' He nodded to Owen. 'I thank you for the news, Captain. I will inform the household.' He began to shut the door.

Owen put out an arm to stop it. 'While your physician sees to your burn, I would speak with Dame Beatrice about her late factor.'

'About Sam Toller? She had nothing to do with him. And why now? No. As I said, she is with the physician and my father.'

'You *said* the physician was here to see to your burn.'

'And my father. Now if you will—'

'Have you learned anything new about Sam Toller's death?'

'I— No. I thought it had been established that he drowned.'

'The rumor about Dame Magda—'

'Oh that. Women's gossip. I can see no reason the Riverwoman would push Sam into the water.'

'Your choosing to replace Dame Magda with Master Bernard was merely a matter of preference?'

'My— What does that have to do with Sam's death? What are you implying?'

'I merely refer to Sam's widow's claim that he had gone to confront Dame Magda about your father's illness.'

'I'd not heard that.'

'No? So why did you replace her?'

'I hardly think—'

'Folk are seeing a connection.'

'The truth is Father was not improving under her care. I had heard good things about Master Bernard, so I hoped Father might benefit from a different approach.'

'Ah.'

'You heard that it was more than that?'

He read nuances. Owen would watch himself. 'Your name was

mentioned in connection with a letter that the archbishop sent to the abbots and priors of York condemning Magda Digby.'

'*My* name? But I've never met the archbishop. Why would I have anything to say about matters of the Church?' Now he was decidedly uneasy. 'I assure you I have nothing against the Riverwoman.'

'Perhaps my bailiffs misunderstood.'

Gavin's expression eased a little.

Owen thanked him for the information. 'I will return tomorrow to speak with Dame Beatrice. If you would inform her.' He walked away before Gavin could disagree.

He had much on his mind as he walked through the now-quiet streets. Having not seen Lettice Brown among the neighbors crowding round the fire, he headed back to the King's Staithe. The cool of evening drew a mist off the river, shrouding the charred buildings, pressing down upon the watchers the grim stench of wet ash, burnt timbers, rushes, and all that burned with homes which hours before had sheltered families.

Holding high a lantern, Alfred led the way toward the charred remains of the Brown home beside Old Bede's. It looked as if a section of the warehouse wall had collapsed on what had been the Brown house. Owen remembered the warehousemen working to tear it down.

'Her husband came staggering home to this, drunk as usual,' said Alfred. 'We had to drag him away. A family took him in. No one has seen his wife.'

Owen would order a search of the rubble in daylight. For now, he asked who else was unaccounted for. A child, who had been visiting his aunt. People prayed he'd merely lost himself in the confusion and would be found.

'Smells like rain in the wind,' said Hempe, appearing out of the mist. 'I pray someone's taken the child in for the night. There's a hope Goodwife Brown is with her daughter out on the king's road. She is expecting a child any day. Go home, my friend. Sleep. You've had a rude welcome home and face a long day ahead.'

Grinding roots, tying sprigs together to be hung from the rafters to dry, mixing powders and lotions for tomorrow's rounds, Magda did not pause in her work as Einar described meeting Bird-eye and how he had been invited to St George's Field for archery practice. He had not expected such a welcome, was much taken by Captain Archer. Clever of Bird-eye. She was glad he'd met Einar. Though a brief encounter, the young man was now in his eye. Clearly he meant to gauge the character of the young man, and quickly. He had sensed something. She looked forward to talking to him.

Asa sat up, reciting her oft repeated criticism of Owen Archer. In truth, it had little to do with Bird-eye and much to do with Asa's long-ago obsession with one of his comrades in arms whom she'd found hiding up on the moors. He had never returned her affection, but she had woven a tale that blamed Bird-eye for his friend's departure. It was ever the way with Asa. She moved through life dragging behind her a burden of grudges, adding to it with every new encounter, folding each slight with tender care and tucking it away so that she might drag it out at a later date, keeping it fresh and ready should she ever re-encounter the accused. Magda doubted that she need warn Bird-eye. He had witnessed the damage Asa had done to his friend and would remember her well enough. But she would avoid providing Asa the opportunity to attack Owen when he came to call. It was high time she coaxed Asa out of the nest. But as she observed her visitors she saw that she might not need to take such action.

Asa patted her pallet, inviting Einar to perch beside her. Eying the narrow space, he chose instead to crouch down, though it meant Asa must shift so she might not be overheard. Magda counted it fortunate that her daughter assumed her hearing had dimmed with age. Setting aside mortar and pestle, Magda took up a quieter task, blending powders.

'What have you learned?' Asa whispered. 'Any news?'

Einar gave a little breathy laugh. 'I've not gone into the city. But Sunday, with the captain's invitation . . .'

'Move about, listen to the gossip, the rumors.'

'Do you have a plan?'

'How can I? I know nothing of his movements.'

'You wait for me to tease him out? The burden is all mine?' Einar's whisper was loud with impatience. When Asa thought to appease him with a pat on the cheek, he flinched. He was not so fond of the woman.

'I will see to my tasks,' Asa retorted, her voice breaking. She glanced at Magda, who hummed under her breath as she worked.

'You will leave here?' Einar asked.

'Soon. Some shifting to do.'

'Into the city?'

'As you refused to share lodgings.'

Einar said nothing.

An uneasy partnership. Not surprising. Magda did not yet know who they were hunting, and whether Alisoun's mandrake root was part of Asa's incomplete plan. For now, she focused on Asa's 'shifting.' She could well imagine all that might disappear from shelves in the night. She added a few new ingredients to the mixture for Asa's evening tisane. While she slept, deeply, safely, Magda would work.

Einar took the first opportunity to depart, asking if he might accompany Magda on her rounds in the forest sometime soon. She smiled and said he might come any time.

'Am I also welcome?' Asa asked.

'Patience. Magda has a distance to cover and thou art hobbled at present.' She chose not to mention the donkey cart. She wanted to observe Einar on his own.

When Asa fell into a deep sleep, Magda went to work doing her own shifting, tucking behind the false wall in the darkest corner all that she would need for the next few weeks as well as those ingredients difficult to replace. What was left on the shelves would not be missed, or too heavy for her to carry in her condition. Unless Einar chose to assist her. It would be interesting to see whether he did. Kneeling to the packs next to Asa's pallet Magda found one empty. Asa would be busy in the morning. From the other Magda drew out the items, putting aside those medicines she would rather not be responsible for having left in her daughter's possession, including far too much ground willow bark – she had already crippled herself. Disappointing not to find Alisoun's mandrake root, though she found ground mandrake root, which she also confiscated. Satisfied that she had done what she could, Magda put all she'd removed into the hidden cupboard and closed it up. At peace with herself, she went to feed Holda more milk, then tucked her into bed with her, falling asleep to deep purring.

FO U R

Secrets

Owen woke to familiar street sounds. Rolling over, he discovered Lucie gone. Light slanted through the shutters. How late was it? His first morning waking in his own bed after a month away, and he had much to do. He intended to call on Mayor Graa before being summoned, preferring to be the instigator of an investigation rather than have it assigned him, particularly when dealing with an official whose sympathies were rarely with the common folk. On the landing, habit took him into the nursery. With eye closed he imagined his little ones here, their bodies warm with sleep, their familiar scents, giggles, whispers, shrieks. How he missed them. He was grateful they were away, safe – he prayed he was right about that.

Descending to the hall, he paused at the garden window gazing out on a soft dawn rain. Not so late. Yet as the kitchen door opened he heard low voices, then Lucie approaching. She wrapped her arms round him, resting her head against his back.

'A long day ahead for both of us,' she said.

'You will be in the shop?'

'Yes. Jasper will not have Alisoun to help.'

'You are glad to return to your work?'

She kissed his neck. 'Yes and no.'

He turned to hold her close and kiss her mouth, her cheeks. Laughing, she pushed away.

'We have guests.'

'I heard voices.'

'George, Alfred, Brother Michaelo.'

'Quite a company. Any news?'

'The missing child was found, frightened, but unharmed, and returned to his aunt, God be thanked. But Lettice Brown has not been seen. Michaelo will tell you more of that.'

*   *   *

Assignments agreed upon, Owen set off for Thomas Graa's home, Brother Michaelo accompanying him as his scribe and his extra eyes and ears. Owen had come to appreciate the monk's powers of perception and his knowledge of the wealthy and the powerful in the city and shire. On the way Owen asked whether Archdeacon Jehannes had said anything of a letter written by Archbishop Neville.

'Which would mean his secretary, my cousin Leufrid.' Michaelo sniffed. 'Unholy beggar.' Hard feelings from an old wound. When Michaelo had first come to England from Normandy a large sum of money had been entrusted to Dom Leufrid, with which he was to buy his cousin a place in an influential abbey. Instead, Leufrid had pocketed the money though he claimed he'd spent it in gaining Michaelo's entry into St Mary's, York. 'Without ever having met Dame Magda he accepted the word of an anonymous letter writer complaining of her sorcery in the city, expressing his fear that God would look away when the pestilence arrived in York.'

So Carn had been right, the archbishop had sent such a letter. 'Did Dom Jehannes have any thoughts as to the letter writer?'

'He says he does not. But there is the matter of a letter he wrote to the Bishop of Lincoln while we were at court asking what he knew of Bernard the leech.'

'The occasion of that inquiry?'

'Whispers of just such accusations regarding Dame Magda and then her daughter, Dame Asa, originating from the man, though apparently he denies it. And no, Dom Jehannes did not speak with him. So he was curious. But he's not heard from Bishop Bokyngham.'

'What was the essence of Neville's missive?'

'He merely quoted gossip and warned against women who weave charms and spells while calling themselves midwives.' Michaelo bobbed his head as they passed several friars haggling with a merchant.

'No specific orders?'

'No. Just spreading rumors.'

'Jehannes's reaction?'

'He doubted the authenticity. He has written to His Grace, enclosing a copy of the letter and sent it by a messenger who is to deliver it directly to Archbishop Neville and no other, particularly not Leufrid.' A little smile. 'I wrote it out for him in a fair hand.'

Owen grinned. 'Well done. Were there any specifics cited?'

'As is his wont he added a positive suggestion, urging the revival of barefoot processions in the parish churches on Wednesday mornings.'

To Owen's mind the processions would fan the flames of fear, but he could see the benefit in the comfort such expressions of penance might bring and said nothing.

'I will bring you a copy of the letter when I write up today's report, Captain. Suffice to say none of it is believable.' Although Michaelo had not always approved of Dame Magda, he held her in high regard ever since the late Archbishop Thoresby had insisted on her being the healer by his side in his final illness. She had given the archbishop much comfort and ease in his last days.

They continued in companionable silence, Owen noticing the temper of the city, what seemed as usual, what suggested a fearful undercurrent. Michaelo's short cape with hood protected him from the gentle rain and shrouded his face, but Owen could see that his eyes also followed passersby with quiet interest.

'I had forgotten about the grave in your garden,' Michaelo said, quietly. 'I came upon Dame Lucie kneeling beside it this morning. Thinking she was tending a flower bed I approached, but she was weeping. I regret disturbing her.'

Owen took a breath before he spoke. The grave of her first husband and their child. Thoresby had granted her permission to bury Nicholas Wilton in the garden that had been his masterwork. Indeed, he had arranged for the ground to be consecrated. Before his death he had instructed Jehannes to move the tiny coffin of her firstborn, Martin, there as well, a gift Owen had feared would be more curse than blessing. 'Martin was an infant when the pestilence took him. He has been in her thoughts of late.'

Michaelo crossed himself. 'I will light a candle this evening.'

'Bless you.' Owen said no more, overcome by the image of his beloved kneeling in the soft rain tending the grave. He remembered her fear when their children burned with fever in late autumn, a depth to it that he prayed he did not come to understand, his own terror being overwhelming. The fear he'd experienced in battle was nothing compared to that he had felt for his children. Moving out of the way of a cart brought him back to the present.

Not far beyond the crossing for Ouse Bridge with all its bustle and business the city seemed to fall away as Castlegate opened into beautiful gardens. Thomas Graa had carved out a city manor near his warehouse at King's Staithe, the house surrounded by gardens of graceful trees, well-kept flower and herb beds, and meandering walkways that continued across Castlegate, tumbling down to the bank of the Foss.

'Beware a mayor who so flaunts his wealth,' Michaelo said. A peculiar remark for one who wore finely tailored robes except when ministering to the poor.

A servant answered the door, bowing them in, inviting them to wait in the screens passage. Family activity could be heard in the hall beyond, a child demanding that his parents clout a servant who denied him a second helping, a woman trying to reason with him in a tight voice. Michaelo muttered something that Owen did not strain to hear, for someone approached, calling out for wine in his parlor. Three cups. The servant returned from round the carved wooden screens to lead them into the hall, directing them down the side, well away from the family gathered near the hearth – children, two young women, an older woman, several hounds lounging about their feet.

Another wall of wooden screens, solid, so as to afford some privacy, enclosed Thomas Graa's parlor, a room with a large table and several high-backed chairs, a shelf behind the most cushioned chair holding rolls of documents and piles of tally sticks. Graa arrived as Michaelo set his wax tablet and stylus on the table. He was a compact man, though tending toward portly in the midsection, with bushy light brown hair surrounding a bald spot, nails trimmed, hands pink and soft. When he moved, he gave off a scent of rosewater.

'A scribe? Is that necessary?' Though irked, he spoke in his usual soft, melodious voice.

'Knowing I can trust Brother Michaelo to record what he hears, I can devote all my attention to you,' Owen said, matching the calm, friendly tone.

The mayor gave him a nod, his expression shifting between satisfaction and uncertainty. After the courtesies, in which Graa asked after the prince's health and expressed his relief that Owen had not lingered at the royal court, he spoke of the damage to his warehouse the previous evening and asked whether the fire-starters had been apprehended. He did not ask about casualties, neither did he express concern about those who had lost their homes and their few possessions.

'You have heard that Lettice Brown is missing?' Owen asked. 'That hers and several other homes were destroyed?'

A raised brow. 'I had not heard about the woman. Should I know her?'

'Her home is next to your warehouse.'

The mayor frowned. 'The laundress with the drunken lout for a husband?'

'A fair description.'

'Poor woman. I warned her husband when he built that shed they call – called a home that he was trespassing on my property with a building unsafe for habitat.' Gesturing as if to say what can you expect he went on to complain about the entire street of unsafe dwellings. 'They were warned. Now they will demand recompense. But she is a good woman. We have used her on occasion, after large events when there is much to launder. Quick and efficient. I pray you find her.'

Owen asked whether he or the council had any leads on the death of Sam Toller, Wolcott's factor.

Graa frowned. 'Toller? Oh, yes. I have heard various rumors, but I am quite certain the man simply drowned.'

'How can you be certain?'

'It happens all the time, Archer. You've lived on the river long enough to know that. And who would wish to kill the factor of a dying man? We are Christians in York.'

Michaelo cleared his throat. Owen asked if he might hear the rumors.

'Some said his wife argued with many of the tradesmen and folk at the market. But would they not then go after her rather than her husband? Common gossip, not worth considering. And there are those who believe the Riverwoman disposed of him, some nonsense about his confronting her with proof that she has been slowly poisoning his employer. But my wife and many of the wives of the council members assure me that is slander.' A sigh. 'Though I must say, many worry that the Riverwoman is bringing a curse on the city. Edwin Cooper the loudest of them. Doesn't his son serve the bailiffs?'

Ignoring the question, Owen said, 'I understand Cooper complained that his wife had bad dreams.'

'Yes. And that during the Riverwoman's ministrations his wife talked in her sleep as if bewitched.'

'It wasn't Dame Magda who attended her, but her daughter.'

'Ah. Perhaps he did mention that.'

'Did his wife spout the devil's words in her sleep?'

'I've heard only that she suddenly talked in her sleep.'

'Has your wife never complained of you talking in your sleep? A man with so many responsibilities? In truth, I do recall your story of how—' Owen grinned. 'Forgive me, but it was a good tale about the goat.'

Graa reddened. 'That was different. But you make a point. Though he did say she had not done so before taking the Riverwoman's potions.'

Asa's, but pointless to correct him. 'Any other complaints?'

'Something about a poppet found in his wife's bed after she had been taken to the nuns. You know the sort of charm, dressed to look like the person.'

Alisoun's mandrake root? 'I do not suppose you saw it?'

'I did not speak with him directly. A fellow merchant mentioned it. I would have you look into it, Captain. See if there is anything to these various complaints.'

'Who was this merchant?'

He shifted on his chair. 'I cannot recall. I did not think it of any import.'

Yet he'd mentioned it now. Owen held his tongue, reminding himself that he would do best not to antagonize the mayor. 'Are there others complaining about Dame Asa's or Dame Magda's practices?'

'Asa is the daughter?' Owen nodded. 'You know how the women are. One begins her complaint and others must outdo her with their own wild tales of spells and charms, folk becoming far more ill than they were before her ministrations, taking up strange activities, women becoming too bold, men weakening.' Graa cleared his throat. 'But it's their souls about which they are most

distressed. As if they were not already damned as gossips. Look
into it, would you? We pay you for such protection, eh?'

Brother Michaelo and Owen went their own ways at the end of
Castlegate, the monk heading back to the minster close, Owen
turning toward Edwin Cooper's beyond St Crux.

The laborers at the cooperage pointed the way to their master,
but warned that he was in a foul mood. Owen stepped into the
workroom, his boots sinking into the thick carpet of sawdust on
the floor, the light dim. He followed the sound of hammering
and cursing to a workbench lit by an east-facing window where
Edwin was pounding out bent nails. Over time Owen had heard
many a tale of the man's simmering anger at the world from his
son Ned, but he had never had cause to observe it. He was
debating whether it was best to leave and try another day when
the man glanced toward the door, peered as if to be sure of
Owen's presence, then threw down the hammer with a muttered
curse.

'You know how to sneak up on a man, Captain Archer.' Pulling
off his work gloves he turned and leaned back against the counter,
beefy arms folded across his thick middle, eyes hostile. 'Been
expecting you. Come to berate me for harsh words with the
daughter of your friend the Riverwoman, I warrant.'

'I am here at the request of Mayor Graa. I wish only to speak
with you about your troubles concerning her.'

'The mayor?' He straightened, dropped his arms. 'Well then,
you might want to sit over here.' With wary glances, the cooper
led Owen to a table on which sat a jug and a stack of small wooden
bowls.

Once they were settled, bowls of ale before them, Owen told
the man that all he needed were details of what his wife suffered
under Dame Asa's care.

'I knew something was amiss when the wife kept talking in her
sleep as if awake, fretting about the children – on several nights
the ones who died young, and claiming that I – nonsense, all of
it nonsense, but fearful speech, excited and stumbling about her
words as never before. And then she was all over bruised and
bitten as if devils were pinching and biting her, cutting her. And
I thought that was the cause of all that nighttime chatter, you see.'

'Did Dame Celia complain of being hit and bitten? Did the servants speak of it?'

'Nay, but we're good Christians all in our house. Nothing like this has ever happened here.'

'I understand Bernard the leech bled your wife for a time. He would have applied leeches and possibly small cuts to assist the bleeding,' Owen said. 'That would leave such marks.'

A grunt. 'I suppose he did. But that was long before that woman trespassed. Infernal hag, claiming to heal Celia when all along she was stealing her soul.'

'Why would she do that, do you think? Her mother Dame Magda was midwife to all your children, and you benefitted from her care not so long ago. What would cause her to turn against your wife?'

Edwin gave a mirthless laugh. 'You think to twist my thoughts.' He poured himself another bowl, but offered none to Owen.

'Not at all. I am trying to understand.'

'I've not yet told you the worst of it, the doll the maidservant found at the foot of my wife's bed when helping her pack up for the priory. Celia refused to believe the Riverwoman's daughter would put it there. Said the Riverwoman would never use such a thing. Who, then? She would not hear of blaming any of the servants. So who?'

'Might I see it?' Owen asked.

'I burnt it straight away, cursed thing. I'll not have such devil work in my home.'

Owen coaxed a description, but it was so vague as to be useless.

'And then of a sudden my wife begs to go to the priory.'

'I understand that was Dame Magda's suggestion.'

'You see? Crafty hag. She slipped in while I was about my business of a morning. It was Master Bernard came to me about it.'

Spying on the household? It seemed to Owen a curious undertaking for a leech.

'Who recommended Bernard to you?'

'Well now, it was Gavin Wolcott. He said he'd heard much good about him, and his father Guthlac liked him.'

'Do you know how Gavin made his acquaintance?'

'Master Bernard's? Out of town, I think. Wolcott's party told him of old Masterton's death, that there was need for another physician in York. Saurian is getting old. Oft refuses to come out after dark.'

'So Bernard was seeking work?'

'I see what you're doing. You want to push the blame on him. Well, the Riverwoman is your friend and I understand you must do what you can to protect her. And her spawn. But you're captain of the city now, and you've a duty to us. You will find plenty folk with tales of her misdeeds. And in such times, with God testing us so sorely as might come to pass this summer, you must do your duty.'

'Whose misdeeds – Dame Magda's or her daughter's?'

'Matters not a whit. Both are witches.'

Arrogant little man. Owen controlled himself, forcing a blank face and a submissive nod. 'Which is why I am here. If I might speak with your daughters and the servants—'

The man shook his head. 'I'll not have you upsetting them with your twisty questioning. I've told you all that we will say on the matter. I don't thank you for pulling my Ned away from his work here in the yard to chase round after you and your mate Hempe. He'd never have helped the Riverwoman sneak into my home had you not filled his head with ideas.'

'The Riverwoman's daughter, you mean. Do you know that Ned sneaked her into your home?'

'It was not my wife or my daughters. They are Christian women.'

Rising, Owen left with a mere nod of courtesy.

From Cooper's house Owen headed to the King's Staithe, where he found George Hempe talking to the laborers unloading a merchant ship.

'Any witnesses to the start of the fire?'

'No. Late in the day, no ship arriving at that time, the staithe was quiet, it seems.' Hempe nodded at Owen's expression. 'You're thinking what I'm thinking. Well planned. And you? Learned anything?'

'Little. You've spoken with the warehouse workers and the neighbors?'

'I went round with your man Alfred. He puts folk at ease. No one noticed anything out of joint that day.'

'Then it's time I talked to Sam's widow about the witnesses, watch her reaction. Was it you who spoke with her?'

'Poole. As coroner for Galtres, where Sam was found. I warn you, Gemma Toller is a shrew.'

Owen found Sam's widow working in a small kitchen garden behind her home, jabbing at the weeds as if thinking that would convince them not to re-seed. Dressed in a gown of faded blue, worn and patched, she was a handsome woman despite the hostile eyes and pursed lips. Bitter about her husband's attentions to Beatrice Wolcott, the woman did prove coarse in her accusations, but even more so in pointing the finger at Magda as the murderer. Yet as she spewed her venom Owen was distracted by how she spoke, the hesitations and repeated phrases, slightly corrected, as if she were misremembering something she had learned by rote. She did have a helpful, hopeful piece of news – Lettice Brown was away at her daughter's home outside the gates for her first lying in. By the time he left the house he was convinced that only her resentment toward Beatrice Wolcott and her fear of what would become of her and her children were real. Nothing in her claim that Sam accused Magda Digby of poisoning Guthlac Wolcott and that he was pushed into the river from Magda's rock was true. Nor did she believe it.

The witnesses were quite clear about seeing Sam return that night, their stories matching, though one had seen more than the other, believing she had glimpsed someone, she thought perhaps two men, shadowing Sam as he strode angrily toward the staithe muttering curses. They now disagreed on the exact words Gemma had shouted after Sam, as well as his retorts, but both assured him that the man showed no signs of impairment as he stormed off, tossing back as many curses as Gemma showered on him.

And yet Gemma swore he had not returned that night. Why? Was someone silencing her, or did she have her own secrets?

At midday, Owen, Alfred, Crispin Poole, and George Hempe congregated in the York Tavern to share what they had discovered. Precious little, for all their digging. Though Alfred's conversation with one of the folk helping clear the debris from around the mayor's warehouse might be of use. From a family of charcoal-burners, he brought a childhood of closely observed burnings to his view of the fire.

'Began at the corner of the Browns' house closest to the ware-house so he thinks it might have served a double purpose, burning both the house and that part of the warehouse. And he's quite certain it was set. "Who builds a fire in a corner of the house so far from the fire circle?" That's what he said.'

'What was kept in that corner of the warehouse?' Owen asked.

The man had not known. Hempe offered to speak to some of the warehousemen. But Owen preferred to do that himself as he'd already spoken to Graa.

Crispin Poole cleared his throat. He had been quiet up till now. 'I keep an ear pricked for news of the forest, being coroner,' he said. 'It's rumored that Dame Magda has guests. Her daughter Asa and a young man who seems to be living somewhere just upriver from her home, on the north bank. Do you know of them?'

'Alisoun mentioned something of it. I've yet to speak with Dame Magda. I thought to call on her later today.'

'I would appreciate to hear what you learn,' said Poole. 'As I said, the young man is said to be living upstream in the forest.'

'You have complaints of him?'

'Just wondered.'

'I will find out.'

With a nod, they all parted to go about their business, to meet here on the morrow at the start of their day.

Beatrice Wolcott set aside a stand of embroidery as she rose to greet Owen in a sweetly melodic voice, directing a servant to pour wine. Small, plump, pale, with rosebud lips and large darkly lashed eyes, she was a comely woman, clothed fashionably, very like a noblewoman Owen encountered long ago at Kenilworth Palace. A disagreeable experience.

'Captain Archer. Gavin told me to expect you.'

'You are most kind. Might I offer my condolences for your losses.' He saw that he confused her. 'Your children, factor, and now your husband's decline.'

She bowed her head, taking a deep breath. 'You are kind to acknowledge it. It has been a difficult time. I pray you sit, have some wine with me.' Through lowered lashes she appraised him as she resumed her seat. 'How might I be of help?'

'If I understand correctly, Dame Magda cared for you and your husband after the deaths of your young children. But of late his son Gavin sent her away. I am told that on the night of your factor's death he had gone to accuse Dame Magda of sickening your husband.'

She gave an alarmed gasp. 'Who told you that?'

'His wife.'

'Of course. That woman,' she said through clenched teeth.

'Is it true?'

'No. But . . . Can I trust you to ensure no one in this household learns what we say?'

'Of course.'

'I sent him with money to beg Dame Magda to see Guthlac. I am so worried.'

A fresh twist. 'Did she come?'

'No. I waited, but neither Dame Magda nor Sam came, not that evening, nor the next morning.' She looked away.

'Might I ask why you sent him rather than one of your servants?'

A blush. 'As you know so much you will have heard that Guthlac's son forbade Dame Magda to interfere with Master Bernard's treatment. Gavin styles himself the young master of the house at this time, so to ask them to go against his orders might be a fearful thing for them. I chose not to do so.'

'Nor to go yourself.'

'Go myself? Leave the city without escort?'

Owen took a sip of the wine and changed the line of questioning. 'Was the dismissal of Dame Magda your husband's wish?'

'Yes. The illness made him fear for his soul, and he came to agree with Gavin that to admit a pagan into the house might be a danger.'

Gently put. 'But you do not agree?'

'I have little say in this, it seems. But no, and anyone who truly cares for Guthlac saw the folly in employing Master Bernard. As soon as he began to bleed Guthlac – within days I saw the change. Within a fortnight he could not rise from the bed himself.' Tears started up, her bottom lip trembling.

'How did Gavin meet Master Bernard?'

'I know better than to ask him.'

'Did you confer with your friends regarding this leech, so new to the city?'

A blush. 'I am not on such intimate terms with anyone.'

'Not even your neighbor, Emma Ferriby?'

'She is too fine to speak with me.'

Owen grew impatient. No one could meet Emma Ferriby and think that. But he let it pass.

'How did Sam Toller behave when you last saw him? Did he seem worried?'

'Sam? May he rest in peace.' She crossed herself. 'He was worried about my husband, his decline.'

'Nothing else?'

Biting the side of her mouth, she made a face as if begging patience. 'He and Gavin were at odds. He felt my husband's son presumed too much in making decisions about Guthlac's business.'

'Was he correct in objecting?'

'It is not my place.'

'So you did not discuss business with Sam.'

'No. Oh, no.'

'Yet you sent him on an errand.'

'He is – was family, Captain. He oft dined with us. And he ensured that the household ran smoothly while Guthlac and I grieved our children. He was a kind man.' A sudden intake of breath, a tear.

Shades of the noblewoman at Kenilworth. But surely this was genuine, if he could only overcome his prejudice. 'Forgive me,' he said. 'But one more question. How did you learn of Sam's death?'

'Crispin Poole informed me, a message for my husband. Of course I had feared . . .'

Owen rose, thanked her, and asked if he might pay his respects to Guthlac. He'd noticed a servant leaving a room off the landing of the solar, exiting by a door to the outside stairs.

A hand to her throat as she rose. 'But why?'

'I need a clear picture of all that has been happening, and as your husband's health is an unfortunate part of these events I hoped merely to see him, how he is.'

With a little sigh, she acquiesced, leading him out and up to the solar. With care to be quiet she opened the door the servant had used. It was a large bedchamber with a wide window, shuttered, a small brazier keeping the room uncomfortably warm. She stepped up to the bed, lifting the limp hand of a wizened old man. Owen worked to see the gruff Guthlac Wolcott in the form before him. The shrunken man's eyes fluttered open, the eyes vacant, drool slipping from his mouth as he moved it ineffectively.

'My love, Captain Archer is here to wish you well.' She smiled up at Owen, the lamplight catching the tears in her eyes.

Owen stepped closer, murmuring a prayer for Guthlac's swift recovery. Once back out on the steps, he thanked Beatrice and apologized for the necessity.

'Gavin is living here now?'

'He is. I am sorry if you wished to see him. He is away for the day.'

He thanked her again and departed.

Matthew Brown lay face down in the burnt remains of his home, the blood from three stab wounds to his back soaking into the ashes beneath him. He reeked of ale. Owen imagined him drinking the day away and then returning to see whether his home was truly gone, or whether the misfortune had been a drunken dream.

'And I was dreading the pestilence,' Hempe muttered as Alfred filled them in on how he was found.

'God be thanked his wife – widow is away, or so says the widow Toller,' said Owen.

'A pair of widows now,' said Alfred. 'Who will break the news?'

'Are we certain that she did not return?' asked Hempe. 'That we won't find her dead as well?'

'She would have come hurrying home at the news,' said a woman standing in the street. 'I fear they are right, we are punished for seeking the aid of a pagan healer.'

'Who has said that?' asked Owen.

The woman crossed herself and scurried off.

'She cannot think that God stabbed one of his children in the back,' said Hempe.

'The question is, who did stab him?' said Owen.

On his way home, Owen noticed that what had been an undercurrent of fear was now on the surface. Furtive glances, muted greetings, small groups huddled together whispering, children's hands held tightly as parents hurried them along. His job would be the more difficult for it.

Lucie pressed Owen's hands, looking deep into his eyes. 'You could not foresee Matthew's death. You'd no cause to expect it.'

She'd held his one-eyed gaze, steady in her conviction, as Owen ran through all that he knew of the fire – very little, and of Lettice and Matthew Brown – even less. As far as anyone knew they had no connection to either Sam or his wife, so no obvious connection to Sam's murder. And it was still possible that Lettice Brown might be alive. He took a deep breath and allowed that Lucie was right. He wasted time blaming himself for Matthew's murder. But he did now have two murders to solve. And Guthlac was dying – was that another? He told Lucie of the man's condition.

'Perhaps we might—'

She nodded. 'Though it sounds as if we might be too late, I will call on them on the morrow, offer some tinctures that might strengthen him.'

Hoping for better news, Owen asked Lucie about her day in the shop.

'Dame Marian came asking for anything I have found of help to the victims of pestilence and those attending them. One of the lay workers has the fever and boils and the infirmarian expects it will quickly spread to the community outside the walls where the lay workers live.'

So the Death had reached Clementhorpe just beyond the city walls. 'God help us.' Owen crossed himself. 'Is Marian well?'

'She is. Radiant with well-being and clearly at peace with herself and enjoying her place in the community. Seeing her now makes plain how weak she was in body and spirit when she came to us in winter.' Dame Marian had been brought to their home for safe-keeping after a months-long ordeal. She had been weak, confused, and despairing of being accepted back into the Benedictine order. But under the guidance of the precentrice she was now responsible for the music in the services at St Clement's Priory throughout the day. Her angelic voice and musical talent had transformed masses at the priory. In a matter of months she had drawn folk from around the city to their small chapel.

'Why is she running errands for the infirmarian?'

'Because she bided with a plague sufferer the past summer without succumbing to the illness. She has offered her services in the infirmary should she be needed.'

'I am sorry I missed her.'

'As was she. She offers her support for Magda in any official inquiries. If she is needed, she will speak, write, whatever is most effective.'

A heartening bit of news. 'Had the priory received the archbishop's letter?'

'Their chaplain did. It was shared in chapter. Dame Euphemia, Crispin's mother, expressed outrage and most of the sisters followed, though in more subdued manner. There are a few who disapprove of consulting a pagan healer, but Marian excused them as generally lacking good sense.'

Brother Michaelo had not brought Owen a copy of the letter, nor his written record of the morning's conversation with Mayor Graa. He hoped he would also include a copy of Jehannes's letter. Perhaps on the morrow. Pestilence, the murders, a physician stirring up ill feelings against Magda, just when the people needed her. 'It is an ill wind that blows,' he muttered.

'We knew the pestilence would come, my love.' Lucie lifted his hand and kissed his palm. 'Take heart. Each time it comes it takes fewer folk.'

'Until the time when it strikes with as much force as the first time. Damnation. Why did we not stay at court? Move with Prince Edward to Berkhamsted Castle in the countryside? Eat sugared fruits and drink fine wine. Stroll through the gardens, sleep as late as we wished, make love all the day.'

Lucie reached over to stroke his cheek. 'That would not have changed our fear for our children, and all whom we love.'

He caught her hand and rose to draw her into his arms, his comfort, his anchor, his advisor.

Magda stepped out of the airless shack, lifting her face to the soft rain as she considered where she might move the family within. The heavily pregnant woman's children had summoned Magda at dawn, thinking that her moans were a sign the birth was imminent. Soon, but not yet. And there would be two babies suckling at her breasts, not one. Helen and her husband had exchanged frightened looks at the news. The flimsy shed, too easily set aflame to permit a fire within, would not do for the birth. Nor was it roomy enough for all the little lives dependent on its shelter. Unfortunate that

Einar had taken Old Shep's cottage. But there was another, a little
farther upriver, near Graa's forest property, not as well maintained,
half the roof caved in, but a far sight better than where Helen now
slept. There was yet another place, but they were not in need of
that sort of sanctuary.

Approaching her home, Magda saw Owen Archer standing with
the lads who watched her coracle. They stood straight and tall,
proud of his notice. Bird-eye was their hero. If he was requesting
their help, he would get it. By the time she joined them they were
shaking their heads, pointing toward the river, gesturing as if
describing someone crossing to the other bank.

'They took your coracle, Dame Magda.' A laceration on the
lad's cheek had bled onto his much-mended shirt.

'Did one of them cut thee?'

'No. Tried to chase them and fell on the rocks.' Head lowered,
ashamed.

'Dirk was brave,' the youngest of them piped up. 'He rushed
at the man shouting that your dragon would tear him apart for
stealing your coracle.'

Bird-eye crouched down as if to look more closely at Dirk's
cheek. 'I'd wager they sleep poorly tonight, eh?' Leveling his one
eye on the lad, he drew his gaze, managed to win a grin. 'You
showed great courage, Dirk.' The lad would savor that for years
to come. Rising, Owen looked round at the others. 'I need one of
you to find Bailiff Hempe, tell him what happened, and that I need
a few men to search the south side of the river. If they find the
coracle they should return it.'

Dirk offered, but Owen insisted Magda see to his wound first.

'Fen will do it for thee,' said Magda. The lad had a keen memory
for detail.

The lad grinned.

'Tell the gate keeper you are working for me,' said Owen. 'And
I count on all of you to let me know at once if the coracle disap-
pears again. I will tell the gate keeper that you are working for
me.'

Five proud lads vowed he could count on them.

'Come, Dirk. Magda will see to that,' said Owen. He nodded
to the others. Fen hurried off on his mission.

At the river's edge Magda paused, sensing a presence on the

far bank. Einar? Asa? She closed her eyes, reaching, reaching, but failed to grasp any clear image.

Before joining Magda in the hut Owen circled the rock, checking that her heavier boat was still hanging beneath the eaves. He stood for a while, taking a good look at the shore on either side, upriver and down. The lads said it was the young man and the older woman who walks with a cane. Owen did not need to guess who they were. They said Einar had come along the bank from the forest as he had done of late, scooping up the coracle to carry it with him to the rock. Asa had come out of the house dragging two fat packs. Einar had lifted them into the coracle loudly complaining about the weight of the packs, then helped her in. They had been low in the water as he rowed her across the river. On the far bank they moved into the underbrush, Einar carrying both packs on his shoulders and the coracle over his head. He was strong. But then he would be if he was good with the bow. Owen wondered whether Einar would come to St George's Field the next day.

Crossing by a window he heard a lad, not Dirk, telling Magda how Dame Asa had ordered him to leave. A higher voice than Dirk's. The lad said he'd taken Holda with him, fearing for her safety. Because of the stolen coracle he'd had to wait until the tide was out to return her.

'She had milk and a bit of gruel at my house. Did I do right?' Magda assured him he had.

When Owen stepped into the house he found a tow-headed urchin holding out his hand for the coin Magda held.

'Canst thou return early in the morning? On thy Sabbath?'

An enthusiastic nod. 'Ma says Sabbath is for those with full bellies, not the likes of us.'

The two lads left, the younger one clutching his coin, Dirk sporting a tidy bandage and clutching a small pot of salve. Owen watched them slog back to shore, ready to come to their aid if the water overwhelmed them. But, though wet, they made it to the bank unscathed.

'The lad was caring for someone here?' he asked, settling onto a stool near a dying fire. Magda nodded to a kitten in a basket lined with a bit of blanket. It could not be much more than a few weeks old. 'She is a patient?'

'Child feared the kitten would be drowned. Brought her to Magda for safekeeping.'

'You will keep her?'

'It is never a matter of choosing a kitten, but of being clear that one would welcome a willing companion. Time will reveal Holda's decision.'

That Magda had already named her suggested she knew what the kitten would decide. A wise young being, to choose such a companion. 'Shall I stir the fire?'

Magda nodded as she poured ales for both of them. When the fire began to snap she placed a small pot on a stone near it. 'A patient's fee.'

It smelled good. He would not keep her.

'Thou art looking well after thy long journey, Bird-eye.'

'The prince's hospitality could not be faulted, and both the journey and the sojourn were the better for Lucie being at my side. Another time I would speak with you about it at length.'

'Thou art ever welcome. Thy children are well at Freythorpe?'

'They are. Eager to see Alisoun.' He took a long drink, then set aside his bowl. 'You've heard about the fire in the city? Lettice Brown's house destroyed, and no sign of her, though it's possible she is away caring for her daughter.'

'Magda heard.'

'Just a few hours ago we found her husband Matthew in the rubble. Murdered. Stabbed in the back. He had been alive this morning, drinking at a tavern until mid-afternoon.'

'The house set fire one day, Matthew murdered the next.' Magda looked troubled.

'I do not believe it is chance,' said Owen. 'But why? Do you know the Browns well enough to help me in any way?'

'Lettice's daughter's time was close. She may well be away. Matthew was a man disappointed by the challenge of life. Thou dost carry a heavy burden, Bird-eye. The folk look to thee for salvation. Wouldst thou speak of the other cares that weigh on thee?'

She listened without comment to Owen's litany of problems, unless asked. About Beatrice Wolcott's behavior she said, 'A young woman who learned early that men treat her well if she is orna-mental, keeps a household running well, and never questions or contradicts them.' When he was finished, she said simply, 'Caught up in the storm so soon. Yet the worst is ahead, the manqualm and the fear.'

'The fear is here. And the pestilence is at the gates. It has come to Clementhorpe,' he said. He told her of Dame Marian's offer.

'Magda is grateful. The time may come . . .' She told Owen of the plague death near Easingwold.

'Carn told me. So it surrounds us.' Owen stared into the fire, wishing— He did not know what he wished. So much. 'I find myself doubting that Matthew's murder and the burning of his home arises from the fear.'

'What, then?'

'That's the rub. Until Matthew's murder I thought the fire had been meant to destroy Thomas Graa's warehouse, or that part of it near the Browns' home. But why then murder him?'

'So many questions.'

'Living so near, might whoever set the fire suspect Matthew witnessed something that would incriminate them? Or that Lettice knew something and might have told him?'

'Why Lettice?'

'A laundress knows much that happens in households.'

'In which case she is in danger if yet alive,' said Magda.

'How did Sam behave the night he came to you?'

'Ill at ease.'

Owen told her what Beatrice had said of his mission.

'He said naught of that. He warned Magda not to enter the city. But the warning had not been his intention until he sat there with Magda.'

'What changed?'

'Magda does not know. He had money with him. Perhaps Dame Beatrice had sent him.' Seeing Owen's frustration, Magda touched his arm, waited until he looked her in the eye. 'Thou hast been home but a day. Such inquiries take time. Thou hast burden enough without adding more weight with thine impatience.'

He was about to respond when she reached out and gently touched the patch over his blind eye. The needle pricks eased. She moved to touch his jaw beneath the beard, and he felt the muscle release. Withdrawing her hand, she breathed with him, slowly, deeply. Owen closed his eye and allowed some time to pass in companionable silence.

'I saw Guthlac today,' he finally said. 'He is incapable of either discovering anything or expressing such an anger.' He described what he'd seen.

'Difficult to hear. It need not have been so.'

'Had you seen any sign such a decline would come?'

'The deaths of his young children weakened him, but he was gaining strength and had every cause to expect an active life for some years.'

'Could the leech Bernard have purposefully weakened him to his present state?'

'If thou hast a suspicion that he is a danger, or that someone has acted to harm Guthlac, it is thy charge to find the truth.'

Could she not, just this once, speculate? Owen struggled to hide his reaction, but she would sense it, of course she would. 'I ask because you were caring for him.'

'At the time of their bereavement Magda sat with them. But a fortnight past the harvest moon Beatrice felt there was no more need.'

'You were not caring for them? Gavin did not send you away?'

'No. Beatrice had been sending a servant to fetch the physicks, then one day she said she would no longer be doing so, her mistress thanked Magda and wished her well.'

Not the stuff of rumors. 'You had not seen Guthlac since autumn?'

'Magda saw him from time to time. He would hail her on the street.'

So he had been out and about. 'When did you last see him?'

'No more than a week before Magda heard the tale of her being sent away.'

'And he was well then?'

'Well enough to be out on an errand.'

They sat in silence for a while, Owen turning various possibilities over in his mind. When Magda suggested he needed his rest, he bestirred himself to ask about Einar and Asa.

'I met him,' he added.

'So he said. Asa would darken his heart toward thee. The invitation to St George's Field was clever, but perhaps not enough.'

'I understand she would have Alisoun believe he is her son, but that is not so.'

'Of little importance. Magda believes they share a common mission, pursuing someone in the city. Who it is, what they want with him, and why they arrived when they did – none of that is clear. It is puzzling that Asa would journey now, when it pains her to walk. She says she came for the healing, but her distress was not their purpose. At least not that distress.'

'What do you mean?'

'A long time she has suffered, taking more and more willow bark for the pain until her blood pooled in her feet, blackening them. She knew to stop the bark, mix a potion to thicken the blood, lie with feet propped up, rest. But instead she continued, worsening her condition with a journey. Magda did not turn her daughter away, doing what Asa knew to do. Now Asa leaves before her blood has thickened. To pursue whoever it is in the city. Given her history, she intends to punish them for betraying her.'

'About what?'

'Magda does not know.'

'And Einar?'

'A mystery.'

'You believe they mean trouble?'

'Of some sort. Whether to Magda, to this man, both, Magda knows too little to guess.'

Owen muttered a curse. Magda pressed the middle of his forehead. 'Look within, trust thyself.'

'The prince summoned me because he believed I had the Sight. He wanted to know what lies ahead for him and for the realm.'

'Thou hast a gift, a seeing, but it is a selfless tool for thy work. For healing the community. As Magda's is for healing the body and spirit. Folk want it to be more. A power. Something to help them rise above.' Again she pressed the middle of his forehead. 'Thou hast gathered the questions. Now thy work is to follow where they lead.'

'While keeping my one good eye on all in the city. And out here.'

'Magda will see to Galtres. Thou hast more than enough work in the city.'

A shower of needle pricks, gentler than before, yet an alert. 'Why do I feel as if you know more than you are saying?'

'No doubt that is true, for thee as well. Asa and Einar puzzle Magda. She must shelter a mother about to birth twins. The manqualm creeps close.' Hearing the weariness in her voice Owen regretted his irritation. 'This is a dark time, Bird-eye. There is much work to do. Magda asks a favor of thee.' Taking some coins from somewhere in her skirts she offered them to him. 'Magda is caring for a family of five children, two about to be born, the father crippled. They need clothing. Good but modest cloth, so that they might make new clothes. And some to make clothes to sell.'

'So that you need not come into the city. Of course. I will ask Lucie.'

'Thou art a good friend, Bird-eye, doing this kindness despite thy frustration with Magda.'

She had noticed. Waving away his apology she stepped outside with him, walking to face the south bank. He joined her, curious as she stood still, studying the bank upriver and down in the fading light.

'What is it?'

'For a moment before returning to the rock Magda sensed someone over there. Almost it felt her calling to Magda.'

'Asa?'

Magda shook her head. 'Whoever it was, she is gone.'

FIVE

Arrows

At first light, Magda packed her basket with all she might need through the morning, including a skin with wine mixed with herbs to warm and calm, and set off upriver. She stayed close to the bank, slipping in and out of the morning mist as she pricked her ears for the sound of someone moving along the far bank. Across from the nest of the swans she settled on a piece of wall to afford the presence she had sensed the opportunity to reveal herself. The wine was for her, to warm her after a night in hiding.

Mother Swan perched to one side of the great nest, a wing draped over the cygnets. She watched Magda for a moment, then tucked her head into her feathers. Father Swan was away, fishing, Magda guessed. Rustlings in the underbrush and in the limbs overhead, the occasional caw or cry, the steady rush of the river lulled Magda to a deep quiet. She was fighting sleep when a louder rustling in the undergrowth on the far bank caused Mother Swan to look behind her, alert to danger. Magda was now wide awake.

A woman peered out from behind a bush, then stepped out onto the bank. Magda lifted a hand in greeting, her heart gladdening to see she had been right in sensing it was Lettice Brown. She need not have bothered putting a finger to her mouth and looking round, for why else would Lettice be creeping about in the under-brush. Magda motioned for her to walk along upriver to a place from which Magda would row her over.

It seemed she might be sheltering many in the forest.

The small coracle, hidden deep within the tangled roots and limbs of an old willow, had served many a friend. Putting the wineskin in the vessel, Magda placed her basket in the hiding place, then carried the lightweight boat and the rough oar to the bank. The river widened and slowed here as it curved, not a chal-lenge at this hour. Within a few strokes she fell into an easy rhythm. At the far bank she held out her hand to steady Lettice as she stepped into the coracle. The woman shivered, the chill deep in her bones. Her damp clothing and exhaustion suggested she had not found shelter for the night. Magda handed her the wineskin with the whispered assurance that it would warm her with but a sip, then set off toward the willow. At the bank, Magda stepped out first, then assisted Lettice, guiding her to lean against the willow while she retrieved her basket and hid the coracle.

'Dame Magda, I must warn you . . .' Lettice whispered as she fell against her.

'Later. Come now, before thou art seen.' Magda held the wine-skin up to the woman's mouth. 'A sip.' Lettice took more than a sip. Never mind. It was not far now.

Magda grasped Lettice's arm to steady her after several stumbles. At the tall holly hedge she stopped, lightly touching the glossy leaves, then awaiting a sign of welcome. In the archway a moth hovered, gazing her way for a moment, then turning and leading them in. She led Lettice through the hedge and out beneath ancient oaks.

'Where are we?' Lettice whispered, gazing up into the thick canopy.

'A safe place,' said Magda, assisting her to a mossy hillock in a clearing. Brushing back thick vines that covered a heavy oak door, she pushed it wide and reached in for a lantern hanging inside, opening a shutter to illuminate a large room beyond. 'Step within.' Heavy oak beams supported the sod exterior, vertical beams making possible a dividing wall completed by heavy cloth. It would be snug and warm once the fire dried it out. Lettice moved into the room, touching the table, benches, the few pots, ladle, wooden bowls, cups, and spoons, the cupboard shelves with jars of grains, dried mushrooms, and beans.

'Thou might rest here,' said Magda. 'There are beds in the room beyond.'

'Who lives here?'

'Thou wilt live here for a little while.' Magda smiled at the questions in the woman's eyes. 'Few know of this place. It is not easily found.'

'It is a fairy dwelling?'

'It is as real as Magda and thee. Come. Sit.' Fetching a wooden cup, Magda filled it with the comforting wine and handed it to Lettice after she lowered herself on to a bench.

Gazing round with wonder tempered by fear, Lettice drank deeply.

'There is firewood by the door. From there thou wilt see a brook. The water is fresh and cool. Magda will bring some in now and build a fire to warm thee. Thou shouldst lie down to sleep a while.' Lettice was already listing and fighting to keep her eyes focused. 'Tomorrow Magda will bring thee clean clothing and more food and wine.'

'You are leaving?'

'For a little while. So that thou might rest. If thou dost wake before Magda returns, do not venture beyond the brook or out of the holly hedge toward the riverbank. Thou shouldst stay out of sight.'

'You believe I am in danger?'

'It is thee who believes so, is it not? Why else didst thou hide along the riverbank through the night?'

'How did you know?'

'Magda sensed thee across the way in the twilight.'

'My house was destroyed by fire, and my husband—'

Magda put an arm round Lettice. 'Come. To bed.'

'But I must tell you—'

'When thou art rested.'

As Magda settled Lettice in a bed, layering blankets over her, she asked about her daughter's delivery, the baby's sex, the name chosen for him.

Lettice whispered of her guilt about leaving Matthew alone. 'I could not take him. I could not trust him to refrain from insulting her husband.' She spoke of Matthew's drinking, how he was ever disappointing her, but how handsome he had been, how clever. He was her first love. Her parents had disapproved, but he had convinced them with his honeyed tongue that he would go far. He would soon own one of the ships he loaded and unloaded at the staithes. As her words slurred together, Magda told her that what she most needed now was sleep.

'The end of thy tale can wait until later. Rest now.'

Lettice slept.

Sunday morning mass in St Helen's was crowded, folk bringing their children for blessings after a boy in the parish of St Denys', Walmgate, collapsed with fever the previous afternoon, his feet blackening, and by midnight boils in his armpits burst. Within hours, he was dead.

The parish priest, Jerome, had taken Owen aside at the church door to assure him he would not preach according to the dictums of the archbishop, that he had prayed over it and God's message had been clear, he was a shepherd of his flock and in such times the people needed their trusted healers, not only Magda Digby but all the midwives in the city.

'The archbishop ordered you to preach against the midwives?' Owen asked.

'It is rumored he sent such a letter to the abbeys and priories, and therefore some of my fellows believe we should warn our parishioners against the women. But I will not do so.'

'Bless you, Father. Our parish benefits by your pastoral care.'

Overhearing and apparently guessing his urge to withdraw and speak to Michaelo, Lucie slipped her arm through Owen's and guided him in to stand among the faithful. 'Time to confer after mass. We have much to pray for.'

Knowing she was right, Owen bowed his head and did his best to nudge his mind toward prayer.

With the pestilence now in the city they had left Jasper to see to the customers who would pound on the door of the apothecary despite it being the Sabbath, begging for the cures they believed had worked for them in past visitations. Brother Michaelo attended him. He had offered his services the previous evening when he had delivered copies of the archbishop's letter and Dom Jehannes's response.

'I saw the terror in the eyes of the people in the minster yard, with rumors of sickness in Clementhorpe and Walmgate,' said Michaelo. 'And many still believe it was a plague house set fire near King's Staithe. All the worst for Dame Magda's absence.'

Owen had puzzled over that, noting that she was just without the walls.

'A difficult journey for the sick,' said Michaelo. 'It is the solitary folk, those left behind, who huddle in the minster yard. They see to one another to a point, but they do not risk going outside the walls seeking help for fear they would be shut out.' So the monk hoped to learn what he could by assisting in the apothecary. 'Though I would as lief Dame Magda returned, I am glad she protects herself. I pray I might be of some good.'

Lucie had, of course, offered him simple supplies, which he accepted with gratitude. His charity work touched her. Owen saw it as an extension of Michaelo's nightly work among the poor in the minster yard, and guessed he might embrace it as penance, atoning for the pleasure he took in his reception in Prince Edward's household, his reluctance to depart for home. Still, Owen, too, was moved by the gesture.

The archbishop's letter had also motivated Michaelo. Neville had mentioned the poor who slept in the minster yard, claiming that they offend the dignity of the great cathedral and should be removed. He'd also chided the Abbot of St Mary's for feeding the poor outside the gate and encouraging the 'vermin city'. No wonder Brother Michaelo wished to assist in the apothecary so that he might be of help to the poor.

The letter puzzled Owen. Alexander Neville was known to be a litigious man, but King Edward had expected his brother Sir John to prevail upon him to temper his behavior.

Dom Jehannes's letter to the archbishop was, in contrast, quiet, respectful, quoting the pertinent parts of Neville's missive as he expressed his concern that news of it might lead the parish priests to preach against the very healers needed as the pestilence returned. He suggested the resumption of penitential processions in the churches on Wednesdays, as had been done in the last visitation of the pestilence *to the great comfort and soothing of souls of the people of York*. He also addressed the issues of the poor, pointing out that the letter had included no suggestions as to how the religious communities might perform their Christian duty of giving alms to the poor if the poor were banished. Or perhaps a letter would follow suggesting where the people might be relocated? He added that if the purpose was to keep the pestilence from the city, it was already too late.

As Michaelo had said last night, quoting the Sermon on the Mount, *Beati mites quoniam ipsi possidebunt terram.* Owen had disagreed with putting Jehannes in the category of the meek, thinking him rather fierce in his gentle righteousness. But he did see the point, the meek inheriting the earth having always suggested to him that the humbler, gentler path created a more lasting change.

'Will you still go to St George's Field today?' Lucie asked Owen as they joined the throng leaving church.

He heard in her voice that she already knew the answer. 'Do you want me to tell Jasper to stay here?'

'No. I encouraged him because I thought the fresh air and the activity would be good, and that has not changed. He's been shut up in the shop so much and likely will be so through the summer.' Lucie looked up at Owen as he held open their front door. She touched his face. 'But of course I worry. For both of you. And just as I understand why you must go, I feel we must allow Jasper to make his own choice.'

*   *   *

Her morning's visits completed, Magda headed back to collect the
donkey and cart, and then Helen and her family. Lettice's tale of
her marriage made her think of her own first love. Sten. He, too,
had been handsome. Tall, strong, his wild dark hair worn long,
often braided, rings in his ears, gold bracelets on his arms. A bard,
he claimed to be, and a healer, a magician. How she had loved
Sten, foolish young twig of a girl as she had been. *Maggie, my
love, we will sail the seas together. To the ends of the earth we
will sail, collecting rare plants, gems, spices, and magical creatures
for healing and transformation.* She laughed to herself, remembering how his descriptions carried her away on dreams of exotic
lands. Lettice's expectations for her marriage had been as foolish,
considering Matthew. In all the years Magda had known of him
he'd demonstrated neither the cleverness to move beyond common
labor nor the ambition to better himself. Their children had married
better men, though humble, thanks to Lettice's reputation as a hard
worker. Magda and Sten's children were the only beauty resulting
from their passionate union. Yrsa, kind, clever with her hands,
winning the eye of a carpenter in Scarborough. Kind, that is, to
all but her mother, whom she blamed for Sten's desertion with
her twin Odo. Magda had not corrected her, did not try to explain
that Sten had proved to be a lazy dreamer who lost his passion
when his charms were not enough to coax coin from wary
customers.

At the dip in the forest track that marked the path to the sanctuary – a path invisible to those who did not know to search for
it – Magda was glad to see no sign of passage since she had
covered her tracks in the morning. Lettice was safe as she could
be for now, and while walking Magda had come up with a plan
that would give the frightened woman more ease in the sanctuary
while also providing shelter to the expectant mother and her family,
including her crippled husband. Humming, Magda continued on,
looking forward to a cup of ale and a bowl of the stew she carried
in a pot in her otherwise empty basket, made by the daughter of
an elderly patient she knew to be a fine cook.

Jasper chose to accompany Owen, remarking as they walked what
a help Brother Michaelo proved, comforting folk as they stood in
line and smoothing tempers. The monk had stayed to provide the

same service to Lucie. 'I admire him for his willingness to help
the poor, but I'd doubted that he could provide much comfort.
This morning he proved me wrong. He says it is a penance and
a practice of humility,' said Jasper, 'but I believe God called him
to this, as he did Brother Wulfstan long ago.'

Not so long ago, in Owen's mind. Not long enough. God be
thanked Lucie needed Jasper in the apothecary or his son would
be out ministering to the sick as well, as his mentor Brother
Wulfstan had done. Blessed work that took his life.

'I pray he is sturdier than Brother Wulfstan,' said Jasper.

'I believe Brother Michaelo has reserves of strength we never
guessed,' said Owen. Indeed, Michaelo continued to prove himself
a talented, resourceful man who helped in innumerable ways. He
had promised that after Jasper returned from archery practice he
would do some sleuthing among the parishes regarding the perceived
orders from the archbishop.

Jasper shifted the conversation to memories of the first time
Owen had taken him to practice at the butts, his hair colored a
bright red, his clothes padded to disguise his shape. That time the
danger had been from a fellow man, the sort of danger Owen
understood. Yet he had failed to protect Jasper.

Wishing to speak of something less troubling, Owen described
Einar, recruiting Jasper's help in observing him should he appear.

The day was overcast, but with a subtle warmth beneath the
cool of the morning that promised sunshine later. Owen hoped
the cloud cover lasted through the practice so that he need not
squint with his one good eye. He would prefer not to make a fool
of himself adjusting another's aim.

At first attendance was sparse, but within an hour Owen glanced
up while training a particularly challenged young man to see that
at least half the usual complement had arrived. He called to Jasper
to take over with the young man. Having begun his training with
Owen at eight years, his son was now an accomplished bowman
with strength and a refined technique.

'Before you go,' said Jasper, 'I wondered if that is Einar.' He
pointed out a young man just arriving, making his way through
the crowd, pausing to look round.

'Good eyes,' said Owen.

'I should like to meet him,' said Jasper.

Owen lifted an arm, motioning to Einar to join him. The young man hurried through the crowd, at the last moment ducking a stray arrow.

'Dangerous out here,' said Einar. 'But I see far more capable bowmen than I've seen elsewhere. You've led them long, Captain?' He seemed easy in the crowd. Whatever his reason for running from Magda, it was not that he was being hunted in the city.

'I've had the training of them for over ten years, when I am here,' said Owen.

'King Edward should be grateful. Though I doubt he will be leading armies across to France again. Nor will his heir.'

Spoken with a certainty that interested Owen. 'You know something of the prince?'

'Rumors.' Einar looked toward the pair beside them.

'My son Jasper assists me in training. Now show me your stance, Einar, then shoot.'

Einar took the bow from his shoulder, chose an arrow. Taking his position, he glanced over at Jasper, who was adjusting his charge's posture, and copied the instructions. He'd understood. The shot went wide, to the edge of the butt. When one of the lads who collected the arrows brought it to him, he thanked him and began to take out a coin.

'No need. The city pays them,' Owen said, nodding to the lad as he withdrew behind them.

'Dangerous work.'

'I've trained them to watch from behind the shooters. More legwork for them, but we've not yet had a casualty, though a near one, a fool who did not pay attention to whether the field was cleared.' Owen stepped closer. 'Some advice?'

'I welcome it.'

While Owen adjusted Einar's stance and his grip on the bow he examined the young man's clothing. Plain, but well made out of good wool. Dyed after some wear, old grease stains taking the new color unevenly. He suspected livery turned into everyday clothing. With his manner of speaking, northern but with a more recent polish with hints of London, the dyed clothing suggested he'd been in service in the south, and not long ago. Owen wondered what had brought him north. Returning to kin? Asa was not so near a relation. And why?

Einar's next shot came close to the mark.

'Well done. You learn quickly.'

A few more adjustments, and on the third Einar hit the mark. He had turned to Owen, but was distracted by something beyond him.

'Who is that man, the merchant with the blue feather in his cap?'

Owen looked. 'Gavin Wolcott. How did you know he's a merchant?'

'His garb?' A crooked grin. 'A lucky guess.'

Owen did not believe it.

Jasper joined them. 'You're good,' he noted after introducing himself.

'Your father corrected me. Forgive me, I've spied someone I have wished to see.'

Jasper leaned over to Owen to whisper, 'The man standing with Wolcott is Master Bernard, the physician.'

'You become my eyes, son.' Owen watched them. The leech seemed to be arguing with Gavin, his gestures clipped, close to his body, but bristling with anger. Tall, slender to the point of gauntness, shadowed eyes.

Einar had lingered. 'What did you call him?'

'Master Bernard,' said Jasper. 'He's a new physician in town. The one rumored to have called your kinswoman Dame Magda a heretic.'

'He calls himself a physician?' Einar seemed to find that amusing.

'Do you know him?' Owen asked.

'Do I? No. No. But look at him – is he a man to inspire healthy habits?' Einar glanced up at the sky. 'It is later than I thought. Next Sunday?'

'You are staying in York?'

'Much depends on whether I might find work.' Einar kept sliding his eyes toward the arguing pair.

'Where are you lodging?'

'Old Shep's house, near Dame Magda's.'

'Would you be willing to come into the city for work? I might ask some folk.'

That caught Einar's attention. 'Would you do that?'

'Come to the apothecary tomorrow.' Owen was thinking about Michaelo. He might observe the lad. A way for Owen to keep him close, possibly second-guess his intentions thereby preventing harm to Magda or others.

With a surprised, *Thank you, I will*, Einar hurried off. Gavin Wolcott was now setting himself up at the butts being used by other merchants' sons, but the physician was gone. Einar did not pause by Wolcott, but disappeared into the street.

'Would you like me to follow him?' asked Jasper.

'I would, yes. But stay hidden and do not engage. Just see where they go.'

Leaving his bow, glove, and quiver of arrows with his father, Jasper wound his way through the crowd and out onto the street. He called to a former classmate, describing Einar and asking if he'd seen which way he'd gone.

'That way,' he pointed. 'He's following the leech with the sly eyes, the one spreading lies about the Riverwoman. Lives across Foss Bridge off Walmgate.'

Calling out his thanks, Jasper hurried on, caught sight of Einar as he crossed the bridge. Running to catch up, he saw Bernard farther along. A woman hailed Jasper, asking whether the shop was open, whether he was headed to someone with the pestilence— *Stay away*, another one implored, *we need you healthy*. He shivered, answering with brief but courteous words, as his father would do. Just past St Denys' church the physician slipped into an alley. Einar seemed to nod to himself and begin to turn away, but he saw a gray-haired woman hurry as best she could on her cane toward the same alley, disappearing into it. Jasper had crept close enough to hear Einar mutter, '*Merde!*' and follow them. Asking a passing woman whether she knew where the physician Bernard lived, Jasper was told to stay away from that alley.

'Pestilence,' she hissed. 'The Riverwoman has cursed the good leech's neighbors for spite, pagan witch.' She spat and crossed herself, hurrying on.

Torn between returning to report to Owen and trying to learn more, Jasper crept to the head of the alley. At the far end, where some light fell through a crossing, Einar paced back and forth, then paused, leaning toward the light, as if listening. Now Jasper, too, heard the voices of a man and a woman, the woman's coaxing, the man's whining. But he could not make out their words. Time to return to St George's Field.

On the way there he encountered his acquaintance and asked exactly where the leech lived.

'He has lodgings in the Fuller home, next to the plague house. Mark me, he will run away, fearful lest the pestilence see that it missed his lodgings. It's the one that juts out at the side almost to the roof of the plague house.'

Jasper crossed himself as he hurried on.

Helen and her crippled husband Fergus rode in the cart, Magda and the children walking alongside. The family would protect Lettice Brown from curious eyes, and she would feel useful. Magda had discussed her plan with Fergus, knowing he would consider the burden with care. After some thought, he agreed, setting the family to packing up what little they owned and readying themselves. They would say nothing of Lettice until close to the destination – children chattered loudly when excited. They would be calmer once put to work to right the place and make their mother comfortable. Though there would be little to right, the parents would count on the children to fetch and carry and settle all for the first night.

Bringing the donkey cart near the ramshackle huts, Magda watched as the family approached, friends waving them off with kind words and prayers. Fergus and Helen were loved and respected in this community of folk who found his tragedy terribly familiar. While cleaning a watermill on his landlord's property he had slipped into the millrace, his leg crushed before his fellows managed to pull him away. Once he could no longer work he and his family were evicted. Magda had worked on Fergus's leg when he first arrived with his family, but though she relieved much of his pain the leg was mangled and he would always require a crutch, and move slowly.

The children chattered and rushed off to explore the woodland as they moved deep into Galtres, always returning when one of their parents called out to them. But as they drew near the turnoff for the house, five-year-old Tess tugged on Magda's hand. Her eyes were pools of fear. Magda picked her up.

'The trees are going to swallow us,' Tess whispered.

'Nay, little one, they will shelter thee in loving arms as they do all the creatures of the woodland and the delicate plants that nourish and heal folk. Thou art embraced by them, but they will not hold thee against thy will.'

The child gazed up into the canopy as a wren settled on a branch above them. 'They take care of the birds?'

'They provide food and shelter.'

'Dame Magda, she will tire you,' Helen said.

'Tiring is not the matter,' she said as she lifted the girl up into her father's reaching arms. 'Magda must guide thee now along a subtle track. Call for thy sons.'

Handing the girl to her mother, Fergus called the boys to follow the cart closely now.

In a moment, Magda guided the company off the main track onto a path that set the cart bouncing. Just beyond a great oak she directed them to leave the cart and walk the rest of the way, which was not far. The eldest boy helped his father out of the cart while Magda supervised the other two in assisting their mother.

'Walk with care. Watch the roots beneath thy feet,' Magda warned. As they walked she took the girl's hand and, pointing out the abundance of beauty all along the path, led the family through the ancient hollies, where they came upon Lettice sitting on a rock beside the beck, leaning to rinse out a pot.

Seeing the little family, Lettice rose with surprise. Magda made her introductions, explaining how they were to help one another.

When Magda departed a while later she hummed to herself, content with her morning's work.

As he left St George's Field with Jasper, Owen shifted through what he had learned from his son and from Harry Green, one of the night watchmen, who had been standing near Bernard and Gavin as they spoke and overheard some of the exchange. According to Harry, the leech blamed Gavin for the temper of the sermons preached in the churches that morning across the city. *They know my name. I told you I must not stand out. I told you.* Gavin had shushed him, assuring him that folk would be grateful for the warning, but Harry said from the look of him Bernard was not appeased and went away angry. He was not certain where

Bernard lodged, but had heard it was in Walmgate. 'Doubt you will long find him there, that is how frightened he was.'

Jasper's news that the leech lodged with the Fullers concerned Owen. Jack Fuller's work as master of a small trading vessel meant he was often away for long stretches, leaving Janet Fuller alone with her daughter, an invalid. And what did Asa want with Bernard? For it was surely she whom Jasper had seen following Bernard down the alley, then speaking to him. He might be wrong in concluding that Jasper had overheard Asa and Bernard talking, but Owen felt in his bones he was right.

As they turned into St Helen's Square, he wondered at the quiet. No one stood without the apothecary awaiting entrance. Jasper noticed it as well, and, hurrying to the door, found it locked. Owen was already pushing open the gate to the rear of the shop off the York Tavern yard when Jasper caught up to tell him. The workshop door was shut as well.

'The house,' said Owen, hurrying to the kitchen door, which was open on the pleasant summer day. That Kate glanced up from her spinning with a smile was reassuring. God be thanked. No bad news, no one ill.

'Captain, Jasper, I will bring your bowls to the hall. Dame Lucie and Brother Michaelo are there, sharing a meal.'

'They shut the shop?'

'Someone in the parish complained about the apothecary being open on a Sunday. Father Jerome came to warn them.'

'You see, Da? Everyone's gone mad.'

Owen clapped Jasper on the back. 'We cannot tell folk how to think. We can only go about our business. Come. Eat with us and tell your tale.'

Lucie and Michaelo sat in the window open to the garden. On the table were a loaf of bread, a dish of cheese, a tankard of ale. With a happy sigh Owen poured himself a bowl and settled at the table, breaking off a chunk of bread and helping himself to cheese.

'The archbishop's letter?' Owen asked, nodding to the document in Lucie's hands.

'Yes. I'd not read it earlier.'

Jasper took his ale over to Lucie, reading over her shoulder.

'He chided the abbot for giving alms to the poor? I cannot believe it,' said Jasper. 'For such a thing to come from the pen of an archbishop, a condemnation of charitable acts.' His voice broke in his distress.

Owen felt for this son of his who oft felt the pull of a religious calling. 'Neville seems bent on antagonizing the heads of the religious communities in York. His brother Sir John will not be pleased to hear of this.'

'Am I to inform him?' asked Michaelo.

'I believe I am duty bound to inform the prince, who will undoubtedly inform Sir John.'

Owen and Michaelo exchanged a look.

As Lucie joined Owen at the table, sitting down beside him, she asked Jasper about his time at St George's Field.

'He has quite a tale to tell,' said Owen, nodding to Jasper to take the floor.

'Might Dame Magda's daughter have thought to convince the leech how wrong he is about her mother?' Michaelo suggested when Jasper was finished recounting his adventure.

Owen agreed that might be so but for the enmity between Magda and Asa.

'A daughter's resentment can fall away when others attack her mother,' said Lucie. 'And so it might be with Asa. Did she not come seeking Magda's healing?'

'Or was it an opportunity?' asked Owen, more to himself than to the others. 'Magda herself is uncertain about their purpose in coming to her. And there is the matter of the stolen mandrake root. In any case, we're more likely to learn something from Einar than from her.' Owen described his idea about the young man assisting Michaelo among the poor.

The monk sniffed. 'You believe I might need help aiding the poor in the minster yard?'

'If that were my purpose, any extra pair of hands would do to carry your basket and lantern,' said Owen. 'I am asking you to see what you make of Einar, whether he is here for good or ill, whether he poses a threat to Dame Magda.'

'I think it a good plan,' said Lucie.

Michaelo stared out the window for a moment. 'Very well,' he said at last. 'If he comes to you and agrees to the work, tell him where he might find me.'

'As for this troublesome leech Bernard, do you know the priest at St Denys'?'

Michaelo turned from the window. 'You think to learn more about the leech from Dom Jerome?' A sniff. 'I know him well enough. The sort of cleric who connects all the ills of the world to Eve and her daughters. I would not be surprised to hear it was Jerome who inspired Bernard's accusations regarding Dame Magda, or fanned the flames.'

'Even more reason to speak with him.'

'You would be wasting your time. Besides, I've only just returned from speaking with several parish priests, both those who heeded the archbishop's call to strike out at Dame Magda and those who did not. Quite a few did. And went further, extending the condemnation to all those women who gather herbs in the hedges and woodlands to concoct what they deem "unholy potions". They threaten to refuse the sacraments to such healers and any parishioners known to consult them.' Michaelo looked to Lucie.

'You believe I might be considered in that group?' she asked.

'I fear so.'

Owen cursed.

'God help all in the city,' said Lucie. 'With people already eyeing their neighbors with suspicion and fear in this summer of pestilence, such sermons would cause more tragedies like the fire near King's Staithe.'

'Apparently the sermon at St Denys' was particularly vicious.' Michaelo nodded to Jasper. 'The woman who warned you no doubt listened to Dom Jerome's slander this morning. Or heard of it. Someone is spreading chaos in the city.'

'Some one? That would be quite an effort,' said Owen, 'and to what purpose?'

'I do not know. Yet how else to make sense of it?' asked Michaelo.

'Who would wish to turn folk against healers when all are so frightened by the pestilence?' asked Jasper.

Who indeed?

Michaelo rose. 'I must go. I need to complete the letter to His Grace.'

'You anticipated my agreement?'

'I know you well, Captain.' Michaelo departed through the garden door, turning left toward Davygate.

'What have I done,' Owen muttered.

Lucie laughed.

'It amuses you?'

'You begin to seem natural partners. Such a face! Do you pretend you are not glad of it?'

Was he glad of it? Michaelo's efficiency would speed the message on its way, and the sooner the prince took action, the better for all. Time and again while with the prince and his lady Lucie had steered Owen to a clearer understanding of the undercurrents in the conversations, the glances exchanged about the table, the whisperings, the subtle gestures. He'd thought himself trained in noticing all this, but Lucie oft corrected him, and saved him from not a few missteps.

'You are right. I will learn to catch myself in my complaints of him.'

It was Jasper who now laughed as he rose from the table. 'He has a way with him at times that would madden the mildest of men. We will not chastise you for moaning now and then.'

'I thank you,' said Owen. 'Where are you headed?'

'The workshop. To finish a few tasks for the morning. Then the garden to dig out the drainage ditch behind the garden shed. It collapsed in the last storm.'

'Leave the digging to me,' said Owen. Tiring his body often cleared his head and he had much to ponder.

When they were alone, Owen told Lucie of Michaelo's promise to light a candle for Martin this evening.

'I thought he might have seen me at their grave,' was all she said.

They sat in a loving silence while he completed his meal, then she led him out into the garden to offer guidance on the digging. Listening to her, seeing the soft sunlight brighten her brown gold hair, he fought the temptation to beg her to stay away from the shop for a while, until calmer heads prevailed in the city. He had no right to deny her autonomy. And for all he knew, her presence would inspire more than it angered, might draw some folk back to their senses. But what of visiting the Wolcotts?

'About calling on Dame Beatrice . . .'

'I meant to say, considering this morning's sermons it would be best if you were the one to offer the Wolcotts my medicines.' Lucie smiled and touched his cheek. 'Forgive me for not saying so sooner. I will go prepare them for you.'

He took her hands and kissed them.

SIX

Service

As the shadows lengthened in the garden, Ned Cooper had burst through the gate breathing hard as if from a brisk walk. While Owen wiped down the spade and put the tools in the garden shed he'd listened to Ned's account of finding Magda's coracle hidden in the underbrush near where Asa and Einar had made the crossing. While his partner had returned it, Ned had waited to see whether someone might come for it. He'd witnessed Einar searching, then cursing as he saw the boys crowding round the coracle on the north bank. Owen had sent Ned off with praise, and now, after cleaning off the worst of the mud clinging to him and changing his clothing, he was on his way to call on Gavin Wolcott. Bernard seemed the key and Owen was determined to learn what he could of the man.

The servant who'd answered the door stepped aside for his master. Owen saw the unease in Gavin Wolcott's posture and the set of his jaw before he put on the crooked, self-effacing grin meant to charm. 'Come within, Captain, share a bowl of ale with me. You must forgive my appearance. I have been in the garden seeing what I might do to repair the neglect in father's illness.' Though he was sweaty and disheveled, no soil clung to the man's clothes or shoes, only cobwebs in his hair and a smudge of ink on his chin and right hand.

Dame Beatrice entered the hall and came swiftly toward them. Noticing Owen watching her she gave him a nod, but her focus was Gavin.

Owen commended his host on his apparent skill at gardening. 'After an afternoon digging in our garden I am covered in dirt.'

'No doubt you apply yourself more heartily to the task than I do,' said Gavin, gesturing to the servant who brought a jug and three bowls to the table to pour and leave them. When she was gone, he sipped the ale and asked what he might do for Owen.

'I've a simple question. I understand it was while you were away on business that you met the physician Bernard. Where? What town? Or was it at a fair?' As a merchant, it would have been one or the other.

'Who told you this?' Gavin asked, his genial mask slipping.

Beatrice had taken a seat beside him. 'I fear I erred in speaking of it to the Captain on an earlier visit. With your father so ill I forgot to tell you.'

Gavin scowled. 'Taking it upon yourself—' He stopped. 'We will discuss this when we do not have a guest.' He turned back to Owen. 'I do not consider the first encounter a meeting. I was at an inn with a group of merchants when one of our party fell ill. Master Bernard presented himself as a physician and offered the man assistance. That was in Lincoln.'

'Who fell ill?' Owen asked.

'Why the devil—?'

'Surely it is a simple request,' said Beatrice, giving Owen an encouraging smile as if to smooth any feathers ruffled by Gavin's curtness.

'God's blood, woman, you don't know what you ask. The man in question has suffered the loss of his infant son to the pestilence. I would not have him bothered.'

'Do you mean John Stone of Easingwold?' breathed Beatrice. 'May heavenly angels watch over the baby's tender soul.'

Gavin glared at her.

'I assure you I will not intrude on his grief,' said Owen. 'Regarding Bernard, those in your company were pleased with his care of your friend?'

'We were,' Gavin said through his teeth. 'Quite. And I might have said something to the effect that we were ever in need of skilled physicians. At least, that is what Bernard claims.'

'I sense you are no longer satisfied with him?'

'I understand you have seen my father, how he hangs on to life by a thread.' Gavin looked away.

'Yes. I was sorry to see him brought so low. I pray you, my wife prepared a few items, one that might help strengthen him, the other to ease his breathing . . .' Owen placed the pack on a small table beside him.

'How kind,' said Beatrice. 'Do thank Mistress Wilton for us.'

Gavin cleared his throat. 'I hesitate to try anything more. He has suffered enough.'

'The tincture sealed with blue wax might, as I said, ease his breathing. I will leave them here. A gift. Yours to use or not.'

'We are grateful,' Gavin said, sounding anything but.

Rising, Owen thanked them both and took his leave. But for what was he thanking them? The exchange felt false to him, both Gavin and Beatrice hiding far more than they revealed.

He was still taking apart the conversation, the gestures, the glances, searching for the hidden truth, when he returned home.

'Will you march through the kitchen with nary a greeting?' Lucie asked, startling him out of his tangled thoughts.

He had walked right past both Lucie and Kate without seeing them. 'God help me,' he groaned, bowing his head.

'So troubling?' She took his arm. 'Come into the hall and tell me everything.'

Kate handed him a jug of ale and two bowls.

Shamefaced, he apologized to her as well.

'I saw your face and knew you had no idea where you were,' said Kate. 'I am sorry the city hangs all our troubles on you.'

He followed Lucie out into the hall, where she sat them at the table near the garden window. A bowl of ale and a long narration later, he felt drained, but grateful for Lucie's deep listening. She agreed with his suspicion, though she had no suggestions as to what he was missing.

She had returned to her tallies and lists at the table while Owen paced, still considering the tensions at the Wolcott home, when someone knocked at the door. Owen hurried to answer, surprised to find Einar on the doorstep.

'You came. No, I did not mean you are not welcome,' Owen hastened to say when he saw Einar's hesitation.

'I know you said tomorrow, but— I hoped— Have you any news of work for me?'

'I do.' Inviting him in, Owen described Michaelo's evening work among the poor in the minster yard. All the while he felt the young man's eyes – so like Magda's – boring into him, trying to fathom his purpose.

And, indeed, his first question was, 'Why are you offering this to me?'

'You seemed eager for work. Was I wrong? Does the work of a healer not appeal?'

'It does. Very much. And I need the work. If I show myself worthy . . .' Einar shifted on the bench to face Owen more fully, squinting at him. 'But by now you have heard I stole Dame Magda's coracle to row Asa across the river.'

'I have.' He was curious how the young man would explain himself.

Einar looked down at the hat he held in his hands. 'I witnessed Asa's suffering on our journey here, pain in her feet and an old injury to one leg. Since then I have bowed to her requests. I know Dame Magda urged her to wait awhile, allow herself to fully heal, but Asa would not have it. I tell you this not to excuse my action, only to explain it. I was helping a kinswoman in need. I meant only to borrow it. But someone returned it before I had the chance. Now I cannot prove it.'

'Why her hurry?'

'Why does Asa do anything?'

Owen saw no point in pursuing that. 'Are you willing to do this work I propose? There is no money in it. But if you please Brother Michaelo, he will help you find a place.'

'I understand. You still extend the offer?'

'I do. Well?'

'If the monk is willing to have me I welcome the work.'

'He is willing, and he could use you now.' Owen told Einar where he might find Michaelo. 'Anyone in the minster yard will guide you to him. He will have been there for a time, I think.'

Rising to leave, Einar turned back to ask, 'Do you have any advice for me in making amends with Dame Magda?'

'Be honest. She will see into your heart, and know the truth of it.'

When he was gone, Lucie said, 'He has her eyes, strangely knowing for so young a man.'

'And a presence,' Owen agreed.

'Not so powerful as Magda's.'

'No. Nor might it ever be.'

'Is Asa the same?'

'Not that I recall.'

As Owen resumed his pacing Lucie said, 'You chose not to warn him of Michaelo's sharpness.'

'Why spoil Michaelo's fun?'

With a smile and a nod, she resumed her work.

Seeing the Riverwoman collect her basket and slip out the door, Lettice followed into the soft light of early afternoon, propelled by her sense of guilt. By confessing her fears to Dame Magda she hoped to prevent more violence. She should have gone at once to Bailiff Hempe to tell him what she had seen and what she believed it portended, the dread that had seeped into her bones, but instead she had run for that very terror.

At first when the healer paused Lettice thought it an invitation. 'Dame Magda, I must tell you . . .' But she stopped as the wizened woman seemed to sniff the air, then look sharply toward the river. 'What do you—'

'Hush,' Magda said, 'not now.' She resumed walking, picking up her pace.

Lettice lifted her skirts and hurried to catch up. 'Dame Magda, I must warn you . . .'

The healer paused, glanced back, her blue eyes sharp and clear. 'Magda is needed elsewhere. Smoke. Danger. Not here. She will return when it is Helen's time. Be of comfort to her and to the children.'

And she was gone, disappearing through the holly hedge toward the main track through Galtres.

At the home where Magda stabled her donkey the child's father said he'd noticed a crowd on the riverbank near her rock.

'Much talk of flames, but I saw none. Have a care, Dame Magda. I will escort you.'

'Thou art kind, but there is no need.'

The crowd still clustered on the bank, milling about, mostly children, though some adults among them, all looking toward her rock and chattering.

'Someone shot a flaming arrow onto your roof!' one of the boys shouted as she approached.

'The dragon's breathing smoke!' another added.

She saw it, a trail of smoke from her dragon's mouth that twisted against the deepening blue of the evening sky.

'The dragon ate the flame and breathed it out,' explained a lass. 'That's why he's smoking.'

From others she gathered an idea of what they had seen. A shadow on the far bank, a flaming arrow that appeared to pierce the roof but then tumbled off, the flame put out. It was then that folk noticed smoke streaming from the dragon's mouth. As it still did, rising in slow, languid curls. How excited they all were, and anxious for her safety. She thanked them all and asked after Twig, the lad seeing to her kitten.

'His mother waded out to fetch him. Found him fussing over the fire, worried that he had made a mistake in stoking it in preparation for your return at day's end and caused the bit of smoke,' said a woman standing on the bank. 'He would not come back with her. *Must stay with the kitten*, he said. Though he did step out to gawk at the smoking dragon.'

As she set her things in the coracle on the shore they told her of the return of her own, assuring her it was back on the rock. She was a little disappointed it had not been Einar thinking better of falling into Asa's ways. But there was time for that. She rowed herself over to the house so the lad might row himself back.

On the rock, she made straight for her door with a nod to the dragon and silent thanks. Within, she praised the brave lad and took the kitten into her arms, holding her close to her heart for a moment.

'Back tomorrow?' the lad asked.

'Magda will consider and let thee know in the morn.'

She had shared a bit of broth with Holda and was relaxing by the fire with a sip of brandywine when Einar came calling.

'So late?' she said.

'I could not sleep without admitting my guilt and apologizing for the theft of your coracle.'

'Go on.'

He spoke of Asa and her insistence on leaving, though he claimed not to know what called her to the city with such urgency.

Partly true, but he knew far more than he cared to say. Still, she forgave him, for what was the point of begrudging him when the coracle was back in her possession? He swore he would not betray her in such wise ever again.

In such wise, but he clearly continued to do so in others.

'Wilt thou accept Magda's hospitality?' She indicated a high-backed chair by the fire.

'Your best chair?'

'Thou art a hesitant guest.' She offered him a dram of the brandywine.

He accepted with puzzled thanks, explaining that he had found work that had prevented him from coming earlier. He spoke of helping the fussy crow with the poor in the minster yard, where he had heard whispers of something happening on her rock.

'They spoke of a wonder. Your dragon breathing fire.'

She smiled.

'It is not true?'

'Folk enjoy tales of wonder.'

'On the riverbank I heard the lads speak of a fire. They would not tell me, not after I stole the coracle, and I paid three pennies for one to row me out here.'

'Magda will speak to them. As for the fire, as you can see, the house is untouched.'

'But someone meant to set fire to your home? I hoped to attend you in your healing visits, but I might be of more help guarding the house during the day.'

'Why wouldst thou wish to attend Magda?'

His tongue loosened by a few sips of the brandywine, he spoke of his work with his father, and how he had assisted Asa in Lincoln, how good it felt to help Michaelo. 'I hoped you might teach me more.'

At most but a partial truth. Magda had not sensed him cowed by Asa. Yet there was the one they followed. 'Thou art called to be a healer?'

'I believe I have some skill. I hoped with your guidance I might see whether that is true.'

'Why Magda?'

'We are kin. I have your blood.'

'Skill is not carried by blood. It is learned.' She was not ready to tell him about his great-grandfather and the slender thread of inheritance she sensed in him. Time for that if, once she knew him better, she thought he might make good use of it. It was only a valuable skill if used for good.

'I thought—' He looked down to his hands, seemed to notice how tightly he clutched them, spread his fingers wide. His great-grandfather's hands. 'Would you teach me?' he asked.

'Magda will consider it. Hast thou more thou wouldst speak of?'

He hesitated, then set aside his bowl and rose. 'I am grateful you did not send me away.'

'Art thou biding with Asa in the city?'

'No. I thought to stay upriver.'

She would have a care when she went to the sanctuary in the early mornings. But she had a task for him.

'Wouldst thou sleep here tomorrow night, while Magda is at a birthing? Feed Holda, see that young Twig stays only until thou hast returned from the minster yard.'

'Thank you for trusting me to guard your home.' His smile was as dazzling as Sten's. 'I will not fail you again.'

Magda grunted. 'Easily said.' The smile faded. He appeared to understand that he must prove himself. 'Return tomorrow in the late afternoon to assure Twig thou wilt return at dusk. Bring thy bow.'

'So you do fear trouble?'

'Magda does not fear what is coming. But she is not certain when it will happen. Trust thyself.'

She observed his unease and understood, yet the test might show him who he wished to be.

On a Sunday evening in fine weather Lucie and Owen were accustomed to sitting out in the garden with the household, this night consisting only of Jasper and Kate. The absence of Gwenllian, Hugh, and Emma muted Owen's pleasure as random noises had him glancing round to see what the little ones were about. He was glad when first Hempe and then Poole wandered in, providing a distraction.

Hempe came to report a rumor going round that the archbishop was plotting to rob the folk of their healers so they might succumb to the pestilence and clear the city, allowing the nobles, Churchmen, and wealthier merchants to expand their townhouses and enjoy the amenities of York. No one was surprised by that, considering the day's sermons.

'The fools are stirring trouble, suspicion, resentment, all manner of bad feeling,' said Poole as he caught the gist of the conversation. 'My wife caught one of the servants spinning a tale about Dame Magda as a servant of Satan and lectured him on all the good the Riverwoman has done for us and so many in York. He claimed he was only repeating what some priest said to his parishioners this morning. I say we must not need him if he's so idle he can hear about such so quickly, but Muriel had given him leave to attend church with his family at St Mary's on Castlegate.'

'The mayor's parish,' Owen noted.

'He is not likely to bother himself about it,' said Hempe. 'So, Crispin, did you send the churl off to fend for himself on the streets?'

'No. Muriel believes him sufficiently chastened to continue working for us. I doubt it, but I have assigned him so many tasks he'll not have the breath to spew more poison in my household, nor spread it elsewhere. Such untruths – they cannot be unheard, and they work on folk as they wake in the night and sense Death approaching.'

The mention of Mayor Graa reminded Owen of what Carn had said of his apparent friendship with Gavin Wolcott. 'What business might Graa have with Guthlac's son?'

'Interesting question,' said Hempe. 'I will ask Lotta. She sifts through merchants' gossip with an eye toward what might be of value to our undertakings. If there is something there, my wife will know of it.'

'If it's one of Gavin's schemes she might not see the whole of it,' said Poole. 'He delights in his own cleverness, misdirecting his fellows so that he has few competitors.'

'Lotta has warned me to pay no heed to Gavin's chatter,' said Hempe. 'She says his own father distrusts him – or did so before his illness. It's why he kept Sam Toller on.'

Owen thought of the shadow of Guthlac lying in the great bed. Poor man if that was true.

Lucie was asking Crispin about her godchild when the garden door creaked once more. 'This will be Brother Michaelo? Or Alfred?' she said.

But it was Einar, hesitating when he saw the company. 'Forgive me. I did not mean to intrude.'

Owen welcomed him, motioning to an unclaimed stool, making introductions. In the dark, with only a small lantern adding a soft light, it was impossible to see Einar's expression, but he perched on the stool as if uneasy. Because of the presence of a bailiff and coroner? Lucie offered him ale, but he declined with thanks.

'I thought you should hear what happened at Dame Magda's this evening, Captain. You will all wish to know of it.' He described what he'd heard about the attack on Magda's house, as well as her amusement regarding the tale of the dragon spouting fire or smoke. 'Though it all came to naught I thought you would wish to know.'

Owen thanked him, as did the others.

'You heard about it while assisting Brother Michaelo?' Owen asked, and when Einar nodded he asked whether any had suggested the culprit, or the motive.

'A priest or the leech who started the trouble, that's who most think behind it. Neither seems likely.'

Poole laughed. 'Agreed. From the south bank to Magda's roof? I would like to see any of our parish priests manage such a shot. And the leech – you mean Master Bernard? He strikes me as a weakling.'

'Someone shot the arrow,' Lucie said, sobering all. 'Have you a place to stay, Einar?'

'I do. Old Shep's, upriver from Dame Magda's.'

'And Dame Asa?' she asked.

'She wished to find lodgings in the city. She has some coin to pay.'

'Does she know anyone in the city?' Jasper asked.

Owen nudged him quiet as Einar said he did not know, then rose, again apologizing for interrupting their evening, and took his leave. Owen walked him to the gate.

'Did you find the work to your liking?'

'It felt good to be of use – at least, I think Brother Michaelo found me useful. He said little to me. I am grateful you, Captain.'

'The poor deserve our help. I thank you for telling me of the incident on the river. I plan on visiting Dame Magda in the morning.'

When Owen rejoined the others they were voicing the question that loomed large in his own thoughts – who benefited from attacking Magda?

'I fear that someone more important than the Wolcotts and the itinerant leech are behind this,' Crispin was saying, 'someone who has the ear of the archbishop.'

'But why extend the accusations to midwives and other women?' Lucie asked.

'I don't like to think that someone powerful is behind this,' said Hempe. 'We should set a watch on Magda's house.'

'The poor who depend on her care will be watching out, particularly the lads who guard her coracle,' said Owen. 'But it would not be amiss to have someone watching from a distance. I will pay a visit in the early morning, see it in daylight.'

As Poole took his leave, he asked if he might accompany Owen.

SEVEN

The Dragon Stirs

Owen caught the two taunting the first woman to approach the door of the apothecary, lifting them by their collars and carrying them down the lane and through alleys to the river.

'No! I can't swim!' one cried.

'You think yourself such a clever lad, eh? I have all confidence in your ability to learn by necessity,' said Owen with a laugh.

'We meant no harm,' whined the other.

'Oh, but I think you did,' said Owen.

He had collected a crowd of onlookers, especially youths of

both sexes, giggly and calling out taunts. Both boys had pissed themselves.

'Need help?' Alfred called as he approached. 'I've a few stout men with me.'

'Good. Better to swing them out.'

'No!' cried the first as Stephen grabbed him and swung him out over the water.

'Ready, Captain?'

The second lad's mother pushed through the crowd, cursing her son. 'You piddle-kneed lunkhead,' she shouted. 'I will give you such a beating.' Owen had counted on her anger.

'We will gladly hand him over to you, but first they will sit a spell in the pillories on Micklegate. We want to set an example.'

The goodwife grinned. 'Fair enough.'

Handing the lads to Stephen and Alfred, Owen headed back to the shop.

Crispin met him on Coney Street. 'Caught sight of you carrying a pair of rats to the river just now.' He chuckled. 'Doubt they will cause trouble for a while.'

'Not if their mothers have aught to say.' Owen massaged one forearm, then the other. 'Burly curs. And what a stench.'

'Are we off to Magda's, then?'

'I need a moment with Lucie. Head on to Bootham. I will catch up.'

Owen found Lucie in the workshop assembling herbal nosegays, protection against foul odors that some believed carried the sickness. She motioned him outside.

'Customers are trickling in. I doubt we would have any had you not lured away the troublemakers.'

'That was my intention. But I fear they are not the last, and they'll be adults next time.'

'Do not worry about us. We will manage. You have a city to protect.'

'And if someone comes showering curses on you?'

'I have dealt with Agnes Baker's venom for years, my love, and it has not felled me. Even so, Jasper will stay at the counter and I will assist from the workshop.'

'You promise?'

She stood on her tiptoes to kiss him. 'Did I not just say that
was the plan?'

Her level gaze eased his worry. 'I must be off to Magda's, then.'

'Yes.'

As Owen made his way through the cluster of shacks stretching
from the abbey gate to the bank near Magda's rock, smoke from
cook fires swirled and danced in the morning mist forcing him to
move his one good eye up, down, and about every few steps. Folk
milled about him and Crispin, eager to talk about the incident on
Magda's rock the previous evening. The accounts echoed Einar's
description, though imbued with more wonder at the dragon's role
– for most believed it had eaten the fire and so protected Magda's
home. And though they counted it a blessing that their healer
escaped without loss they worried for their own settlement. What
if the flaming arrow had landed in their midst? They showered
blessings on Owen, thanking him for keeping danger at bay, and,
despite being gaunt with hunger, generously offering him food
and drink, which he declined, begging haste.

Reaching the bank he glanced back for his companion and saw
Crispin leaning on his cane in the midst of a gaggle of small
children taking turns touching the stump of his arm, some with
trepidation, others with giggles. Catching his eye, Owen motioned
that he was ready to cross. While he waited for Crispin to join
him Owen explained to the lad on watch at the boat that he preferred
rowing himself and his friend. When he sweetened the news with
a penny, disappointment turned to delight.

'You drive a hard bargain,' said Crispin, joining them.

The lad grinned and bobbed his head. 'I'll watch for your return.
Make sure the bank is clear.'

Magda stood in the doorway cradling the kitten as they climbed
out of the coracle. 'Thou hast come to see the fiery dragon,
Bird-eye?'

'I would enjoy that, but I see that he is as woodenly inclined
as ever.'

With a barking laugh she stepped aside to welcome them into
the house.

'I will just walk round, check for damage, before I join you.
Go on, Crispin.'

'You should have seen the captain disciplining a pair of street rats this morning . . .' Crispin was saying as he stepped into Magda's house.

Fetching a ladder, Owen climbed high enough to examine the roof facing the north bank. He saw no sign of fire. But on the south side he found the remains of an arrow, mostly the metal head – barbed, with a long shaft, for hunting small game – lodged in a scorched area of a wooden patch he had added a year earlier to cover a worm-eaten spot in the overturned ship. He removed it and searched the ground for remnants of more, finding the blackened remains of another directly beneath where the dragon's long neck was exposed to the south bank. As with the first, it stank of lard, oil, and burnt wood, but the head on this one was badly bent. As he moved the ladder to one side of the creature he apologized for the intrusion. Climbing up, he focused his attention on the carved dragon rather than the height, his half-blindness making him a poor judge of such things, and ran a hand along the wood. Marvelously smooth, and hardly weathered. Peering closer with his one good eye, he detected a scorched patch, but no indentation such as he would have expected. It was as if the arrow had simply bounced off. *You are a wondrous being,* he thought to the dragon.

As he stepped inside with his findings Crispin reported no sign of damage within.

'Yet at least two burning arrows managed to strike up above.' Owen held out the remains to Magda and Crispin, describing the damage to the patch and what might be a scorch mark on the dragon. 'I would expect something around that patch to have caught fire, but I found nothing. Your dragon has but a slight discoloration, as if the arrow bounced off. As you see from this head, the arrow suffered the worst of it.' He cocked his head, gazing on Magda.

Ignoring the question in his eye, she asked, 'Did Einar bring thee news of the attack?'

Surprised by the question, Owen hesitated, and it was Crispin who responded.

'He did. He fears whoever it was might try again.'

'Magda's lads are watching. They are collecting river water to have at the ready should the next arrow land in their midst.'

'But there is more,' said Crispin, telling her about the sermons the previous day.

'Magda has heard it all before. The crows are consumed by the fear of things against which they are powerless, so they beat their chests and spout angry words. Bird-eye and the bailiffs will be busy keeping the peace within the walls. Magda thanks thee for thy concern, thine as well, Bird-eye, but there is no need. Should Magda discover the archer, thou shalt hear of it.'

Owen knew better than to press further. 'We shall do likewise.'

Crispin had picked up what was left of the two arrows. 'These heads are the most commonly used for hunting. Might belong to anyone.'

'Intentionally difficult to trace back to a particular person or group,' said Owen.

With that, Crispin rose. 'I am sure you have other matters to discuss.'

Magda handed him a jar. 'More of the unguent for Dame Muriel to work into thy leg.'

He fumbled with his scrip, but she held up a hand. 'Until thou canst walk without the cane, Magda will take no coin from thee.'

'You believe that is possible?'

'Magda intends it to be so.'

Bowing to her, hand to heart, Crispin departed.

'He is a good man.'

Magda snorted. 'Thou didst not always think so.'

True. 'I had my reasons.'

'All men veer from the better path at times.'

'Am I right in trusting Einar with the poor in the minster yard?'

'Such work under the guidance of the fussy crow might be the medicine he needs to draw out the poison.'

'Poison?'

'There is a darkness in him, but also much light. Thou hast done well.' She smiled. 'And thou canst rest easy about Lettice Brown. Magda has taken her to safety.'

'God be thanked. She was not injured?'

'No. But she is frightened. Magda hopes to hear her tale on the morrow.'

'You will tell me?'

'If it seems helpful, yes. Now go in peace. Magda has a full day with many folk to see over a great distance. Time is precious.'

'You promise to tell me?'

'Did Magda not say so?'

Conditionally. But he would not argue. On the bank he encountered Twig, the lad who watched Magda's kitten, waiting for the coracle.

'I believe you were here last night, when the house was attacked,' said Owen.

The lad stood to attention. 'I was, Captain.'

'Did you see or hear anything that might help us discover who the archer was?'

'No. But I will keep watch.'

'I depend on it. You are a courageous young man, Twig.'

'I'm only here to look after the kitten. It's the dragon protects Dame Magda's house.'

Owen glanced back at the fierce wooden visage. Easy to see why the lad would believe it. Having seen the remnants of the arrow, he himself was half convinced some magic was at work there.

The first timid knock came shortly after Owen departed. Lucie found a young mother at the door carrying a swaddled infant and holding the hand of a little boy. Begging Lucie's pardon she asked if she might shop for what she needed out of sight of the eyes on the street.

'Someone is watching?'

'I saw no one, but I fear— Our priest said— Mistress Wilton, I would not ask but—'

Lucie waved away her apologies and saw to her request, sending her on her way only to find another customer waiting outside the door. And so it went, the most worrisome a man frightened for his wife; she had asked Master Bernard to help her after her water broke and he told her to have her mother deliver her child, that was women's work.

'But both our dams are long dead, Mistress Wilton. That leech would not help her, but he convinced her that midwives are all daughters of Satan and she would not let me send for one. Can you help her?'

Lucie explained that she was no midwife, nor was there any substitute for one. She named several and advised him to tell his wife they were known as pious women. As they were.

Silently she cursed Bernard and the gullible parish priests as yet another visibly frightened neighbor stepped up to the workshop door.

One step and the distant buzz of the folk in the city and Galtres fell away, leaving only the sounds of the woodland and the inhabitants of the sanctuary. A raven's caw was no louder than a child's voice. Scent, too, changed, the mulch beneath Magda's feet rich with season upon season of leaves and animal droppings. It was as if one of the homes of Sten's kin had followed her to Galtres, surrounded by a patch of the ancient wood. In the past she had come here when the world bore down upon her, withdrawing into the peace of this place in which time slowed, seeking the happiness of her years with Sten. Memory, more of a trickster than a guide, hiding the darkness of the time after the birth of the twins, reveling in the long happy days when she hungrily learned what she could from Sten and basked in their mutual passion. But gradually the veil frayed and in rushed the pain. From all that she had learned with him and since, Magda summoned the will to sit with her grief, and, through it, find her own peace in the earth and all creation. By then it was too late to help her daughter Yrsa do the same. She was long gone, married and living far away. But perhaps Magda might now help her daughter's grandson to find his way. If that was his wish. Tonight might provide the chance to see his true intent.

At the beck within the sanctuary clearing Helen's boys were doing chores – gathering kindling, carrying buckets of water, scrubbing bowls, all with a wide-eyed quiet that bespoke a frightening event. To ask might be to stir up tears. Fergus sat astride a stool near the doorway, his crushed leg thrust out at its strange angle, showing his daughter how to grind the grain for flour. He glanced up with a furrowed brow that smoothed only a little as he struggled to rise, telling Tess to go help her brothers at the beck.

'I prayed you would come soon, and here you are.' Tears stood in his eyes.

'Be at ease,' said Magda. 'Thy wife's time has come?'

'I woke to find her pacing the room. Then her pains began. From the start they were worse than ever before, and they have not stopped since before dawn. She says they are still too far apart for it to be time. Dame Lettice is helping, but she needs you, Dame Magda. I have sat here listening to them and she is frightening Helen. She fears that her husband's murderers are coming for her and we are all in danger. Helen tells her you would never place us in the path of such trouble, but she will not hear it. I fear she has already frightened them. I was about to send one of the boys for you.'

'Magda saw their faces. Give the woodland time to draw them into the wonders. Once they see, they will understand they are safe. Thou art safe. All will be well for thee. Now Magda will see to the women.' She stepped inside, pausing a moment to allow her eyes to adjust to the dimness. In the sleep chamber Lettice bathed Helen's face in cool water while the expectant mother stood panting.

'Dame Magda!' Helen cried, breaking away from the other woman.

'God be thanked,' breathed Lettice. 'I have done all I know to do. She must—'

Magda suggested that Lettice go out for some fresh air and a walk about the clearing while she examined Helen.

'Bless you,' Helen said as she eased down onto the bed with Magda's assistance. 'She fears—'

'Thy husband heard. Be assured, this sanctuary will not be breached. It is Lettice who needs the protections about this place, not thy family. But she will be of help to thee when calmed. And thou wilt help her through her first weeks of grieving.' She massaged Helen's head as she spoke, listening to the woman's breathing, waiting for it to slow even more.

When the rhythm pleased her, Magda checked first for breech, but the head was in the right place. Laying her hands upon the distended stomach she awaited the next contraction, feeling where the twin lay as well. 'Ah, there is the second of the pair.'

'I cannot feel two heartbeats,' said Helen.

It was ever difficult to distinguish two, for many reasons. Listening closely, she caught the second, moved her ear along Helen's distended stomach until the second heartbeat was the stronger one. 'Two strong hearts.' She guided Helen's hands. 'One here. The other here.'

'God is good!'

In truth, it was early to rejoice. Much could happen before and during the birth. 'The pains will ease, return, ease, return. Breathe deep and allow thy body to do its work. Magda will return before sunset.'

'I must endure this all day?'

'Thou hast a long wait ahead of thee. Wilt thou allow the woods to ease thee? Walk about the clearing with thy children supporting thee, rest when thou wouldst, then walk again. Listen to the music of the woodland. Watch the wind in the leaves.'

Helen's heart slowed and her breathing lengthened. 'Yes, I will do that, Dame Magda.'

The boys dropped their chores and came running to assist their mother, but it was young Tess who arrived first, eager to show her mother her discoveries.

'As long as I do not need to bend down,' Helen laughed, taking her daughter's hand. The little procession moved off into the dappled sunlight. Fergus smiled after them.

Stepping back into the dim interior, Magda tidied the bed. On a shelf in the outer room she arranged all she would need when she returned at the end of her day. She took a wooden cup from a stack on her way out. 'Watch for Magda just before sunset,' she told Fergus. 'The births will come in the night.'

'Bless you, Dame Magda.'

She found Lettice in the grass by the beck. Kneeling, with hands covering her face, she wept. Magda scooped up water in the cup and added a tonic. With a swirl of the bowl the tonic dissolved and she touched Lettice's hand. 'I brought something to refresh you and lighten your heart.'

While Lettice drew her hands away and accepted the offering, Magda lifted her face to the breeze and listened to the creaks and sighs of the woodland canopy, the bird calls, the rustling of animals and birds foraging in the undergrowth, the chuckling of the beck.

'Dame Magda, I—'

Magda took the empty cup from her hand, set it aside. 'Splash thy face to cool it.' When Lettice had done that she sat back, blinking as if awaking from a dream. 'Now tell Magda what is in thy heart.'

'I frightened poor Helen in the midst of her pains.'

'She says that thou dost fear thy husband's murderers will find thee here? And Helen's family?'

'Yes.'

Magda took the woman's hands, cold from the water. 'What didst thou witness?'

'Only the men discovering poor Matthew in the ruins of our home. One shouted that he had been stabbed again and again.'

'And thou hast a thought to who did this?'

'I fear— I begged a favor that cost my husband his life. I am laundress for many merchant households, as you know. Some for a long while. Guthlac Wolcott's – I have worked for them so long I felt I might ask. Master Gavin was complaining about the men who work in the warehouse. He said what could he expect when they were paid by the mayor, not by him. When I was leaving – I do not know now how I was so bold – I told him my Matthew might see to all the work he needed. He chided me for listening, but surprised me then, telling me to send my husband to the warehouse the next morning.' She swiped at tears. 'Matthew was grateful for the work. But something happened, as it ever does. Matthew was there but a week when Master Gavin stopped me as I delivered the laundry and said to tell Matthew he should not return. Why did he tell me? Matthew would not believe me. He went along as he had every morning. When I came home from collecting my work that day I found him sprawled on the floor, his nose broken and an eye swollen shut. Two of the warehouse workers accused him of stealing and ordered him out, but he refused, telling them he worked for the Wolcotts. So they beat him and threw him out, threatening him with worse if he returned. My poor Matthew,' she whispered, the tears falling freely. 'The next day he went to the Wolcott home, but they would not see him. The servant called him a thief under her breath and slammed the door.'

'What had he stolen?'

'They never said what.'

'Thou didst not ask thy husband?'

'No. And when I went to fetch the Wolcott laundry on my usual day neither Dame Beatrice nor Master Gavin said anything. I dared not ask for fear they would let me go. And now he's dead. Stabbed. Murdered.'

'Thou dost believe Thomas Graa's workers murdered thy husband?'

'I do. And I am frightened for Dame Beatrice and her babe.'

'Her children are dead.'

'God has worked a miracle. She is with child – a laundress knows these things – and her husband is dying. He is so poorly, Dame Magda. I do not know why Dame Beatrice has not sent for you. But what if those men come to their home— The mayor is a powerful man.'

'If he is so powerful, why should he wish to threaten Dame Beatrice?'

Her fears came from a place Lettice could not explain.

'This information would help Captain Archer find the murderers. Wouldst thou permit Magda to tell him?'

'My daughter – with a newborn child I fear for her. And my son – he works in a shop in the city.'

'All the more reason to tell the captain. His men can pursue the ones who might make trouble for them.'

'I thought it best I disappear. Say nothing to anyone.'

'Magda asks too much of thee.' She rose, gathering her things.

'But others might be in danger.'

Magda said nothing.

'Matthew might have heard something that would endanger many,' said Lettice. 'You trust that the captain can protect my daughter or you would not suggest it.'

'Nothing is certain except that thy husband has been murdered. As was Sam Toller.'

Lettice reached down to the water, letting it run across her hand. 'I cannot in good conscience remain quiet. Should I go to the captain?'

'Thou art needed here.'

'Then yes, I pray you, tell him all that seems important.'

Magda left Lettice gathering a few roots and berries to add to a stew for the family. Whispering her thanks to the spirit of the place, Magda continued on her afternoon visitations. On the main track through Galtres she kept an eye out for a trustworthy friend heading to the city. She needed to get word to Bird-eye to come to her in the morning. She had much to tell him.

* * *

Arriving at Graa's warehouse near King's Staithe, Owen watched unnoticed for a while, getting his bearings. Two men were doing an inventory, one calling out the contents of barrels and chests, with estimates of how many items were in each, the other making notes on a wax tablet. Thomas Graa wanted an estimate of his losses from the fire, Owen guessed. Other men shifted items away from the area damaged in the fire. He approached one of them, explaining that he was investigating the fire at the mayor's request, and asking whether they knew who had lost merchandise in the blaze, Graa or one of the merchants who leased space.

'Those who lease, Captain. Not all damaged, but for some it was everything.'

While he was speaking, the one with the wax tablet joined them, clearing his throat and eyeing Owen with unease. 'I tagged what was salvageable and now they are moving it to another area,' he said. 'Is there a problem?'

Owen explained again why he was there. 'Would you know whose merchandise was ruined?'

The first man began to answer, but was interrupted by the clerk, who told him to return to his work.

'We can say no more until I have the mayor's permission to do so, Captain.'

'You do not think he meant for me to ask questions?'

'I do not know which questions he would wish me to answer, and which he would prefer to answer himself.'

'Then I should go directly to Mayor Graa?'

'No! No, that will not be necessary, I assure you. It is a matter of form. You understand.'

'I will return later this afternoon. I advise you to speak with the mayor as soon as possible.'

'But he might be—'

'Or I shall.'

'Yes, Captain.'

The mayor was not likely to rise from dinner until mid-afternoon. Owen would return before then. With any luck the clerk would be out of the warehouse searching for his master, affording Owen an opportunity to look round, catch a worker eager to talk. For now, he headed home.

In the yard of the York Tavern, Bess Merchet called to him from the tavern doorway.

'See the lass creeping round the wagon to slip into your garden gate?' she said, nodding in that direction.

Though the day was mild, the warmest day since early autumn, the young woman wore a long cloak and a hat pulled down to cover part of her face.

'What the—'

'They are frightened, that is what, frightened to be seen giving their custom to a female apothecary. The monstrous clerics have terrified them.'

'Is Lucie helping them from the workshop?'

'She is. All morning. While Jasper sees to those bold enough to enter from the street. Quite a few of those, I must say. To their credit. But it should not be like this. At a time when all are so fearful for their health, it should not be like this. Curse the new archbishop.'

'I will find a way to convince Lucie to take her dinner with me.'

Bess patted his arm. 'You are a good husband.'

A man skittered off as Owen crossed to the gate, clutching a small packet to his chest. He disappeared down the back gardens.

Lucie glanced up at the sound of the gate. The young woman had removed her hat. One of Crispin Poole's servants. Nodding to Owen, Lucie returned to her discussion with the young woman. Owen waited, smiling and bowing to the young woman as she turned to depart.

'Captain. I pray you say nothing to my master and mistress about my cowardice in hiding my presence.'

'If you promise not to repeat the offense, I will,' he said, well aware he would be chided by Lucie as soon as the young woman departed. But the servant agreed, with apologies, and scurried off.

'Owen.' The gray-blue eyes were leveled at him.

'Forgive me, but she was clearly instructed to come to the shop door, not hide back here. Dine with me?'

He expected an argument, but she leaned over and kissed him on the cheek before poking her head into the workshop to call Jasper to join them. Following her, Owen saw that the customer he had seen standing outside was the last for now.

'A messenger came to the shop,' said Jasper. 'From Magda. He is waiting in the kitchen. I told him Kate would feed him.'

'Did he tell you what she wanted?'

'No. He said he promised to tell you, and that is what he meant to do.'

They found a young man about Jasper's age sitting cross-legged on the kitchen floor near where Kate worked at a table. He had just raised a spoonful of stew to his mouth, his other hand clenching a chaser of bread, but lowered them and rose with remarkable agility when Owen entered.

'Finish your dinner,' Owen said. 'Surely there is no rush?'

Kate laughed. 'If you waited until Thatch finished you would never hear his message. I have never seen such an eater! And my brothers can stuff all manner of food into their maws in little time.'

Thatch laughed along with her. 'Oh, aye, Rob is a one.'

'They lived below us until his father found work in Easingwold,' Kate explained.

Owen motioned Thatch over to sit on a bench beside him. 'I'm of an age when I do not trust myself to rise so easily as you from so low a place,' he said. 'Now. Magda has a message for me?'

'She said the woman you seek told her much that you must hear. Come to her on the morrow, early in the morning. Tonight she will be at a birthing. Einar will sleep on the rock.' Thatch screwed up his face afterward, as if testing whether he had spoken all he had tucked away.

'If you see her, tell her I will come.' Owen held out a penny, but Thatch refused it.

'I should pay you for filling my belly, Captain. And the chance to see Kate.'

'You are always welcome, Thatch,' said Owen.

Telling Kate he would eat with Lucie in the hall, Owen gave them peace.

He found Lucie pacing the length of the long table. She had doffed the white coif she wore in the workshop and shaken out her hair so that it softly curled on her shoulders. Christ, she was as beautiful as the day he'd first set eyes on her a decade past. Turning, she caught sight of him and stopped, folding her arms against her. He had expected anger, but her expression pulled him back to a dark time several years ago after she lost a child in a fall. Sorrowful, haunted.

'What troubles you?' As if there were nothing awry. Yet he could not guess.

'I see their fear. The archbishop has stirred up something ugly, menacing. In such a time, the smallest spark and all might go up in flames. He has lit more than a spark.' She waved it away. 'What was Magda's message?' A frown when he told her. 'No hint of the matter?'

Jasper hurried in, sliding onto a bench.

'I have enough to worry over.' He was telling her about the clerk in Graa's warehouse when Kate entered with food, Thatch assisting.

The three fell to the food, hungry after their frustrating mornings. A comfortable quiet settled over them.

'I shall return to the shop now,' said Lucie when she had eaten her fill. 'If folk are too fearful to enter by the shop door, let them see how well they fare with another apothecary.'

That did not sound like Lucie. 'Are you certain you wish to shut out the frightened?'

'In this instance, yes. I will not be bullied by the likes of that bloated weasel.'

'You speak of the archbishop?'

They both turned to the kitchen door, where Michaelo stood, almost smiling. 'I have come to offer my services in the apothecary for the afternoon.'

As Owen retraced his steps to the warehouse he questioned his distrust of Michaelo's comments regarding Einar. Or his lack of comment. He had applied himself and done his best to help. He found nothing of note about the young man. Had something humbled Einar? For he had not seemed so bland when Owen first encountered him with Alisoun. Had he simply been judging a young man setting his sights on attracting a young woman who intrigued him?

'You walk as if you are heading into a storm.'

The comment snapped Owen out of his reverie to find Hempe jogging along beside him. He slowed his pace. 'Thinking.'

'I thought you should know that Dame Asa, Magda's daughter, was assaulted this morning near the minster yard. Early this morning. She went to minister to the poor and was assaulted by a young cleric who accused her of being a heretic like her mother.'

'Is she badly injured?' Owen asked.

'When my man got there the folk who had helped her said she was pushed to the ground and lay there awhile, stunned. The cur who beat her was lying on the ground whimpering. She had managed a few good strikes with her cane while her rescuers held him. I escorted the mewling coward to the dean's house. No man of God does such a deed, I said. He whined that he heard folk in the crowd whispering about who she was. "Born of the Devil," the fool told me. I boxed his ears before I delivered him. And glad I did. Dean John sent me away, benefit of clergy. Pah.'

'Do you know where she's lodging?'

'Not yet. And if she chooses to hide I do not know how I will discover it. I think it was her first time to the minster yard. By the Rood, I wanted to beat that holy beggar into the ground.'

As hoped, the clerk had not yet returned with Graa's response. Indeed, Owen found only a few workers within, none of them the ones he had spoken to earlier. Stepping over to the section that had collapsed, he studied the work, admiring how much had already been cleared away. He said as much to the worker who joined him.

'We work hard here, Captain Archer. But I would like very much to shift to working with the bailiffs. This is steady work, but my back aches most nights.'

'I will mention you to George Hempe.' Though he doubted Hempe would be interested, he could not resist ingratiating himself. 'Mayor Graa will have some merchants complaining, I expect. Was there much loss?'

'For some, not all. I won't forget the look on Master Surrey's face when he found so much of his goods ruined. A few others lost some, but we salvaged more. Master Ferriby's nephew Luke was furious. Claimed his cloth should have been the other side of the warehouse. Wanted to know why it had been moved, but no one could tell him. Most fortunate were the Wolcotts, with little lost, I think. The son moved out two chests of goods just the day before the fire. An angel watching out for him, that is certain.'

Indeed. Most interesting. 'How did Luke Ferriby discover their goods were moved?'

'Came in just to be sure. Found none of it where it should have been. We searched. Found nothing until he discovered some bits in the debris. He will be reporting to his uncle. Master Ferriby's away in the country, but we will hear of it anon.'

Owen thanked him and promised to speak with Hempe.

Ferriby's shop door was open to the warm afternoon. Knocking first on the doorframe, Owen stepped within, calling out a greeting. Luke appeared from behind a tall cabinet. A wonder it was, free-standing, made of some exotic wood said to protect the fabric from insects and dust. When the carpenter installed it Peter and Emma had invited them to admire it – the maker hoped to sell more like it, and the Ferribys had thought it might be something for the apothecary. Luke gave it an affectionate thump and invited Owen to join him in the back chamber where the chairs were more comfortable. On a table was a flagon of wine and two plain wooden mazers, both with a bit of wine in them.

'It is a fine day for guests. You've just missed our parish priest, Dom Paulus. He'd come from the bedside of Guthlac Wolcott. Gave him the last rites. Poor man is expected to die any time now. "A most inhospitable home," Paulus said. By nature a jovial man, but not so today.'

'I am sorry to hear Guthlac is in his last hours.'

'Thanks to the ministrations of that slimy Bernard. To my thinking, it's men like that leech feeding the gossips in the city who are to blame, frightening folk away from the healers who have always seen to us.'

'You've met Bernard?'

'To my misfortune. Arrogant, telling folk what ails them without bothering to listen. He's the one should be chased out the gates and good riddance.'

Offered a mazer of wine, Owen asked for just a little. 'My business should not take long.'

'Ah, forgive me. I was shaken by Dom Paulus, his worry about parishioners spreading rumors not only about the Riverwoman, but now most of the midwives and healers we need this summer. And I'm repeating myself. Forgive me.' He poured Owen a small measure of wine, handed it to him, poured much more for himself. 'How might I help?'

Owen explained that he had been to Graa's warehouse and

learned what had happened to Ferriby's stock, pausing to allow Luke to express his anger, then asking how much access people other than the warehouse workers had as a rule.

'Little. The clerk is a tyrant, terrified of his employer. But I noticed before the fire that Gavin Wolcott and Sam Toller, may he rest in God's grace, well, they seemed to have privileges the rest of us did not. Apparently the young Wolcott has won Thomas Graa's favor, often dining there according to my uncle.'

Owen thanked him for the information, waving off the offer of more wine. The man was clearly feeling the solitude with all the family away. While passing the Wolcott home Owen noticed a servant standing in the shadows beside the house, weeping. Calling to her, he asked whether her master had died. She shook her head, lifting it enough for him to see the blood at the corner of her mouth. Concerned, he went to her aid.

'Who did this to you?'

She backed away from him, shaking her head and putting a finger to her lips. Now he heard, from within, Gavin Wolcott shouting at another servant.

'Is he often like this?'

'No. But he's not like the old master, so kind. I pray you, go. He must not see us speaking.'

In truth, it was not Owen's business. But he thought it a good time to speak with Graa. Hurrying to Castlegate, he learned that the mayor was out of the city for a few days. A family member ill. Convenient.

Late afternoon, no line of folk for the shop. Owen stepped within to find Lucie dictating to Brother Michaelo a list of items to replenish – myrrh, bugloss, butterbur, marigolds. She looked up with a surprised smile.

'You are home early.'

He kissed her on the cheek. 'No dearth of custom?'

'No. Folk seemed comforted by Brother Michaelo's presence in the doorway, welcoming them in, speaking to those who waited.' Lucie touched Michaelo's hand. 'I am grateful to you.'

Though he gave a little sniff, the monk's eyes were warm with pleasure.

'You had success at the warehouse?' she asked.

'A goodly amount. I'd hoped also to speak with the mayor, but an illness in the family has taken him away.'

'I know. His wife was here. I counted it a friendly gesture to seek my help so openly, though Dame Katherine did push through to the front of the line, one of her manservants guarding the door so that she might consult with me without gossips hearing it.'

'Would the gossips have learned anything worth repeating?' Owen asked.

'She wanted whatever might draw the poison from the pustules, and juniper to burn to protect those in the family not yet stricken.'

'For whom?'

'Her sister and elderly mother in Beverley.'

'Has there been any more trouble?'

'Not from the lads,' said Michaelo. 'But a pair of youths showing off for a foul-mouthed young woman hung around the graves in the square calling out insults to the customers. The mere sight of Stephen bearing down on them put them to flight.'

Owen grinned.

A customer stepped into the shop, leaning on a cane. Lucie moved toward the beaded curtain to help him.

'Do you want to send Jasper in from the garden?' Owen asked her.

'No need,' she said. 'I doubt many more customers will appear.'

He had much to mull over with her, but the customer's cane called to mind what Hempe had told him about Asa. 'I will be back in a while,' he said, hurrying off.

EIGHT

Chaos

The fire crackled and snapped, Fergus stoking it as the evening cooled the room. Magda smiled at the sound of the children settling down to food after the long day of distracting their laboring mother with the wonders of the old woodland. As the shadows lengthened and the birds quieted, the family had tucked themselves inside the house, ready for a hot meal and the wait for the birthing. Helen was now lying on her side in the bedchamber, Lettice, calm now, rubbing her back and her ankles. As soon as Helen drank the tisane Magda was mixing they would help her to the birthing stool. The drink would strengthen Helen for the work she must do this night.

Before entering the house Magda had rested by the beck, scooping up chill water in a small wooden bowl, drinking it down, imagining it cleansing her mind of the troubles of the day – illness, life-changing injuries, fear, loneliness, gnawing anger. Closing her eyes, she reached out to Asa, born of her womb, concerned about the jolt she had felt in the midst of setting a broken bone, a sudden sense of her daughter in pain. An attack. Injuries. Fear. With Asa that would quickly turn to anger, and more trouble. *Thou art welcome to come to the rock. Magda will see to thine injuries.* A tumble of emotions, Asa's anger turned inward. Unworthy. Cursed. *Thou art worthy, daughter.* Or she could be, if she could but embrace her artistic gift, if she could see that she might be the healer she yearned to be through her creations. Magda's heart ached for the blindness of her child.

Helen's drink prepared, Magda was tidying the shelf on which she had worked when she sensed Tess standing behind her.

'Will I have a sister?'

Magda bent to lift the child, so light for her age. She smelled the woodland and the aromatic smoke in her hair. 'Thou hast offered up thy wish for a sister?' she kept her voice low, as if sharing secrets.

'I did, and father said it was wrong. I should love my family and not want it different. I do love them all! But a sister—'

'She would whisper her secrets to thee and thou wouldst promise to keep them safe. Thou couldst be her elder, teach her about the world.'

'You understand.'

'Magda does.' She kissed Tess on the cheek and set her down. 'Soon thou shalt see whether thy prayers are answered.' She put a finger to her lips.

A short time later, Helen cried out as the first twin slithered from her. As Magda held up the girl so that all could see, she felt a shiver throughout the sanctuary and a sense of the ground heaving and settling. The others were too caught up in the birth to notice her gasp.

'A sister!' Tess cried.

Magda reached out with her mind, finding the source downriver, near her rock. Torches on the riverbank, Einar standing on the rock. *Open thine eye, Owen.* She imagined Bird-eye glancing up, sensing the trouble. No time for more. Wiping the blood and secretions from the baby's face she blew in her mouth. A weak cry strengthened into a healthy wail.

A fine daughter, she told Helen, then called to Tess to take up one of the small blankets she had cut from an old, frayed one and wrap her sister up and hold her until her mother was ready to do so. The little girl performed her task with delight and pride.

Magda encouraged Helen to push through her weariness to birth the second baby. As the labor dragged on Lettice grew agitated. Magda handed her the bowl of brandywine she had poured earlier.

'A baby arrives when ready.'

Revived, the woman took up her place supporting Helen, who drooped now with weariness yet pushed with each contraction. In a little while the head appeared and the second, smaller girl slipped out. Her cry, when it finally came, was feeble compared to that of her older, stronger sister. When Helen was cleaned and settled with her babies in her arms, their elder sister proudly beside her ready to take a baby if need be, Magda welcomed the men into the room.

'Two daughters!' Fergus exclaimed, beaming. 'You will have all the sisters you wished for, my sweet.' He ruffled Tess's head, then negotiated his way to the other side of the bed to sit by his wife, kissing her tenderly.

Magda stepped outside, lifting her face to an evening breeze, breathing in the green, loamy scent of the woodland. She thought of Einar, Asa, Beatrice, Celia, so many others who would suffer before the manqualm fled at the first hard frost. Many would die, not all from the pestilence. A few would join Sam Toller, victims of violence unleashed by the feckless crows.

A presence joined her, his scent, both earthy and animal, familiar though it had been such a long while since she woke to find him gone. *Thou hast a great-grandson, Sten.* She spoke of Einar, how she had known him. She told Sten of the young man's

complexities, a seeker, yet secretive, uncertain of himself, un-
decided about whether to befriend Magda or destroy her. She felt
Sten's hand on her shoulder, reassuring. But she doubted he could
see what lay ahead for Einar. The young man must find his own
way. Must choose his path.

'Dame Magda! It's mother! She's bleeding again!' Tess cried.

As twilight darkened the streets, Owen bobbed his head to Janet
Fuller.

'Captain Archer. How might I help you?'

He cleared his throat and glanced toward a woman lingering
on the street, watching them. 'My wife sends greetings, and something for Cilla.' Her invalid daughter.

'Bless Mistress Wilton. Do come in.' As she closed the door
she called out, 'We have a visitor, Cilla.'

The young woman, for she was now surely Alisoun's age though
so frail, sat in a high-backed chair by the fire circle, her legs
propped on a stool and wrapped in skins. In the past Janet had
frequented the apothecary regarding her daughter's frail health.
Her husband was master of a small trading ship commissioned by
the Graas and their partners between York and the Lowlands. She
greeted him with a soft smile and a blessing.

'Would you care for—' Dame Janet began, but Owen shook
his head.

'Forgive my intrusion. I do not mean to stay.'

'I pray that Mistress Wilton has not sent you across town in
such times to ask after my Cilla. I regret that I have not been to
the shop in so long. But my lodger—'

'I do have this for Mistress Cilla.' He handed Janet a jar. 'A
salve for her legs, to keep the blood up. But my main purpose is
to ask about your lodger – the leech Bernard, is it not?'

A nervous nod. 'Yes. But he is not in. I believe you might find
him at St Denys'.'

'Ah. Then I shall disturb you no more.'

'Do come again soon, Captain,' Cilla said.

'I will do that,' he said with a smile, and took his leave.

Owen found Bernard pacing before the altar in St Denys',
fingering paternoster beads. Stepping into the shadows, Owen
watched him, getting a sense of the man when he thought himself

alone. Lit by candles arrayed on the altar and a table to one side, the leech appeared broader in the shoulders than he had in St George's Field. Was it simply that he now stood straighter than he had yesterday? As Owen watched, Bernard began talking to himself, a low murmur, the words unclear, but the tone sharp, and he stabbed a finger as if accusing his unseen audience. Owen slipped back out, then returned, pushing open the door with such force the candles danced, letting it slam behind him as he strode across the nave into the light.

Bernard spun round on his heels. 'Captain Archer. You interrupt my prayers.' He kept his voice low, affable, with a slight taste of disdain.

'I am here on official business.'

Lowering his head as if to mask his glance round while he tucked the paternoster beads in his belt, Bernard took a few steps away from Owen, in direct line with one of the doors. 'I cannot think what official business you might have with me.'

'You have made a name for yourself in the city as the righteous savior of those who had fallen under the influence of Dame Magda Digby.'

'I meant to do no such thing, Captain. The cooper made much of a passing comment.' A slight smile, as if pleased with himself for blaming Edwin Cooper for the state of the city. 'I had heard much of it reported by Gavin Wolcott.'

'I doubt that.'

The man bristled. 'Are you here to order me to apologize to the old midwife?'

'I have come to ask about her daughter, Dame Asa. She was beaten today for her connection with Dame Magda. I was told you might know where she is lodging.'

'Dame Asa, you said? I do not know the name, so I cannot think why someone would tell you that.'

Oh, but he did, Owen was sure of it, no doubt from Edwin Cooper. 'Gray hair, an injury has her walking with a cane.' The leech shook his head. 'She was seen at your lodgings. Perhaps she is your landlady's friend?'

'Did Dame Janet tell you I would be here?' When Owen did not respond, Bernard smirked. 'You say she is the daughter of the pagan healer?'

The man mistook this for a conversation. 'Are you aware that Guthlac Wolcott received the last sacraments today?'

Bernard hesitated, caught off balance. 'Yes, poor man. He was so far in decline there was little I could do. That is for whom I prayed when you interrupted me. May God watch over Guthlac's devoted wife. To lose him now, as the Death enters the gates of this great city . . .' A sigh.

'Guthlac wasted away over a matter of weeks, losing strength even to an inability to speak. What struck him down so swiftly? What did Dame Magda not see?'

'His humors were awry. It is the common cause of mankind's ailments, worsening as we age.'

'And bleeding should have balanced his humors?'

'I was too late. By the time I saw him the bleeding could but ease his suffering.'

'There was nothing else? A tonic to strengthen his blood, a—'

'Do you question my training? I know you are friends with the Riverwoman. Or is it your wife, the apothecary's widow, whose conjectures you spout? Does she believe the midwife might have cured Guthlac?'

'The late Archbishop Thoresby would have no other at his side when he was dying.'

'A man on his deathbed should not be permitted to choose his healer.'

Owen was about to retort when he felt a shower of needle pricks over his scarred, sightless eye. Danger. Not here. 'You are clearly of no use to me,' he said.

'Good evening to you . . .' the leech was saying when the door slammed behind Owen.

As he stepped out of the church he looked round, getting a sense of where the danger lay. Not here, and it was not a threat to him. He hastened down the twilit streets toward home, the prickling gaining strength. He was almost running by the time he reached the garden gate, but the sense was still at a distance. Bootham. Outside Bootham. Magda Digby's home. Shaking his head at Kate's offer of food, he plucked his bow and a quiver of arrows from the hook by the door, and asked her to tell Lucie he was headed to Magda's.

*   *   *

At Bootham Bar, Carn eyed Owen's bow. 'You're wise to head out armed. Folk gathered out there one by one, men and women. A cart went through earlier and stopped beside the road. When folk started gathering round it and moving away with torches in hand I sent for the bailiffs. Hempe and several young men are out there now.'

'How many with torches?'

'Twenty, thirty. I could not see all of them from the tower, but they were moving toward the river, torches lit.'

Outside the gate Owen moved off the road toward the river, seeking out a high spot where he might look out over the shacks of the poor toward Magda's rock. Shouts, bobbing points of light, but the only large fire he could see from his vantage point was in the center of the settlement and it was clearly a bonfire. Stringing his bow, Owen hooked it over his shoulder and moved toward the disturbance. He collected a growing gaggle of children nudging one another and whispering his name. One of them told him that Twig was out on the rock, caring for Magda's kitten.

'Thank you for telling me,' he said, hurrying off.

He came upon a woman yanking a scrawny lad by the arm and shouting about her ruined dress, which was far too fine for the settlement. From the boy's arm dangled a sloshing bucket.

Owen grasped the woman's arm and squeezed. 'Unhand him and return to your home.'

She let go the lad, glaring at Owen. 'I will report you to the sheriff!'

Stepping out of range of the lad's swinging bucket, having caught the stench of urine and shit, Owen grinned. 'You are most welcome to reveal that you were here, threatening these folk who have so much less than you.' Releasing her, he continued on.

'Captain!' Alfred hastened to join him.

'One of the lads is on the rock. Have you seen him?'

'No. Someone just started rowing over, then fell back in the vessel.'

Owen pushed his way through the crowd, Alfred on his heels. They passed a line of folk passing empty containers to two women standing in the shallows to scoop up river water and hand the filled containers up another chain that disappeared among the shacks.

'Back there they add piss they've saved. The Riverwoman's idea.'

Clever. Glancing toward a shout he saw one of the small shacks take light, burning brightly. But not clever enough. He called to the line of folk with buckets of water and pointed to the fire. The snake turned. The air was thick with smoke now and he cursed at his intermittent blindness with one good eye.

A small cluster of lads about Jasper's age stood on the shore, one of them holding a torch, several others holding buckets, facing a group of the rioters with torches who were shouting, 'Heretic!' 'Curse!' 'Burn her!' 'Burn the dragon!' A cleric appeared to be leading them.

'Is there piss in this water?' Owen asked one of the lads. At the nod, he plucked the bucket from the lad's hands and drenched the cleric. The fool reared back, cursing most unclerically, his torch sputtering. Grabbing another bucket, Owen aimed at the man who stepped up to take the cleric's place, and, when his mouth was wide open, flung the water and piss. Choking on it, the man dropped his torch at the water's edge. Owen plucked it up and waved it at the shouting group as he backed them into Hempe, Ned, and several others waiting to chase them back to the city. Once that commotion moved away Owen headed upriver toward several men who were running to keep up with Magda's coracle, spinning wildly in the incoming tide. Two of them waded out as the current swung the vessel close, trying to grab it with a long hook. But the current shifted and spun it away. They shouted for the injured rower to rise up and row. Squinting in the twilight, Owen watched the man struggle to sit up. Lifting the torch to illuminate the would-be rescuers, Owen called out to the man in the coracle explaining what they were attempting. Listing to one side, the man grabbed the oar and began to row toward the light, at last bringing it close enough they were able to snag it with the hook. Handing the torch to his neighbor, Owen went into the water to help pull the boat to the shore.

Only when Owen lifted the wounded man and set him upright beside him did he recognize Einar. An arrow pierced his upper left arm. He held him steady until he found his feet and caught his breath.

'Bless you all,' he gasped.

'You gave us a good chase,' one of the men said, laughing with relief.

'Can you describe what happened?' Owen asked.

'I was rowing out to the rock. Was shot from behind.'

'Could you see who?'

'No. Shoved the oar inside and bent down to shield myself.'

'Come. I will row you to Magda's.'

Alfred had joined them. 'The shot came from our side of the river,' he said.

'Find out if anyone saw another with a bow,' said Owen. 'Send someone to tell my wife I will watch through the night. Those who live here, see to your homes. I will guard Magda's.'

Launching the coracle, Owen rowed out to the rock using the incoming tide to assist.

Twig greeted them at the door cradling the kitten. 'How can I help?'

'Sit with Einar on this bench until I call you in.' He would need to search Magda's secret store for brandywine, pastes, and lotions, as well as a tincture to add to the wine. Once he had it all assembled, he stepped outside to fetch them. He found Einar relieving himself in the river. Twig stood near him facing toward the shore. Several homes were alight. Damn those who had so little care for the poor. Damn them.

'Is yours aflame?' Owen asked.

'I don't think so.' Twig hugged the kitten.

'God be thanked. Come. I will need your help.'

The lad seemed glad to turn away from the destruction.

While Twig heated a pot of water and searched for sufficient rags, Owen settled Einar on a cot near the fire, giving him a cup of brandywine fortified with the tincture to help with the pain.

'Sip some of that.'

By the time he had mixed a paste for the wound, Einar was asleep. Owen cleaned the wound and examined the arm, the direction of the arrow. Calling Twig to him, he tested the strength of his grasp. Good and strong. Confident the boy could keep the patient from flailing, or at least dampen the blows leveled at his tormentor, Owen settled on the procedure, waking Einar to explain the steps in full and assigning tasks. The lad asked no questions, simply gathered the things he would need and nodded when ready. Einar assured Twig he would do his best to cooperate.

The tide was high, but it was in, the current no challenge, as Owen rowed Twig back to shore. Smoke still swirled about, embers from the fires snapping loudly in the unusually quiet settlement, punctuated now and then with the cries of fretful children. Watching, wary, ready for more trouble, folk moved among the tumbledown structures, some holding torches or lanterns. Owen learned that Alfred had been unable to discover the marksman, and had returned to the city to stand guard through the night at his captain's home. That was one worry eased. Owen escorted the lad to his mother, who they found sheltering in a home close to the walls.

Twig ran to her. 'Mother? Is our house—'

'One spark and it was gone.' She held him close for a moment, stroking his hair and kissing the top of his head. 'Your father rescued this.' She held out a small battered jar, shaking it. 'Your treasure.'

'We will use it to rebuild,' said Twig, handing it back to his mother.

Owen praised Twig to his mother, describing how much he had helped. 'Bide here with your mother tomorrow, Twig. Einar will be on the rock for a few days.' Michaelo would lose his assistant for a time. Then, excusing himself to permit them their time to grieve for their loss, Owen went back out to walk among the watchers, learning what he might, before returning to the rock.

As he rowed back he made out the figure of Einar standing beneath the dragon, her great claw – but that was not possible. The carving was but a long neck and head. Yet he could swear a great claw rested on the young man's shoulder. When he reached the rock he rubbed his eye, looked again, and saw nothing but the head hanging upside down, leering. Even so, Owen crossed himself and whispered a prayer of protection.

'Is there much damage?' Einar asked, seeming unaware of anything untoward.

'A few homes, including Twig's. We found his mother. His father is walking the watch. Such a loss is devastating to those who have so little.'

'And for what?' Einar cursed. 'I saw the clerics out there. One of them was the one who accosted Asa. He was bragging of it. I punched him.'

'Have you seen Asa?'

'No. I searched for her after I heard of the assault, but I found no one who could tell me where she is.'

Owen noticed how Einar touched his bandaged arm. 'Someone said the leech Bernard might know where she is staying, that she had seen her at his lodgings, but he denies knowing her.'

'Of course he would,' Einar muttered.

A splash in the river. Both of them glanced round, on alert, but saw nothing.

'Where were you headed with the coracle?' Owen asked.

'Here. To Dame Magda's rock. They said Twig was here with the cat. I feared for him. I was halfway across when I was shot.'

The archer had made use of Owen's distraction with the crowd.

'Had you been long on the riverbank?'

'No. I had just come from my work with Brother Michaelo.' A pause. 'You think it was not an accident that he aimed at me?'

'I prefer to talk in the house.' Owen opened the door and stood aside.

Einar stumbled as he bowed to clear the low doorway. Owen caught him and helped him to the cot. It was a wonder he had been up and about at all, much less appearing alert. He was young, yes, but such an injury and the loss of so much blood were bound to take their toll, not to mention the effect of the herbs in the brandywine.

'I will stay the night, wait for Magda,' said Owen.

Eyes closed, Einar said, 'In truth, I could not trust myself to protect the house tonight. But I asked you a question. Do you think I was the archer's target?'

'*You* do not think it an accident,' said Owen. 'Whom do you fear? Bernard, or someone connected to him?'

Einar started, as if Owen had splashed cold water on his face. 'Why Bernard?'

'Who is he to you?'

'Not me, Magda.'

'It was not her but *you* he would have seen on the riverbank.'

'Then I am wrong.'

Owen was not convinced, but the young man was fading. 'Did Bernard lie to me? Does he know Asa?'

'He knows her. I saw them together often in Lincoln. But I know not the nature of their acquaintance.' He spoke slowly, pausing to lick his lips, his words beginning to slur.

'She did not speak of him with you?'

A long pause. 'Not until he departed Lincoln. She claimed he misrep—' Einar looked confused. 'Said he was no leech.'

Owen remembered Einar's amusement when Jasper spoke of Bernard as a physician on St George's Field. 'A barber posing as a physician? It might explain much.'

'I did not know Alan is the one who has spoken out against Dame Magda.'

'Alan?'

'Bernard. I grow confused.'

'Enough for tonight. Rest.' Owen saw that he was settled, then went to check the kitten, snuggled in a basket lined with soft cloth. Asleep. Holda's sweetness turned his thoughts to his children. Pouring a small measure of brandywine, he settled by the fire and let his mind roam free. But he kept returning to the question, Who was Alan?

Magda stood under the stars, reaching her mind toward her rock. Smoke. Three homes of the poor gone up in flames. Bird-eye on the rock with Einar. Quiet now. She would go to Einar, but the new mother might need her in the night. The bleeding had stopped with a strong draft of yarrow and comfrey and Helen now slept, but Magda could not in good conscience leave just yet despite Lettice and Tess hovering about her, rocking the newborns, and Fergus sitting beside his wife, stroking her hair.

Seeing the fires in her mind's eye, Magda was glad she had removed this family from danger before the births.

Waking in darkness, Owen saw Einar stoking the fire, adding a few pieces of wood. They quickly caught, the flames lighting the cot where Owen lay. The kitten had managed to leave her basket and curl up beside him. Observing the injured man rise to fetch some items from Magda's food cupboard, Owen judged him well enough to fend for himself a while longer and closed his eye, returning to slumber. When next he woke it was to a draft from the open doorway. Finding the kitten gone, he bolted from the bed to the threshold. Outside, Einar stood guard over the little being as she was scratching to cover her business.

'Dame Magda's trained her to paw at the door. I observed them together while Asa was here.'

Laughing, Owen moved off beyond them to relieve himself in the river. A turn round the house assured him that it had suffered no damage. By the time he returned to the door Einar had taken Holda inside. Closing his eye, Owen reached up to touch the dragon. Warm, though the sun had not yet hit it.

Inside, Owen poured himself some ale from a jug in the cupboard, noted it was almost empty. He would ask Tom to send some out to Magda. He settled by the fire across from Einar, who was feeding the kitten a bit of milk. 'Does Asa wish you harm?'

Einar glanced up. 'She's no cause to wish me ill. I've been of use to her. Though not so much now.'

'Is it possible she and Bernard are lovers?'

'What? No! She is much older than he is.' But he did not look so certain.

'You are reconsidering?'

'Thinking of the names she's called him, how angry she was when she thought he was here with a wife and child.'

'Janet and Cilla Fuller?'

'She was soon set straight. Folk know Jack Fuller.'

'But her anger . . .'

'Did seem to arise from more than a healer questioning the skill of another. So yes, perhaps.'

'What do you know of him?'

'I think I've told you all I know, other than what the gossips said.' Owen noticed how Einar avoided his gaze. 'There were whispers about him in Lincoln, on the run from some troubles with men's wives. I thought that might be why he left. He does not seem a man who can defend himself. Nor does he seem to want attention.'

Owen laughed. 'He has certainly made himself known here.' But he thought of the exchange with Gavin Wolcott at the butts, and his reaction to Owen the previous evening. Perhaps being infamous was not his choice. 'How did you come to be with Asa?'

Keeping his head down, suddenly fussing with the kitten, Einar mumbled something about happy chance.

'Did you live long in Lincoln? Is that where you are from?'

'No.' The kitten gave a little cry at a sound outside. 'She hears Dame Magda.'

Owen had heard her as well, coming through the shallow water. He stepped out into a soft rain to greet her. 'Your kitten alerted us to your return.' He lifted the baskets from her arms as she passed.

'Have a care with that one,' she said about the heaviest. 'It will be dinner for Magda and Einar.'

'Smells enticing.'

'Thou art fortunate to have Bird-eye to attend thee,' she said to her great-grandson. 'He has much experience with arrows.'

'How did you know about the arrow?' Einar asked.

'Magda will answer thy questions. But first she has much to tell Bird-eye. Wouldst thou step without?'

'You do not yet trust me?'

'Hast thou given Magda reason to do so?'

Owen tensed at the flash of anger in the young man's eyes, but Einar did as he was told. Awkward in his haste to escape into the rain, he barely avoided stepping on the kitten. When he had closed the door behind him, Magda poured warm water from the pot Owen had kept simmering, added a pinch of herbs, and settled by the fire on a low stool. Asking a few questions about the events of the previous night, she listened with closed eyes to Owen's account, and his thoughts regarding Einar, Asa, and Bernard. And the mention of an Alan.

'Alan, Bernard.' She nodded to herself and went quiet for a while, testing her drink, sipping it, still with eyes closed.

Owen rarely noticed the intricate web of lines on her face that mapped her long, rich life. Usually the power of her gaze distracted one from anything else. She had high cheek bones, a long, narrow, delicately arched nose, full lips, much fuller than in most elders, all textured with wrinkles, some deep, most shallow, covering every inch, even her eyelids. A strong face, and beautiful despite being so marked by time. Lost in his own thoughts he started when she spoke.

'Dost thou trust Einar?' Her blue eyes watched him.

He considered. 'Only so far as believing what he has chosen to tell me. The harm is in the omissions. He knows, or perhaps merely guesses, far more about all the troubles of late than he admits, which is why his confusing the names seems important.'

'Magda's sense as well. What Magda is about to tell thee must be shared only with those thou most trusts.' She proceeded to weave a dark tale involving the Wolcott household, Gavin Wolcott's treatment of Matthew, and Graa's possible part in it, Lettice's belief that the fire was meant to kill her for her knowledge of Beatrice's pregnancy, her fear that Matthew was murdered not only for what they might have tried to hide from him at the warehouse but also what Lettice might have confided.

An illegitimate child. 'Might they have kept you away so that you would not see her condition?' Two murders, Sam and Matthew. Both might know too much, Matthew from his wife. Were Guthlac and Lettice meant to die as well? 'Could they have used Bernard to hasten Guthlac's death?'

'Who fathered the child?' asked Magda.

'Might it be Sam?'

'He cared for her, but there was no shame in him regarding her,' said Magda. 'Though his wife disliked Beatrice. He *was* married. Would it not be more likely to be someone who hoped to claim the widow and child?'

'Gavin?' asked Owen. 'But he seeks the respect of the merchants in York. They would not accept his marrying his father's widow.'

'A difficulty.'

'But who else might be the father? Lettice had no suggestion?'

'That is not her concern. She fears returning to the city. There is no need as yet, and thou art now armed with information that might help thee in finding answers.'

'Might I speak with Lettice?'

Magda slowly shook her head. 'Nor wouldst thou learn more.'

'Is there anything else I should know? What of Asa's beating?'

'Beating?' Magda looked surprised. 'Again?'

Owen told her what little he knew.

'Magda had not heard. Have a care with Asa. She would find satisfaction in ruining thee.'

He knew that, yet to have Magda warn him gave him pause. 'Do you have any sense of what Bernard might be to her?'

'He is said to use bleeding for most complaints. It might be all
he knows. Perhaps he sought Asa's advice. She does have a way
of turning friends to enemies. But she has said little to Magda,
and nothing of him.' She glanced toward the door. 'Twig should
be here by now.' When Owen told her why he was not, she agreed
that he should be with his mother. 'Einar will be here today.'

'And tomorrow?'

'Unless he tells Magda all that he knows she will send him
back to Old Shep's.' She rose. 'Thou hast much to do. It was good
of thee to see to the wound and sit with him through the night.
But the city needs thee.'

'The troublemakers might return. Would you accept one of my
men to guard you?'

'There is no need. Magda will not be harmed.' She smiled. 'Her
dragon protects her.'

He remembered how it had seemed the dragon had reached
down to Einar. 'Does he protect Einar as well?'

'She,' Magda corrected him. 'Why dost thou ask?'

He described what he thought he had seen, and her warmth
today.

'That is good,' she said, softly, as if to herself.

'I did see that?'

'If so, it was through thy third eye.' She touched the middle of
his forehead. 'Not this one.' She tapped above his good eye. 'Now
it is time for thee to go.' She led him to the door, calling to Einar
as Owen stepped out into the rain.

Einar came round from beneath the eaves and thanked Owen
for all he had done. 'If you see Brother Michaelo, will you tell
him I will return to assist him tomorrow?'

Owen glanced at Magda. Had Einar overheard her ultimatum?
But she did not seem bothered. 'I will.'

In the shop, Lucie and Jasper dispensed a dizzying assortment of
plague remedies beyond anything they recommended, from pig's
intestines and toads to powdered gems to noxious combinations
of herbs and roots. The morning had revealed more red crosses
on doors. Owen waited in the apothecary workshop, gauging when
Lucie would have a moment to speak to him. Damp from the rain,
he was eager to settle for a moment by the kitchen fire and share

what he had learned while it was all fresh in his mind. But his hopes were dashed when he heard a man describing the wounds his wife had suffered in early morning as she left a birthing and was beaten in the street.

'It was the neighbor came pounding on my door, telling me to come, he had found her in the alley. I feared she was dead. So much blood coming from her head. But she spoke my name and was warm in my arms as I carried her home.'

Owen stepped into the shop. 'I will bring the medicines and see to her.'

The man looked confused.

'I tended wounds on battlefields,' said Owen. 'And I know my wife's remedies. I worked as her apprentice when I first came to York.'

'He did,' said Lucie. 'Edith will be in good hands, John.'

The man sobbed his thanks, and Lucie smiled her appreciation as she prepared a basket for Owen. He brought bandages from the workshop.

When it was ready, Owen kissed Lucie on the cheek as he plucked up the basket. 'I will ask Alfred to come back to watch the shop and house.'

'He watched through the night and went home not long ago.'

'Then I will send someone else until he is ready.' With another kiss he left her, escorting the fretful husband out into the rain. So much for drying out by the kitchen fire.

N I N E

Puzzles

Magda examined Einar's shoulder, nodding with approval at Bird-eye's work both in removing the arrow and packing the wound. But Einar distracted her with a simmering restlessness building toward boiling.

'Thou hast much on thy mind.'

'The captain is not what I expected,' he said. 'I heard that he used a friend lately come from the French court to ingratiate himself with Prince Edward. The friend is now captive at court.'

Resting her fingers on Einar's wrist she looked deep into his eyes. When his pulse calmed, she asked, 'Is the friend of whom thou speakest the musician Ambrose Coates?'

'You know the story?'

'Magda knows the truth. Minstrel is an old friend. Thou hast taken hold of the tale from the wrong end.'

'Will you tell me?'

While wrapping Einar's upper arm in a clean bandage Magda told him how Ambrose had come to her on a snowy night before Yuletide to ask her how best to approach Bird-eye for his help with information he learned at the French court and had undertaken to bring to the prince, at great risk to himself. It was his misfortune to bring trouble in his wake, but Bird-eye protected him and saw that he was safely delivered to trusted members of the prince's household. Magda assured Einar that Ambrose would be content to remain at court, where he would have an audience and a patron.

She watched as the young man grew increasingly troubled. 'Could I have been so misguided?' he muttered. She sensed he felt betrayed and guessed the source of his unease.

'Asa delighted in thine impression of the captain as a treasonous friend.' The deepening of the line between the thick brows told her she had guessed correctly. 'She does not wish to hear good of anyone who has crossed her. Didst thou not see?'

'I did not see how deep it went.'

While creating a sling for his arm she asked what else he needed for the day.

'I will be fine. I have much to think on.'

'Good. Magda hopes thou wilt unburden thyself this evening.'

While preparing her basket for a day visiting the ill she continued her account of Bird-eye, how he took it as his duty to protect the city and, in doing so, the North, how devoted he was to family and friends. Having given Einar much to ponder, she hoisted her basket and departed, reminding him to feed the kitten and let her out when she needed to relieve herself.

The midwife's injuries would prevent her from working for a time, but none of them so serious Owen could not reassure both Edith and her husband John that all would be well. His greatest challenge was convincing John to hold her steady in the chair while Owen set her broken arm. It was not a bad break, and with a small, albeit painful, adjustment she would heal well. When that was accomplished, he completed the cleaning and wrapping of her head wound.

While Owen worked Edith described her attackers – two large men, one sounding much like one of the workers in Graa's warehouse. Nothing to connect them with the cleric who assaulted Asa except in the act. He would seek out the warehouse worker later in the day. She mentioned Bernard, accusing him of inspiring the trouble, expressing her sympathy for Janet and Cilla Fuller— 'Imagine listening to his hateful ideas all the day.'

'You and Dame Janet are friends?'

'Of a sort. I have helped her with Cilla from time to time.'

'Did you know her before she was married?'

'No. She came to the city when she wed Jack.'

Someone knocked on the door. John went to answer it armed with a hefty piece of wood. 'Oh. *Benedicite*, Brother Michaelo.'

Begging their forgiveness for intruding, Michaelo said he had a message for Owen when he was finished.

'I am finished.' Owen instructed John to come to the shop on the morrow to tell Lucie how Edith fared through the night. She would then provide him with what he needed to help his wife continue her healing.

'Come along with me,' said Owen as he strode away from the midwife's home. 'I believe you might make my next stop easier.'

'Of course. But you need to know. Jehannes received a response from His Grace the Archbishop. He assures him that the letter to the abbots and priors was meant merely as a suggestion, and commended him on the suggestion of processions. As Archdeacon of York he gives Jehannes full authority to do what is best. Indeed, he would appreciate his smoothing things over with the Churchmen in the city.'

'He wiped his hands of us and put the burden on Jehannes,' said Owen. 'In short, he disowns us?'

'It would seem so. Might I trouble you to tell me our destination?'

'The Fuller home, where Bernard is lodging. Dame Janet might find your presence reassuring. She seemed anxious last night. And you might have a word with her daughter Cilla, who made a point of inviting me to return – soon.'

'Ah.' After that, they both fell into their own thoughts as they headed for Walmgate.

Bernard answered the knock, narrowing his eyes when he saw who it was. 'Captain Archer. And a monk?'

'Brother Michaelo,' said Owen. 'Have you remembered meeting the woman of whom we spoke last night?'

'*You* spoke. *I*—'

Dame Janet peered round him, then stepped between Bernard and the door. 'Captain Archer. Brother Michaelo. Do come in from the rain.' She glanced at Bernard with a shake of her head and shooed him out of the way. As they moved past her she patted her tidy kerchief, brushed her apron, then planted a fierce smile on her face.

'I pray you forgive me. I was just sweeping out the kitchen. Might I bring you some ale while you confer with Bernard?' Her smile tensed as Michaelo crossed the room to greet Cilla.

'It is you with whom I wish to speak, Dame Janet,' said Owen.

The leech stepped between Owen and Dame Janet. 'See to the girl, Janet.' The woman averted her eyes and retreated a few steps.

'I was mistaken yesterday,' said Bernard. 'Dame Janet does not know this woman you asked after.'

'And who was that, Bernard?' Janet asked.

'Asa,' said Owen, 'a healer lately arrived in York. She was beaten in the minster yard yesterday.'

'Asa?' Janet shook her head. 'I do not know the name.' But she looked long at Bernard, her expression one of loathing.

He wandered away.

'I see. Then I will leave you to your day, Dame Janet,' said Owen. 'I pray you forgive the intrusion.'

'Not at all, Captain,' she said, suddenly friendly. 'I pray your family are all safe and sound? The little ones well?'

'They are in the country for the summer.'

'I am glad for it. I worry for my husband, that sickness delayed his ship. Pray for us, Captain.'

Michaelo had made the sign of the cross over Cilla and joined
Owen. 'I will pray for your family, Dame Janet.'

'Bless you.'

Out in the street, Owen moved through the rain pondering the
words, the gestures, maddened by his certainty that he had missed
an opportunity.

'Apparently Bernard is Cilla's uncle.'

'What?' Owen stopped and stared at Michaelo.

'Though she had not met him before he appeared a few months
past she had heard her parents speak of him. She recalls them
referring to him as "Alan the snake", but her mother tells her she
has confused him with someone else. Cilla thinks not, and prays
you find a way to return when "the snake" is away.' Michaelo
spoke as if in the midst of a conversation, his mouth betraying his
amusement as Owen looked at him in disbelief. 'But she could
not suggest a time when you might be certain of that. She also
mentioned that her father had been long away, and would be
surprised that "the snake" was poisoning the household. That is
another bit of news. Jack Fuller's ship has docked at King's Staithe
and she believes her father will soon evict her uncle.'

'I am in your debt,' Owen said with feeling.

'Mm . . . yes. Will that be all?'

'You are welcome to accompany me to the mayor's warehouse
near the staithe, if you can spare the time.'

'Of course. If I can be of help.'

'I would be grateful.'

Michaelo grinned.

They were soon caught up in the flow of folk and carts leading
to Ouse Bridge, attempting to cross through them to descend to
King's Staithe. Michaelo lifted the hem of his habit, protecting it
from the path the steady rain had turned to mud.

On the staithe Owen noticed Jack Fuller helping another carry
a load down the gangplank from a small ship. Considering the
well-muscled man, Owen guessed he would easily put Bernard in
his place.

Brother Michaelo cleared his throat. 'Is that Dame Asa?'

At the bottom of the gangplank, just out of the way, Asa leaned
on her cane, watching Fuller. As he set down his burden she
gestured to him, but he turned back to the ship.

'It is.'

'She looks nothing like her mother,' said the monk. 'Now Einar, something in his eyes hints of her blood.'

Owen agreed.

'Whatever injuries she suffered healed sufficiently for her to risk the rain and mud,' Michaelo noted.

'Would you follow her?'

'I thought you wished— Of course. Though I am not what one might consider inconspicuous.'

'Nor am I.'

Michaelo glanced at Owen's patch. 'No, that you are not.'

'After the warehouse I mean to return to the apothecary.' Nodding to Michaelo, Owen continued on.

In the warehouse across the way he searched the faces for the one he suspected of beating the midwife, but he was not among the workers.

'Might be at the staithe. Ship's come in,' said the man who had been helpful before. 'His name is Duggan.'

'I did not see him there,' said Owen. 'Where does he live?'

'Don't know, don't want to know. I keep my distance from trouble.'

In the lane in front of the apothecary a cluster of women hailed Owen, asking whether he had caught the men who had beaten the midwife Edith.

'We are still searching. But I assure you Dame Edith will make a full recovery.' He could do nothing about their disappointment except mirror it in his gut.

Inside, Jasper was placing small packages in a woman's basket, reviewing with her what they were and how she was to use them. Juniper for a protective fog in the house if one of them should fall ill. A poultice to draw the poison from the buboes, a lotion to ease the pain. Yes, he had added the emerald powder as she had requested. A plaster for the chest. A strong syrup for cough. A scented beeswax candle for the bedside. There was more in the packages already placed in the basket before he arrived, far more than they would have the time or presence of mind to use once the sickness struck. But folk traded ideas, and some hoped to use everything possible. As the woman counted out a

considerable amount of money, Owen noticed Lucie gesturing to
him from behind the beaded curtain separating the shop from the
workroom. He bobbed his head to the customer and joined Lucie.

'Have you made a fortune today?' he asked.

'Pestilence is sinfully lucrative for an apothecary,' said
Lucie, 'but a fortune, no.'

'Much charity?' He knew his wife. If the customer could not
afford what they needed, she would pretend to tally what they
owed and keep a running count, but when – if – they came asking
for the total she would shoo them away.

'A few who could not pay.' She kissed his cheek and touched
his bearded chin. 'I heard that Guthlac Wolcott is dead, and the
burial tomorrow.'

'From whom?'

'One of the butchers was praying in the church when a servant
came for the priest. He hurried here for more protections from the
pestilence. I assured him that Guthlac was not a victim of
the Death, that he has been dying a long while. But he was too
frightened to be comforted.'

'May Guthlac rest in peace.'

'How are Einar and Magda?'

'She is untouched by the violence. Einar will mend. Will Jasper
miss you if you come with me to the kitchen? I have much to tell
you.'

As he sat by the fire waiting for Lucie, Owen absently stroked the
kitten on his lap. Kate set a bowl of ale beside him. He would eat
after he had discussed with Lucie all he had learned since their
last long talk. But it was Michaelo who arrived first, pushing
back his hood and running his long fingers through the hair that
circled his tidy tonsure.

'At the risk of disrupting your dinner . . .' He paused in the
doorway.

'Come, sit, tell me,' said Owen.

Removing his shoes, Michaelo joined Owen by the fire, holding
his hands to the heat, then tucking them into his sleeves. 'I will
not stay long.'

'You followed Asa?'

'More than that. After you left, the men on the staithe grew frightened when Jack Fuller failed to reappear, muttering about him being the only one not struck down by illness on that small ship, arguing about whether he seemed ill, none of them willing to go up to see what had happened. So I went. He was on the deck, bent over, breathing hard, his clothes soaked with sweat, his neck hot to the touch. When I called from the ship for someone to come help me take him home, only Asa responded.'

'She climbed the gangplank with her cane?'

'She had help. While I debated whether to assist her or stay with Fuller to keep him upright, Janet Fuller hurried forward to assist Asa, calling shame down on the cowering men who were suddenly eager to help. We transported him to his home in Walmgate in a cart borrowed from the staithe, Asa and I leading the donkey, Dame Janet in the cart with her husband and a small chest Jack refused to leave behind.'

Lucie had slipped in while Michaelo told the tale. 'All the men in his ship are ill?' she asked.

'Most are dead.'

'*Deus juva me.*'

'Was Bernard there?' Owen asked. 'Will he care for Jack?'

'Janet promised her husband that her brother would not touch him. Asa and Janet will care for him.' Michaelo nodded at Owen's surprise. 'She said God brought her here at this time for a purpose. Dame Magda had supplied her with what she would need to help those her mother could not.'

'Despite the beating the other day?' Lucie asked, taking a seat beside Owen. 'I pray Bernard does not mistreat her. Unless he has moved out?'

'I did not see him, but I heard nothing of his moving out.'

'Perhaps someone should watch the house?' Lucie suggested. 'I hope she knows that we will provide anything they require.'

'Anticipating your generosity I already told her to send someone to you for anything she needed,' said Michaelo. 'I do not think she will be leaving that house for a day or two. If it is the pestilence, Jack Fuller will die quickly. And then, I fear for Mistress Cilla. She is already frail.' Michaelo rose. 'I will leave you now. I know you have much to discuss.'

Owen escorted him to the door. 'You are not worried for yourself?'

'I have lived through numerous returns of the Death. My bile is too bitter for its tastes.' A smirk.

Owen felt Lucie's eyes on him as he turned from the door. It lifted his heart to see the laughter in her eyes. 'He might be right,' he said.

She burst out laughing. 'Pray God he is.' It was but a momentary jollity. 'I do not think I should like to lose him so soon.' Already her eyes were sad. 'So many dead in the ship.' She crossed herself.

They adjourned to the hall, carrying in ale. Kate would bring in the food.

Settled near the window, Owen began his tale with an account of what had happened at the river the previous evening, Einar's injury. Alfred would have told her much of it, but he knew she would want to hear his account. And then, after answering her questions, he told her of Lettice's fears regarding her husband's death, particularly his treatment by Graa's warehousemen and Gavin Wolcott, and continued on to Beatrice's pregnancy.

'I had not expected that,' said Lucie. 'Poor Lettice, I can under-stand her fear. As their laundress she might very well be silenced. That alone . . .' Lucie paused, frowning down at her ale.

'What is it?'

'I wonder whether you might have been better to take heed of Gemma Toller's distrust of Beatrice's intentions with her late husband. Is it not possible that Sam was the father of her child?'

'Possible.'

'Or you are wrong about Gavin's feelings for her. She is a beautiful woman and far closer in age to him than to his father.' Lucie glanced up. 'Did I understand Brother Michaelo to say Bernard is Janet's brother?'

He told her about Einar's calling Bernard 'Alan' and what Michaelo had learned from Cilla.

'A snake. Dear Cilla,' said Lucie. 'She is so like her mother in everything but physical wellbeing. I tried every tonic I could imagine, as did Magda.'

'What is wrong with her?'

'A faulty heart perhaps. She has ever been weak, any exertion robbing her of breath in short order. Her mind is sharp. When she was younger Janet and Jack arranged for a tutor to come each morning.'

Owen's thoughts turned to his eldest daughter. 'Gwenllian will be missing her classes.' Through winter into spring she had attended a small school for girls. He took Lucie's hand. And so they sat for a long while as the rain gathered strength out in the garden.

'Alan.' Lucie sat forward. 'Janet's brother. He was in service in the household of a wealthy man in London. She never mentioned him but to say an unpleasant encounter reminded her of him. When I laughed at her calling him a leech, thinking it cleverness, she admitted that he was more properly a barber, Alan's master having trained him in bloodletting, but he *was* a blood-sucking worm.'

Owen had noticed how Janet spoke her brother's name as if taunting him. He had thought it was her omission of the Master before it. 'Why would he change his name?'

'Driven from his post? If he posed as a physician there as he has here but has in truth little training . . . Owen, what if Guthlac need not have died? What if his decline and death are the fault of a man posing as a physician?'

'We cannot prove that.'

'But if his London master discovered Alan posing as a physician in London . . .'

'And so Alan fled and changed his name to escape prosecution.'

'Yes.'

'We might be wrong.'

'But if not. Owen, we must stop him before he causes more deaths.'

'And how to you propose to do that?'

'How indeed?' Lucie folded her arms and lay her head down on the table.

Owen rubbed her shoulders, kissed her neck. 'Meanwhile there is still Sam's murderer to hunt down. I will try to speak with Gemma.'

'But you've not eaten.' Lucie sat up, glancing at the door. 'Kate did not bring the food.' She was up and rushing to the kitchen before Owen caught up with her thoughts.

He found her with an arm around Kate, who stood in the doorway to the garden, her shoulders heaving with her sobs. Out in the rain stood her siblings, the twins Rose and Rob. It was clear from their faces they had brought unhappy news.

'Our sister Meg. The Death has taken her and her mistress,' said Rose when Owen drew them into the warmth of the kitchen.

Meg was Kate's younger sister by a year, maidservant to an elderly widow in Fossgate.

Owen left them to Lucie's care and carried the food out to the hall, then called them all in to nourish themselves as they might. He fetched Jasper from the shop, seeing to a last customer before shutting it for a time. The Death walked the streets of York. They all needed their strength.

Rain had slowed by the time Magda stepped out from the cover of trees. All seemed peaceful in the ramshackle settlement on the riverbank. Rowing to the rock, she touched the dragon, nodded her thanks. Within she found the fire stoked and something savory bubbling in a pot. Einar rose as she entered, plucking up his tunic.

'Thou wilt need help with that.' Magda set down her baskets and assisted him, offering a small pack to carry from his belt with items Brother Michaelo might not have. For of course that is where Einar was headed.

'Thou hast cared for those suffering the great sickness?'

'With my father.'

'Thou wilt be of much help to the fussy crow. Return this evening. Magda would check thy wound before sleep.'

Einar nodded and departed.

Magda hummed to herself as she sorted the contents of her basket and set her mind to her visitations on the morrow. Einar was reclaiming himself, she felt it deep within. Soon he would confide in her.

TEN

Patterns

The house showed a plain front to the street, but within Dame Gemma had created a space of color and warmth. Several large wall hangings either embroidered or painted could be drawn over the windows to shut out drafts, and otherwise brightened the walls. Owen took a seat on one of three benches made comfortable with colorful cushions set around the fire circle, accepting a bowl of ale with thanks. He had come so far by choosing his words with care when the widow had opened the door and looked ready to slam it shut, saying he had thought much about what she had said when they had last spoken and had come to believe she was one of the few people who might help him find Sam's murderer. He told her that he was particularly interested in Sam and his work for the Wolcotts.

'I pray you, tell me all that is on your mind.'

To his relief, she had merely nodded and invited him in, offering him ale, even setting out a bowl of roasted nuts. As he looked round, he noticed that on the wall over the entry someone had painted IHR in yellow.

Taking a seat, Gemma followed the direction of his gaze. 'You have noticed the charm,' she said, crossing herself.

It was believed that the initials indicating Jesus Christ might serve as powerful protection. 'Against pestilence?' Owen asked.

'All manner of harm to our household. I gave it a fresh coat of paint after Sam's death, but it is not new.'

'I was also admiring the wall hangings. You painted them as well?'

The small smile in a face drawn down in distrust transformed her for a moment. 'I have not always been a shrew, Captain. It is only in the past several years that taking joy in beauty deserted me. When worries beset me I can no longer see God's gifts, only the pain ahead.'

At a loss for how to respond to such a statement, Owen chose merely to say, 'I am here to listen, Dame Gemma,' and settled in to do just that, bowl of ale in hand.

'I owe Dame Magda an apology. I fear it might have been my hateful words that incited the priests to preach against her and the other midwives. I am searching for a way to undo the damage I caused them. And all who depend on their care.' She dabbed at tears with a corner of her apron. 'I have prayed to God for his forgiveness. But the damage is done.'

'What changed your mind?'

'I never believed it an accident, that he slipped and fell into the river. But I knew it was not Dame Magda who pushed him. I feared the true murderer would silence me. So I accused her to protect my family. My daughter and her little ones. My son.'

'Protect you from whom? Have you been threatened?'

'I dare not say.'

'I can protect you. I have the bailiffs and their men at my command. But I need to know from what or whom we are protecting you.'

'We are unimportant. And with the great sickness—'

'All the more reason to act now to prevent more violence.'

She rose to fuss with the fire, poking the logs, then walked toward the window at the side of the tidy hall and stood for a while, gazing out. Owen waited, helping himself to the well-spiced nuts, washing them down with ale. He was about to ask if perhaps he should return later when she turned and hurried back to her seat, beginning to speak even before she settled. 'It's the Wolcotts.' Smoothing her apron, she closed her eyes. 'I feel as if I should begin with "long, long ago", as I did with my children when I spun them a tale.' A tear escaped down her cheek, and another. 'Would that it were a tale. Then I might change it and my Sam . . . I regret every word I spoke to him in anger.'

On an impulse, Owen reached out to touch her hand. Pressed it. 'I will do all in my power to protect you and your family. Tell me first about your children, before we forget. Their names, where they live.'

She smiled at him, telling him of her daughter, wed to a stonemason and lodged in the minster close with their three children, and her son, an apprentice to a goldsmith in Stonegate.

The tale she spun was far more than Owen had expected.

'At Michaelmas two years past Sam told me that Guthlac Wolcott and his son Gavin had decided to double his pay. He spoke the words as if telling me of the death of a dear friend. And from then on he was troubled in his mind. I was forbidden to spend the additional money – it went to the church. We did far more than pay the tithe. I resented him for that. Our son might have benefited, and we might have helped our daughter, with her three young ones. Sam's new piety – I took it into my head that he and Dame Beatrice – she is so lovely, and so young. It was just after the first child she bore Guthlac, and soon thereafter she was again with

child. Sam's long days, often I was abed when he bothered
to come home. I became convinced that both babes were Sam's.
I could not believe such an old man had sired two such beautiful
young ones.' She crossed herself. 'Wicked thoughts. I told no one.
But Sam was so uneasy in his mind, and I was frightened.' Only
now did she withdraw her hand with a soft apology, taking a sip
of her ale.

'You told Sam of your fears?'

'I accused him. He swore it was not true. But I would not hear
it. I said all his misery was his own fault.' She closed her eyes as
tears fell. 'I became so bitter. So bitter. My friends fell away,
weary of my biting words, my complaints. They saw us prosper—
I did put coins aside and fixed up the house, dressed Sam and
myself in clothing befitting his status. They saw no cause for my
anger.' Looking up at Owen, she seemed to search his face.

He could not imagine her finding anything but concern. And
sadness. If Lucie were to push him away he would be lost.

'You said you would not hear him out. He tried to explain?'

'He swore I was wrong about Beatrice, but that he feared for
her. She was between two who had plans for her, and she did not
realize her peril. He feared, too, for Guthlac, when they engaged
Bernard.' She crossed herself. 'May God welcome my Sam into
eternal bliss.'

'What do you know of Bernard?'

'He is evil, Captain. I know evil when I smell it.'

'Who engaged him?'

'Gavin worked to convince the old master that he was imperiling
his soul by having a pagan healer in the house. Sam came home,
worried for Guthlac, saying Beatrice would not stand up for her
husband. So of course I attacked him for that, told him she was
a whore who destroyed our love.' A sad laugh. 'But after his death
Lettice Brown told me I was wrong about Sam. It was Gavin who
was her lover. Lettice— May God watch over her. What happened
to her, her husband, her home, I cannot but wonder whether she
was being silenced. I pray she is safe, though how she might have
escaped . . .'

He might ease her mind, but it was not his choice to make. Nor
did he entirely trust her. 'What did Sam say of Gavin?'

'He despised him. Grasping, greedy, dull-witted. I begged him to respect his master's heir, else he would be without work when Guthlac died.' She sobbed. 'But the old man outlived my Sam.'

All the while he listened, Owen sensed a falseness, a woman pretending fear and a sad simplicity, but in truth shrewdly spinning a tale. He poured her more ale and waited for her to signal she was ready to continue. When she had drunk down a goodly amount of ale he asked, 'Do you know Janet Fuller?'

She crossed herself. 'Poor Janet. To have that leech as a lodger. I'd prayed her husband would throw him out, but now, so ill . . .'

'Did she ever speak to you of a brother?'

'That lout? Alan, in London. Why?'

'I cannot say. What do you know of him?'

'His master was a physician, trained in Italy. But so they all claim to be. He trained Alan as his assistant, entrusting him with bloodletting and simple cures. She said he seemed quite proud of it all when he wrote to her.'

'What was the occasion of the letter?'

'He said he might have cause to return to York, there was some trouble in London. His master was a foreigner and under suspicion. Janet's husband did not want him in their home, but she did not know what recourse she would have were Alan to come when Jack was away. Perhaps that is why she took Bernard as a lodger.'

A foreign physician, trouble, an assistant fleeing London. 'Do you recall when Bernard arrived in York?'

Gemma closed her eyes. 'I cannot recall. I was caught up in my own worries. I am sorry.'

'You have been more than helpful,' said Owen. He rose. 'I will speak with Hempe, arrange to have your home and those of your children watched until we have caught your husband's killer.'

She had risen as well, pressing her back with weariness. 'You believe me?'

'I am grateful,' he said, bobbing his head as if nodding.

'Bless you, Captain. Bless you.'

Owen stepped out into a late afternoon heavy with the day's rain yet crowned with a deep blue, and a sun bright where it found a way into the overhanging stories of the crowded street. He breathed in deep and set off at a brisk pace for the shop and Lucie's counsel. On Coney Street he encountered a small pulsing knot of men and women shouting curses. Pushing his way into their midst he found Goodwife Keene, an elderly midwife, cowering as she covered her head with her arms against the blows two youths and a woman rained on her. Yanking the two youths out of the way he caught the arm of the offending woman and held it until she looked up, stepping back with a snarl as if she were a mad dog interrupted in battle. Agnes Baker. For years she had whispered ugly rumors about Lucie, who had done her the great disservice of saving her from herself. Agnes had appeared far too often to purchase certain physicks that calmed the mind and eased pain. After witnessing her stumbling about as if drunk and having difficulty when dealing with customers, forgetting what the person had requested, unable to recall what was available, Lucie had refused to continue to dispense those physicks in more than single doses.

'What has the goodwife done to provoke you to violence?' Owen asked.

'Captain Archer,' she sneered. 'I cannot expect you to respect God's word.'

'And what word would that be, Goodwife?'

'He condemns heretics!'

'I know Goodwife Keene to be a pious Christian. She embroiders cushions for the good monks of Trinity Priory and attends Mass there every Sunday. Perhaps you might learn about your neighbors before condemning them.'

Alice Keene was beyond words, nodding her head while still ducking from expected blows.

'I shall speak with your parish priest, Dame Agnes, tell him of your violence to a good Christian woman. And as for these youths . . .' Owen turned to the two young men held now by the crowd. 'Ah, one is your son.' With a hiss Agnes Baker tried to snatch him away, but the man and woman holding him would not give him up.

'Curse you, Owen Archer,' Agnes hissed.

'Now who is the one cursing Christians?' Owen asked. He took her son by the collar and shook him, letting him go with just the right amount of force to set him rolling on the pavement. 'Be off with you and take your spineless offspring with you.'

He turned away, not trusting himself to say more. Agnes was the very model of a venomous gossip.

The other youth, Warren, was well known to all the bailiffs and their men, and a regular in the pillory at Trinity Priory. 'I see that your last turn at the pillory taught you little. But to beat your elder, a woman who has helped safely deliver far finer citizens of York than you will ever be – even I did not expect such cowardice from you.' He caught him up by the shirt, shook him as well, then tossed him away, knowing the lout would lick his wounds and scurry home only to sin again. 'As for the rest of you, I am sorry to see that fear has made cruel fools of you.'

Crouching to Goodwife Keene he helped her straighten while an onlooker, clearly contrite about doing nothing, collected the items that had rolled out of the midwife's basket and offered to carry it home.

'We will go first to the shop so that I might see to your scratches,' he told Alice Keene.

'I pray you, do not bother with me,' she said. 'I will clean myself at home.'

'The mood in the city is ugly,' said Owen. 'I will not rest easy until I have seen to your injuries and escorted you home.' He thanked the woman who held the basket and took it from her.

In the apothecary workshop Lucie saw to Alice's facial injuries – deep scratches on her face, the work of someone's fingernails, and a bruise beginning to color on her broad forehead. She prepared a comfrey paste that would soothe the scratches, a St John's wort salve for bruises, telling her to check herself for other injuries once she was home, a feverfew powder for the headache to come.

After escorting Alice home, Owen headed to the York Tavern. He would have preferred going straight back to Lucie to tell her all he had heard from Gemma Toller, but she had deliveries to store after closing the shop.

Seeing his face, Bess drew him into her quiet space next to the kitchen and poured two goodly cups of brandywine, handing him his and tilting her head, ready to listen.

'Where to start?' he wondered.

'Not a comforting beginning.' She took a drink. 'I understand you sent Agnes Baker and her loathsome eldest off to do penance for their sins. We may never see them again. I toast you for that.' She lifted her cup to him and took another drink.

'Not surprised you heard. Folk are on edge. Guthlac Wolcott is dead.'

'I heard. Not pestilence, but folk won't believe it. And being buried out in the kirkyard here. We will be busy with folk wanting to drink and gawk.' She knew more than Owen did. 'Though the family has suffered much this past year – the little ones, then their factor's death, now Guthlac, I have a bad feeling about that son and the young wife.' She leaned toward Owen, studying his face. 'I see you have somewhat to say about that. Tell me.'

While Owen was telling her about Gemma Toller's suspicions regarding Beatrice's children, Hempe arrived.

'Tom told me you were here,' he said. 'I hoped for a word.'

Bess motioned him in, fetching another cup from the shelf behind her, offering him brandywine. She summed up for him what Owen had just said.

Hempe shook his head. 'She told you all that? How did you charm her? She never said aught of use to either me or Poole.'

'We disregarded her as a shrew,' said Owen. 'Which she may be, with a purpose. Or she may provide insight. I've not yet decided.'

'What changed your mind about her usefulness?' Hempe asked.

'It was something Lucie said when we spoke of Dame Beatrice's condition.'

Bess gave him a look as if to say, of course. 'What of Guthlac's death?' she asked. 'Did she find blame with Bernard?'

'I sensed no opinion on that except that Bernard may not be who he claims.' Owen told them what he knew and suspected.

'Fled trouble in London and changed his name?' Hempe said softly. 'And climbed from barber to physician, educated in Italy.' He held out his empty cup for more. 'Might he be an executioner for those willing to pay well?'

'I wonder,' said Owen.

'Did I hear you say that Dame Beatrice is with child?' asked Hempe. 'Is Gemma certain?'

'Dame Magda is,' said Owen. 'And there is more.' He told them the rest of what Lettice had told them, of her conviction that the Wolcotts were behind her tragedy.

'God in heaven,' Hempe whispered.

Bess shifted in her seat, setting the ribbons on her cap dancing. 'Bad seed, that Gavin. I have always thought that. To think that

he would so coldly plot his father's death. And what of his friendship with the mayor? Is Graa part of this?'

Owen marked that Bess knew of the friendship. 'No one has
suggested so. But the warehousemen who beat Lettice's husband
were Graa's men.'

'So we keep this investigation to ourselves until we know what
is what,' said Hempe.

They spoke more, Hempe talking of disturbances throughout
the city. When Owen rose to leave, he declared his intention of
calling on the Fullers the next morning, after the burial.

'I pray you, do not cross the threshold,' said Bess. 'You do not
want to bring home the Death.'

Hempe rose as well. 'Lotta and I will attend the vigil at the
Wolcott home tonight. For a short while. Dame Beatrice attended
Sam's requiem, and would have come to the vigil the night before,
I think, but that she knew of his widow's animosity toward her. I
will tell you whether I notice anything of interest.'

'Have a care, both of you,' Bess warned.

Owen was not entirely pleased to see Brother Michaelo sitting by
the garden window in the hall as he headed into the kitchen.

Lucie looked up from the bowl of warm water in which she
was washing her hands.

'A timely arrival. I have just come from the workshop.'

'I see we have a visitor.'

'He said he will not stay long,' said Kate. 'He wishes to speak
with you about Einar. To warn you. How is Goodwife Keene?'

'She is shaken,' said Owen. 'I think midwives will be hesitant
to attend births until folk calm, and I cannot blame them. The city
might promise protection, though even if the council would agree
– which is doubtful – we cannot be everywhere.' A weariness
wrapped him and pulled him down as he took off his boots. He
wanted nothing so much as to slump up to bed and sleep. Yet he
knew sleep would elude him. His mind was noisy, desperately
racing about trying to disentangle the threads of thoughts and order
them. 'It is too easy to point at a female healer in accusation. Yet
a man such as Bernard leaves a trail of ruin behind him and all
are silent.'

Lucie walked over to take his hand. 'It is ever so. And men of the Church are ever ready to point at women and absolve men. Come. Let us hear Michaelo's news.'

Michaelo set aside a bowl of ale and rose with grace from his seat near the fire in the hall, bowing to them. 'Forgive the intrusion, but I felt you should hear of Einar's behavior tonight.'

'Trouble?'

'Distress. I told him how Asa had walked onto the ship to attend Jack Fuller. How she had called for help guiding him home, and then stayed with him even though Master Bernard might return and take umbrage at her presence. He groaned and kept muttering, "No, no, I must stop her." Thinking to comfort him I told him I understood that he feared for her, that the Death might take her. But he corrected me. "She means to punish him for using her and then throwing her aside."'

'Punish Bernard?' Owen asked.

'Yes. He would say no more, but his mind was not on the folk we attended tonight. I wished he would go to her.'

'And did he?'

'No. He went to Dame Magda. Seeking her advice.'

'I hope that is true.' Another thread tangling the riot in his head. Bernard had used Asa? He remembered what Magda had said, that the leech might have sought Asa's advice. 'I mean to call at the Fullers in the morning. After Guthlac's burial.'

'Have a care,' Michaelo said softly. 'I would not have you fall ill.'

'Nor I,' said Lucie.

Once again he promised not to cross the threshold. 'I am moved by your concern, Michaelo.'

'You have much work to do,' said the monk.

'I do. And there will be much more.' He told him about the incident with Goodwife Keene. 'We have gone far beyond a few troublemakers.'

'As I said, you cannot be spared.' Michaelo rose as if to leave.

'Stay a moment,' said Owen. 'There is something I would like you to hear. It will not take long.'

Kate knocked, then entered with a jug of ale and two additional bowls. 'I thought you might have need of this. And I will bring bread and cheese if you like.'

'Bless you, yes,' said Lucie.

Settled near the window for the refreshing evening breeze, Owen told them of what he suspected regarding Bernard.

'A physician in London. The need to flee,' Michaelo said. 'You are thinking of Monsieur Ricard's execution for treason against Prince Edward. That Alan was in his household and changed his name as he fled.'

'Am I too eager to make a connection?' Owen asked.

'Eager?' said Lucie. 'I cannot think you welcome such trouble in the city. I, too, thought of him.'

'I question the prince's choice in men for the search,' said Michaelo. 'That they would lose the trail when he has done everything to be conspicuous.'

'Not his intention, I think,' said Owen. 'At St George's Field he exchanged angry words with Gavin Wolcott, accusing him of endangering him by spreading rumors about him.'

'Gavin Wolcott,' Lucie whispered.

'There is more.' Owen told them all that Gemma had confided, as well as Magda's news of Beatrice and Lettice's fears.

'A web,' said Lucie. 'All spun by the same spider?'

'Or several conjoined for mutual benefit,' said Owen.

'Shall I compose a letter to the prince?' asked Michaelo.

'I would hope to have this resolved long before a letter might reach him, he acts, and his men arrive, but yes. At least he will be alerted. Thank you for offering.'

Michaelo rose, bowed. 'I shall bring the letter in the morning. We might discuss it while we watch the burial.'

When he was gone, Lucie began to pace. 'Asa and Bernard, or whoever he is. He was here weeks before she arrived with Einar. Can that mean something?'

'I wish I knew.'

Lucie continued to pace. Owen settled back to fill his stomach.

'The day went well?' he asked.

'I am pleased to say the shop was busy, and no one made a fuss about waiting. I turned away a few who asked me to act as midwife, assuring them that there were sufficient experienced midwives in the city. But hearing of what happened to Goodwife Keene I wonder if they will hesitate to attend births until – until what? I pray for the city.'

'You have all you can do to care for the shop,' said Owen. 'You cannot add midwifery to your tasks.'

'No. Nor was I tempted.' She held out her hand. 'Shall we go to bed, my love? I missed you last night. After I show you how much, we might talk more.'

Owen thought that an excellent plan.

Magda had sensed Einar's agitation from the doorway, but continued ladling stew. He sat down and took the bowl she offered but forgot about it on his lap, letting it cool as he began to unburden himself.

'Asa has— Do you know the Fullers? He's a—'

'Riverman. Yes.'

'Fuller's ship docked today. Asa was on the staithe and heard that he was unwell, no one would help him, fearing the Death. Brother Michaelo assisted her in helping him home. Asa means to bide there, caring for him. I cannot— I must stop her.'

'Did she not tell thee that was her wish, to help those all other healers shunned?'

'She said nothing of it to me. But Bernard? No. If it were anyone else I would admire her action. But the leech. I do not trust her motive.'

'Dost thou know what it is? Or art thou guessing?'

'In truth, I am guessing. She's kept much from me. For a long while in Lincoln she said nothing of her work with Bernard.'

'She worked with him?'

'Yes. And now hates him for taking her up and then discarding her.'

'In what way did he take her up?'

'He proposed they work together, that they would share what they knew, each would learn. Asa feels he received all the benefit for he knew little more than bloodletting. And then he left Lincoln without a word.'

'That is why she cursed his family when she found him.'

'You know of that?'

'Such loud words spoken on the street – all York heard the tale of the gray-haired healer shaking her cane and calling down curses on him and his kin.'

'And now she pretends to help them. But that is not her intent. We must stop her.'

'With or without Asa, the family will feel cursed. Jack Fuller
has brought home the manqualm. His beloved daughter, gentle,
frail Cilla, may succumb. Thou dost not necessarily know Asa's
heart. She might choose to do for the Fullers what Bernard cannot.
Prove her worth to the city while shaming him.'

'I wish I could believe that would satisfy her. But I cannot. I
should have told all that I knew to Captain Archer.'

'Go to him in the morning. Tell him all you wish him to know.'

'Will you come with me?'

'No. This is thy mission, not Magda's.'

'At least let me tell you—'

'Eat now. When Magda changes thy bandage, that will be the
time to talk.'

ELEVEN

W hose Vengeance?

A summery morning had coaxed Owen out into the garden,
where he had walked the paths, collecting debris, plucking
out stray weeds before breaking his fast. He paused beneath
an apple tree, remembering his first spring in this garden, the
feeling of having come home after years in the service of the old
duke. This tree had reminded him of his mother, how she pampered
and tended the fruiting trees in their small garden. How closely
he had watched her work, just as his children followed Lucie
around the garden, curious and eager to help. His precious little
ones. What were Gwen, Hugh, and Emma doing now? Were they
playing in the old orchard at Freythorpe? Did they think of him?
He bowed his head when the bells rang for Guthlac's mass, saying
a prayer for the man's soul.

The quiet moment was shattered by Hempe clattering through
the gate, his bald head uncovered, hat crushed in his hand.
'Something is not right about Guthlac's death and this hasty burial.'

'We bury folk quickly in a plague summer, you know that.'

'Still.'

'What troubles you?'

'Last night Lotta and I called on the Wolcotts to honor the vigil, sit up for a while with Dame Beatrice. It was warm in the room, a window open to allow his soul to escape and I knelt there for the air. Gavin kept slipping in and out of the room – I could hear him out in the garden. And every time, Dame Beatrice would look up – something about how she did, she was not mourning, she was – anticipating? It felt wrong, all of it. When we departed I slipped out back and there was a cart piled high with belongings, a manservant standing guard. He said that after the burial Dame Beatrice wished to go to her parents. Master Gavin would escort her there while they were burning the bedding of the late master and purifying the house. Lotta was annoyed with me for behaving as if I suspected them of some crime, and when I told her what the servant had said she thought it a kind act on Gavin's part. Of course the young widow would find comfort in her parents. But Lotta woke me this morning. "I just remembered that her parents are dead," she said. "Beatrice's. Folk whispered when they were wed, that young child to that old man, that her brother was eager to marry her off. She and his wife were always sparring." I was forgiven for my distrust.'

'Where are they headed?' Owen wondered. 'And what is of such value in that cart it must be watched?'

'And isn't it curious that Master Bernard neither sat the vigil last night nor attended the service this morning.'

'I heard the bells chime the end of the service. Did you stay throughout? Are they on their way to the cemetery?'

'I did not stay. I needed to see you, talk this over.'

'He might have arrived late—' Owen thought about Asa tending Jack Fuller. 'Or there might be trouble at his lodging. I mean to stop there after the burial.'

'Might we go now? We might pass the procession on the street.'

'I need food, my friend. I've not yet broken my fast. Come. I will not be long.'

He found Michaelo in the kitchen, talking to Lucie. Nodding a greeting to Hempe, the monk proffered Owen a wax tablet. 'I propose this letter to the prince.'

Owen read while he ate bread and cheese and washed it down with some ale. Short, succinct, stating the details so that Prince

Edward might decide whether or not to send an envoy. His only quibble was vowing to take Bernard – Alan – into custody and question him, holding him if his suspicions seemed justified. That might be Owen's intention, but to promise such to the prince was unwise.

'Say that the man will be watched, questioned, and prevented from leaving the city.'

Michaelo nodded. 'Perhaps I might add, "should he survive the sickness in his household."'

'A grim practicality,' said Owen as he returned the tablet, 'but unnecessary. How soon can you send it?'

'Archdeacon Jehannes knows of a messenger heading south on the morrow. It will travel with him. I will deliver it for you to sign and seal before I see to the sick in the minster yard.' The prince had given Owen a seal specific to his correspondence so that all might know to expedite it.

Thanking him, Owen took Lucie aside to tell her what troubled Hempe, and where they were headed.

'I will watch Guthlac's burial, tell you if I notice anything of note,' she said. 'You might ask Michaelo to accompany you. He mentioned calling on the Fullers to offer help if they needed him. If they do not require him, I could use him in the shop today. Jasper wishes to walk the prayer procession in St Helen's midday.'

Bess and Tom Merchet stood in the tavern yard with their staff and a few others, quietly awaiting the burial procession. Owen and his companions were turning into Coney Street when they met the solemn processional. They pressed close to the building to make room. As the coffin passed, Owen bowed his head and crossed himself. Gavin and three other merchants served as bearers, walking in solemn gait behind the priest and two clerks, one holding a crucifix aloft, the other carrying the censer. Dame Beatrice Wolcott followed, her eyes lowered, hands pressed together in prayer. Behind her were a few neighbors and a small group who seemed to turn out for all burials. No sign of the leech.

'Any word from your watch on the Wolcott home?' Owen asked Hempe.

'I have two on the watch, one who can see the front of the house from the Ferriby yard, one who can watch the area in the back garden, and the loaded cart. The one in front saw a man arrive late in the night with a package, large and apparently heavy, drawn quickly and quietly into the house. The one watching the cart saw that package placed in the cart before dawn.'

'Any thoughts on what it contained?'

'None. Perhaps something from the warehouse?'

'So late at night?'

'I know. During the day I have only one watcher posted. Less conspicuous. He's playing gardener at the Ferriby house,' said Hempe. 'The letter to the prince. You are convinced the leech is the Alan that His Grace seeks?'

'I am, yes.'

'God help us.'

After knocking on the door to the Fuller home Owen stepped back, assailed by a pungent cloud of juniper-laden smoke wafting from a shuttered window. It would ever be a plague smell to him. Michaelo murmured a prayer.

Janet Fuller opened the door a crack to peer out, her hair wild about her, clinging to her sweaty face. 'Captain Archer and Bailiff Hempe.' She seemed to choke on their names. Swinging the door wider, she said, 'And Brother Michaelo. Bless you for your kindness yesterday.' As the monk stepped forward she held up a hand to stay him. 'This is a plague house. My Jack is beyond help. God will soon call him. Cilla fell ill this morning.' Her voice broke. 'And Asa, he beat her so badly I fear for her.' She bowed her head. 'To pay such a price for her kindness. Her friend Einar is with her.'

'Who beat her?' Owen asked.

'My brother. Alan.'

'Is he here now?' Hempe asked.

'No.'

From an arm's length back Owen tried to peer beyond her, but he could see little in the dimly lit room. 'But Einar is here?' he asked.

'Yes. He has seen to her, comforting her where she lay after the beating. She was in such pain. I did not know what to do. I feared if I moved her I might cause more injury.'

'If you would tell us what happened,' said Owen. 'When was Alan here?'

'He returned late in the evening. I was sitting by my daughter's bed behind the screen, holding her hand and singing to her while Dame Asa lanced Jack's boils. The stench of it—' Janet sobbed.

'And he beat her?' Owen asked.

A sharp nod. 'He pulled Dame Asa from the chair where she sat by my husband and threw her against the wall. She lay there unmoving. But he kept beating her. Kicked her, struck her with the chair, stepped on her right hand until I heard— Mother Mary, stomping and grinding and shouting that he would save the world from her sorcery, her vile drawings, the poppet curses, her thievery. But he is wrong. Alan is the devil's foot soldier, not Asa.'

Deus juva me, Owen silently prayed. The brutality. 'Do you have any idea what provoked such a rage?'

'At first I thought it was the knife she was using. She went searching for a sharp one and found one among his things. When he went for her I tried to stop him. I feared he would cause her to slip and hurt Jack. But he was too quick for me. He wrenched the knife from her hand. Made her bleed. God help me, I cursed him and ordered him out. "You wait," he said to her.'

'What did Asa do?' Hempe asked.

Janet pressed a hand to her eyes. 'What was it she said?'

Behind Janet Owen heard Einar's voice, speaking softly.

'I remember,' said Janet. 'She called after him that she knew who he was and had told the sheriff. He cursed her but went on out of the door. I prayed he was gone. Then I heard him on the steps to the solar.'

Alan knew his secret was out. 'And Asa?' Owen asked.

'She took another knife from the scrip on her girdle. But her hands were shaking and I took it from her, gave her wine. She drank it while I cleaned the black poison from my love's groin.' A sob.

'Take your time,' said Owen softly. He turned to stare down a curious neighbor, who scurried off.

Janet found her voice. 'All the while we could hear him up above, stomping about and raging. God help us. I went to calm my daughter. She was begging me to go out into the street and call for the night watch. We were arguing when he rushed in and set upon Dame Asa.'

Owen doubted the night watch would have been of much use

by then. 'The knives. Are any of them still here?' He hoped they might carry some proof of Alan's connection to Monsieur Ricard, something that would convince the sheriff that 'Master Bernard' was indeed Alan Rawcliff. Why else would Asa taunt him?

'I will look on the table,' said Janet.

'And the poppets he mentioned. Did you see any?' Owen asked. 'Or drawings?'

'I have,' said Einar, appearing behind her. He held up what Owen guessed to be a mandrake root dressed in drab clothing, like Alan's. 'Asa stole Alisoun's mandrake root and made a poppet, a curse. From what Cilla said about what he was shouting, Asa had tucked it in his bedding. He must have found it last night. Asa had told Cilla about it. Assured her it would frighten him away. He threw it at Asa before he grabbed her hand.'

'You knew she meant to do this?' Owen asked.

'She spoke of it. I knew she had the root with her when she left Dame Magda's home. And I found this folded up in her scrip.' Einar gave Janet a paper to pass to Owen.

Glancing at it, Owen recognized Asa's work, though the skull-like head surrounded by writhing vines came from a far darker place than the flowers and animals with which she had decorated her home up on the moors. He tucked it into his scrip.

'Did you find any knives?'

'I was not looking for them,' said Einar.

'Where is your brother now?' Owen asked Janet.

'He must have run out into the night when I went to the kitchen for a cleaver. He was gone when I came back and has not returned, praise God.'

'We must take Asa to Dame Magda,' said Einar. 'You can search her scrip then.'

Owen looked to Michaelo. 'Can you and Einar fashion a litter and bring her out? Hempe and I can then take her.'

'I will take her,' said Einar. 'If Brother Michaelo would stay with Dame Janet.'

'Of course,' said Michaelo.

Janet protested.

'I pray you, permit me to be of help,' said the monk. 'I have been among victims of the sickness and have not as yet fallen ill, nor do I have family to protect.'

'Are you certain?' When Michaelo nodded, Janet said, 'Bless you,' and stepped away.

While Einar led the monk to Asa, Janet checked the table by her husband, returning to say Alan must have taken the knives.

As expected. Owen asked if she had all she needed, listened to her requests, promised to return with them after Asa was settled.

Hempe nodded. 'It is a long way through the city to Magda's rock. I will fetch a cart and alert my men to search for – I will tell them Bernard. It is how they know him. When you go through Bootham, ask whether the gatekeeper saw him. That will be one less task to assign.'

With a nod, Owen settled on the step to await Hempe's return, trying to imagine where Alan might flee. A frustrating endeavor, for he hardly knew the man. He rose to pace and think, but his mind kept turning to the brutality of Alan's attack.

When Hempe at last appeared leading a donkey and cart, Owen hurried to him. It was a rickety thing, lurching to one side. Seeing it, Owen asked Janet for a hammer.

'You will find one in the shed behind the house.'

It was the work of a few minutes to repair the axle well enough for the journey.

'The carter will be pleased,' said Hempe. 'I paid him far more than this is worth, and now you have repaired it.'

'For the moment,' Owen said. 'As you say, it is a long way.'

Einar and Brother Michaelo brought Asa out on a board that likely served as the family's table. She was wrapped in a shawl, but with enough of her face visible to see the swelling, the bruises, and the caked blood on her forehead. Those were only the visible injuries. Though Asa did not appear to be conscious, she gasped and moaned as they tilted the board to lift it up into the cart. Owen curled his hands into fists imagining what he would do to the cur when he found him.

Owen would remember little of the slow journey across Foss Bridge and through the city that warm, sunny morning. On such a summery day one would expect the streets to be filled with people young and old finding cause to be out enjoying the warmth on their skin, the light. But if they crowded the streets he traversed they must have made way, for he recalled no obstacles. Neither did he remember any conversation with Einar, and Asa did not regain consciousness for all the motion. He was lost in combing through all that he had heard or thought about Alan in search of missed warnings. Never had he imagined the man capable of the violence he had inflicted on Asa. Why had he not anticipated it? Because he called himself a healer? His pose of piety? Owen had never imagined the man could be so easily provoked to physical brutality. Even a man facing death for treason – to beat a woman with such brutal intent felt far beyond anything he might have expected. Or was it? How many men beat their wives after being crossed in far more mundane ways, often not by her but by someone else? Too many. And a man accused of treason was a desperate man.

A thought gnawed at him. Was he no better than the folk who easily believed violence of women healers, curses, spells, but would never so accuse a physician, leech, barber? Alan's contempt for female healers – had that not been the warning sign? Owen might have guessed. He might have warned Asa.

'God go with you, Captain Archer.'

Owen snapped to attention at the greeting from the gatekeeper at Bootham Bar. Not his friend today but Oswald, younger, less experienced, though diligent and trustworthy.

'Plague death?' Oswald asked, keeping his distance and holding a cloth to his nose.

'A victim of a brutal beating, not dead, God be thanked. Have you seen the leech Bernard come through?'

'Master Bernard?' Oswald shook his head. 'Not today. But he would be at the Wolcott burial, would he not?'

'He was not. I thought perhaps he had been summoned from the city.'

'If he was, not in this direction. Most folk head out this way to consult the Riverwoman.'

'As do I.'

Oswald waved them through, wishing them Godspeed.

'She has not moved,' said Einar from the cart.

'Better that she not suffer the journey. Did you give her something to help her sleep?'

'Dame Janet gave me valerian powder in wine to dribble into her mouth. But she has not awakened since the beating.'

'Did you examine her? What are her injuries?'

'You can see the gash on her head, and bleeding either on or inside that ear. Her lip is split in two places, her nose broken. She has much pain along her right side. I would guess he broke some ribs. Her right forearm and hand are bruised and swollen, and her right foot lay at an uncomfortable angle. I did not trust myself to move her much. Dame Janet had covered her with a blanket and tried to give her water, dribbling with a spoon.' He groaned. 'It is my fault. If I had told you all that I knew—'

'Not now, Einar. I need you here with me, aware of everything you do, everything you hear. We will talk later.'

At the river, after Owen checked that Asa's bindings were secure, a group of men offered to help transport her to Magda's rock. They knew the river, they assured him. The tide was not fully in and they knew where to walk. Lifting the board on which she lay out of the cart, they gently set it on the water. Owen and Einar followed the men as they floated Asa to the rock.

Twig came out to watch, the kitten in his arms. 'I will put out the trestles,' he said, disappearing within. At the rock, Owen and Einar took either end of the board. Thanking the men who had guided Asa across, Owen bowed to the dragon and led the way into the house, setting it on the trestles by the fire.

'Dame Magda said she would be back at midday,' said Twig. 'She expected to be needed here.'

After Owen removed Asa's bindings he set to cleaning her so he might gauge the extent of her injuries. The blood on her face appeared to have come from a gash in her temple rather than from within her ear, preferable, but still dangerous, and likely the reason she did not wake. Into the hot water he poured a mixture of agrimony, ivy, and dock root for deep cleansing, having Einar hold a padding of cloth soaked in the mixture to the wound while he wound a clean strip of linen round her head. Twig fetched a cushion for Owen to place beneath her head, supporting her neck. The swelling made it difficult to determine just where there might be breaks in her forearm, hand, foot, and leg, so Owen did little more than clean them with the mixture and applied poultices of nepte leaves with chervil and comfrey, as well as a little arnica from Lucie's garden. All the while, Einar had spooned into Asa's mouth a weak mixture of poppy milk and valerian in wine.

Magda would be a better judge about how to proceed. Asa was

her daughter and had recently been in her care. With luck the swelling might go down by the time she returned. Not knowing the extent of her internal injuries, Owen dare not move her to a bed where she might rest in more comfort, but he folded a blanket and gently lifted her shoulders to slide it beneath her, then covered her with another.

When Asa seemed settled, her breathing improved, Owen insisted on examining Einar's injured arm. The young man had removed the sling in order to help carry Asa out of the house and place her in the cart, which made sense at the time. Einar winced at Owen's touch.

'A lot of swelling,' Owen noted. 'Are you in much pain?'

'Dame Magda says it is healing well.'

Avoiding the question meant a yes to Owen. 'That was before sitting up all night attending Asa, then carrying her out.' He removed the bandage. As he'd thought, the activity had reopened the wound. But he had expected worse. Changing the bandage should be sufficient for now. He added a little salve for good measure.

'Before you leave I want to talk, Captain.'

'I mean to stay until Magda returns. She may need me.' But the change in the young man's voice, a tremor, a hesitation, caught Owen's attention. 'If you're worried about Asa, her breathing is good. And her heart. She may fully recover.'

'It's not that. There is much you must know.'

Owen did have questions. 'Come out into the air.' He instructed Twig to let them know if there was any change in Asa. Stepping out, he chose the side of the house looking toward the south bank and settled on a bench, stretching out his legs.

Einar joined him. 'I might have prevented Asa's injuries. I knew Bernard's temper, had experience fighting with him.'

'You? When?'

'It is a long tale.'

'I am aware that he is not who he claims to be, that he is Janet Fuller's brother, Alan. I was looking for him this morning. I thought to find him at the Fuller home.'

'I did not know their relation until last night, at the Fuller home. God help me. I went to protect the family from Asa.'

'Brother Michaelo told me.'

'I was right that, hating him as she does, she meant to do

something to goad Bernard – Alan. But I was wrong about what that was. It seems she was of much help until he attacked her.'

'Was he still there when you arrived?'

'No. You need to know about Alan. I encountered him in London. I am sure of it.'

'Go on.'

'When my father fell ill he sold his medicines and his tools for bloodletting to pay for food and shelter, letting me shift for myself in continuing our work. I found my way to London, stealing just enough to get by, thinking to apprentice to a barber. But I knew no one. I could find no honest work, so I fell in with thieves. I was good at it. Worked my way into a band that robbed the finest houses. When a French physician was arrested for treason I volunteered to be first one through the house, report what was there. I hoped to find all that I needed and to set myself up as a traveling barber. I found the house filled with silver and much that would bring a good price, but no tools. Beyond the master's bedchamber there was a stairway down to a smaller building. When I stepped through the door I heard someone, slipped in unnoticed, watched him emptying the room of medical implements and supplies. He knew what to take.'

'All that you wanted.'

'Yes. So I attacked him. He was stronger and faster than he looked. Better fed. He beat me and ran off, dropping a few of the smaller tools in his haste. I was not so badly beaten I missed out on them and some silver. With coin in my pockets I went to the taverns. I learned that the king's men were searching for a man named Alan Rawcliff, the French physician's assistant. He'd escaped before they raided the house. Sounded like the man I'd fought. I started hunting him, thinking I could catch him with the stolen items and be rewarded.'

'What was the physician's name?' Owen asked.

'Ricard.'

The Frenchman who had slowly poisoned Prince Edward. Owen had been right about Alan's identity. 'Go on.'

'I picked up his scent in Peterborough, but he'd already moved on. Someone thought to Lincoln. And he'd changed his name to Bernard. In Lincoln I heard of a woman who said she was Magda Digby's daughter working with a barber named Bernard. That's how I found Asa.'

'She was working with him?'

'Yes. Making good money. He spoke well, dressed well, found his way into the homes of far wealthier folk than she might. But he knew little beyond bloodletting. She offered to train him as they worked together. I learned all this by following her. She was friendly to me, permitted me to stay with her, but made it plain that I should not nose about her business. I might have warned her then that he would not stay.'

'He disappeared?'

'She was furious, as you can imagine. And he had taken some of her medicines. A while after he had left Lincoln, the king's men arrived, searching the city for a traitor. Their description of Alan Rawcliff, assistant to the traitor Monsieur Ricard, matched Bernard, even down to Asa's belief that he'd never done more than apply leeches and administer simple remedies, which is what he'd done for Ricard. Like I said, I'd already guessed who he was, but now I knew. A few folk whispered of Bernard the barber, but as he was gone it seemed no one told the king's men that he might have been there. The city merchants and Churchmen wished to avoid trouble in Lincoln. Asa was excited. We would hunt him down and turn him in.'

'She took up your cause.'

'She did not know I had already been on the hunt. Or – perhaps she did.' He opened his palm. 'This knife was in her scrip. It has Monsieur Ricard's mark on it. So do the tools Alan dropped. She might have seen them and noticed the mark, known this knife was proof.'

'It does explain why he snatched it from her. How did you trace him to York?'

'A chance conversation with a taverner at the edge of the city a few months after he left. He seemed eager to gossip about travelers, so I asked about Bernard. "Ah, the sly barber sold himself to a York merchant as a physician educated in Italy. Rode off with him."'

'The taverner said nothing to the king's men?'

'I did not ask. To my shame I thought only of how Asa and I might benefit from his trouble if we followed him to York.'

'Did he mention what York merchant?'

'Called him a young fool traveling with several others who were angry with him when they discovered he had invited Alan along.'

'So you told Asa where he had gone . . .'

They had then come to York, and in short order heard of the
rumors about Magda Digby, some of the accusations so close to
Asa's manner of speech that Einar realized Alan must be using
her confidences. He said nothing until he met Magda himself and
found her not at all how Asa had described her, but rather a woman
from whom he wished to learn, a woman of wisdom and honor.
When Asa complained about Alan, Einar laughed at her.

'By then she disgusted me as much as he did. I hoped that with
Dame Magda I might learn healing. If I could convince her that
I am called to it . . . So I told Asa that once I ferried her across
the river I wanted no more to do with her.' He bowed his head.
'She did not deserve what she's suffered.'

'No.' Owen said nothing for a while.

Einar rose, stepped down to the edge of the rock, stuck a hand
in the water. 'I like it here on the river. I pray Dame Magda will
forgive me.'

'You have told her all this?'

'I did. But all she said was that you were the one to hear it.
She did not throw me out, but she will.' A heavy sigh.

'You said Asa used Alisoun's mandrake to make the poppet.
She knew Alan feared them?'

'She said they held a particular terror for him.'

'When did she steal it?'

'I don't know. She showed it to me the day I rowed her across
the river. She stole a number of household goods from Dame
Magda as well.'

'I thought she had used the mandrake root earlier,' said Owen.
'There was another, or so Edwin Cooper claimed.'

'I know nothing of that.'

'No matter. How long were you here in York before going to
Magda?'

'A fortnight or more. Asa tried to find work, but the fear of
strangers was already spreading in the city and she found few
who would open the door to her. Folk hurried past her on the
streets, cloths over their mouths, though she looks neither ill nor
unkempt. Dame Celia Cooper seemed to welcome her, and she
hoped that might lead to more work. For a time it did. Until
Cooper threw her out and his thugs beat her. She cannot move

fast with her bad leg. Lincoln is a city on a steep hill. Several
years of climbing it visiting the sick crippled her. She expected
York to be easier for her, though the journey from Lincoln was
difficult. But despite having the coin to pay, the only lodging we
could find here was up a steep set of steps often slippery with
rain. She tried to come down only once a day and back up in the
evenings. But it meant she was out on the streets all day, walking.
After the beating she decided it was time to find her mother and
ask for help.' Einar settled on the bench beside Owen. 'I cannot
think where Alan's gone.'

'Nor can I. If he's in the city, Hempe's men will find him.'

They were interrupted by Twig, stepping out to tell them that
Asa was moaning and licking her lips.

'Let me help you with that. Oof! That's a load.' Jasper laughed
as he backed through the beaded doorway to ease his side of a
large package down onto the floor where it would be out of the
way.

His companion bobbed his head to Lucie. 'Mistress Wilton. I
am Tomas the weaver.' His accent identified him as a Fleming.
'This is the fustian the captain ordered for the Riverwoman.'

She had forgotten. 'Bless you for delivering it.'

'I try to keep busy. It is hard at present, with the sickness. Folk
do not like to come near foreigners.' He and his family had lived
in York a long while. But Lucie knew it was true the Flemings
were avoided.

'Did the captain pay you?' she asked.

'More than enough. I have coins to return.' He counted them
out, placing them on the table just inside the door. 'We were glad
for the order. Will the Riverwoman be making clothes for the
poor?'

'She is giving work to a family in need of it. Enough for them,
and sufficient to make more to sell and display their skill.'

'If I might be of help. We have a table at the Thursday market
and we could display some of their work. Good for them, good
for us.'

'I will tell Magda of your generous offer.'

He bobbed his head and withdrew, thanking Jasper for his help.
Curious, Lucie untied the cord and lifted the waxed cloth to

reveal a fustian unlike anything she had seen in shops, so soft as to seem far costlier, yet with a tight weave for long wear. She would see what she might do to stir up more business for Tomas.

'I could borrow Bess's cart and take it to Magda this afternoon,' said Jasper. 'I would like to see her.'

'And Asa?' They had heard of Owen's solemn progress through the city and out Bootham, gossip spreading fast.

'No. Just—'

'You need not explain. For months you have been chained to the shop with little chance to stretch your legs and see something else. I accept your offer. Remember to take the coin.'

In the early morning Magda had been called to a home halfway to Easingwold. A child had tumbled from a roof. Setting the bones of a young child was ever the most difficult, and Magda had been weary of heart and spirit by the time she went to the glade to see how Helen and her twins fared. The family's joy cheered her, and when the children invited her to share a meat pie they had made from their father's catch she welcomed the chance to prolong her time in the healing place. So it was that she turned home long after she had intended. She had not forgotten that she would be needed, but she had sensed Bird-eye's presence, and knew that whatever the problem, he could cope until her return.

Raven chided her along the way, urging her to walk faster. Asa, then. Magda reached out to her daughter, finding confusion and pain, a great deal of pain, but no anger. Broken bones, broken spirit. Tears. She quickened her pace, but a flood of memories slowed her – Asa's childhood of broken bones, torn skin, loosened teeth, sprains, screams, curses, high fevers, but never tears. By the time she bore Asa, Magda knew that children survived illnesses and injuries that felled older folk. Some criticized her for allowing her child to run wild. But Asa *was* wild, a creature of the moors, buffeted by winds, nurtured by storms and inconstant sun. Four-legged animals and those with wings spoke to Asa more clearly than the two-legged folk among whom she lived. She'd sought out the ancient trees, sitting on their roots through the day, drinking in their wisdom. Among her own kind she was ever ready to erupt in fury, chilling in her delight in cruel barbs and japes. She had only disdain for her brother

Potter, but she had loved her father, whom all called Digby. He carved and chiseled life out of wood and rock, humming as he worked, or weaving stories as folk in the village brought out their own work to listen. Strong, a man of few words when he was not telling tales, he comforted and cajoled his wild daughter, encouraged his quiet, curious, awkward son. When Magda felt the call to go south to the forest of Galtres, Digby had blessed Potter's decision to accompany her, expecting both to return before long. Asa had cursed both of them, angry about their defection, though except for her mother's healing skills she had wished to have nothing to do with them. And she had cursed Magda again on her return, blaming her for both the deaths of her father and her brother. Now she came for healing. The pungent scents of the woodland rooted Magda in the present as she remembered, propelling her homeward.

By the time she greeted the dragon, Magda had heard from her lads how Bird-eye and Einar had brought Asa strapped to a board, unconscious, how the men had floated her to the rock. In the house she found Bird-eye bent over Asa, whispering to her. Magda joined him, looking down on her daughter, drinking in the pain that radiated from her body and her heart. Breathing it in, breathing out a promise of ease. In and out as she made a cursory exam of the bandage obscuring Asa's forehead, the eyes blackening over the broken nose, so swollen she must breathe through her mouth. Her eyes opened. Blinking.

'Mother.' Mouthed more than spoken. One hand fluttered, the other lay quiet, swollen and discolored. The forearm as well. Tears came.

'Who did this to thee?' Magda lifted the blanket to examine her feet. Same side swollen and discolored.

'Alan, who calls himself Bernard,' said Owen.

'Provoked him,' Asa whispered.

'Perhaps. But it was his choice to accept the bait and attack thee. Where is the pain?'

'Everywhere.' Asa closed her eyes, squeezing out the tears.

'The most serious injuries are all on her right side,' said Owen. 'Forearm, hand, and foot may be broken, and possibly the lower leg. The ribs on that side as well.'

Magda leaned close to listen to Asa's lungs. She glanced up at

Einar. 'Thou didst a good job of moving her with care. Ribs might be broken, but they have not punctured her lung.'

'God be praised,' said Einar.

'Thy god had naught to do with it. Take credit for thy choices, Einar.' Looking down at Asa, Magda invited her to rest quietly while she and Owen discussed how to proceed.

Asa reached for Magda with her uninjured hand, pressing her arm. 'Forgive me.'

'Hush now. Rest.' Magda stroked her daughter's cheek and turned away, motioning to Owen to follow. 'Einar, stay within Asa's sight. Lay a comforting hand on her. Twig, thou hast done well to keep the water hot. Hast young Holda eaten?' The kitten now ate small portions of meat throughout the day.

'Just a while ago.'

'Many thanks for thy care this day. Come again tomorrow if thy mother can spare thee.'

Bobbing his head, Twig slipped out the door.

Now they might speak without guarding themselves. While Owen listed all that he had observed, Magda began to mix powders and poultices, preparing for the likeliest events. There was much work to do. 'Canst thou assist Magda until evening, Bird-eye? By then Einar should be sufficient.'

'I will stay as long as you have need of me.'

Shortly after nones Jasper brought the Merchets' cart round to load the fabric. At the shop counter, Lucie measured out cloves and sprigs of juniper for a young mother who could barely speak for the fear choking her, but who had gasped out wishes for Owen's safety, having seen him escorting Asa through the city. She jumped as a young man hurried into the shop. Lucie held up her hand, signaling him to wait, and finished filling the woman's basket.

'Pay me later,' she said. 'Go home to your children.'

Whispering her thanks, the woman hurried out, skirting the young man.

'Brother Michaelo sent me. He needs these items for Dame Janet. I am to wait.' He handed Lucie a torn piece of paper with a list of items for soothing poultices for the buboes.

'How is Cilla?'

'These are for her. She's badly, Mistress Wilton, and her father's gone. A while ago.'

Lucie's heart hurt for Janet, who would be left alone in her grief. She was measuring the items when Jasper came to tell her he was leaving. She gave him the news.

'Should I stay?'

'No. There is no line at the door. Go. I am eager to hear what you learn.'

Waking Asa from a restorative sleep, Magda told her that she and the captain must see to her deeper injuries, warning her that there would be pain. Broken bones to set.

'I can bear it,' Asa whispered.

With a feather-light touch, Magda placed her hands on Asa's swollen forearm, sensing the heat, feeling for any breaks in the flow of blood through the limb. She did the same over the hand, staying longer, the bones so intricate. Now she told Einar to do the same. She saw his reluctance, his doubt, but he extended his hands and she softly talked him through it, inquiring about what he felt. He missed the extent of the damage in the hand, misinterpreted a break in the forearm, but he had some ability, which she had expected after what he'd told her of his father, how folk believed him to be a gifted healer because of his uncanny ability to read a body with the lightest touch. In his eyes she saw his hunger to learn more.

Next Magda adjusted Asa's shift so that she might place bare hands on the swollen rib cage. A possible break there. Wrapping it would support her when she coughed. She moved down to the leg. Though swollen and no doubt painful, and the ankle twisted badly, she sensed no breaks. It should not bear weight for a while, but would heal if packed and bandaged with a poultice of comfrey and arnica like what Bird-eye had applied. She commended both men on their gentle handling, and Bird-eye for the poultice.

'Not as bad as I feared,' said Asa with an attempt at a smile.

Drawing Owen to her worktable, Magda confided that splinters of bone in the arm would render the setting painful but she could not risk a strong sedative. Since childhood Asa responded to physicks in ways one could not anticipate.

'Such a brutal attack,' said Owen.

'And the victim an aging woman with brittle bones. Magda will depend on thy strength to keep her still. She will feel the splinters, and the broken bones in her hand will shift painfully as Magda sets her arm.' She saw his concern. 'Afterward thou shalt wrap the hand in bandages dipped in a healing paste. Magda will wait a few days for the swelling to lessen before she dares splint the fingers.'

'The hand will never heal well enough for her to draw, will it?'

'No.'

She held his arm as his anger flared. 'Calm thyself, Bird-eye. There is much work to do. Thou canst hunt this man after Asa sleeps with more ease. Now remove thy shirt. This will be bloody and hot – the fire must be stoked to keep Asa warm. She might lose much blood.'

'You will open her?'

'Likely the arm, yes.'

The procedure was as difficult and grueling as Magda had predicted. For it happened that Asa's splintered bones could not be set until Magda removed some of the fragments impeding her work, a long, painful, bloody process. After hours in the warm house, his mind and body devoted to supporting Magda, Owen escaped into the afternoon air, drinking in the breeze from the river, resting his attention on the sound of water, feeling his fatigue.

Magda followed. Lifting her face to the sun she rose on her toes, stretched her arms toward the sky, and let out a long sigh. Owen marveled at the short, slender, aged woman, so agile and graceful after hours bending to difficult surgery. And to subject her own daughter to it – he did not think he could do it. Yet he knew it was the only hope for Asa to have use of the arm and hand. Uncertain as that was. Magda's eyes were calm now, but it seemed to Owen that the worry lines in her aged face were deeper.

'I bow to you, Dame Magda. I have never seen such fine work. Far more men would have survived had you been the surgeon in the camps.'

'Healing soldiers so they might return to the battlefield? Magda would find it difficult to bear. Wouldst thou have the stomach for it now?'

With surprise, he shook his head. 'No. I would not.'

She smiled, her wrinkles deepening around eyes and mouth.

'Thou hast a great heart, Owen Archer, and thou hast given much of thyself today. Calm thyself before thou goest into the city.'

Turning back toward the house, Magda touched the dragon's head, and for a moment it was as if the two became one, woman and dragon, completing each other, a being of fire and water, her scales aglow, hovering in the air, then gracefully diving into the river, but also Magda the woman Owen had always sensed, a warrior woman but with wise eyes that drew him in, clearing his mind of doubt. In that moment he saw the enormity of what she had been teaching him all the while, understood how he blinded himself to the subtleties that would help him in his work. Out of doubt. And fear. He blinked away a tear of frustration, and Magda stood before him as the healer she presented to the world. Nodding to him, she went inside.

Owen lingered, pacing and shaking out his legs and arms, fighting to sustain the vision, allowing himself to see the connection he'd sensed between Magda and Einar, how the young man had known without her saying what she needed of him, and how Owen's own gift was valuable in a different way. He saw it so clearly now, how he had brushed away his knowing that Gemma Toller, Beatrice Wolcott, and Gavin Wolcott were lying. As he had known from the beginning that the leech was dangerous. He was arguing with himself when he heard his son calling to him.

Jasper stood on the riverbank, pale hair glinting in the sun. Behind him, a donkey cart. Cupping his hands over his mouth he was calling, 'I've brought Dame Magda's cloth!'

A task forgotten. Lucie must have taken it to hand. Owen motioned for Jasper to wait there and ducked inside to see what Magda would wish him to do.

'The family is in Galtres, are they not? It is a heavy load to carry far,' he warned.

Einar glanced up from where he was assisting Magda in wrapping Asa's rib cage. 'I could deliver it in the morning.'

Magda nodded to him. 'Bring it here. Einar will take it tomorrow in Magda's cart.'

Owen stepped out to motion Jasper across. 'Use the coracle. We'll take it back together.'

He felt the calm slipping away.

TW ELVE

So M any Q uestions

O wen seethed, itching to find Alan, pin him to a wall, and take his time describing the damage he had inflicted on the body of a woman who was in his sister's home tending to a man dying of the pestilence, the feelings churning as he answered Jasper's questions about Asa's injuries, Alan's violence, Einar's part in all of this.

It was with some relief that Owen took his leave of his son. Learning that the death had taken Jack Fuller, his body removed by friars, and that Cilla Fuller would likely soon succumb, Owen first went there.

Two friars tended a fire in the yard while Janet stood in the kitchen doorway hugging herself, ignoring the loud, vicious remarks of a man and woman watching from a neighboring yard. Still seething, Owen walked over to them and said he was recruiting folk to help dispose of the dead. As they seemed idle, he would submit their names.

Muttering curses, they retreated – not to the house where they stood, but to a yard farther away.

'They marked my house with chalk weeks ago, spreading a rumor that my Cilla carried the pestilence.'

'Your brother did nothing about that?'

'He said not a word. I scrubbed it off.'

Despite the enormous losses she had suffered in the past day she presented an orderly appearance head to toe. Only the hollowed-out eyes betrayed her, empty, as if walking with the dead, not the living. Owen expressed his sorrow and asked if there was anything he or Lucie might do for her. She thanked him for silencing the couple, and for the offer.

'Brother Michaelo was so kind, and Dame Lucie refused money for the physicks I requested. Today the friars appeared on my doorstep, six of them, and offered to help me with the bodies of my husband and daughter. When I told them that my daughter was still alive one of them offered to attend her while two of their brethren took away my Jack.' She crossed herself. 'And the others are cleaning and burning Jack's clothes and bedding.'

'It is good to hear of such kindness in a dark time,' said Owen.

'So many have been kind. There will be a mass in the morning. I expect another in a few days' time, though Cilla being so sickly she might stop breathing at any moment.'

'I am sorry.'

She patted his arm. 'When I have grieved, I will find a way to help my neighbors, for surely the Death walks among us all now.' She took a breath. 'Have you found my brother?'

'No. I have just come from Dame Magda's.'

'Forgive me. I did not think to ask. How is Asa?'

'Resting. Magda has done what is possible for now.'

'Will she recover?'

'She has much healing to do. Would you permit me to arrange for someone to watch your house? For your protection?'

'While the friars are here Alan would not dare come.'

'We cannot be certain. His actions might be part of something larger.' Seeing her fear, he begged her forgiveness, 'But I would be remiss if I did not warn you.'

'I am grateful, Captain. I pray you do whatever you think necessary, and if there is anything I might do, I trust you will tell me. And if I might beg a favor. Take Alan's things. I will not be able to sleep in that room until it is all removed and I have scrubbed it.' She turned, nodding to him to follow her up a narrow set of steps to the solar, where an oil lamp burned. 'I have touched nothing. All but the table, shelves, bed, and chair is his. He had two packs tucked beneath the bed. You are welcome to them.' She nodded to herself as if satisfied that she'd said all she intended, and moved toward the steps.

'Was Asa a help to you?'

She turned, a hand on her stomach. 'She was a great help, so gentle with both of them. That Alan would do this— God forgive me, but I meant to kill the animal. I fetched a cleaver from the kitchen.'

'He saw you with it?' Owen could well imagine Alan turning on her.

'No. He fled while I was gone. Leaving her there. I feared he had killed her. I don't understand. Did he know her?'

'For a short while.'

'The young man. Einar. Is he her son?'

'No. A cousin.'

'He has a good heart. The friars said he has been assisting Brother Michaelo with the poor who sleep in the minster yard and then he walks to an old shed in Galtres to sleep. If he needs a place to stay in the city he is welcome here. Would you tell him that? Perhaps he might suffice for my protection as well.'

'I will tell him, though I would prefer to use one of my men for the watch.'

'Whatever you think best. I will be down below with my daughter. Bless you, Captain. I will not rest easy until Alan is in the castle dungeon. But at least my home will feel free of him when his things are gone.'

'Your question about Alan and Asa— Has your brother ever been with a woman?'

She gave him a puzzled smile. 'Do you think he would confide such a thing to me? If he has I pity the woman. Do you think he and Asa might have been lovers? Perhaps he felt betrayed by her? I will pray for her.' She left the solar, closing the door behind her.

On the table Owen found tools for bloodletting, most with the mark Einar had pointed out, and bowls of leeches. Many appeared dead. There were a few physicks for simple complaints – feverfew powder for headache, mint and fennel seed for the stomach. A paltry selection for a physician, or even a barber. Perhaps he had removed the rest.

Reaching beneath the bed, Owen found but one pack. Worn leather, well used. Considering what little he'd found it would hold all that Alan had left behind. He used the few items of clothing to pad the items from the table – a few shirts, London-made, one much darned, hose, also darned, a hooded cape of waxed cloth for rain, a fine ivory comb missing a few teeth, a razor.

Before leaving, he took a turn round the room, lamp in hand, searching for anything misplaced.

'You found only the one pack?'

Owen had not heard Dame Janet return.

'Just this, yes.' Something occurred to him. 'Did he explain why he did not wish anyone to know who he was?'

'What do you mean? He did not deny he was my brother.'

'Had he ever before used the name Bernard?'

'It was our father's name. He said he had taken it in honor of him.'

Loath to cause her more pain, Owen said nothing. 'I will send someone to watch until he is found.'

She nodded, stepping aside so that he might descend before her.

He turned at the top of the steps. 'Was he carrying anything besides the poppet when he came down last night?'

'No. Nothing.'

'He was wearing his cloak?'

'No. You found none?'

Owen shook his head.

'What does that mean?'

'Perhaps he already planned a retreat and stored the second pack elsewhere.'

'But he had only just learned that Jack was home.'

Owen hesitated before his next question. But it could mean much to the widow. 'Brother Michaelo mentioned a small chest your husband was keen to keep with him. Is it still in the house?'

'I had not thought to check.' She hurried down the steps.

Owen paced, thinking of the package delivered to the Wolcott house in the night. Janet returned, crestfallen.

'Gone. What will I tell the Graa family? They entrusted the ship and crew to Jack. How did he dare? And when? Jack returned just hours before he died.'

'You said you went to the kitchen for a cleaver to defend Asa and he was gone when you returned.'

'Of course. And the chest was just beneath the table beside my husband's pallet. The fiend! May God damn him to eternal suffering,' she hissed.

'I will find it, Dame Janet. Tell me what it looks like.'

She measured it in the air, a small chest, as he would have expected. 'I had his initials carved on it, Captain. JF. And a rose to remind him of me.'

'May God watch over you and your daughter. Might I attend the mass in the morning?'

'I would be honored. It will be at St Mary's in Castlegate. I
cannot abide the parish priest at St Denys'.'

The sun was low in the sky, the streets evening-dark. Cool breezes
whispered around corners, signaling an end to the warm spell.
Owen shifted the pack on his shoulders as his mind raced, searching
for a clue as to where Alan might hide his belongings, and Jack
Fuller's chest of papers and coin. Nothing in Alan's belongings
suggested such a place. But Hempe's report of the delivery to the
Wolcott home drew him there.

Voices of guests could be heard in the Wolcott yard. He passed
it, slipping into Ferriby's yard next door. John, the 'gardener',
nodded to him.

'Plenty folk coming and going at the street door, but not the
leech,' he said. 'Heard him prattling at folk in the parish often
enough I know his voice. I've listened for him, and he's not been
there.'

'Have you heard anything of interest?'

'Servants moaning that when the young master and the mistress
leave early tomorrow they're to scrub down the house and close
it. The rest is much moaning about all the work, some tears for
the old master.'

Peering through the hedge, Owen noticed the cart Hempe had
mentioned, loaded, covered, ready for a morning departure. He
saw no one about.

'The cart is not guarded?'

'Has been. I expect all the household is caught up with the
guests.'

Leaving the pack of Alan Rawcliff's belongings with John,
Owen told him to stay close to the hedge, then slipped through
into the Wolcott yard, ducking behind the cart. He waited, listening
for footsteps or any sign he had been noticed. When he deemed
it safe he untied a corner of the cover on the cart. The sun still
cast light in the garden, the contents of the cart visible – bedding,
cushions, a few chests of the sort that commonly hold clothing.
Hearing footsteps, he crawled into the cart, dropping the end of
the cover he'd lifted. He held his breath as the footsteps came
close but then continued moving away from the house. Someone
heading for the midden, he guessed. He lay still. The person

returned, hesitating for a moment near him, then continued to the house. Slithering out, Owen peered up, and, seeing no one, lifted the cover more. He had felt something that might be a small chest beneath some cushions. Too dark beneath the cover and the cushions to see any carvings to identify it as Fuller's, he shifted a larger chest to search beyond it. More footsteps, and voices. Again he climbed in, dropping the cover over him. The men were discussing protections against the pestilence. One said he had participated in a penitential procession in his church. The other scoffed, arguing that once the pestilence was in the city no amount of penance would push it out.

The first said, 'Penance for my sins, not those of all the city. I know plenty deserve to be afflicted.'

'Afflicted? You make light of the Death? There is no other end to it, you know.'

'I know of two survived it.'

'Pah. They thought they did is all.'

The men moved past, heading for the midden again, Owen guessed. He moved a foot to ease a cramp and reached down to rub it, stopping as they returned.

'Did you hear Wolcott's leech beat the Riverwoman's daughter? She would have died but Captain Archer took her to her ma.'

'Is that why we have not seen him today. I would hide, too, if that one-eyed Welshman caught me out.'

'Too bad the captain did not stay at the prince's court.'

'Why? The city needs a protector.'

'Protector? He's spying for the prince and who knows who else.'

'They say the Riverwoman's dragon survived burning arrows without any damage.'

'Mind me, those who tried to burn that witch's house will all be dead of the pestilence before the harvest.'

'So might we all.'

Their voices fading, Owen eased out, dragging the small chest to the light. Fuller's initials, and a rose. What did it mean? Alan was paying to leave the city in the cart? Did he believe the sheriff would act on Asa's word? Or might he truly fear Magda's wrath?

Handing the chest through the hedge, Owen had returned to the cart to retie the cover when he heard footsteps. Ducking down, he heard Gavin Wolcott questioning a servant.

'Where did you see him?'

'Near the hedge.'

'Carrying something?'

'I thought, but might have—'

'My apologies if I alarmed you,' John called out from the direction of the Ferriby garden. 'I was on the ladder trimming the top of the hedge. My shears flew out of my hand.' He waved the old shears. 'Found them.'

Gavin cuffed the servant and stormed back into the house.

Owen silently cursed as the servant began to pace and mutter curses, some to the 'young master', some to the Ferriby gardener. Though he managed to retie the cloth over the cart when the man turned away, Owen dared not leave. He waited for what seemed hours until Ferriby's nephew Luke came strolling into the yard, hailing the serving man by name. Eager to complain to a sympathetic friend, the serving man grumbled away as Luke led him round the side of the house, motioning with a hand behind his back for Owen to take advantage of the distraction. In a flash, Owen was through the hedge, thanking John for fetching Luke.

'That was clever. As was your feint with the shears.'

'I noticed them talking earlier and prayed Luke would agree. He will expect you to await his return, share a bowl of ale with him.'

'Gladly.'

Retrieving the pack and chest, Owen went into the shop. He did not wait long. Luke arrived, chuckling to himself.

'You saved me from a long, long wait, or worse,' said Owen. 'I am grateful.'

'I was glad of the chance to help, Captain. I confess I enjoyed it. I am not fond of Gavin Wolcott. Nor are any of the servants in that house. They are sad the mistress is deserting them. Time for a bowl of ale?'

'I was hoping you would ask.'

Owen settled on a bench, leaning his head against the wall but quickly straightening as he realized how easy it would be to fall asleep right there. Luke busied himself filling two bowls to their brims from a large jug, handing Owen one while already sipping from the other.

After a long, welcome drink, Owen asked whether Luke had heard from his uncle. 'Will he stay at the manor through the summer?'

'No. He plans to move back and forth. He cannot abide being away from the business. Not a country man. I do not think the mistress will be glad of that. She has an idea that somehow folk carry the sickness from place to place even if they do not seem ill.'

'It would explain how it spreads through the land.'

Luke looked doubtful. 'What did you find?'

'Something that does not belong to either the Wolcotts or the person I believe delivered it to them.'

'That will be the man you are hunting, Master Bernard?'

Owen grinned. 'You are a shrewd one.'

Luke put a finger to the side of his nose. 'I'll say naught about it. I have itched to search that cart. I suspect much of the merchandise Gavin Wolcott "moved" in the warehouse was brought to the house. And I'd not be surprised to find others' goods tucked away as well.'

'You think him a thief?'

'If you've ever tried to look into his eyes, well, you can't. Shifting all the while, looking here, looking there, anywhere but facing you. Sam Toller despised him, you know.'

'Did he?'

'With good cause, I think. Even his father distrusted him. He had Sam carry on his trade while he was mourning his children – not Gavin. I say you will find that Sam Toller was pushed into the Ouse for his curiosity.'

'You know this?'

'Cannot prove it, but the man was loyal to Guthlac and wary of Gavin, that he told me over many a tankard of ale.'

'What of Dame Beatrice? Did she trust Sam over Gavin?'

'Could not tell you. Sam admired her, and pitied her. She loved her children.'

'And her husband? Did Sam pity her for being wed to a man so much older than she?'

A wince. 'He never said as much, but something made me think he did. I could not swear to it. Nor whether she was unhappy. I always thought her oddly unfriendly to Dame Emma, the kindest of women.'

Finishing the bowl of ale, Owen thanked Luke for his help, and his information. 'I have much to do before nightfall.'

'I am glad to help. I will miss the "gardener" when Gavin and the mistress are gone.'

Slinging the pack over his shoulder and lifting the chest, Owen took his leave. His stomach growled as he turned back toward the Fuller house. But there was much to do before he turned homeward.

Janet Fuller wept to see the chest. 'My Jack was so proud to be master of a ship.'

'Would you inspect the contents, tell me whether anything is missing? Go inside, where it is comfortable.'

'You should not come into the hall, not with Cilla—'

'I will wait here.'

While he stood without, watching the street, Owen glimpsed a familiar lope and hailed Alfred.

'Any sign of the leech?'

'No, Captain.'

'Are you headed home?'

'I was. But if there's aught I might do for Dame Janet and Cilla . . .'

Hearing how Alfred's voice changed when speaking Cilla's name, Owen wondered whether she was the young woman he had once hoped to wed. 'Stand watch until I find someone to take your place?'

'Gladly, Captain.'

Janet appeared, a smile assuring him that all was as it should be. 'Alfred. Are you to guard Cilla and me tonight?'

'As long as I am needed, Dame Janet. How is Cilla?'

Owen slipped away, turning toward the Cooper house, not too far. Edwin supported Alan. Might he hide him?

With the waning light, he noticed lamps lit in many homes. One burned in the kitchen of the Cooper house. Several men congregated in the cooperage yard, two rolling new barrels to a pile beneath the eaves, two watching, talking in low voices.

'Is Edwin Cooper about?'

'Aye, he is. But what he's about, well, see for yourself.' The man gestured toward the workshop.

The shutters on the window beside the door were opened. On the floor, illuminated by a lamp on a worktable he glimpsed a man's bare backside, hiding some of the naked woman beneath him. Cooper cried out, begging God's forgiveness as the woman beneath him laughed. Owen recognized her as a servant in the household. Much ado here, but nothing to do with Alan Rawcliff.

Nodding his thanks, Owen turned toward Hempe's house. He would ask him to send someone to relieve Alfred's watch, arrange for help with tomorrow morning's plan, and then go home. He needed Lucie's clear-eyed counsel. He would leave the visit to the mayor's home till morning, when he passed it to attend the mass for Jack Fuller. Near the bridge he encountered a pair of friars praying as two men loaded several corpses onto a cart. Victims of the pestilence, from the stench. Covering his nose and mouth with a scarf he, like all folk in the city, wore round his neck right now, Owen hurried along.

It was only when Owen entered his own gate and saw Lucie, Jasper, and Kate sitting by the fire, heard the murmur of their talk, that he felt his stomach unclench. He had turned away Lotta Hempe's offer of food and drink in his haste to make certain all was well at home.

'Have you eaten?' Lucie asked.

He could not recall when or what he'd eaten. Certainly not at Magda's. Nor since then. He vaguely remembered some bread snatched up as he left for the Fuller home in the early morning. 'No.'

While Kate prepared a bowl of stew and cut bread Owen poured himself a mazer of ale and sank down before the fire. Lucie stood behind him, massaging his temples.

'We will talk,' she said, 'but first you must eat and rest awhile.'

He took a long drink. 'He calls himself a healer,' he growled.

Lucie shushed him. 'Eat first. Jasper told me the extent of Asa's injuries. I know, my love, I know.'

He woke with a start, finding himself stretched out on the settle in the kitchen, a blanket covering him, his head in Lucie's lap. She smiled down at him.

'You slept a few hours. I am glad.'

Sitting up, he moved his shoulders, remembering eating and starting to tell her of his day, the heaviness. He did not remember lying down. *I grow old*, he thought. 'And you? I trapped you?' He spoke softly, thinking that Kate must already be abed.

She laughed, her eyes merry. 'Seeing your confusion I am tempted to say yes, but in truth Jasper, Kate, and I took our work into the hall so that we might talk. Now that they've gone to their beds I settled your head on my lap. I have not sat here long.'

He was glad of that. 'Worry kept you wakeful?'

'Asa's suffering. The beatings of healers. That man hiding somewhere. You need not whisper. I convinced Kate to sleep up in Philippa's old room. You were telling me about Gavin Wolcott's plan.'

He rose and stretched, poured a little more ale. Stood leaning over the back of the settle. 'I believe he is running off with his father's, and possibly others', goods. To Graa's property in Galtres? Would anyone think to search there for him? I will be watching for him at Bootham.'

'You believe he has more to hide than Jack Fuller's chest?'

'Luke Ferriby believes so.' He told her what Luke suspected. 'But I wonder whether Fuller's chest had been put there by Alan for his own use. I expect to find Alan hiding in the cart. Or the chest was a payment for his trip out of the city.' But Owen was not satisfied with that. There was more, he was sure of it.

Someone knocked on the kitchen door.

'So late?' Lucie whispered, crossing herself. Of course she would fear the worst.

Owen opened the door to Brother Michaelo. The monk looked worse than Owen felt, agitated, his face drawn, his eyes pleading.

'Forgive my calling so late, but the poor in the minster yard—'

'You would not be here without good cause,' said Owen, standing aside, motioning him in.

'Dom Jehannes wished me to inform you that two of the king's men arrived at St Mary's tonight, asking about a Master Bernard, lately a barber in Lincoln.'

'He is suddenly much sought after,' said Lucie.

'I hope to find him in the morning,' said Owen.

'You know where he is hiding?' Michaelo asked.

'I believe so, though it might involve a chase. But this concern I see on your face – surely it is something else?'

'Anna, the cook. She has fallen ill. We fear it is the Death.'

'Come, join us at the fire,' said Owen.

'Have you what you need to ease her?' Lucie asked.

'She— Her husband asked if you might mix the headache physick for her. It calms her, and she trusts it.' He stood near the fire, but did not sit.

'I am happy to do so.' Lucie rose, staying Michaelo when he would follow. 'I will not be long.'

'Is she showing signs?' Owen asked. 'Boils?'

'Not yet. She is wheezing, fevered, muttering of demons.'

From the door Lucie said, 'That might be many things. Do not despair.' She stepped out.

'If my work among the poor in the yard brought it into the house—' Michaelo's eyes watered.

Such an affection for a woman about whom he often complained.

'I think with shame of Brother Wulfstan, a man I poisoned, who lived only to die among the sick in the last terrible visitation of the pestilence,' said Michaelo. 'He kept himself apart from his fellows so that the abbey suffered few deaths. And I witlessly return every night to Dom Jehannes's home.'

'As do so many others,' said Owen. 'Where else might you go?'

'I might bide among the poor.'

'Have you discussed this with Jehannes?'

'He said I would do no such thing.'

'Let that be an end to the idea.'

Michaelo lowered himself on to a chair, shaking his head at Owen's offer of food or drink. He spoke of Einar, how helpful he was proving. He had assisted Michaelo this evening, with less vigor than usual but still attentive, speaking as they walked of Asa's injuries, Magda's skill, Owen's calming presence.

'Mine?' Owen asked. 'Magda anchors me. And Lucie. Has the pestilence taken any of your poor?'

'Several in the past few days. It has sunk its claws into the city.'

'May God watch over us all.' Owen wondered about Freythorpe. No manor was completely an island unto itself. If the air carried it, why could it not move from farm to farm? Or if folk carried it, villagers might go to market, bring back the sickness, a child working elsewhere bring it home to the family, traveling tinkers, friars . . . If it were in the water . . . His stomach complained. He pushed himself to think of something else. 'How did Jehannes hear of the king's men?'

'He supped with the abbot.'

'Did he meet them?'

'He was introduced as he made his departure. Not the two who escorted us north. King's men, not the prince's. But they met you at court, intend to consult you.'

'I would beg a favor. Would you meet me at Bootham Bar at dawn with two horses? Hempe will be bringing men on foot, but I mean to ride out after Gavin Wolcott and would like your company.'

'Wolcott? Why?'

'I want to see where he is taking a cartload of goods, not all of it his.'

'I am no soldier, Captain, you know that.'

'You proved an excellent tracker when last we rode out into Galtres.'

A small smile, a nod as if to say, *So I did*. 'I am happy to be of service.'

Lucie returned, handing Michaelo a wrapped parcel. 'You said she trusts my physick. Did she try something she thinks she should not have trusted?'

'I would not know.'

'You might ask. Fever would be unusual from a potion, but it is possible.'

'I will.' Michaelo rose. 'I am grateful, Dame Lucie.' He touched Owen's shoulder. 'Dawn at Bootham, two horses.'

When he had departed, Lucie pulled Owen to her, holding him for a long while. He stroked her head, understanding that she, too, had been worrying about the children at Freythorpe.

When she released him she reached for his hand. 'Come to bed?'

'Oh yes.'

On the way she asked about Michaelo's parting comment. Owen explained. They spoke of the king's men, wondering whether Alan was aware of his danger.

'I pray he is not,' said Lucie. 'A cornered animal is all the more vicious.'

Asa had awakened after sunset, thirsty and in pain. Magda made a soothing tisane, adding more milk of poppy. Sleep is what her body needed, and her heart. Rest. Forgetfulness. She sang to her daughter, songs Asa had loved long ago.

Einar returned from his evening work with Brother Michaelo

about to fall asleep on his feet. Magda fed him and put him to bed, then sat with the kitten. In the quiet she gathered her thoughts, how she would proceed for the next few days, testing whether she still felt at ease with her decision to send Einar with the cloth. She could not judge without such a test how strong Sten's blood was in him. If he returned with the cloth, having failed to find the glade, he need not know she had tested the strength of the bloodline over time. If he should succeed, she would present it as a choice he might make. She did not prefer one outcome over the other. He had steady hands, moved quickly but with care when called on while she and Bird-eye had worked today, calm despite Asa's moans and the extent of her injuries. If he wished to learn at her side, she would agree, no matter what happened in the morning, but not at once. He must spend time alone to discover the path to which he was called.

When Holda grew so limp that she almost slid off her lap, Magda settled her in her blanket-lined basket and stepped outside. A few fires burned on the bank, but elsewhere the dark enveloped the city and the river. A heaviness in the air, little breeze, a slight scent of rain. Dry until morning, then a drizzle, no storm. She closed her eyes and let her senses travel far and wide. Within the city walls she felt the pulse of fear and sorrow. A few points of joy, soft, not buoyant. Anger crawled in the shadows, pointing, blaming. In her mind's eye she saw the sisters of St Clement's downriver kneeling, heads bowed in prayer, rising to join their voices in song. She smiled as the dragon slipped into the water, closing her eyes to follow her down into the cool depths.

When at last she returned to her own fire she added a small log, cold after frolicking with the dragon, and covered Einar with a second blanket. Asa waked, murmuring prayers of penance. Magda helped her to more of the poppy juice, smoothing her brow and whispering about Raven, who had announced her coming, ever watching over her. A small smile. For the moment, her daughter found peace. It would not last.

Owen woke before dawn. Lucie must have risen earlier, her side of the bed cold. He dressed and stood on the landing, listening. Two familiar voices, Lucie's and Jasper's. No strangers. No new problems. Returning to the room for his eye patch, he headed down the steps to begin the day.

'You will eat before you set out to track the Wolcotts,' said Lucie.

'I will. As much as you can spare, Kate,' he called as he headed out the door to the midden. The air was thick, dew heavy on flowers and leaves, the sort of morning when one wished to cover mouth and nose against the pestilence-laden miasma. By the time Owen stepped back into the kitchen his hair and his clothing felt damp. The fire welcomed him, and Lucie's kiss. He had just settled by the fire and plucked up a chunk of bread when someone knocked. Kate set a bowl of ale beside him and went to the door.

'Bailiff's man. I'm here for the captain,' said an unfamiliar voice. 'I stood watch in the Ferriby garden through the night, and I think— Captain!'

'Step inside,' Owen said in a quiet voice, glancing out into the yard as the young man stepped in.

'Forgive me. I did not think about who might listen.' Blushing, the young man took off his cap and held it over his heart.

'Your name?' Owen asked.

'Roland, sir. I mean, Captain.'

'Come. Talk to me while I break my fast. Are you hungry?'

Roland's eyes lit up, but he folded into himself. 'I must still report to Bailiff Hempe—'

'You can surely have a bowl of ale and some bread,' said Owen. 'A bit of cheese. Sit.'

Kate handed Roland a bowl of ale.

'I am most grateful.' He perched at the edge of a bench near Owen. 'Mistress Wilton,' he bobbed his head as she settled by Owen.

'Drink a little to wet your throat before you deliver your report,' said Lucie. 'I can hear by your hoarseness that it would be welcome.'

Eager to please, the young man did as he was told, and then launched into a description of something long, heavy, and unwieldy being carried out to the cart before dawn, two serving men struggling with it, Gavin Wolcott holding a lantern and directing them in a hushed voice, glancing about often, as if fearful of discovery.

'A rolled-up featherbed, I think, but so heavy, and heavier in the middle than the edge, the way it sagged. They put their burden down on the ground so they could uncover the cart, moving things about, all as silently as they might. The longer they worked, the more Master Gavin looked about, shushing them for every noise louder than a whisper. When they lifted it to load it into the cart it was tilted for a moment and – I might be making a fool of myself but I swear I saw a foot poking out.' Roland gulped the rest of the ale.

'You think they were moving a body?'

'I do, Captain. A dead one. It never twitched, not in all that while on the ground, and when they almost dropped it.'

'Any stains on the featherbed?'

'Nothing so dark as to make me think of blood, if that is what you mean. But the lamp was not so bright . . .'

'You did well to tell me of this, Roland. Have they left?'

'Might have by now. The men were tying it down and Master Gavin had gone in to fetch Dame Beatrice. My mate John had come to keep me company till daybreak. I left him to watch.'

'Good. Go back, and if they're still there, follow them to the city gate. If they've chosen Bootham, you will see me there. If not Bootham, as soon as you see where they are headed make haste to find me there and tell me all that you noticed. I'll go after them.'

Rising with a chunk of bread still in his hands, Roland nodded to Owen, Lucie, Kate, and hurried out.

'Do you think they have murdered Alan Rawcliff?' Lucie asked.

'I mean to find out.'

TH IRTEEN

Journeys

Armed with his bow, a quiver of arrows, and a dagger, Owen departed just as the city was waking. Carn greeted him at Bootham as he was looking out for Oswald, the young day guard.

'Bailiff Hempe took men through a while ago, five of them yours, three on horseback.'

'Horseback?' Owen was glad to hear it. 'Anyone else leave the city?' The gates should not open before dawn, but Carn was in the habit of opening a little early for those departing the city.

'Not long after your men young Wolcott drove out with his father's widow. On their way to her parents. Taking her as a kindness.' When Owen cursed under his breath for missing them Carn mistook it. 'I agree. Seems soon, Guthlac buried only yesterday. But she was all draped in veils, as was her maidservant, and they clung to each other as if deep in mourning.'

'How long ago?'

'Not long. They won't yet be far into the wood, not with that load. Seems to me a foolhardy undertaking, driving such a heavily laden cart along the track through Galtres. The carthorse seemed restive. Probably the squeaks and the cries of the women. You are expecting trouble, I'm guessing.'

'I mean to be ready if it should arise,' said Owen. 'How many in Wolcott's company?'

'Besides the women and the young master, a manservant guiding the horse.'

'Any other travelers before or after?'

'After them, a carpenter and apprentice with a cart full of timber for a farm near Easingwold. Pulling it, they were. A long journey for them. Not long after two laborers. Said they work a night watch in the city. Rough sorts. Then a clerk from the minster who was called home to his dying mother. Red eyes, almost tripped over his own feet.'

The timber. That would usually be coming into the city, not out. Owen would look out for them. The laborers from Graa's warehouse?

'Did you recognize the grieving clerk as being from the minster?'

'I cannot say as I did, for I thought him a priest, calling him father. He corrected me.'

'And the carpenter. Was he familiar?'

'No, but I do not know all in York.'

'I owe you some of Tom Merchet's ale,' said Owen.

Carn's weary face brightened. 'I will be waiting, Captain.'

'If a young man name of Roland comes looking for me, send him to assist the bailiffs' men on the riverbank by the Riverwoman's rock.'

'My shift is over as soon as Oswald arrives.'

'Tell him to pass on the word.'

'I will. He's a good lad.' He motioned toward something behind Owen. 'Here's Brother Michaelo with two fine horses. For you?'

'*Benedicite*, Carn, Captain,' said Michaelo. 'Am I late?'

'You arrive at the very moment I need you,' said Owen. 'Come. Our prey has escaped the city.'

Carn waved them on through. 'May God watch over your hunt.'

Owen cringed at the too-loud clue as to their intention.

'The poor in the minster yard will be grateful for the meat,' Michaelo called back in a volume matching Carn's. 'Fool of a Scot,' he muttered as he turned back to Owen.

'I thank you for that.'

Outside the gate they moved off to the side so they might adjust the saddles and prepare to mount.

'Fine animals,' Owen noted.

'From the abbey stables,' said Michaelo. 'Dom Jehannes is standing surety that no harm will come to them.'

Perhaps misguided confidence. Owen did not expect the day to go smoothly. 'How is Anna this morning?' he asked.

'She said she slept well and her head no longer pounds. She is grateful for Dame Lucie's physick.'

'Her fever?'

'Still hot, but she thinks it might be easing. We pray Dame Lucie was right, it need not be the Death upon her.' Michaelo mounted.

Owen continued to fuss with the stirrups. 'That is good news.'

Michaelo leaned down toward Owen, lowering his voice. 'Forgive me, but should we not be in haste?'

'And alert anyone watching that we are on a mission?' He watched as Michaelo understood. 'We will take a leisurely pace toward the woods, chatting amiably as we watch for trouble on the riverbank near Dame Magda's house.'

'My mistake.'

Einar led the donkey and cart out of the yard, getting acquainted with the animal. It felt good to stretch his legs and breathe in the scents of the forest, feel the cool air on his skin, even the mist. All night the fire in Magda's home had burned hot, a comfort at first, but later waking him in a sweat. He had taken the blankets

and moved as far from the fire as possible. And though he woke
with icy feet and hands he'd stayed in his corner until Magda
called to him to observe her examination of Asa.

This morning her face and all exposed skin on her right side
were darkened with bruising. But the swelling in her hand had
eased a little, and he helped Magda removed the temporary bandage
so that she might apply an unguent on the bruised and swollen
hand, misshapen by the mutilated fingers.

'When will you set them?'

'Later this day, before thou must leave to assist the crow.'

Einar imagined the agony Asa would suffer in the process.
'Michaelo is more of a phoenix, rising from the ashes,' he said,
hoping to wipe away the image.

'All clerics are crows to Magda.'

'He is different.'

'Thou couldst say that of each one.'

When would he learn that arguing with Magda would circle
back on him?

When the examination was finished, she had sat with Einar as
he ate, explaining how to find the earthen house in the woodland
glade where he was to deliver the cloth. Her directions were like
none he had ever received. He must move at a slow pace once the
track dipped, feeling for the subtle shift in the scent and listening
for the moment when it seemed as if the woods hushed at his
approach, the trees stilled. He was then to turn toward the river
on a path that he might doubt was truly a path leading anywhere.

'Thou wilt understand when thou seest it,' said Magda. 'Leave
the donkey and cart in the clearing beyond where the path bends
round an ancient oak. Shoulder thy load and walk from there. The
house is not far.'

'How will I know it?'

'It is the only one on that path. If thou canst not find the path,
return to Magda and she will take it another day.'

'You doubt me?'

She had smiled and touched his arm. 'It is not thee whom
Magda doubts.'

And that had been that.

Considering Alan's violent temper, Einar had taken up his bow
and a quiver of arrows for the errand.

'Magda warns thee to leave all weapons but a short knife in the cart.' She had not smiled then.

'Why? This family to whom I deliver the cloth would object?'

'Not them. Promise Magda thou wilt leave all weapons in the cart.'

'But someone might steal them – or Nip, now I think of it. A donkey is valuable.'

'No one will steal thy weapons from the cart. Nor Nip. Magda warns thee to follow her directions.'

'I swear I will.'

He'd felt uneasy then, even more so now. Her riddles confused him. But he was determined to succeed.

The woods were quiet so early in the morning. On the way he would walk Nip and the cart, not ride up high where the noise of the wheels might mask his sense of the quieting. He would ride in the cart on the way back. He had been walking for a while when Nip grew restive as two men, bent beneath the weight of their sacks of wood, waddled toward them.

Einar eased the cart to the side of the track to permit the pair to pass. They blessed him in barely discernible mumbles as they slowly went by. Something about them prompted him to stay put until they were out of sight. He was glad he had, for once he resumed he quickly sensed a change in the air, an enveloping quiet. To his left he saw a faint trail, as if the underbrush had grown over what was once a deeply rutted track. Softly encouraging Nip, he guided him on to the path and beyond a great oak. There he found the clearing Magda had mentioned, complete with an old trough in which the water looked clear. Cupping his hand, he tasted it. Fresh water.

'There you are, Nip. Refreshment.' Slipping his weapons into the cart, tucking them away in a corner, he backed up to the rear of the cart and crouched down to lift the pack of cloth to his shoulder. With a promise to return soon, he continued down the track which grew more defined, smiling as he heard the sound of water over rocks and felt the coolness as if near a waterfall. The trees shivered and sighed above him.

In a few moments, Owen mounted and moved off toward Galtres, Michaelo riding on his right, his sighted side. That would allow them to converse, but once they began to track the cart in the woods Owen would order him to his sightless side. He told him what he'd learned from Carn. 'Are you armed?'

'For riding into Galtres? Of course. A dagger. Where is the leech?'

'Carn did not mention him, but I believe he hid beneath the cover on the cart until out of the city. Or was hidden.'

'His payment for hastening Guthlac's death?'

Owen glanced at Michaelo. 'You begin to think like me.'

A raised brow. 'What of the others whom Carn mentioned? Do you expect them to join up with Wolcott?'

'The laborers, yes. But not that cart. I do not believe they mean to pull such a load through Galtres. They're headed to the river-bank. They will find two of my men there. I thought someone might think to distract me a second time.'

'Building what?'

'The question is, what might they burn?'

'God help us.'

'Another two of my men will meet us a short way into the woods, the fifth farther along.'

'The three on horseback.'

'That would make sense.'

While they rode at an easy pace Owen told Michaelo all that he had learned of Alan Rawcliff, Einar, and Asa.

'An unpleasant pair, Gavin and Alan,' Michaelo noted. 'We know the latter will not hesitate to resort to violence. What think you of Gavin?'

'He practices at the butts on Sundays. A fair shot.'

'Not so good as you, I pray.'

'No. But if he has the advantage that might not matter.'

For a while now Owen had kept his good eye – unfortunately causing him to twist to the left – on a cart being pulled with some difficulty across the uneven ground toward the riverbank. From a distance he could hear the racket it made. A good thing, for the pair pulling it seemed unaware of the trail of folk moving in silent fellowship to form a barrier behind them and close them in.

Owen pointed to what was happening.

'You look pleased,' said Michaelo.

'I am glad to see that the minds behind all this are too arrogant to be careful.'

'Arrogant?'

'They do not expect us to see the pattern. No need to try a new strategy, just repeat what they tried before, an attack on Magda's house and the folk she protects. They believe me to be ever-vigilant on her behalf.'

'You are. But you see far more clearly than they do.'

'I thank you for that.'

When almost level with Magda Digby's rock they came upon the grieving clerk Carn had mentioned, sitting on a log by the side of the road as if overcome. Brother Michaelo offered a prayer.

'A dark time for us all,' said Owen.

The man kept his head down as he muttered a *benedicite*.

At the edge of the wood Owen guided his horse behind a tree so that he might watch as the mourner rose and started running toward his fellows in the cart. Seeing he meant to warn them, Owen spurred his horse to chase down the man, leaning over to grab him by the tunic and yank him up across his pommel, which pressed into the man's middle, forcing the breath out of him. He lay quiet while Owen rode back to join Michaelo.

'Does he breathe?' Michaelo asked.

'With difficulty. But he will not ride long.'

Michaelo crossed himself as he guided his horse to Owen's blind side without needing to be reminded.

'What am I looking for?' he asked.

'Tracks of a cart. Anything else that might suggest whether they are alone. If it seems of note to you, tell me.'

Not far from where he'd left Nip and the cart, Einar came upon what looked like a tall hedge of holly. As he stepped through it he experienced an inexplicable sense of coming home. The track became soft beneath his boots with a cushion of old leaves fallen from great oaks and willows. He spied two boys filling buckets at a stream.

The elder stood up sharp when he noticed Einar and demanded to know who he was.

'I am Einar. My kinswoman Magda Digby asked me to bring this cloth to your house. Is it far?'

'The cloth!' The younger grinned from ear to ear. 'We're all to have new tunics. I'll lead you. It's not far.'

Attempting to run, the lad made the water slosh so wildly in the bucket that Einar offered to carry it, but the lad laughed and slowed down. The hedge and the ancient trees within encircled a glade green with grass and moss, a carpet that heaved up in the middle to create an earthen house. In front of the open doorway sat a man whittling.

'Dame Magda sent me,' he called out. 'I am Einar, her kinsman, and I come bearing cloth.'

'Welcome! My wife will be pleased. But you were not followed?'

Einar laughed at that. 'Only if they received Dame Magda's instructions, and believed them.'

The man nodded his head. 'I am Fergus.' He shifted the leg that stuck out straight at an odd angle for comfort. When Einar realized that he could not rise without the walking stick leaning behind him, he offered to carry the cloth inside.

A woman appeared at the door, older than the man, sweet of face but with frightened eyes. 'Who is this, Fergus?'

Explaining, with Einar's help, Fergus convinced her – Lettice, he called her – that Einar was a friend to them, and Magda's kinsman.

'May God watch over you,' she said at last. 'And may he bless you and Dame Magda for your kindness.'

She held out her arms for the cloth, which Einar still balanced on his shoulder.

'It's heavy. Where shall I set it down?' he asked.

She'd begun to argue with him when a younger woman appeared in the doorway carrying an infant.

'Do stand aside and permit the young man to place that heavy load on the table,' she said with a smile in her voice.

Lettice obliged. Inside the doorway Einar paused, amazed by the space. A girl laughed at his expression.

'It's magic!' she said as Einar set the pack on the table.

'Now you know that Dame Magda does not like that talk of magic,' said the woman holding the infant. As she spoke, the thin cry of another infant rose up from somewhere in the depths of the remarkable house. 'She is jealous that I am carrying her twin sister. I must go to her. Bless you.' She smiled at Einar. 'I pray you give our thanks to Dame Magda. Will she be here later today?'

'If you need her, I will make certain that she has word,' he said. 'I will sit with her daughter while she is out.'

'I would be grateful,' said the woman. 'I pray you tell her that Helen's milk is slow.' She blushed to say it.

'I will, Dame Helen,' said Einar.

The woman thanked him and withdrew into another room. How large is this house? Einar wondered.

'Sit with her daughter?' Lettice said. 'What is wrong with Dame Asa?'

'She was beaten by the leech A— Bernard.'

'God help us,' she whispered. 'Is it bad in the city?'

'With the sickness folk are fearful. Priests have spoken out against the midwives and other women healers. Dame Asa and others have been attacked.'

'May God have mercy on us all. Has Mistress Wilton closed her apothecary?'

'No. And the bailiffs have men on watch to prevent more attacks.'

'We are most fortunate to be here,' said Fergus, leaning on his walking stick in the doorway, one arm round the young girl.

Einar apologized for speaking of trouble in front of the child.

'No need,' said Fergus. 'She understands that the world is not always friendly, do you not, Tess?'

The girl nodded, but Einar saw the fear in her eyes. He knelt to her. 'You are safe here, little one. Without Dame Magda's instructions I would never have found you. Never.'

'Why is she kind to us?' Tess asked.

'She is kind to all.'

He was rewarded with a little smile, which warmed him.

Not far into the woods Owen paused to listen, then softly made the sound of an owl. Alfred and Stephen emerged from behind a great tree, leading horses.

Michaelo sighed with relief.

'Who is this slung across your lap?' Stephen asked.

'Meant trouble to Dame Magda,' said Owen. 'Truss him up, gag him, and leave him where you waited. We can fetch him on our return.'

The man found breath enough to cry out as Stephen yanked him down off Owen's horse. But he was quickly gagged and bound and left to enjoy the soft rain that had begun to fall. The tree would protect him from most of the moisture.

The four continued on until they encountered a pair of woodsmen bowed beneath loads of kindling. When asked they mentioned passing several carts heading north, but only one with women.

'Two of them, one crying so pitifully,' one of the men said. 'Grieving for her husband, so said the man escorting her.'

They had passed them a while back. Since then only a man and his son with a farm cart, and a young man with a donkey cart. The latter had a bow and quiver of arrows, like Owen.

Vigilant for men laboring under such heavy burdens. Owen nodded to Stephen, who moved to block their way. Alfred dismounted, handing Owen his reins. As one of the men scuttled to the side Owen caught him and shoved him to the ground. His partner tried to shrug off his load and run, but Stephen used his horse to pin the man against a tree. Alfred's cursory search of the packs revealed bows, arrows, and torches. Within moments the pair were trussed, gagged, and tucked away, their loads sorted for items best not to leave near them.

'We'll need a cart for all the miscreants,' Michaelo muttered.

'The nights are mild. We might let them sleep beneath the stars.' Owen handed Alfred his reins and moved on.

Michaelo hurried to join him on his blind side. 'Am I still to be watching for signs of a cart?'

'Yes.'

They rode in silence, Stephen and Alfred riding single file behind.

'Why would Gavin Wolcott risk so much and involve so many merely to steal the goods that would have come to him by right?'

'If folk guessed that the children born to Beatrice were his, not his father's, including the one she now carries, he would lose his good standing in the city. The deaths of the two little ones in the autumn would be seen as God's judgement.'

'Yet they clearly learned nothing.'

'A desperate couple with everything to lose, so they flee. But they cannot get far.'

'Because you saw through the ruse.'

'Too late to save Guthlac.'

'You cannot save the world. But was the old man so blind he could not see what was between his son and his wife? And why did Bernard – Alan – assist him?'

All good questions, for though Owen had theories he had as yet no answers.

Within moments of Einar's departure Asa had begun to weep and beg Magda's forgiveness.

Her voice but a whisper, her words poorly formed because of swollen lips and jaw, she clutched at Magda's neck with her uninjured hand, pulling her close so that she might hear. 'I am to blame for Bernard. I poisoned him against you. Forgive me.'

'Hush now. Lie still while Magda changes thy bandages.'

Asa had refused anything that might calm her so that she would have a clear head, though she now willingly drank down a cup of broth laced with herbs to dull the pain.

'I thought to twist him to my purpose,' she said. 'Told him I taught myself the spells and charms you kept from me. Said the power was in our blood.' One eye was swollen shut, but the other watched Magda for a reaction.

'Spells and charms in thy blood?' Shaking her head, Magda cut the bandage on the ruined hand, softly whispering words of comfort as she peeled away the cloth sticky with healing and soothing pastes.

'You are whispering a charm now.'

'To calm thee. It will work if thou dost find comfort in it. It is nothing without the rest. If Magda relied on charms thou wouldst die from thine injuries.'

Less swollen, the hand no longer hid the extent of the damage. Magda breathed deep and returned to the charm, calming herself as well as her daughter.

Twig, playing with the kitten near the window that looked out to the riverbank where he lived, cried out in dismay.

'What is it?'

'A fight on the bank. They pulled two men to the ground, one of them carrying a lit torch. Someone took it from him and doused it in the river. I think they meant to start a fire. Now our folk are searching the cart, holding up torches and wood for a fire. But there's something else and someone just pulled their shirt up over their mouth and nose.'

Magda had joined him at the window. She watched a man in the cart struggling to rise. Those searching the cart backed away.

'Pestilence,' she whispered. The two had brought not just fire
but also the manqualm to the folk on the riverbank. With a hand
on Twig's shoulder she spoke of it, told him that she would go
to the man as soon as she had finished changing Asa's bandages.
She thought to send the boy to his mother, but he was safer on
the rock.

'Thy dam will be worried, but Magda needs thee here. Thou
canst go to her when Einar returns. He will not be long.'

Twig stood tall. 'I will come for help if Dame Asa needs you.'

Patting the lad's shoulder, Magda returned to her now sleeping
daughter. She worked quietly, quickly, wishing to tend to the man
brought in the cart before someone took him into their home.

As Magda opened the bandage around the shattered forearm
Asa stirred, whimpering in pain. Lifting a cup to her lips, Magda
urged her to drink.

After a long draught she lay back with a wince. 'Everything
hurts. But the arm is the worst,' Asa said. 'I heard the boy. Go to
them, Mother, the people who watch over you. See to them.'

Magda heard the whisper of wings, a faint caw, then a knock
on the door. One of the older boys from the bank, breathless,
shivering a little for his soaking from walking across from the
bank.

'A man in a cart, Dame Magda. Sick. Some of the women
thought to carry him to the bonfire in our midst. Others argue he
will bring the Death. We gave him water.'

'A kindness if he is burning with fever.'

'He is.'

'Go!' Asa called hoarsely.

Gathering her things, Magda went with the lad, rowing across.

On the riverbank folk opened a path for Magda to the man lying
in the cart. She smelled him long before she saw his flushed and
sweaty face. 'Stay back,' she barked to the crowd. 'Bring water.
And a bowl thou canst spare. It must later be burned, with all that
touches him.' She saw the regret on faces as they eyed the cart.
Peering at what else was in there, she saw what they coveted – the
wood brought for burning would shore up a flimsy shack. Why
bring such good timber? 'Where are the two who brought this
cart?'

A man and a lad of perhaps sixteen years were dragged through the crowd before she could warn folk to stay clear of them. They showed the beating they'd received, but neither of them were flushed with sickness. Yet. She recognized the older one from Gavin Wolcott's lodgings before he moved back into his father's house. But the lad was unfamiliar.

'Where didst thou find this sufferer?' she asked them.

'In hell, witch!' the boy slurred through swollen lips.

The man kicked him, bobbed his head to Magda. 'Plucked him from the minster yard.'

She guessed that the cart and timber were also from there. 'The firewood? Torches? Didst thy master provide them?'

The man bowed his head and said naught.

'Boy? Thou hast plenty wind to curse Magda. Dost thou work for Wolcott as well?'

'Burn, witch!' the boy shouted.

Magda raised a hand to stop the one about to clout him. 'Let him be. He will sicken soon enough.'

That hushed the boy, who glanced fearfully at the cart.

But Magda was busy now that she'd been offered a wooden bowl for the medicine she would mix for the sick man. Taking a stump from the cart, she placed it so that she could use it as a table on which to mix the herbs with some wine.

'Canst thou sit up enough to drink?' she asked the sick man.

Nodding, he managed to pull himself up against a pile of torches. From her basket she took a cloth bag and a small jug. Pouring some of the wine into the bowl, she emptied the contents of the bag into it and stirred, all the while talking to the man, learning his name, assuring him that he would be more comfortable after drinking the potion. When at last she handed him the bowl he lifted it to his lips with trembling hands.

'A little sip, then wait a moment, then another. Do that until thou hast finished it.'

But he drank greedily, swooning before he'd emptied the bowl. She retrieved it and helped him settle. Touching him gave her the information she needed. The stench came from his groin. Pulling a jar and a clean rag from her basket, Magda hummed as she smoothed a rosemary scented paste onto the rag, offering it to the man. 'Tuck that where you feel the stickiness. It will soothe thee.'

The man, moving more slowly now, did as instructed, then lay quite still. He would die in the night, but in more comfort. Climbing onto the cart, she began to arrange wood and planks to cover the man. Someone joined her, a man she recognized as having recovered from the sickness years ago. Nodding to him, she stepped aside and let him complete the project.

Passing through a quiet place in the wood Owen felt himself relax. It did not last. From far ahead he heard a shout, another. Two distinct voices, one startled, one angry. And then a woman's scream. Owen nudged his horse into a canter he could safely handle as the woods closed in round them. Michaelo fell behind, and soon it was Alfred who rode beside him. He heard nothing now, and thought he might slow to listen. But he soon caught a fresh cry, nearer and more sustained, not the woman this time but a man, outraged. Sudden silence. Owen steadied his horse, then moved forward at a steady pace, close now. Very close. A rattling, squeaking noise. A cart moving fast. Too fast for Galtres. The track narrowed ahead and could at times be treacherous with old roots exposed. Owen held up a hand to signal he was slowing, listening to the cart, fainter now, watching for signs of where it had paused for whatever had occurred.

There it was, tracks of a cart, underbrush flattened. He moved on, even more slowly now. After a time he called a halt, listening. 'What was the last you heard the cart?' he asked.

'A while ago,' said Michaelo. 'A rattling and groaning that bespoke a rough patch of track.'

Stephen agreed.

'Ride as quietly as you can now,' said Owen. 'Ears pricked. They might be off the track. We do not want to miss them.'

'Captain,' Michaelo called softly, pointing toward the trees on Owen's blind side.

From the woods a large man limped out from the trees, holding the reins of a horse with his one hand. Crispin. Owen lifted his arm to call a halt. Crispin had offered to ride out before dawn and wait, meaning to follow if the cart came through. As he had an official interest in the woods, if seen he had a plausible reason to be there. Closer now, Owen saw a man slumped on Crispin's horse.

'Who?' he asked.

'John. One of yours, I believe,' said Crispin. 'Wriggled his way out of Wolcott's cart, trussed, and could do nothing to break his fall. He's addled, but I believe he was taken while watching the Wolcott house.'

Alfred dismounted and approached, lifting the man's chin. 'Yes, this is John. He relieved Roland this morning.'

'He's a good man. His quick thinking was a big help to me yesterday. His escape from the cart went unnoticed?' Owen asked.

'Wolcott had dismounted and was arguing with the three men walking ahead. One was supposed to be leading the horse but kept wandering up to talk to his mates. Wolcott said they were slowing him down and he ordered the two to follow behind.'

'Are they now?'

'Yes, and having a time trying to walk fast enough. But John grew restive and I worried we would give ourselves away. I don't think they are far ahead. The two women have been very quiet.'

'Do you want to head back to the city with John?' Owen asked.

'No. I want to see this. I'll follow behind.' He looked up at the horse. 'I could use help mounting.'

Alfred came to his aid.

Owen ordered Stephen to go first, keep a steady pace, quick enough, but not so quick they gave themselves away. He held his breath now as he listened for sounds of a cart. And there it was. Stephen lifted a hand, nodded. Michaelo whispered a prayer. Owen strung his bow.

FO URTEEN

C onsequences

A customer stepped aside with a cry as a man rushed into the apothecary.

'You must come! It's the widow Wolcott!' Breathing hard, the intruder leaned on the shop counter, gulping air. On his sleeves, bloodstains.

Luke, Emma Ferriby's nephew. Lucie wiped her hands and drew

him aside. 'You said the widow Wolcott. But Dame Beatrice departed the city this morning.'

He shook his head. 'No. Someone else.'

Jasper came out of the workroom. 'I can watch the shop.'

Lucie motioned Luke to follow her out to the garden, depositing him on a bench. 'Sit.'

'No time. She is bleeding.'

But Lucie was already on her way to the kitchen, where she told Kate they were going out. 'I think I will need your assistance.'

'Mine?'

'Jasper must tend the shop. Come.' Lucie picked up the basket of supplies she kept by the door and hurried out.

The rumble and squeak grew louder, and the sound of boots striking the road in a brisk march. Close now. Alfred guided his horse to one side of the track.

'Weapons?' Owen asked Crispin.

'If those two had bows I would have seen them. Knives and brawn, if we're lucky, an axe if we're not.'

Nodding, Owen whispered to his mount to calm it as they eased past Alfred. Ahead, the trees thinned, revealing the men hurrying to keep up with the laden cart. Three people were clearly visible on the seat, two veiled women and Gavin Wolcott. Owen notched an arrow and aimed at Wolcott's shoulder, but before he let it fly a woman turned round and called out a warning. Wolcott raised his bow, an arrow notched, but had to rise and turn round to shoot.

In that pause Owen hit Gavin's shoulder, the impact toppling him forward onto the horse, who skittered. The men in the rear began to charge Owen and his men, but halted at a woman's scream.

'The cart! Gavin has fallen beneath the cart!'

Alfred and Stephen surged past Owen to take the men.

'Captain, down!' Michaelo shouted behind Owen.

As he pressed himself to the horse's neck something rushed past. Looking behind him he saw an axe lodge in a tree.

'The man who was leading the cart,' said Michaelo. 'He has a knife now.'

Straightening with his arrow ready, Owen aimed at the arm

holding the knife, then the man's thigh. As the man fell he was pushed away by Gavin, who was crawling out from beneath the covered cart. One of the women clambered down to help him while her companion stumbled down off the cart and hobbled away.

'I'll stop her,' Michaelo called out.

Owen, arrow notched and ready, walked his horse toward the woman leaning over Gavin. Rearing up, she bared her teeth at him. No veil covered her head now. Gemma Toller, her face and the front of her gown bloody. In her hand she held a substantial knife, and the way she wielded it, the discipline with which she raised her arm – she knew how to throw it. There was nothing for it but to immobilize her. As the arrow struck her upper arm her eyes widened in disbelief and she slipped down onto Gavin. That should keep him down for a moment.

Dismounting, Owen moved to the cart, untying a corner of the cover as Crispin rode up to him, John riding pillion.

'The roll of bedding is on the other side,' said John.

As Owen stepped over Gemma she reared up, grabbing for him.

Crispin raised his walking stick and struck her in the head. 'I never did trust her.'

Stephen and Alfred dragged their two men toward the cart, both bound hand and foot, dumping them on the track and then dragging Gemma and Gavin out of the way. Michaelo followed them, leading a woman who stumbled along on a tether to his saddle. Not Dame Beatrice, but one of her maidservants.

'Where is your mistress?' Owen asked.

'I do not know,' she sobbed. 'He told me to dress that woman in my mistress's gown. He said we must protect my mistress, that she was accused of murdering the old master, so this woman was pretending to be her.'

'Can anyone tell me where Beatrice Wolcott is?' Owen growled.

One of the men who had followed the cart was sitting up now. 'That whore? I tossed her in a shed where she'll rot as she deserves.'

'How dare you!' the maidservant cried. 'My mistress is no whore.'

'No? She slept with his son to bear Wolcott brats. What would *you* call her?'

Stephen silenced him with a kick to his chin.

Gemma Toller struggled up to fall upon Gavin, pounding on him with her fists. 'What have you done with her? What have you done?'

Crispin used his stick to push her off the man. 'You might have asked after her earlier,' he said.

'I did. Gavin— He said Beatrice was leaving in a separate cart by Micklegate Bar. We will be hanged for this,' Gemma whimpered.

'Likely,' said Crispin.

Owen shushed him, told Stephen and Alfred to tie up the prisoners, motioned to Michaelo to help him search for the man rolled in bedding. The monk dismounted, tying the reins to the cart.

The roll was where John had said. As he pulled it toward him Owen could feel that it did indeed contain a body, one that twitched, then jerked as he handled it. Once on the ground he cut the cords holding it together and opened it. Inside, Alan Rawcliff lay unconscious, bruised and battered, his shirt stiff with dried blood.

In a garden shed she lay, clammy with a fever, her heartbeat fluttery, her feet and hands cold. A gentle rain was falling, seeping through the ruined roof of the shed and dripping on Beatrice Wolcott. But that was not what soaked her skirts. She cradled in her arms a slip of flesh, bloody, still connected by the cord.

'Blessed Mary and all the saints,' Kate sobbed.

Lucie whispered a prayer for the dead child, then, bending to the woman's ear, said, 'Beatrice, can you hear me?'

The eyelids flickered. Her lips moved, but no sound emerged. The bottom lip was split as if she had been hit, her cheek and chin bruised.

Kate drew Beatrice's upper body onto her lap and Lucie knelt to her, filling a small bowl with wine, dribbling a little in the woman's mouth.

Beatrice coughed, gasped, then licked her lip. 'More,' she whispered.

Warning her to just sip, Lucie dribbled more as she told Beatrice who they were and that they had come to help.

'Too late,' she whispered, turning her head to the side, closing her eyes.

'Beatrice? I need you to wake.' Lucie tapped her cheek. 'You must wake.' But the woman was still. Yet her heart beat, and she breathed, shallowly. Where there was breath there was life.

It took more work turning round the cart than it had redistributing the contents to make room for bound and injured passengers. But a widening of the track farther on helped. Soon the solemn party turned back toward the city, John and the maidservant on the seat of the cart, Stephen riding beside the carthorse.

'Was this the plan all along?' Michaelo asked Owen. 'Gemma and Gavin?'

'If so, I fear we will not find Beatrice Wolcott alive.'

Michaelo bowed his head and began to pray.

Alert to noises or furtive movement in the woods to either side as he rode, Owen could not understand Einar's sudden appearance. One moment there was no one to either side of the track ahead, the next he was halting the company to make way for Einar, who was leading Magda's donkey cart out from – where? Owen saw no path. Was he truly so depleted by the fight with Wolcott and his party that the young man and donkey cart could be upon them before he noticed? And from where?

'Delivering the cloth?' Owen asked.

'Yes.' Einar stared at their overflowing cart. 'So many injured. An accident? Do you need help?'

'I could use the cart,' said Owen. 'We're taking these folk to the castle jail. But the leech I must deliver to the king's men at St Mary's Abbey.'

'Alan? They know about him?' Einar sounded disappointed. Perhaps realizing in that moment his missed opportunity. He might have delivered up the man to the prince.

'Help us deliver him,' said Owen. 'I know Magda would not deny me the use of her cart that far, and for the leech who battered her daughter.'

Einar nodded. 'Gladly. I will accompany you and return the cart afterward.'

With Alfred's assistance, Owen transferred the still unconscious Alan Rawcliff to Magda's cart.

'His lips are cracked,' said Einar. 'I have water.'

As Owen lifted Alan's head, Einar helped him drink. But though he swallowed, he did not open his eyes.

'Did you drug him?' Owen asked Gemma Toller.

'I don't know. I did not know he was with us.'

Gavin Wolcott did not stir.

The maidservant wriggled in her bonds. 'If I help you, will you let me go free?'

'I can promise nothing,' said Owen, 'but I will tell the sheriff you willingly helped us.'

She hesitated. 'You will do that?'

'I promise.'

'They gave him something to drink in his wine. From the jar of physick for the old master,' she said in a rush, as if racing against second thoughts. 'Then when he was stumbling about howling that he was betrayed those two men hit and kicked him until I thought he must be dead.' She indicated the two who had followed the cart.

'Did Gemma Toller witness this?' Owen asked.

'I told you—' Gemma began.

'No. She came this morning.'

'Is the physick still in the house?' Owen asked.

The maidservant shook her head. 'Packed in the cart. If you loose my hands I will find it for you.'

He freed her hands. Out of a trunk she lifted several men's shirts, a few cushions, two decorated mazers, finally drawing out a pouch that she handed to him. Within was a small covered pot tied closed. He opened it and sniffed – too many scents for his limited knowledge, but he was confident that either Brother Henry, the abbey's infirmarian, or Lucie would be able to identify the contents. Entrusting the Wolcott cart and the captors to Crispin Poole, Owen led the serving maid to Einar's cart, helping her into the back with Alan.

'Call out to us if he wakes,' he said. He meant to take her to the Wolcott house to see to Beatrice, if she yet lived.

With Einar seated on the cart, Owen rode to the front of the group and led them out of Galtres.

After praying over the stillborn, Lucie wrapped him in rags that Luke had brought from the Ferriby home and handed Luke the bundle to bury in the garden. Malformed and premature, the child would not have lived even if a midwife had been present. It was Beatrice who might have benefited from proper care, and Lucie cursed Gavin for his cruelty to his father's widow. Beatrice still did not wake, and grew colder despite the fire they had stoked in the Wolcott kitchen where she now lay.

A pounding on the door. 'Where is the thief? I will have his head!' a man shouted. 'Come out, you coward, and face me.'

Lucie rushed to silence the intruder and discovered the mayor, Thomas Graa, his round face purple with rage. He took a step back when she appeared. 'Mistress Wilton?'

'If it is Gavin Wolcott you seek, he is gone,' she said, 'leaving his father's widow to suffer alone in a filthy shed.'

That quieted the man. 'Dame Beatrice? What has happened?'

'I do not know. Luke Ferriby came searching for—' she paused, realizing the mayor had no idea Owen had been watching the Wolcott house, 'his gardener. He discovered Dame Beatrice in a faint in the shed and came for me.'

Trying to peer past Lucie into the room, Graa said, 'Gavin has gone mad. We must hunt him down.'

'My husband took men to track him.'

'The captain? Excellent. Best thing we have done, offering Archer the captaincy.'

'My concern is Dame Beatrice.'

'Ah. Of course. I will send a cart to fetch her, bring her to the sisters at St Mary's in Castlegate.'

'That is kind of you,' said Lucie. 'But I thought to take her to my home, where I might see to her.'

'Of course. Yes. That is good of you. I will send a cart to carry her to your home.' He turned away, muttering to himself. 'That monster. Fled with our goods. Damn him. I thought him such a find young man. How I could be so wrong . . .' He paused, turning back to ask, 'And Bernard the leech?'

'I know nothing of him since he beat the healer attending Jack Fuller,' said Lucie. 'I pray my husband discovers him with Gavin Wolcott. Now I must return to Dame Beatrice.'

'My servants will come with the cart to assist you.' Graa hurried off.

*   *   *

As Owen led his men and captives out from the cover of the trees he discovered a crowd on the riverbank. He did not see the cart from the morning. Glancing back, he called Michaelo forward, asked him to find out if their men needed help.

'I will go,' Einar offered. 'I would see whether Dame Magda needs me.'

'And if she does need you?' asked Owen. He looked to Michaelo. 'I want the others to press on to the castle. *You* will accompany me to the abbey.'

'Of course,' said Michaelo.

Einar insisted on accompanying the monk to the riverbank.

'But you've no horse,' Owen pointed out.

With a laugh, the young man began to run, graceful and fast. If Magda was a dragon, her great-grandson was a wolf, thought Owen. Michaelo rode after him.

'Ah, youth. Such grace. And speed.' Crispin and the others had pulled up beside Owen. 'We will await their return, should you have need of us.'

Owen glanced at Gemma Toller, quietly weeping. He noticed that the talkative one had a fresh gash on his forehead and lay with eyes closed, jaw slack.

'Gave you trouble?'

Stephen grinned. 'You might say that.'

'Michaelo's returning,' said Alfred.

Seeing the monk's solemn expression, Owen rode to meet him.

'The two in the cart brought a man dying of the pestilence to toss among the folk on the riverbank, unholy monsters,' said Michaelo. 'One of the ones I've attended in the minster yard. Magda has eased the poor man's last hours. I offered to send for the friars.'

Owen nodded. 'No trouble now?'

'Your men hauled off the two and others who arrived to set fire to the settlement and Magda's house. They await you at the castle.'

'Einar?'

'He waded out to Magda's rock, suddenly worried about Asa, who has been alone but for the boy Twig. He asks that we return the cart to the bank, and Magda's lads will see to it.'

Curious. He had seemed keen to accompany them. But it was

no time for questions. 'Do you know how to guide a donkey cart?'
Owen asked the maidservant.

'I do, Captain.' She clambered up to the seat and took up the
reins.

Waving Crispin and the others on, Owen fell in behind them,
Brother Michaelo beside him, the cart following.

Brother Henry, the infirmarian, sniffed the contents of the jar.
'Milk of poppy and – I am not certain. Allow me to take some
to study.' He tipped a spoonful into a cup. 'But Dame Lucie might
better answer you.' He nodded toward Alan Rawcliff, who lay on
a pallet in a corner of St Mary's infirmary guarded by one of the
king's men. 'Whatever it is, he will recover. At present he plays
cat and mouse with the king's man. He opened his eyes quite
wide for a moment, fixing them on his guard. When he realized
he was no longer a free man, he shut them tight. Rest easy. You
have brought an evil man to justice. I will see that he is in sufficient health to survive the journey to Westminster and answer for
his crimes.'

Owen retrieved the jar. 'It is for Gavin's trial I would know the
contents. He used it on his father. Guthlac did not survive it.'

'Poor man,' said Henry. 'The king's man shared with me the
Bishop of Lincoln's report. Several mysterious deaths linked to
our guest. A most dangerous fraud, not only for practicing without
sufficient knowledge but for causing so many to shun the skilled
midwives in our city.'

Owen thanked Henry and took his leave. Brother Michaelo
waited outside the infirmary, peering in for a moment before
following Owen out. He had been refused entry, Brother Henry
remembering only too well the time Michaelo had poisoned his
teacher, the gentle Brother Wulfstan.

'Do you miss the abbey?' Owen asked.

'As I would a thorn in my boot.'

Michaelo maintained a stony silence while Owen recounted his
conversation with Brother Henry. It was only when Owen grew
quiet that the monk cleared his throat.

'Einar was slippery about where he had been with that cart,' he
noted.

'You asked him?'

'I did. He appeared out of nowhere – did you notice?'

So it was not a matter of Owen being distracted. 'What did he say?'

'The donkey was lagging, so he moved off the track and found water for him. When I began to ask more questions he hurried away.' The monk was quiet a moment. 'One of Dame Magda's riddles made flesh.'

Owen remembered Magda and the dragon becoming one. 'He is her kinsman.'

'Much more so than Asa, it would seem.'

They had left the maidservant in the screened passage of the abbot's house, watched by a novice. They found her curled up on a bench, asleep.

While awaiting the mayor's cart, Lucie searched the house for the medicines she had sent with Owen the other day and clean clothes for Beatrice. She found the medicines untouched, but the only items of clothing left behind were a threadbare gown and an old wool cloak on a hook in the kitchen. They must do for now. With Kate's help she removed surcoat, underdress, and shift, washing Beatrice as best she could with the little water left in the bottom of a jug, then dressed her in the too-large gown, wrapping the cloak round her for warmth. Kate tucked heated stones wrapped in a torn blanket inside the cloak. She added the strengthening tonic to a cup of rainwater.

'Why would he take her clothing?' Kate wondered aloud.

'None of this makes sense to me,' said Lucie. The silence of the house had given her chills. It felt as if it were watching, waiting. She was glad to hear a cart rattle into the yard. Even better, it was Owen's voice calling out to her.

Luke entered first. 'Look who I found.'

Owen was right behind him. 'Is she alive?'

Lucie was glad to see him. 'Barely. If Luke had not found her when he did . . .'

A woman rushed past him, kneeling beside Beatrice.

'Mistress! I was so worried.'

'Her maidservant,' Owen explained.

Lucie drew her away. 'You can be of most help by telling me how long she has been so ill. Was this pregnancy more difficult than the others?'

The woman shook her head. 'The baby was not a problem. We were to say nothing of it. She tried to hide it, and I do not think she ate enough for two, but she had no sickness. What happened?'

'She lost the child.'

The woman sobbed, 'No!' and tried to wrench away from Lucie, who shook her.

'Go outside and calm yourself. We are taking care of her.' Lucie let go and nodded to Luke, who led the woman into the yard.

'Luke told us how he came to you,' said Owen. 'The mayor's cart waits outside. He says you are bringing her home?'

'I can see to her there.'

'She may be part of the plot.'

She saw the concern in his eye, knew that he foresaw the pain of giving Beatrice up to the law. 'I know, my love. But no matter her part in the deception she was abandoned and came close to death. She can be questioned when she is strong enough. I trust that you will ensure the sheriff knows of her ordeal.'

FIFTEEN

Revelations

It seemed a sign of grace when Captain Archer offered Einar the chance to help deliver Alan into the hands of the king's men. But while he stood on the riverbank he had caught a movement on Magda's roof, the dragon moving its head as if beckoning him across the water.

Brother Michaelo was asking him about his sudden appearance on the forest track.

Einar answered vaguely as he stared at the dragon. Once again it beckoned to him. 'I must see to Asa,' he said.

'But the wagon,' said Michaelo, 'the abbey.'

Einar waved him off. 'I trust you and the captain.'

He waded into the river, muttering a curse as he discovered the current strong with the tide. As the water deepened he began to swim, all the while arguing with himself. It was mad to think a dragon masthead could move, could beckon him. But he'd seen it do so. As he pulled himself onto the rock he heard in his head, *On the far side. The boy cannot hold her much longer.* He scrambled to his feet, pausing to shake off some of the water. *Hurry!* the voice – a female voice – said in his head. Glancing up as he passed the dragon, he swore she nodded. And then he heard the boy.

'Dame Asa, you must not do this.'

The fear and weakness in Twig's voice cut to his heart. Einar sprinted to them, dropping to his knees and taking hold of Asa's shoulders. How had she the strength to pull so?

'You can let go now, Twig, I have her. Bless you.' Einar leaned down to whisper in Asa's ear, 'Forgive me. Forgive me for not telling you all I knew about Bernard.' He felt her hesitate and used the moment to pull her away from the water, falling onto his back with her above him. She blinked, bringing her eyes away from whatever had been calling her.

'Forgive?' she whispered.

He eased her to one side and rose, bending to lift her in his arms. He carried her into the house, nodding to the dragon as he passed. She nodded in response.

Twig stoked the fire and heated water. He helped Einar settle Asa on the bed. The bandage on her hand was soaked, of course, but with blood as well as river water.

Einar set about fixing a calming draught for her and told the lad to pour himself a bowl of ale.

'Mother will not like to smell it on my breath.'

'Tell her I insisted you drink it for warmth and calm after you saved a woman's life and almost fell into the water yourself,' said Einar. He smiled as the lad drank. 'You are a hero this day, Twig. All will hear of this. You have rewarded Dame Magda's trust in you a hundredfold.'

'I'm no hero. I was afraid.'

'That's part of being a hero. You followed your heart, not your head. Your heart told you that her life was worth saving, fear be damned.'

The lad beamed. Einar patted his back. 'Now. I must change her bandages and I will need your help. Are you sufficiently recovered?'

A flash of alarm as the boy glanced at the bloody bandage, but he straightened, puffing out his chest. 'I am.'

Asa's moans pierced Einar's heart, and as he worked his remorse over his betrayal of her consumed him. Only when the mangled hand was freshly wrapped did he notice Twig's distress.

'Too much blood?' he asked softly.

The lad shook his head. 'I'm not brave. I saw something and never told anyone because I should not have been where I was. And a man died.'

Magda stepped away as the friars lifted the dying man into their cart. They would take him to a building at the friary where they tended those dying of the pestilence, including their own. Time at last to return to Asa in this quiet moment before the Death revealed itself among the folk on the river. They had been touched. Weakened by poverty, many would succumb. Too many.

'Dame Magda,' Twig's mother called to her as she pushed through the onlookers, the lad stumbling to keep up as she pulled him along behind her. 'My son has a confession to make.'

At last. Magda had been aware for a long while that the lad held something inside. She guided them toward the riverbank, and the coracle. Another with much on her mind waited there. Lettice Brown.

'I watched Einar's encounter with Captain Archer and his men,' said Lettice. 'They had Gavin Wolcott, Bernard the leech, Gemma Toller, and the men from the warehouse. They can no longer harm me. I am ready to tell the captain all that I know.'

Gemma Toller among them. Magda nodded to herself. She looked to Twig. 'Dost thy confession pertain to the Wolcotts and the Tollers?'

The boy mumbled a yes.

'He saw the men grab Sam Toller and toss him into the flood,' said Twig's mother.

'Go together to the captain,' said Magda. 'It is time he heard all.'

Returning from the castle late in the afternoon, Owen stopped in the apothecary to see how Jasper was coping. No line of customers in the lane, a few in the shop. Jasper glanced up as he spoke loudly to an elderly man who cupped his ear to hear his instructions and gestured toward the workroom.

Owen found Lucie there, crushing roots in a mortar.

'Back at work so soon? What of Beatrice?'

'Edith, the midwife, is with her.'

'How did she become involved?'

'I sent Luke Ferriby with more of the unguent and a message that I might need her advice about Beatrice. She returned with him. With her arm still immobile she cannot deliver babies, but she wants to help and suggested she sit with Beatrice. They are up in the guest room.'

'This is for Beatrice?'

'A purgative.' Brushing her hands on her apron, Lucie drew him to the bench near the garden door, well away from the shop. 'Jasper and I tested the contents of the jar the maidservant gave you. We found rue and feverfew, which Edith agreed would cause the excessive bleeding and cramping. But there is something far more dangerous I did not mention to her – hemlock.'

'So they *were* poisoning Guthlac.'

'And then Beatrice, yes. I had put her soiled clothing in a sack and brought it here in case we might salvage any of it. She had worn a sleeveless surcoat over her gown, and beneath it was a stain smelling strongly of the mixture in the jar. I will not call it a physick, it is such a jumble, as if Alan added anything that might cause harm.'

'Bless you.' It was just the proof Owen needed to hang Gavin if Alan Rawcliff and Beatrice Wolcott pointed the finger at him. Would they cooperate? He stood up, rubbing his face. 'I pray you get some rest.'

'And you. We thought we would shut early. None of us have eaten since early morning.'

Owen stepped out to see whether Jasper needed help. He was talking quietly to Twig and a woman who must be his mother, nudging the lad forward, kindly but firmly. Behind them stood the missing Lettice Brown. All three were out of breath.

'Lettice!' Lucie rushed to her, taking her hands. 'God be praised.'

'Dame Magda took care of me, body and soul,' said Lettice. 'And now, knowing what Captain Archer did today, I feel I can speak out without endangering my family. But first I pray you allow this young man to speak. His heart is heavy.'

'It will be best if we go to the house,' said Lucie, guiding them through the workshop and across the garden.

Kate looked up with surprise. 'More for late dinner?'

'We will not be long,' said Twig's mother. She drew her son down onto a bench by the fire. 'He's a good lad, my Twig. Saved a woman's life today. But he's confessed something you need to hear, Captain Archer. Said nothing before because he was where I had forbidden him to go, you understand. But it's been gnawing at him.'

'Well?' Owen asked. 'You know you can trust me, Twig.'

The lad nodded, but Owen could feel the fear rolling off him.

'You are brave to come forward. And I am grateful for anything you can tell me that will help bring the murderers to justice.'

'We sneak into the city some nights when the tide is out. We find things stuck in the mud. But we all know we shouldn't be there. Folk drown.'

A *tsk* from his mother.

'Go on,' said Owen, crouching so they were eye to eye.

'I saw a man hit on the head and tossed into a boat. The men rowed him upriver for a while and then threw him overboard, rowed back.'

'When was this?'

'The night that man went missing, the one fetched up on the bank, the one Dame Magda found.'

'Where was he when they came upon him?'

'Under Ouse Bridge. We watched it all, me and my mates. Swore to each other we'd say nothing.'

'Would you know the two men if you saw them?'

Twig shook his head. 'It was too dark. But they were big.'

'Thank you, Twig. This is important. But that's not all, is it? Your mother says you saved a woman's life today?'

'Dame Asa. She meant to go in the river. I held her till Einar came.'

'That was brave of you. When you're grown, if you need work, come to me. I can always use a man of honor and courage. Till then, no more walking the mud flats at night, eh?'

'I swear.'

Owen rose, looking to Lettice.

'I would speak with you alone,' she said.

'What would you say to speaking with me and Bailiff Hempe? Gemma Toller is in his custody. I would like her to hear what you have to say as well.'

Her face drained of color. 'I pray you, not the castle jail.'

'I would not ask that of you. She is at Hempe's home, being tended by Dame Lotta.'

A small smile. 'I will go. Yes.'

While Lettice had told them all she had confided in Magda and spoke of her fear for her children and their families, Gemma Toller silently wept.

'I know this is painful to hear, and harder still to admit having a hand in it,' Owen said to Gemma, 'but I would know how you thought to escape punishment.' He looked to Hempe, who had questioned Gavin and the others at the castle. 'Do we know that Gavin gave the order for Sam's death?'

'He confessed to that after the two men spoke at length of their orders, how they had followed Sam to Magda's and back home that night.' Hempe looked at Gemma. 'Do you see the full extent of your lover's vile plan?'

'How will you live with this?' Lettice murmured, as if to herself.

Gemma stared down at her hands. 'I saw only his love for me, dreamed of how it would be when we were together. I believed Beatrice and Sam had betrayed me, that her two children were Sam's. Now— God help me, I remember how Gavin seeded my suspicion. He would begin to say something, then shake his head as if he had forgotten and look on me with sad eyes. Soon I was begging him to hide nothing, tell me the worst.'

'And did he?' Lotta Hempe asked. 'Did he accuse them outright?'

'Yes.' Gemma's voice shook as she faced her own willful destruction.

Lotta looked to Owen and her husband. 'Might it be true?'

'We hope to wring a full confession from him,' said Hempe. 'And the leech may know much.'

'Or Dame Beatrice, when she can speak,' said Owen.

Lotta asked Lettice if she needed a place to stay. Thanking her,

Lettice said that for now she had a home, and people who needed her.

Magda rowed back to the rock with a heaviness and sat for a long while beneath the dragon, thinking of what Twig had witnessed. Until the dragon touched her arm, urging her to attend her daughter.

Asa lay on the pallet with eyes closed, her breathing ragged. Einar held her uninjured hand. Magda mixed a soothing tisane for herself, and sat down by the fire, sipping and waiting for her thoughts to calm. Holda climbed onto her lap, turning and turning until she settled in a graceful curl, her purr cloaking Magda in stillness. She reached down with her thoughts, sensing the solidity of the rock beneath her home.

Einar spoke into the silence. 'We almost lost her.' His voice was as ragged as Asa's breath. 'Twig held on to the end of his strength. Did he tell you?'

'He did.' Magda watched Einar stroke Asa's curling gray hair, evincing a tenderness absent until now. Plucking Asa from death might have reminded him she was as vulnerable as anyone else. Or something had shifted for him in the glade.

'My fault,' he said. 'I might have warned her of the leech's treachery, but I saw no benefit for myself.'

While he spoke Asa's breathing changed.

'Art thou certain she did not know who he was?'

'It must be so.'

Setting the kitten in her basket, Magda gathered cushions. 'If thou wilt assist.'

As he lifted her upper body so that Magda might place the cushions beneath her, Asa opened her eyes.

'Better?' Magda asked.

'Easier to breathe,' said Asa.

Magda rested a hand on her daughter's chest, feeling the waves of anger, resentment, confusion, despair. 'To speak the truth oft brings ease of heart. Is he right, Asa? Were you unaware that the leech was Alan Rawcliff, servant to the prince's poisoner?'

A tear appeared. Another. Asa's lips trembled. Magda held a cup of soothing tisane to her mouth. She drank a little.

'She might need—' Einar began as he rose.

But Magda hushed him and motioned for him to sit.

Asa turned her head, looking to Einar. 'In Lincoln, one of the king's men came to me with an injury. As I attended him I asked about the man he sought. By then I knew enough, guessed more. All seemed to fit him. When we arrived in York and Bernard – Alan – sent me away,' a deep, shuddering breath, 'I went to the sheriff. Told him all, and to write to the bishop of Lincoln if he doubted me.'

For a moment, Einar said nothing, looking round the room as if searching for an explanation, then back at Asa. 'I cannot believe—' He reached out as if to hit her but caught himself, withdrawing his hands. 'You knew all that time?' He kept his voice soft, but his eyes accused her.

Asa whispered a yes.

'Is it thanks to thee that the king's men are here now?' Magda asked.

'Sir William called the guards to remove me. I was nothing to him. Why should he believe me? I meant to return with the knives. The king's man had drawn the French traitor's mark for me and there it was, on Alan's knives. On yours as well, Einar.'

'You searched my things?'

Asa was quiet a moment. 'I am glad they have come. Now he will face his doom.'

'You are consumed by resentment,' said Einar.

'And you by greed.'

'I have changed.'

'Have you?' Asa's words were cut short by a moan.

'Unlike you I can learn,' Einar said.

'So you strut now. Cock of the walk? But you are the one who might have warned me when you first came to Lincoln. You might have warned the bishop, the sheriff.'

'You have no right— Even if you were my mother. Another lie. You do nothing but lie.'

'We traveled as mother and son. Have you forgotten?'

'But you thought to fool Dame Magda?'

Asa turned her head away, and in her silence Magda sensed that Einar had filled a void for her daughter.

'You are all lies.'

'No son of mine would so betray me,' Asa whispered.

'Betray *you*?'

'Silence!' Magda commanded. 'Bickering like two selfish pups fighting over a bone.' She took the cup of tisane to her worktable, adding milk of poppy to the mix. Rest and an easing of the pain were all she could do for Asa at present. When the pain receded she would look beneath the bandage to assess the harm her daughter had done herself. She did not look forward to what she likely must do.

As they prepared for bed, Owen told Lucie the version of the story Gavin chose to tell.

'He claims Guthlac urged the leech to attend her, fearing she was unwell. Denied any knowledge of what procedure Alan might have performed or what medicines he administered. Claimed he did not know Beatrice was with child until Gemma told him of the blood in the bed. Sam's children, all of them, he swears, and poor Gemma, so betrayed, had pushed her husband into the Ouse in a moment of anger.'

'He denied that Gemma was his mistress?'

'No. He says she was so distraught about her husband's affair with Beatrice. He'd gone to comfort and quiet her and fell in love.'

'But quite ready to accuse her of murder. How bittersweet.'

'The two men caught with him swear he hired them to follow and kill Sam. Gavin tried to wriggle out of that, but failed.'

'What now?'

'Find out what Beatrice and Alan have to say. Do you think she will talk?'

'I pray she does.'

While Asa slept, Magda listened to Einar's account of his day, in his hesitations and long pauses witnessing his confusion, his doubt, but also a hunger to understand.

'Was it a test?' he asked.

She placed one of her hands on his and held his gaze for several heartbeats.

'What are you doing?'

'Tasting thine experience of the glade.'

'You can do that?'

'Art thou not able to feel another's heartbeat with a touch?'

'Yes, but . . .'

'Much the same.'

He shook his head. 'You made it clear I might not find the glade. Why is that?'

'It is protected from all but a few. Those abiding there would not have found it without Magda.'

'A spell?'

'Some would call it that.'

'Your spell?'

'No. Magda found it so.'

'Are they able to leave?'

'Lettice Brown left, did she not?'

'Can she return?'

'If accompanied by one of us. Magda will escort her in the morning.'

'I would be happy to do so.'

'A kind offer from the penitent. But soon thou shouldst take thy leave of this place.'

Her words saddened him, as she had known they would.

'I hoped to stay here and learn by your side.'

'Thou art not yet ready.'

'I found the glade. You said others would not. Not without you.'

'That is true. Thou hast proved thy blood. Yet that is but a small part. Hast thou the will? The heart? Thou must seek the answer. Discover thy heart's yearning. Watch thyself. Learn where thou art called, and for what.'

'A quest?'

She smiled. He was young, his head stuffed with tales, ballads of noble deeds, quests of honor. 'Of a kind.'

'Is that how you came to healing?'

'By following the heart's inclination. Magda was younger than thou art now when she left her village and walked north, into the forests, though the moors were all she knew. But she could not resist the call. Long she walked, moving deeper and deeper into the trees.'

'Alone?'

'Yes. One day her scent was caught by a bear clan.'

'How far north did you walk?'

'How far, or into when? The years remain a mystery to Magda. She heard them coming for her and scrambled up a tree.'

'But bears—'

Magda nodded. 'She learned. They climbed up now and then to see where she was, but stopped far short of her perch. Each time she climbed higher. They seemed content to wait beneath while she grew weaker and weaker. She had climbed as high as she dared, until the limbs swayed in warning that they could not hold her long. The next time one climbed up to her, snuffling and grunting, his scent stronger and stronger, she could do nothing but close her eyes and cling to a branch murmuring spells of protection, honoring the trees, asking for their help. At long last the limb shook with the weight of another and she looked at her attacker. She would face him down. But on the limb, so close she could hear his heart beating slow and steady despite such a climb, was a man. He reached out a hand and assured her she had nothing to fear.'

'A shape-shifter?'

'Or did a frightened girl expect a bear?'

'You don't know?'

'Does it matter?'

'I want to understand.'

'Would it make thee kinder? Wiser? Life is a mystery, Einar, a thing of wonder. Honor it, and it will treat thee well.'

He was quiet, and she sensed him thinking back to the glade, moving through it, tasting it, feeling it. The blood was strong in him.

'Was that Sten, my father's mother's father?' he finally asked.

'Yrsa's father, yes. And Odo's, her twin brother.'

'I never heard of Odo. What happened after Sten found you?'

'His people took Magda in. They followed old ways, so much forgotten on the moors, their healing skills beyond anything Magda had ever thought could be. She stayed and learned, at first from Sten, later from the women of the village. In time they quarreled. He did not like what they were teaching Magda, how she was changing, choosing to work for the good of others, not herself. One day he left, taking Odo with him. Magda stayed a while, but Yrsa begged to go in search of her twin and her father. The women encouraged Magda to take Yrsa away, to bring all that they had taught Magda to her people on the moors. There Yrsa might forget her loss when she met her kin. So Magda went. But nothing ever truly consoled Yrsa. She wed young and moved away.'

'Meeting Sten's people and staying to learn from them, that is what your heart chose.'

'And then to use what they taught as a healer.'

'I should go north. To the forests.'

'If that is where thy heart takes thee.'

'Coming here was not enough?'

'Remember what called thee here. Thou hoped to seize Alan Rawcliff and earn the prince's gratitude.'

Einar took a deep breath. 'Greed brought me here.' He rose. 'I need air.'

Magda waited, drowsing by the fire.

'What of Asa?' he asked when he returned.

'Each person follows their own path, for good or ill. Crossing Asa's path brought thee here. But thou must find thine own.'

'I will go to Old Shep's,' he said.

She said nothing, letting him go away to take in all she had said. It was good.

SIXTEEN

A Desperate Yearning

Owen woke before dawn, alone in the bed. Shrugging on his clothes he stepped out onto the landing. Lamplight spilled from the room in which Beatrice slept. He heard Lucie's voice, another, a mere whisper, responding. He moved closer.

A murmured exchange, then the rustle of movement and Lucie appeared in the doorway, her hair tumbling about her, a shawl over her shift. 'Beatrice is awake and wishes to speak with you.'

Glancing in, he saw her sitting up against cushions holding a cup to her lips. Had Lucie slept?

'She is willing to tell me all she knows?'

Lucie stepped outside, telling Beatrice she would be right back. 'Yes. She called it shriving. For her soul.' Her eyes were shadowed, and he saw traces of tears.

'Her story moved you,' said Owen.

'She has told me little. It is Michaelo's sad news. Goodwife Anna died in the night.'

Owen crossed himself. 'It was the pestilence?'

'Yes. I am angry with myself for giving him false hope.'

'He wished to believe.'

'I mentioned that you might have need of him. She has agreed to have both of you present. Shall I ask him to come up?'

'Michaelo is here?'

'In the kitchen. Kate is coaxing him to eat something. Go prepare yourself. Then bring him up?'

Michaelo sat bolt upright in front of the kitchen fire. He stared at nothing, a cup of ale forgotten in his hands. He had not even bothered to shave his tonsure or his face this morning. 'Such a strong woman.'

Owen remembered the strong hands with which Anna had kneaded the back of an injured man, giving him comfort. 'She was. But the sickness respects no one.'

'No.'

Heading out for the midden, Owen found himself praying for his children, tears in his eyes. That was the one thing his ruined left eye could still do – produce tears. Back in the kitchen, while he ate a piece of bread with cheese and washed it down with ale Michaelo spoke of Anna's suffering, the long night, her death in the early hours. He saw that the monk had brought his writing materials.

'Are you certain you are ready for work?'

'I need to be of use.'

Carrying a pitcher and several bowls, Owen led him up to the solar. Beatrice greeted them with a *benedicite*. Owen noticed Lucie's late aunt's paternoster in the woman's lap.

'I do not deserve all that you and Dame Lucie have done for me,' Beatrice said. 'I have sinned against God and caused so much pain.'

Owen took the seat near the foot of the bed. 'I am glad to see you so recovered.'

Michaelo stationed himself beneath the window.

Lucie placed a table in front of him, then returned to her own seat across the pallet. 'You wished to unburden yourself to my husband,' she said.

Knowing she must still be weak, Owen considered what would be most useful to hear. 'Could you begin with the plans for yesterday morning?'

'I was to leave the city by Micklegate Bar with my maidservant and a manservant, going to my family home. Gavin would send for me when he was settled in Leeds under a new name.'

Interesting detail. 'Why did that not happen?' Owen asked.

She shook her head, her face so pale Owen thought she might faint. Lucie bent to her, asking what she needed.

'To begin afresh with dear Guthlac. To have the chance to refuse his gift of children.'

'His gift of children?' Owen asked. 'I don't understand.'

Her fingers sought the beads in her lap. 'My husband knew he could not give me children. He offered an alternative, to lie with his son.'

Owen glanced at Lucie and knew by the subtle shift away from the woman that she shared his surprise about Guthlac's part in the triangle. But that was a priest's concern, not his.

'I saw that he meant it as a kindness, and – God help me, I took it as such.' Her voice broke. 'How I came to think it a little thing, confessed and washed away afterward— I knew it was wicked. I knew we would pay dearly. But for it to be our babies, my Geoff and Mary, my sweet ones . . . How they burned with the fever. As if to burn out the sin in which they were conceived.' She sobbed. 'They died in my arms.'

Lucie took her hands. 'You should rest.'

'No. I must tell you now. I fear I won't find the courage again. I've never confessed my sin because I could not promise not to sin again. I knew that I would. I missed my babies. I prayed for another. And I loved him.'

Owen gave her a moment before asking, 'What was Bernard's part in all this? Where was he to have been yesterday?'

Her face had flushed with the confession, and now the color rose sharply. 'When Gavin brought him to the house— From that moment I feared for myself and my husband. Gavin assured me that Bernard understood my husband's condition far better than the Riverwoman. He made much of that in front of the leech. But in truth Gavin and my husband had forbidden Dame Magda in our home long before Bernard came. They feared she knew of our deception, that the children could not be Guthlac's, that their deaths of the pestilence were our punishment for our grievous sin.'

'You know little of Dame Magda if you believed that.' Lucie's voice was quiet, not accusing.

'But what was Bernard's part in this?' Owen asked.

'For his services he was to receive a goodly sum. I do not know how much.'

'He, too, would go to Leeds?'

'No. Gavin assured me that he would be no part of our new life. I realized he did not trust Bernard, and the man knew it. He confronted Gavin. They had a row the night before the funeral. Loud. Ugly. Gavin said he sent him away.'

'Did you see him leave?' Owen asked.

'No. But Gavin told me he did.'

'We found the leech rolled up in a rug in the cart, drugged with the physick he had used on your husband.'

'Gavin did that? No. Is the leech—'

'He is recovering, and will answer for his crimes.'

Clutching the beads, she crossed herself. 'God forgive us.'

'What of Gavin's relationship with Gemma Toller?' Lucie asked. 'Did you know about her?'

'Not until that night, the night before our departure. Gavin gave me brandywine to calm me. The pains were coming. He said it was grief and worry. But all would be well. I should rest before the journey. I remember the pains worsening, but then I slept. When I woke in the early morning, before light, the pain was much, much worse. I called for help. *She* came. Sam's widow. She wore one of my gowns and I thought it must be a dream. She shook me and told me to dress, it was time to depart. She tore the bedclothes away. When she saw the blood she ran from the room. Two men pulled me out of the bed and carried me out to the garden. I thought they meant to bundle me in the cart but they put me in the shed. I could not— Did Gavin never mean to wed me? Did our children mean nothing to him? Why was Sam's widow there?'

Owen had heard Gemma's side. That she had always been the one meant for Gavin. But how to tell this woman the truth? He could not, not now.

'I am grateful for all you have told me, Dame Beatrice. It will

help me when talking to Gavin and Bernard.' Owen glanced at
Michaelo, who nodded that he was ready. 'Rest now. When I feel
I know the truth of the matter, we will speak again.'

Lucie handed Beatrice the bowl, urging her to drink deep.

The cruelty of Beatrice's treatment slowed Owen's steps as he
turned toward the castle. When he snapped at a child racing past
he judged himself too angry to confront Gavin Wolcott just yet.
Instead he turned toward St Mary's Abbey. The king's men would
prevent him from murdering Alan, but he might frighten him into
confessing his part.

'The infirmary?' Michaelo looked doubtful.

'Surely Brother Henry will permit you to perform your duty
for me,' said Owen.

With a shrug, the monk followed him to the abbey.

The infirmarian's bleary eyes told a tale of a difficult patient.

'Alan wakes?' Owen asked.

'Yes, God help us. When he understood where he was and why,
I have never heard such language, spewing curses in ear-piercing
shrieks as he fought against his restraints and accused us of sending
him to his death. I quieted him with a soporific, but not so much
that he cannot respond.'

'Has he been questioned?'

'By one of the king's men, yes. He loudly denies assisting
Monsieur Ricard. Says he has never heard the name, nor will he
admit to being Alan Rawcliff. He answers only to "Master
Bernard".'

'The king's men believe him?'

'No. They are eager to speak with you.'

'I know little more than I did last night. Except that his physick
poisoned the womb of Beatrice Wolcott, killing the child she
carried and bringing the mother perilously close to death. Albeit
her condition was worsened by her abandonment to suffer the
miscarriage alone in a cold, dark, filthy shack.'

'He did that?'

'Not the abandonment. That is another's crime. He is still in
the infirmary?'

'Sadly, yes. Abbot William refused my request to move him
where he might be isolated and spare my other patients.'

Owen glanced round, saw three monastic patients, two of them elderly. 'Poor men.'

'I provided them with waxed cloths to place in their ears to dull the sound, and a sleeping tonic last night.'

'You are a kind man.'

The monk's usual gentle smile made a brief appearance. 'I am called to heal, not to torment. But enough of my woes. You will wish to speak with Alan.'

'I want a written record of his confession. Will you permit my secretary to attend me?'

The gentle eyes hardened. 'You do not mean Brother Michaelo?'

'I do.' Owen held his gaze, gently, but firmly.

After a moment's hesitation, Henry bowed. 'For you and His Grace,' he said.

Michaelo slipped quietly behind Owen, becoming his shadow as Henry showed them to a screened corner away from the windows looking onto the gardens. Standing before the narrow break in the screens was a muscular man in royal livery. He bobbed his head to Owen and Michaelo, standing aside to allow them through.

The bruises on Alan's face remained, but the swelling had eased and his cold eyes were trained on Owen.

'Come to gloat with an audience, Archer?'

'No. To talk. My secretary will record what you say.'

'You waste your time.'

'I see. You think your argument so weak that you would not consider an exchange of information that might ease your punishment?'

'Prince Edward show mercy?' The man's rasping laughter dissolved into a coughing fit.

A novice hurried through the opening with a cup. 'Honeyed water,' he said to Owen, who nodded his approval.

The young man knelt beside Alan's pallet, assisting him in drinking for his hands were bound beside him. Owen took the opportunity to position a stool where he might see Alan's face, then waited. When at last Alan turned away, the novice rose, bobbing his head to Owen and slipping out.

'Gavin Wolcott blames all on you.' A lie for which Owen would do penance. But if it revealed the culprits . . .

'Greedy whoreson. What information do you need to hang him?'

'Tell me all that you know of Wolcott's plans. Exactly what he hired you to do.'

'His father was dying. Poisoned by the witch. He needed a leech, that is all.'

'You cannot hide behind your lies. His Grace Prince Edward has sent men throughout the realm searching for you as part of the traitor Monsieur Ricard's household. Your flight was your first mistake. Now he has reports from Bishop Bokyngham of Lincoln regarding your crimes in his city. Poisoning Guthlac Wolcott, his widow, and his unborn child are merely additions to the case against you.'

'I poisoned no one.'

'Then tell me what Gavin Wolcott hired you to do. And what you know of his plans.'

Lucie glanced back over her shoulder, touched Jasper's arm. 'Will you finish Dame Felice's requests?' she asked. 'I am needed in the workroom.'

With a smile to melt the iciest of hearts, Jasper suggested an addition to the elderly woman's remedies for aching joints.

Slipping away, Lucie joined Owen in the back. 'What is it?'

'I need a moment of your calm so that I don't march to the castle and murder Wolcott.'

'Shall we walk in the garden?'

'Alan tells a darker tale than Gavin,' Owen began. 'He says he started with bleeding, as Gavin wished his father to weaken just enough not to interfere.'

'Is that not what Gavin told you yesterday?'

'Ah, but when Beatrice told Gavin she was with child he wanted Guthlac hastened to his death before folk in the city noticed her condition. Alan claimed that he balked, but Gavin offered him considerable wealth in property. He then mixed a physick and gave instructions for a minimal dose. Nothing lethal. He says that it was Gavin who began to double and triple the dosage.'

'Nothing that Alan Rawcliff can prove,' said Lucie. 'But his duty was to refuse to continue treating Guthlac.'

'He seems to feel he did what he could. Yet when I persisted he admitted some concern about how often he replenished the physick.'

'Do not grace the concoction with that word. Poison is what it was. And he failed in his duty. So he learned the art of poison from his master?'

'It seems Gavin Wolcott provided most of the ingredients.'

'Which is why you found nothing in his things,' said Lucie. 'And Beatrice? Did he echo Gavin's story about her?'

'Alan Rawcliff swears the children had all been Gavin's and that he used Beatrice until she had signed over all her property, then meant to kill her. But Alan had nobly refused to provide more of the physick.'

Lucie took Owen's hands. 'Magda would tell you to look through your third eye. You can sense where the truth lies.'

'But when I am so angry . . .'

'That is why we talk it through, my love.'

He pulled her into his arms whispering into her hair, 'How was I ever so blessed?'

She held him close, listening to his heart. Strong. Steady. 'I have all faith in you.' Stepping away, she kissed his cheek and nodded. 'They disgust you.'

'Gavin cruelly used Beatrice, as did his father. I am certain of that. Alan saw an opportunity for sufficient wealth to create a new life. Gemma coldly left Beatrice in that condition. And Beatrice . . .' Owen stopped. Lucie saw the pity in his eye. 'I cannot see why she would permit Alan to continue to attend her husband when suddenly a healthy man was so weak. She is not completely innocent of her husband's death.'

'Once stepping onto the dark path . . .' She pressed Owen's hands to her heart and kissed his forehead. 'I will bring you some brandywine to warm you while we talk more. Sit here, or pace the garden paths. I will return.'

Sir William Perciehay, sheriff of Yorkshire, wished Owen and the king's men to ride out to the manor on which he was hiding from the pestilence. As it was they who were extending him the courtesy of the report they felt no obligation, declining his invitation and instead sending a messenger with a letter summarizing Owen's assessment of the case against Gavin Wolcott, Gemma Toller, Alan Rawcliff, and the various servants and warehousemen, including the supposed archer, a former warehouseman Gavin had met on

Graa's property in Galtres, whom Hempe and his men were chasing down. He made special mention of the conflagration caused by Gavin's firing of both the warehouse and the Browns' home, such a blaze in a city being a particular danger. Brother Michaelo's fine work.

Owen and the king's men met instead in the mayor's chamber on Ouse Bridge to hear Owen's assessment. He did not wish to say it all twice.

Graa listened with growing unease. 'A viper in our midst,' he hissed once, then busied himself brushing imaginary crumbs from his lap, swirling the wine in his mazer, anything but meet Owen's gaze.

Ignoring his discomfort, Owen completed his account without pause, after which he answered a few lackluster questions. As Graa cleared his throat and began to rise, Owen addressed him, suggesting he extend a public apology to Magda Digby and the other female healers for failing to come to their defense.

'A public apology?' The mayor's voice crackled with indignation. 'I had nothing to do with this. It is the archbishop who should do penance,' Graa said, 'surely not the civil authority.'

'The archbishop does not maintain the peace in the city,' said Owen. He looked to the king's men. 'And it would seem that your failure to apprehend Alan Rawcliff when he was in Lincoln was a part of this business.'

Minor knights, the two looked to the mayor for his support. But Thomas Graa was nodding.

'Indeed, it was not you who apprehended him, but the captain of York. For that, I and my fellows on the council should be commended on our wise decision to elevate Owen Archer to the position,' said Graa.

'We knew nothing of Rawcliff's presence in York until the sheriff wrote to Bishop Bokyngham,' said the king's man Sir John. 'And then your archdeacon. It was the bishop's negligence while Rawcliff troubled his city that brought this on York.'

Graa looked down his nose at them, muttering what was clearly an insult. Owen had stopped listening to the chattering jays.

Saying he had completed his duty in the matter, all but arranging the escort for Dame Beatrice when she was moved to the infirmary at St Clement's on the morrow, Owen gave a curt bow and departed.

*   *   *

Eyes closed, Magda was one with her dragon, diving into the rich brown water, welcoming the flow against her skin, her hair riding the currents, replenishing body, heart, and mind. Her daughter's hand was lost, too damaged to repair, too painful and potentially poisonous to leave as it was. With a grieving heart she had removed it, with Einar's steady assistance. Cauterized and bound, the rest of the arm would now heal. While Magda tended it she must cope with her daughter's furious grief. But Asa would live. A gift? Perhaps not. And so Magda sought release, racing through the waters, spinning, leaping, diving, one with her dragon.

'Dame Magda?'

A jarring return to the bench, once more an old woman wrapped in layers of wool, hair bound. She had known Einar would be wakeful, but could not resist the swim.

'I will leave in the morning,' he said. 'Unless you feel you need me—'

'Thou art better off without Asa.'

He planned to stay in the city with Janet Fuller, assisting her and Brother Michaelo in seeing to the victims of the sickness. In the autumn he would leave on his quest. He had asked whether Magda would accept him as a student were he to be drawn back to her.

'Magda and thee will talk more before thou dost depart.'

'But will you?'

'Magda has not rejected thee. Only advised thee to be certain.'

'How old was Yrsa when you returned to your people?'

'Five turns of the seasons.'

'Then I may be away a long while. Will you—'

'Be here? Alive? If not, thou wilt find another teacher. Perhaps thou wilt find them in another place.'

'I cannot imagine.'

She smiled at that. 'Thou art attempting to control rather than accept what comes. Be at peace. Thou hast a good heart. Thy way will be true.'

He bowed to her. 'I don't expect to sleep, and both of you need your rest. I will spend the night at Old Shep's and leave from there.'

'Take the bag Magda packed for thee.' Powders and unguents

for the sickness. She touched his cheek. 'Courage. Trust thine own heart.'

When he left, she joined once more with the dragon, diving down into the silken depths, warmed by the fire within.

It was a hideous vision of Alan with burning eyes melting his face, bat wings protruding from his back, thick thorny vines spilling from his mouth and hands, crawling with spiders and rats. In Asa's characteristic way the vines crept insidiously over the page entwining animals and people, crushing or strangling them. Owen crumpled the paper in his hand. He had thought to show it to Magda. But it would be enough for him to describe it.

'Asa drew that?' Lucie asked, her voice sharp with horror.

'Alan Rawcliff's soul, I think. She'd kept it in her scrip. I imagine she had meant to show him.'

'That and the poppet. She was taunting him.'

'I will burn it.'

'Yes, do. But not in the house. The brush pile in the garden. I will ring it with angelica.'

The smoke rose, curling into the soft summer sky. A sudden draft caught it, pulling it away.

'God's grace is upon us,' Lucie whispered.

'Amen,' said Owen.

Clasping hands, they prayed a Hail Mary, *ora pro nobis peccatoribus* . . .

'She never understood the purpose of her drawings,' said Owen.

'And now it is too late? She will lose all use of her hand?'

'She has lost the hand itself, I think.' He had dreamed it in the night, a terrible price.

He stayed in the garden to work on the trench, working up a healthy, healing sweat, letting his mind go quiet, this simple task his most ambitious goal for the morning. The early June sun was warm overhead when a familiar voice called to him.

Peter Ferriby stood beneath the linden. Leaned against it, wiping his forehead.

Tossing his spade aside, Owen went to him. 'Are you ill?'

'Old, that is what I am. A long ride, then the walk here, and my legs are ready to give out in protest. But I wanted to bring news.'

Owen was drawing him to the bench beneath the linden when Lucie hurried out from the workshop, her lovely face set in a determined smile. '*Benedicite*, Peter. I pray your family are well?'

'Yes. They all love the country. Yours as well. I have brought news of all three.'

'Come. Sit with us,' said Owen. 'I will fetch some ale. But first – our children are well, you say?'

'God help me. These old bones,' said Peter as he lowered himself to the bench with a wince. 'Well? Bless me, yes. More than that, thriving. Gwen and Hugh are daring adventurers. You will have your hands full with that pair. A jester and a fine hawker, your son. She enjoys the hawks as well, and is a fine rider. Both my boys have declared their undying love for Gwen and spend their visits vying for her attention. Emma tumbles about all the day with your steward's children, a riotous brood.'

Lucie took Owen's hand, pressed it. 'That is good news.' Her voice husky with emotion. 'I am grateful. Dine with us?'

'Gladly. My nephew's told me of his exploits in your service. I take it the burning of the bedding was the least of the happenings next door.'

'Oh, indeed,' said Owen. 'It is quite the tale.'

AUTHOR'S NOTE

For many years Joyce Gibb, a friend with a keen eye for character and continuity, worked closely with me as I wrote the first drafts of my books. She died after a long stretch of declining health on Christmas Eve 2019. A few months earlier I told her that the next Owen Archer would be the book she requested time and again, a Magda tale, one in which the Riverwoman played a central role, one in which I would delve more deeply into her past, her origins. I regret that I waited so long that she read only a very early draft of the first chapter. I dedicate this book to her.

In the first months of 2020, as the world became aware of a new, dangerous, highly contagious virus, I panicked. I had set the book in the midst of a recurrence of the bubonic plague. Now I would have the discomfort of writing about a frightening pandemic in the midst of one. My first instinct was to change the setting. But the atmosphere played to my purpose, a time of raw fear that stirred superstitions and fears of hellfire, a perfect backdrop for the people's ambivalence about Magda Digby, a woman who seemed a mythical being, not a Christian, a woman they sometimes feared yet relied on for her skills as a healer and midwife. So I stayed the course. As it turns out, the writing gave me an outlet for my own anxieties, and being in Magda Digby's head and heart provided comfort in an unsettling year.

Who is Magda Digby? She has been a part of this series from the beginning, first manifesting in a brief scene in a graveyard in *The Apothecary Rose*, a character stepping out of the pages of medieval romance to mourn the death of her son. In later drafts her role grew as I realized her potential. She was the archetypal elderly woman living on the edge of a village/town/city/wood, a healer, a wise woman, with a mystical aura, ever an enigma. A counterpoint to the pragmatic Owen Archer. Mystical or other-worldly elements were unexceptional in medieval romances, a mix of Christian and old folk beliefs. Richard Firth Green's fascinating and highly readable *Elf Queens and Holy Friars: Fairy Beliefs and the Medieval Church* (University of Pennsylvania Press, 2016) discusses this at length, with wonderful examples. By the late fourteenth century fairies were increasingly demonized by clerics, which saddens me. Imaginations open to mystery seem far healthier than those cramped by clerics with ink-stained fingers desperate to demonize all but Church doctrine. No wonder Magda Digby had no time for them. As you see, although she began as an archetype, Magda quickly deepened into a unique individual.

Is she a witch? What is meant when labeling someone 'witch', not in the sense of name-calling, but when claiming that someone practices 'witchcraft', depends on when and where it occurs, and who is doing the labeling. So what was going on with the idea of a witch in Magda's time? In England in the late fourteenth century neither the concept of witches nor the burning of witches was yet well formed. The precursor in the Church was the accusation of heresy. But how had the country women with a deep knowledge of healing herbs, roots, barks, fruits, long accepted as important for the health of the community, come to be considered heretics? What was contrary to Church doctrine about plant lore? Abbeys boasted extensive herb gardens. Was it because the occasional charm was included? How did that differ from the birth girdles or saints' relics people sought for protection during childbirth or illness, or the holy water priests sprinkled on fields to bless the crops? And who would their accusers be? As a crime writer one of my first questions was, who benefited from the downfall of these women? Certainly not the community who depended on them. Perhaps particular members of that community who had no need of them? One group came to mind: the members of religious communities with their own infirmaries (and medicinal gardens). But why did they care?

I consulted one of my favorite trustworthy sources, Jennifer Kolpacoff Deane's *A History of Medieval Heresy and Inquisition* (Rowman and Littlefield Publishers, Inc., 2011), and found chapter 6, 'Medieval Magic, Demonology, and Witchcraft', to be particularly helpful. I was grateful to find her simple definition of magical practice: 'the exercise of a preternatural control over nature by human beings, with the assistance of forces more powerful than they' (185). Right away I saw the key issue – 'forces more powerful than they'. It's interesting that she adds that 'for the historian, magic is particularly tricky to study because (like heresy) it is more concept than reality, and because our sources are (like those on heresy) so often written by authors hostile to their topic' (186). And she quickly gets to the meat of the issue, that clerical theorists became increasingly worried about how prevalent and accessible all this was as all levels of society, from the healer to the priest to the court astrologer, used a mix of charms, blessings, herbal remedies, signs, and sky for all sorts of situations. They believed that although a monk might be trusted to be using all of this with God's blessing, an illiterate woman living in the woods might be highly susceptible to evil forces. What was important was not so much what a person *did*, but who they *were*. Clerical thinkers delved into esoteric books of magic, alchemy, and astrology, and it was these who attached the concept of demonology to the work of folk healers. What strikes me as absurd about this is that they were the ones flirting with 'secret' books, not the midwives and other female healers, who did not have access to libraries housing such items – not to mention being far too busy to spend their days bent over books, and often illiterate. I'm oversimplifying, but for my purposes this helped me think through how the very people who had depended on the character Magda Digby, the Riverwoman, for healing might be persuaded to turn on her in a time of pestilence if they were convinced by someone in whom they placed some authority that her healing skills came to her from infernal sources and God would punish them for seeking her aid.

It would be more than a century before the concept of a witch was fully explicated in the *Malleus maleficarum* (or *The Hammer of Witches*, written in 1486). Some might call Magda a witch, but more likely they would consider her a pagan or a heretic, and a danger to their souls.

What do I think? Magda might as easily be described as having some fairy blood as being a witch. She has little patience with charms and spells, and is far more caring and compassionate than many baptized in the Church. If you were to ask her who or what she is, she would smile at the question. She is as you see her. Her calling is to heal.

And yet there is the dragon, her indifference to religion, the air of mystery. Let's leave it there.

ACKNOWLEDGMENTS

This book is dedicated to my friend Joyce Gibb who worked closely with me on every book from *The Riddle of St Leonard's* through an early draft of *A Choir of Crows*. She died on Christmas Eve 2019. There is more than a little of Joyce in the character of Magda Digby, the Riverwoman.

I am grateful for advice, feedback, encouragement, and deep reading from Louise Hampson, Mary Morse, Molly Seibert, Michelle Urberg, and my agent Jennifer Weltz. Mary in particular stepped in to fill the void left by Joyce, discussing early ideas, suggesting sources, cheering me on – a precious gift. Thank you to Sara Rees Jones and the members of The Northern Way project for information about the pestilence in York. Working with the team at Severn House is always a joy – special shout out to my wonderful editor Kate Lyall Grant.

In this crazy time I've been fortunate to be sheltering in place with my favorite human, Charlie Robb (thank you for the maps!), and my favorite feline, Maggie, whose kitten energy revs me up and keeps me laughing.

And thank you to all the readers who buoy me throughout the year. Be well!